A Fate of

Two Crowns

Eleni James

OF LIGHT AND SHADOWS

For all those fighting invisible
illnesses and battles nobody sees and
still show up in the world

...

I see you. I am you. Keep fighting.

Delomere Mountains
Academy Hall
Village
River
Pool
Gym
Primms
Techs
Drithm

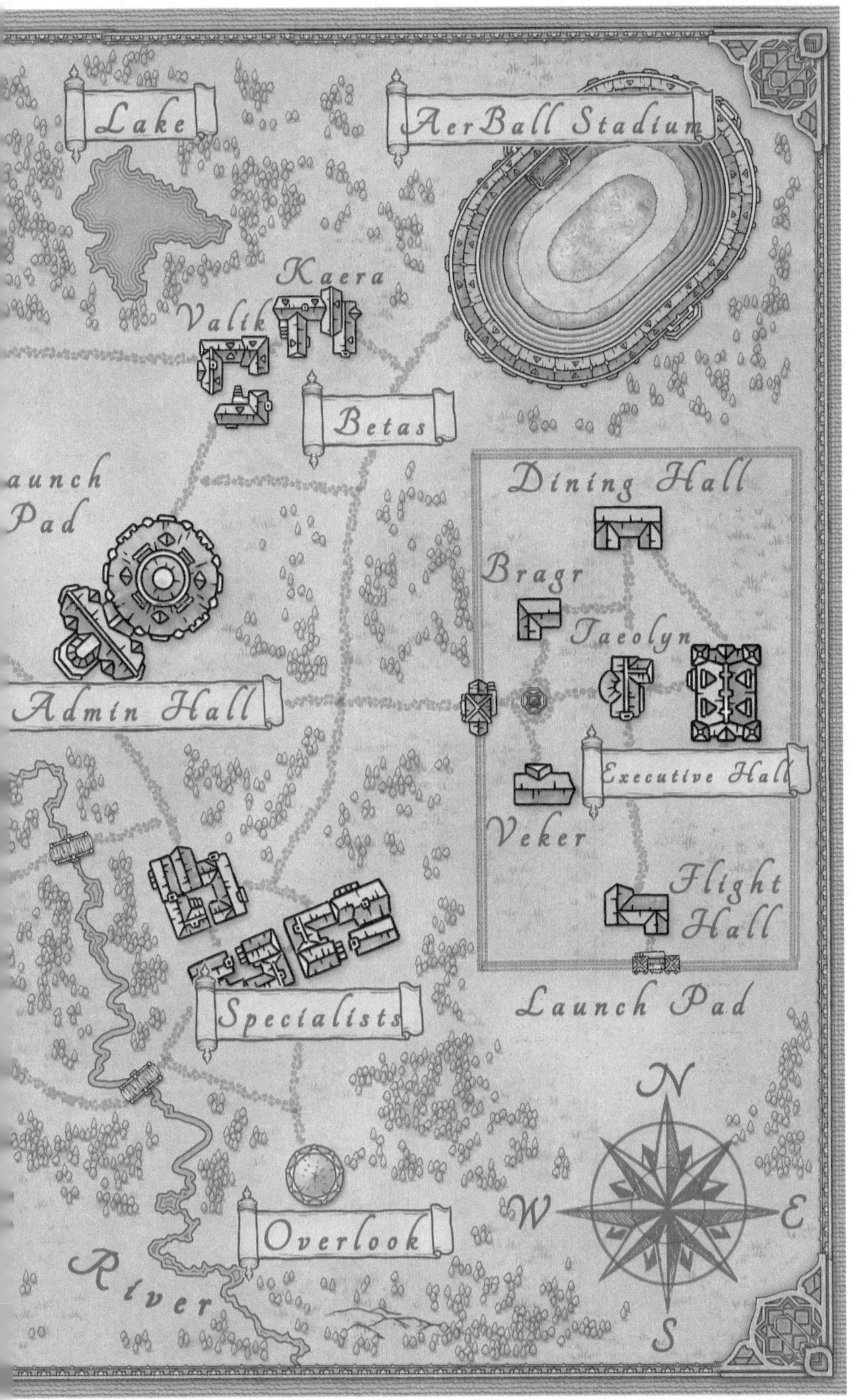

Lake
AerBall Stadium
Kaera
Valik
Betas
Dining Hall
Bragr
Taeolyn
Launch
Pad
Admin Hall
Executive Hall
Veker
Flight
Hall
Specialists
Launch Pad
N
W
E
Overlook
River
S

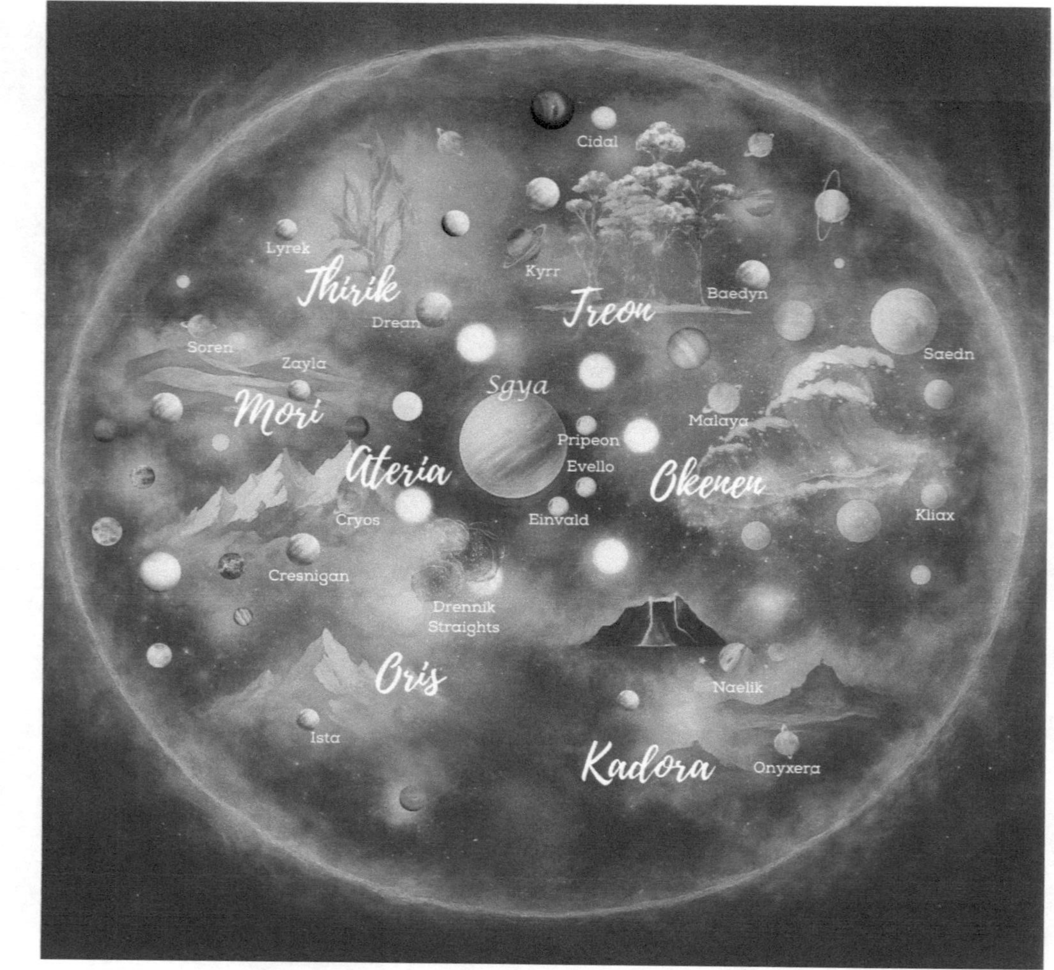

Cidal
Lyrek
Thirik
Kyrr
Treon
Baedyn
Drean
Soren
Saedn
Zayla
Sgya
Mori
Malaya
Ateria
Pripeon
Evello
Okenen
Cryos
Einvald
Kliax
Cresnigan
Drennik
Straights
Oris
Naelik
Ista
Kadora
Onyxera

Kingdoms Guide

Treon Kingdom:

King Bastian & Queen Amaya
Princess Raea (Soraea)

1. Kyrr (capital)
2. Baedyn
3. Kronox
4. Rayek
5. Lludc
6. Gowden
7. Cidal
8. Zinus
9. Lundr
10. Cerus
11. Nylund
12. Rugden
13. Brov
14. Aterran
15. Trao
16. Dionek
17. Telon
18. Tithys
19. Kao
20. Euron
21. Neptyn
22. Kallik

Ateria Kingdom:

King Alexi & Queen Sava
Prince Boyce, Princess Aolyn

1. Cryos (capital)
2. Bahn
3. Ashum
4. Matera
5. Papirene
6. Cresnigan
7. Zinik
8. Sagchyl
9. Straxver
10. Draerr

Okenen Kingdom:

King Aki & Queen Priana
Prince Anders, Cole, + Princess Clara

1. Malaya (capital)
2. Saedn
3. Darya
4. Oxorion
5. Orcleus
6. Kliax
7. Silas
8. Aquarion
9. Sedgesea
10. Kolari
11. Sinek
12. Demeter
13. Eshe
14. Nyx
15. Azuris
16. Maren
17. Fimme
18. Morak

Kadora Kingdom:

King Garrek & Queen Nalana

1. Naelik (capital)
2. Hraun
3. Terria
4. Onyxera
5. Mystel

Mori Kingdom:

King Osiris & Queen Meganna

1. Zayla (capital)
2. Ia
3. Ven
4. Chyr
5. Ulen
6. Feandra
7. Soren
8. Hespin

Thirik Kingdom:

King Urik and Queen Mara

1. Drean (capital)
2. Lyrek
3. Ithacane
4. Brinvek
5. Teger
6. Ozeri

Oris Kingdom:

King Huntr & Queen Isobel
Prince Felix

1. Ista (capital)
2. Nokorane
3. Latva

Planet of the Gods:

1. Sgya

Sgya Moons

1. Evello
2. Einvald
3. Pripeon

Academy  Structure

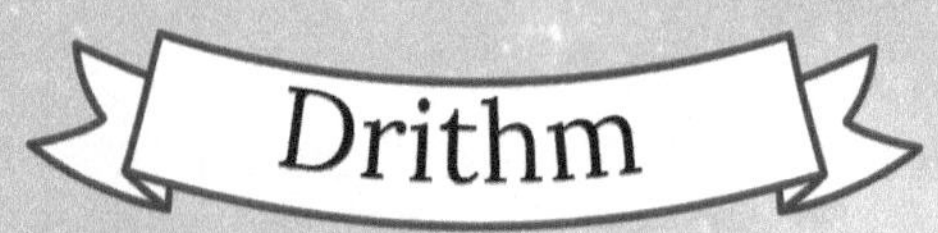

Orders

Primms	Technicals	Betas	Specialists
Ages 10-12 year olds	Ages 13-15 year olds	Ages 16-18 year olds	Ages 19-20 year olds
(introductory level)	(early academics, combat, technical skills)	(intermediate level)	(advanced specialization & leadership prep)

Executives

Ages 21-22 year olds

(final collegiate-level training)

Bragr Dorm

Taeolyn Dorm

Veker Dorm

About the Book

This book contains explicit content and dark elements that may be triggering. For a full list of warnings, see the last page.

Spotify Playlist

Apple Music

soraea

A cold sweat plasters my nightgown to my skin, a scream still tearing at the back of my throat. I sit bolt upright, lungs burning, desperate for air that feels thin and sharp. My eyes, blurred with the remnants of shadows and distorted faces, snap open to the familiar mist swirling outside my windows, the palace gardens a ghostly haze below. Sleep, I know, will not return.

This restless waking is new, replacing the sound sleep of my childhood. Over the past year, that sense of security has dissipated like morning fog. Now, an invisible tension hums in the air, a warning I don't understand, vibrating deep within my own core. Even the planets within our system seem restless, their weather patterns shifting bizarrely. The magic that once flowed freely feels unstable, sensing an impending change. It's a whisper of the world, and only I seem to hear it.

one

. . .

MY BACK SLAMS into the mat with a loud thud, forcing the air from my lungs. Pain radiates through my chest as I fight for another breath, the weight of my Nakata-plated corset heavy against my ribs. I breathe, allowing the adrenaline to fade, counting to three before my eyes open. I inhale my first full breath.

"You're distracted," he admonishes. "Let's go again." Light hazel eyes look down on me with such love that I feel the potential Bond rippling in the air between us. It's faint, almost impossible to detect, yet definitely there. It's only been present for a few weeks, but I already find comfort in it. Kellan reaches out, pulling my body off the mat and straight into his broad chest.

"You know, you could always just–"

"What? Take it easy on you?" he chuckles. "Not a chance. Let's go, Tierson, no holding back."

I fight the urge to roll my eyes. Instead, I roll my shoulders, step back, place my feet exactly as I was taught, and launch at him, my small dagger lifted to strike. Before I reach his energy shield, his right arm shoots out, wrapping around my raised one. He twirls me so quickly my back presses to his front, my arm pinned across my chest, my own dagger nearly at my throat. I swallow a groan of frustration.

The scent of salt and cinnamon fills my senses, and memories of us stargazing, wrapped in large blankets, flood my mind with a comforting stroke. I lose myself in the vision before my eyes open, remembering where we are.

This dimly lit room, with its exposed wooden beams and sparse sparring mats, is our private gym. It was my idea to freshen up here before our official first day as juniors at Drithm Academy.

"Those are old moves, Raea," he chuckles against the shell of my ear. His breath caresses my skin, sending warmth through my whole body. My chest heaves from losing every second of this sparring match, but the frantic beat of my heart? That is all him.

As my right foot gracefully sweeps behind him, I forcefully nudge his foot forward. He stumbles back, and I slip away, not hesitating when I swing my practice blade at his throat, piercing his energy shield.

"Old moves, huh?" I ask, smiling as the third bell chimes, signaling the end of our session. "Time to go." This time, I reach out, taking my best friend's hand as I pull him up.

At six feet tall, he stands a whole foot above me. The comfort of our bodies connecting like this is a feeling I know well. Kellan and I have trained together since we were five. The veil protecting our system is declining, and the threat of attacking shadow forces looms, creating an urgency in our training. Despite my parents' best attempts to *protect* and coddle me, I won the argument to train. What started as a silly *let her get it out of her system* now drives me to train three days a week, hoping I'll be ready if the shadows come. I step back, catching my breath, before leaving the mats ahead of him.

Leaving the sparring arena on the west side of the school grounds, a cool breeze, thick with damp soil and pine, washes over us, chilling our sweat-soaked bodies. My senses are alive as we follow a narrow, well-worn path toward the check-in table for our new Order. This fresh start fills me with excitement. I'm eager to reconnect with friends and classmates after being away for three months.

After eleven years at the academy, we form a tight-knit community here—as close as possible under our system's strict social hierarchy, especially with my royal title. The line stretches with faces from across the system. Nobility from all seven kingdoms attend Drithm.

Pine trees arch overhead, casting dappled shadows across the path as we walk toward the academy gates. This place feels as much like home as the palace on Kyrr. If I follow the trail to my right, I know I will end up at the Specialists' dorm yard. Drithm Academy consists of five Orders, each building upon the last, culminating in Executives—our collegiate level.

Our time at the academy begins with Primms, for students ages ten to twelve. Technicals, or Techs, follow for ages thirteen to fifteen. Betas is for ages sixteen to eighteen. Specialists, my favorite Order, is for nineteen and twenty-year-olds.

Finally, the Executive level is for twenty-one and twenty-two-year-olds.

As the path ends, the administration building's white facade gleams in the sunlight, its glass rotunda sparkling, flanked by grand wings that rival capital structures. Intricately carved oak doors, framed by a large archway, stand beneath colossal sculptures of our gods, Astor and Calia, welcoming all who come to learn. Above, vibrant flags mark each Order and dorm.

"Ah, Princess Raea, it's wonderful to see you again," Professor Ainslyn greets us as we step into the line near the academy's entrance. Junior and senior Executives shuffle in behind, their chatter filling the air as they catch up from home. The professor stands tall and commanding, his warm, tanned skin, kind dark brown eyes, and short-trimmed beard marking him a seasoned warrior. Once among the system's strongest, his path changed after a tragic mission explosion left him with a prosthetic leg. Rather than disappearing, he channels his expertise to shape us into capable warriors as our weapons and combat professor.

"Duke Hyston," he acknowledges with a polite nod. I catch a glimmer of mischief in his eyes as he winks at me before striding to the front where the senior Executive student takes roll and distributes dorm assignments. Kellan nudges my shoulder playfully, a grin spreading across his face. Professor Ainslyn and I have always shared a special rapport; last year, I passed the insanely difficult Hallo gun test—an achievement few students manage. He often praises my abilities, both on and off campus.

I lean against the sturdy trunk of an ancient tree and pull out my Prism. With a click, I capture a selfie with Kellan, our faces lit with genuine smiles despite our sparring-mussed hair. I upload the photo to The Link, the hottest communication and photo-sharing platform.

"So, what dorm do you think we will be assigned this year?" Kellan asks, bouncing on his feet with nervous energy. I quickly upload the photo for Cassia, my publicist, then slip it back into my bag. This year's Executive Order promises to be the most challenging, and I want to focus on my schoolwork.

"Probably Taeolyn, maybe Veker," I reply. The wind makes me shiver now that I'm cooled off. "I doubt they put us in Bragr," I add with a shrug; that dorm is typically for nobility from the outer regions and lower-ranked nobility—those first to see battle should the veil fall. Taeolyn is the dorm where the royals are almost always housed. In fact, I can't think of a single royal who hasn't been in Taeolyn. He takes a lock of my bright white hair, tucking it behind my ear.

"Is it wrong that I want Veker? It's all I've ever wanted." I tilt my head up at my best friend; he's never admitted that. Veker is the dorm often given to nobility who work in higher technical positions.

"But then we'd be in different dorms." A familiar, unwelcome nausea tightens in my abdomen—the constant cramps I've had all day, a prelude to my unbearable cycle. Tonight, I'll need to visit the school healers.

He sighs. "I know, and I'd hate it, but I also—"

"Look at him," a man taunts from behind us. "Hyston trying to lay claim already." I hear a few snickers as I glance over my shoulder and spot King Aki's sons from the Okenen kingdom, Anders and Cole Rykerson, standing three people back in a circle of their friends.

Their group stands out among the rest, each member exuding a ridiculous amount of arrogance. The young women surrounding them, with their simpering smiles and hair-tossing gazes, immediately grate on my nerves.

Cole, the younger brother, possesses an effortless charm. With his athletic build, award-winning smile, and striking blue eyes framed by blonde waves, he embodies his role as a star athlete. He moves with a confidence that has most women flocking to him, school and kingdom regulations be damned.

Then there's Anders, the older, undeniably more formidable brother. He stands taller than the rest, arms crossed over his chest with commanding authority. His expression remains cold and calculating as he glares at Kellan. A blonde girl I don't recognize daringly runs her hand up his chest, but he seems oblivious. He's all hard lines and dark magnetism, and something stirs inexplicably low in my belly. Before my gaze can linger, his sapphire blue eyes lock onto mine, sending a wave of shame coursing through me. *Shit.*

I quickly avert my gaze, feeling the awareness of his scrutiny burning into my back. Anders and I have never spoken, our paths rarely crossing at the academy's classes or occasional balls. Yet, his presence always looms like a shadow—lingering, watchful, surrounded by an entourage, and seemingly oblivious to anyone who doesn't bow to him. His arrogance is legendary, and I've made it my mission to keep my distance; the princess of Treon has no intention of falling into his trap and becoming fodder for school gossip.

Five long years have passed since King Aki's transport mysteriously vanished, leaving his family without answers. I sympathize deeply with the Rykerson brothers—the thought of losing my own father, who means everything to me, feels unbearable. King Aki was, from my recollections, a well-loved, strong ruler. It bewilders me how his sons have morphed into such arrogant, insufferable heirs.

Kellan, revered among students as one of the strongest warriors, earned the title of Weapons Master for swordsmen last year, in Specialists Order and he offers no such sympathy or patience. "Shut it," Kellan snaps.

The crowd around us collectively gasps, giggling with oohs as the air thickens with building tension. "See you on the mat, Hyston," Cole replies with cruel satisfaction. I turn to face Cole just in time to notice

Anders elbowing him in the side in silent reprimand. I snort out my amusement, gaining Anders' attention.

His intense gaze snaps toward me, pinning me in place. The air thrums, a vibration echoing through my bones. In that single, electrifying moment, our gazes collide, and a powerful ripple of energy resonates between us, binding our fates in a way that terrifies me. Disbelief crashes over me like a tidal wave. It's just the Bond, I remind myself, even as a profound stirring deep within me—something that has slumbered my whole life—now awakens.

"Next," Izak, the senior Executive, calls out, his tone flat and laced with boredom. "Names, please," he sighs. I feel a chuckle bubbling up, but I fold my lips in, biting down the giggle. Izak knows precisely who we are, yet the ritual of formality must be upheld.

With a barely contained smile, I declare, "Princess Raea Tierson, Treon Kingdom." As I speak, I extend my wrist, showing the detailed tattoo that marks my identity, my family crest tattooed on my skin.

"Duke Kellan Hyston, Treon," Kellan chimes in, mirroring my gesture. His tattoo, while similar in concept, is a simple black replica. All of the nobility in my realm bear the Treon crest on their wrist.

Izak nods somewhat absently, tapping on the tablet. Without looking up, he asks where we'd like our tracker placed. I tap my forearm, where I have chosen to place the temporary tracker every year since Primms. The cold metal tip presses into my skin, and I brace myself for the momentary burn. Using nanotechnology, the tracker is placed, and the screen on the device turns green. Kellan takes his in his shoulder.

"You both are assigned to Taeolyn," Izak says. "Please make your way to the dorms for orientation. Next," he calls out again, shifting his focus to the person behind us without missing a beat.

"Knew it," I squeal, bouncing on my toes. I've always hoped that once we reached the Executive Order, we would be assigned to Taeolyn. It's where both of our parents were placed. I don't miss the way Kellan's shoulders fall, just an inch, before he wraps an arm around me—his smile soft, meant to placate.

"I'm sorry, Kel," I say as we hover beyond the table. "I know you really wanted Veker."

He shrugs, checking the time. I'm bummed for him, yet a touch of satisfaction warms me: we'll graduate together, having spent our entire academy years side by side.

A sudden, warm voice interrupts my thoughts. "Ryker, how nice to see you," Professor Ainslyn calls out from behind me. *Ryker?!* Please don't tell me Anders seriously goes by his last name. "Has your brother also been placed in Taeolyn?"

A deep, velvety laugh tumbles through my body, igniting all my nerve endings and putting my body on alert. I refuse to turn around and look, knowing it will only feed his inflated ego.

"No, he's been placed in Veker. I don't need his antics messing with *my* dorm." *His dorm?* Gods, the sheer arrogance of his statement makes my skin crawl. He may be nearing his coronation after graduation, but he's still just a student.

"Very well, I will see you during orientation then," Professor Ainslyn says, his voice drifting off as we head toward the Executive dorms.

After a few minutes, we pass under the wide stone archway that spans the path and then some. Just beyond the magical wards—which only allow Executives to enter—sit the three glittering dorms in all their glory.

The Executive Order is the pinnacle of Drithm Academy.

Directly ahead, the beautiful white facade of Taeolyn Dorm ascends several stories. Its striking design stands out, adorned with grand terraces where students lounge against balustrades draped in delicate vines and blossoms spilling from window boxes—an atmosphere of pure elegance. Pristine white stone, tall arched windows, and ornate designs intertwine with clean, flowing lines, creating a perfect harmony with nature. The many terraces and window boxes brim with vibrant plants and trees, effortlessly blending architecture with the surrounding forest.

To my right, Veker Dorm makes a bold statement with its towering walls of sleek black marble. Light filters in through its glass dome, illuminating the interior with a natural brightness that accentuates its modern design. The dorm exudes an aura of intimidation and innovation. On my left, Bragr Dorm stands in stark contrast to its neighbors. Its dominating structure resembles a barracks more than a traditional dormitory, with towering stone walls and turrets rising at each corner. The design screams of cold, damp climates and blood-soaked battlefields; preparing for war, I'm sure that living in a barracks feels right at home.

Beyond them, the campus spreads out. Nestled behind Bragr, the warm aroma of baking bread and roasting meats drifts from the dining hall, its arched pathways a welcoming bridge connecting all three dorms. Further to the right, beyond Veker's shadow, the Transport Hall stands like a shiny beacon for the Sky Division hopefuls. Directly behind Taeolyn, the Executive Briefing Hall stands as the campus's central hub, a network of bridges and covered walkways pulling everything toward its authority.

A palpable thrill fills the air as students arrive at their assigned dorms. I find myself swept up in the collective enthusiasm, recognizing familiar faces. This is it. Our final Order here at the academy. Home for the next two years until graduation. These are my friends, my people—the last glimpse of our "childhood" before we receive our roles within our kingdoms, likely never seeing each other again. For nearly half, this is their final year.

Reaching the top of the stairs, an arched entrance adorned with glass doors glides open with a satisfying slicing noise. Inside, the central chamber expands before me, revealing five expansive levels. Natural light floods the space, pouring through tall windows and bouncing off the white stone. Lush greenery adorns every corner, and an ancient fern tree—its branches reaching like welcoming arms— stands at the heart of the room. Cozy seating encircles its trunk, while the gentle sound of trickling water fills the air from small fountains decorating each level.

Grand staircases ascend toward the upper three levels where our bed chambers are located. Near the back, a glass-encased elevator waits. This main floor is the epicenter of life at Taeolyn. For the next ten months, until I return to Kyrr, this is home.

Being at school feels refreshing. Here, I shed the weight of royal obligations, simply another twenty-one-year-old student. No formal curtsies or forced expectations bind me. I am just a part of a group immersed in politics, history, and the shadow of a potential war—and my personal favorite, flying. That is, if I can convince the Sky Division professor to let me.

"Find your mailbox for room assignments on your device," a lady announces with weariness. She stands taller than I do, her chestnut hair cascading gently to her shoulders, partially obscured by a navy cloak. She appears younger than most professors, perhaps an Executive-only instructor or a recent addition. As she waves a single hand, I notice the Bonding mark tattooed up her left middle finger and hand. It takes me by surprise; I have never had a Bonded professor, meaning she is also nobility.

Kellan and I work our way through the crowds of familiar faces, saying hello and offering a wave or a hug as we brush past toward the far wall, where our student mailboxes are located. Spotting my name along the first column dedicated to royals brings a rush of excitement that I actually belong here.

There are currently only three kingdoms represented by royal children at Drithm: my own kingdom of Treon, Okenen, Anders' and Cole's, and Ateria, Princess Aolyn's kingdom. These mailboxes contain a personal tablet that we'll use to keep track of classes, take notes, and submit assignments.

Over the years, Aolyn and I have become fast friends despite a royal decree discouraging close friendships, especially between royals of the opposite sex, out of fear that the royal houses might actually Bond.

It's not like the Lumos Bond is dictated through friendships, but fear is a powerful thing. A century has passed since it's happened, so the rule seems unlikely to apply, but rules are rules.

Activating my tablet, the blue Taeolyn crest appears before a login screen. I log in to my school account and find that I have been assigned a room on the fifth floor with Princess Aolyn as my dorm mate.

A touch of nostalgia settles as I realize she begins and ends her time at the academy as my dorm mate. Class schedules will be distributed with our division assignments, splitting the Executive Order's three distinct dorms into nine separate groups.

Kellan and I ascend the stairs together, the scent of nature and old books filling the air. On the third floor, he stops, turning to me with a warm smile, but I see the disappointment just beneath.

"See you in orientation." He heads toward his assigned room. I want nothing more than to ensure his happiness this year, yet I sense the blow of not being placed in Veker will cast a long shadow. My own relief, however, is laced with a potent dread. Anders Rykerson is also assigned to Taeolyn. Ten months. My heart hammers the words, a frantic drum against my ribs. *We are in the same dorm.* And suddenly, the thought of graduation feels a lifetime away, stretching out before me, long and utterly inescapable.

two

. . .

AFTER CLIMBING the stairs to my room, I open the door, stepping into the palatial room I will call home for the next two years at Drithm. It seems that I'm the first one here. My bodyguard, Kuron, and my handmaid, Mera, have ensured that all my belongings are perfectly arranged and unpacked.

Taking a moment to fully absorb my new room, I spin in place and can't help but feel a sense of fullness, a sense of joy, and a sense of finality. *I'm finally here.* I move through the room, which looks more like a sanctuary than a dorm, and smile.

My gaze drifts to the windows, where elegant white drapes cascade from the ceiling, currently held back with a golden rope. The large windows let in a soft, natural light, filling the room with a gentle glow of sunlight.

I smile softly, noticing that Mera has already laid out my school uniform for the day on a dresser near the closet. Inside the large walk-in space, Mera also unpacked and organized my clothes, neatly displaying my dinner gowns.

A giddy noise escapes me when I wander into the connecting bathroom, noticing that we each have our own. It's rare for students to have living arrangements such as these, but I gladly accept this upgrade. My bathroom is stunning, its architecture beautifully reflecting the same style as the rest of the dorm, with white stone and arched entrances.

Noticing the time, I quickly rinse off and then dress in my uniform: stretchy black pants and a fitted black shirt. I spritz my favorite mist and style my hair into six braids, tying them back into a long ponytail. My natural waves cascade down my back. Feeling refreshed and ready, I grab my tablet and Prism, slip them into a bag, and exit my room. However, I collide with a solid wall just as the door clicks shut behind me.

The collision knocks the wind out of me, sending me stumbling backward and off balance. Before I hit the wall, two firm, calloused hands grip my arms, steadying me. My heart races as I look up, and up, into a pair of intense sapphire blue and silver eyes.

Oops.

"Princess," Prince Anders drawls, his voice rich, resonating somewhere deep in my bones and uncomfortably low in my stomach. A strange current of energy courses through my body, and I can't help but tilt my head slightly to get a better look at him. His eyes swirl with an otherworldly quality, catching me off guard. The movement is so subtle you wouldn't be able to see it from a step away.

I've never met anyone with eyes like his. When he blinks, the moment vanishes, and I remember who we are and the fact that we aren't friends. Can't be.

"Anders," I respond curtly, though I manage to nod politely even as I take a step back, as if some distance will quell the heat pooling in my stomach. The moment I inhale, I'm hit with an intoxicating wave of scents: the briny tang of raging seas, vibrant notes of citrus groves, and warm and woody sandalwood mixed with something distinctly masculine. The aroma envelops me, heady and rich, and for a reason I can't quite explain, I feel the overwhelming urge to lean in and fill my lungs with more.

The amused look he gives me is enough to make me flinch inwardly, but I mask it, maintaining my careful composure. "Running late to orientation?" he asks mockingly, with a raised brow and a slight quirk on his gorgeous full lips. He crosses his arms over his broad chest, just below where his buttons hang open, revealing sun-kissed skin.

The action and realization of how close he is makes my throat dry.

"No, I will be early if you'll just excuse me." I pivot on my heel, desperate to put as much distance between us as possible. Just as I think I've managed to get away, his arm shoots out, hooking around my waist and yanking me back toward him. Heat and energy flare where his arm makes contact, and I silently curse him.

"Wrong way, Princess," he purrs, his words dripping with a smoothness that sends a fresh wave of tingles across my skin. The way the 'S' rolls off his tongue feels like a magnetic pull, awakening me. Blushing furiously, I turn away from him, acutely aware of the flush in my cheeks, and begin walking in the opposite direction, determined to get away quickly. I don't have time to consider my reaction because humiliation burns worse. Much to my annoyance, his long strides keep pace with me, shadowing my every step.

"Don't you have some women to flirt with or a mirror you need to brood in front of?" I toss over my shoulder, annoyed that I can't seem to move fast enough.

He snorts. "Jealous?"

I *almost* laugh. "Did your mother drop you on your head as a baby?" I stomp around a corner. "You do realize that the system doesn't revolve around you?"

He grips my elbow, swinging me around so fast I nearly collide with him again. "You're a feisty little thing. Where's the beloved princess that has the whole system wrapped around her finger?" My nostrils flare with barely contained annoyance.

"Has it ever occurred to you, Prince Anders," I say with a saccharine smile, "that maybe it's just you that I don't like?" His eyes narrow, and he clenches his jaw. I inwardly do a little dance for getting under his skin.

He steps closer, our bodies nearly brushing, and I have to tilt my head to look up at him. "Do tell me, Princess," he says with an icy, calm voice. "What is it about me you don't like? You don't even know me." *True.* Not that I'm willing to admit it. I know enough, and he doesn't realize that women love to talk. Talk and talk and talk. And who is the number one source of gossip? The annoying prince before me.

"I know enough," I retort, spinning on my heel and yanking my arm out of his grasp.

I only get two steps before he responds, "I thought you knew better." My steps falter, but I refuse to give him the satisfaction of turning around. "Don't believe everything you hear." Shame and annoyance prick my body as I storm away. Am I acting childish? Yes. Is he correct? Also yes. Do I want to apologize? Nope.

Ignoring him as best I can, I navigate toward the second-level classrooms, where holographic signs hover over each door, announcing which room is dedicated to each subject. The sounds of chatter and laughter echo off the walls, alerting me to my destination. Still, it's the palpable tension between Anders and me that commands my focus—that and the storm brewing between us.

Down the long hall toward the back, I find the bridge to the Executive Hall almost instantly, thanks to the crowd, and make my way across, only to get stuck at the entrance. I can feel the heat of Anders at my back as we are met with a bottleneck of students from all three dorms shuffling into the same space.

The hall is bigger than any other Order's. Arched windows make up the back wall, overlooking the forest behind it, with long, thick drapes running the height of the wall. There's a dais located in front where professors are already gathering.

The room is shaped in a semi-circle broken into three colors. Veker is positioned to the right, featuring its deep forest green seats. Bragr is positioned to the left, with its light ivory seats, and the navy blue seats at the center of the room are reserved for Taeolyn.

"Raea," Kellan waves from ahead. I shake off the strange buzz of energy and make my way over to him. "Hey, I saved us seats." He wraps his arm around my shoulders as we turn up the stairs behind us into the Taeolyn section and find seats along the third row on the second level.

There's a hum in the air as students trickle in and find their friends. Around the hall, the seats are filling up with juniors and seniors. I scan the crowd, taking in the sight of familiar faces and noting who has been placed where. It's one of my favorite things about the first day back.

My kingdom is the largest, and as the sole heir, my parents keep me secluded when I'm not in school. I just want to fit in. I want the other women to like me, but it feels like I'm always the outsider. When I try to join in, everyone typically grows quiet, out of respect or annoyance, I'm not sure. So I watch. I watch, and I smile and remind myself I'm blessed to have the friends I do.

The hall grows louder while Kellan recounts his first meeting with his new dorm mate. It's all I hear before his voice is muffled because, as much as I shouldn't, I can't keep my eyes off Anders, especially now that he's not looking my way. It's then that I really *notice* him for the first time, or at least allow myself to.

Since I last saw him over a year ago, time has been kind to him–too kind, really. His face is carved into sharp angles, impossibly gorgeous, and his locks of dark brown hair, nearly black, are styled in a way that looks effortlessly perfect. I can't help but fantasize about running my fingers through it, tousling those silky strands just enough to see his reaction. The thick, dark hair contrasts with his piercing blue eyes.

Anders' complexion is a rich, sun-kissed olive shade, evidence of long days spent on sandy beaches at home, where his palace resides. As if this weren't enough to enthrall me, the tattoo wrapping around his left arm catches my eye. It's a blue and black octopus that is said to safeguard the Okenen kingdom. The design clings to his bulging biceps, stretching over his skin and peeking just above the edge of his collar, leaving me to question what other tattoos might be hidden beneath layers of clothes. His other arm bears the crest of his kingdom tattooed on his right bicep. I want to trace it with the tips of my fingers.

He stands tall, towering over most of the other students and staff around him, and it's impossible to ignore the sheer strength radiating from him. Even in the all-black uniform, the outlines of his toned muscles are evident in the firm contours of his torso, the definition in his arms, and the powerful build of his thighs in his combat pants. An inappropriate desire spreads through me as I drink all of him in, imagining what it would be like to be pressed beneath his weight.

Anders is, without a doubt, the most attractive person I've ever met. It's a shame that he doesn't have a sparkling personality to match.

For a minuscule second, I allow the defenses of my mental shield that protects my Bond to open. I have been practicing over break to visualize and construct a white iron gate to conceal the Bond that flows aimlessly about. But when I let those gates open, I'm immediately overwhelmed by a surge of intense light so powerful that it has me gasping for air. Startled, I slam my mental gates closed, shutting him out. There's no way I can entertain my Bond with him. Not now, not ever.

"Raea?" Kellan asks, breaking my gaze.

"What?" I ask, only now realizing I haven't heard anything he has said for the last few minutes. Embarrassment washes over me. *What the hell was that?* My eyes snap back to Anders one last time, and I find him staring back, something dark lurking in the depths of those beautiful eyes despite his emotionless face. *Did he feel it, too?*

"I asked if you've received your schedule yet," Kellan says, brows knitted together. Sweat begins to bead, pooling on my lower back, and I shift uncomfortably. They need to turn on the air.

"I think we get them in Divisions." *Why do I feel so breathless?* The question is there on the tip of his tongue, but the projection of a voice cuts it off before he has the chance to ask.

"Attention. Attention!" Chancellor Xara calls out over the speaker, saving me from my flustered thoughts. My eyes swing to the dais, finding the Chancellor looking around the room. I exhale a breath I didn't know I was holding, noting her vibrant amber eyes against her ebony skin, her jet-black hair braided into a tight crown. She is fierce and loyal, a leader I admire. The room falls silent as I settle into the comfortable seat. "Great, you all listen," she chuckles alongside the students.

"Welcome back to another year of Drithm Academy. Most of you know each other. Some are transfers from other schools. I expect you all to act like the nobility you are. You are now in your dorms; next, you are assigned to your divisions. Seniors, you maintain your assigned divisions from last year.

"As Executives, you are the leaders, the oldest, the example for younger students, bearing the most responsibility. This year's dorm leaders are as follows." Only then do I notice other students mingling among the professors—all except Anders. His hands tuck into his pants, a look of pure boredom on his face, as if he has somewhere else to be. As a prince, he attends far worse meetings, yet he could at least try to appear happy.

As a royal, it's ingrained in us that everyone watches. It's unfair, a simple fact. Every movement is judged and scrutinized, and people wait for a slip-up. I know what one little mistake can mean—the media's whispers of "spoiled princess," "unstable heir." Anders belongs up there, acting as Okenen's future; he *is* their future.

"Taeolyn, your dorm leader is Prince Anders Rykerson." *What?* My heart stutters, a physical jolt. Only now do I realize how daft I am. Of course, he is. The sheer arrogance of his early stance, the way he commanded attention even then...it all clicks into place. *His dorm.* I huff a disbelieving laugh, leaning back as my thoughts flee.

Energy ripples up my spine, the jolt so quick I almost hiss. I bite into my bottom lip, reaching for Kellan, half expecting static to zap him. To my playful annoyance, nothing happens. Kellan's brow lifts in question as I pout like a petulant child whose prank failed. He chuckles, snaking an arm around me, tugging me closer until my head rests on his shoulder. "You're warm," he whispers.

"It's just hot in here." He looks at me like I've lost my mind, but I settle onto his shoulder again, uncaring.

"Veker, your dorm leader is Lord Elex Morrison." Elex, slender and impeccably dressed, steps forward. He looks ready for an intelligence meeting. "Bragr, your dorm leader is Lady Corine Cazl." The tall redhead steps forward, arms behind her back, nodding like she accepts orders.

"For some of you, this is your final year as a senior Executive. You will take on leadership roles, working alongside our kingdoms to learn what awaits after graduation or begin transitioning into selected new roles. Your king makes the final choice." She pauses, glancing around the room at the two hundred or so students. Her eyes connect with mine, a soft smile crossing her face. Though our relationship is not always smooth, she often puts my parents in their place when they overstep in the name of "protecting" me.

"As Executives, we brief you on current happenings; we do not shield you. So it is my duty to explain today's events." The room falls unnaturally quiet. "As we understand so far, the veil had a momentary loss of power, lasting no more than five minutes." Whispers spread through the crowd. "During that time, a temporary loss in magic occurred throughout the system. Reports are still being assessed, but it appears that one of Terria's volcanoes in Kadora has erupted, reaching a nearby village. Efforts are underway to recover survivors." Gasps, then a cry, ripple through the room. My stomach sinks, my mind whirling with questions. We know the veil weakens, though even the best scientists and historians cannot fully explain why. "We will update you as more information comes in. Keep your tablet on you. Continuing on."

After Chancellor Xara finishes introducing this year's classes and professors, we are dismissed into our dorm halls. With Kellan at my side, we make our way to the top of the stadium seating, finding our places along the edge. The Taeolyn hall is smaller, its purpose the same, but now it is Anders' territory.

I have spent years waiting for this moment. This is the height of excitement in my life, the closest I get to freedom. Once I graduate, I spend my days shadowing my mother, attending luncheons and events with a fixed smile. No more hiking forests, no more monitoring intelligence channels, no more piloting transports. I plan to make the most of these two years.

The room comes alive with conversation on the veil as juniors fill the empty seats, waiting for division assignments. "This is so exciting," I whisper. Kellan chuckles, squeezing my hand once before letting go.

Anders stands at the front of the room with a few other students. I recognize only one—Trysten Asgir, Anders' best friend. Trysten, also annoyingly handsome, is tall, like Anders, and toned with muscle. His lighter brown hair, similar to coffee with milk, is long on top and shaved down the sides, hanging to the right and framing his whiskey-shade eyes. Tattoos cover both arms. I'm sure he's a heartbreaker, too. Why do all these men have to be so infuriatingly good-looking? Calia should reserve such looks for men with personalities to match.

Trysten's father is King Aki's best friend and second-in-command. I have no doubt the role falls to his son when Anders assumes the throne after graduation. It's unprecedented for such a young royal to step in, especially with Queen Priana still alive and ruling, but she announced last year she plans to step down to let Anders rule in his father's stead alongside his future Queen. The poor woman who Bonds with Anders better have enough personality for both of them and be ready to carry all the emotional weight of that relationship. The only thing I've heard Anders is capable of is the occasional brooding and standing there like an intimidating statue of boredom while women throw themselves at him.

"Okay, listen up," Anders says. A hush falls over the room. Two students find their seats, as two more make their way to the front—one of them Princess Aolyn. A smile crosses my face as I watch my friend take her place. Her bluish-black hair, longer now, hangs loose like a curtain to her waist. She wears a striking black gown, not the standard issue; its dark hue is a stark contrast against her pale skin and ice-blue eyes lined with coal. She is devastatingly gorgeous, the kind of beauty that commands a room. She has high cheekbones, an oval face, and a perfect cupid's bow on her pink lips. She must feel my attention because she turns, finding me immediately, offering a quick smile before turning back toward Anders.

"We have a long year ahead. Your workload doubles that of other Orders. You have more classes and more training—not just in your division, but all three. You are assigned a division you study with for the rest of your time here. As a division, you attend classes together, train, eat, and learn to rely on each other. These are permanent; there is no changing them. So don't ask. You rise or fall as one. As my dorm, I expect you all to get along. No fighting, no petty arguments, no drama. And gods, no damn Bonding—you know the rules." He tucks his tablet to his side, gazing around the room.

"On the weekends, you may head into the village in groups of three. Check in with the admin office first to ensure your trackers are active, and be back before midnight." Hushed voices spread through the juniors. We've never left campus on our own. I can't wait. Exploring new cities and villages is a favorite pastime. However, it can often be a daunting endeavor due to security concerns.

He pauses, swiping a hand through his hair. It should mess up the style, but now it looks even better. Ugh, of course. Anders' face grows serious. "With this most recent update on the veil, it's important to train for whatever may come." The veil was created by our gods, Astor and Calia, to protect us from their siblings. Almost a thousand years have passed since Astor and Calia left us, using all their energy to create the veil to keep Kane and Ravana from finding us. History paints the twin shadows as consumed by a spite so venomous they turned on their own people they were meant to protect. There's something about the whole thing that leaves me with an unease I can't place.

"War may come. It may be in our lifetime. It may not be. Without the help of the gods, we're on our own. When you graduate, you head home to your kingdom. I'm here to make sure you learn everything you can before then."

Right. Reality hits me square in the chest; I am not here to play. These are my people, part of my kingdom or not, and if the veil rips, they will seek refuge here in Treon. Every bit of knowledge I learn could save a life—maybe even my own. I squeeze my hands, nails biting into my palm, counting to ten, letting the wave of anxiety flow. Anders sets his tablet down, shifting his posture, but nothing changes the dread and apprehension in the air. It is so thick you could cut it with a knife.

"Divisions split into groups of roughly twenty juniors and twenty seniors. No transferring once placed, so don't call Mommy or Daddy to rescue you." The room chuckles. Anders commands a room, I realize, but he's still a cocky, arrogant asshole. Sweat slides down my spine beneath my corset. I wish I weren't wearing it, but rules; it's the only way I attend school.

Anders' eyes find mine and hold as he calls out the first division assignment. I tilt my chin up, ignoring the slight smirk on that handsome face. "Sky Division, your leader is Trysten Asgir." Anders' gaze leaves mine as Trysten steps forward, arms crossed. "If your name is called, make your way up here with your tablets for your assignment and schedules. First selected..."

Just kidding. They're back to me. "Raea Tierson."

All eyes swing. My heart stutters and stops. *Me?* My parents don't want me flying. They pulled me from flight school in Specialists; only Chancellor Xara's insistence that it was essential to Drithm courses finally allowed my training to proceed. Sky Division means I graduate with aeronautics and flight time for my own transport. My parents, who wanted me in Intel, won't be happy.

I inhale, regaining a steady heart rhythm, and stand. I feel everyone's eyes. I wish I were normal for once. This should be exciting, but it fills me with dread. Half the room is probably wondering when my parents will appear. The other half probably thinks my parents pulled strings.

I will my body into submission, taking the perfect posture, squared shoulders, and a confidence that's nothing but a practiced facade. I stop before Trysten. His eyes cascade down my form-fitting black custom uniform—my favorite, a little tighter in the bust, showing more curves this year. I hold steady under his perusal, unwilling to show how exposed I feel. Everyone assumes they know me from news articles, seeing me as the spoiled brat who gets everything. They don't know how hard I fight behind the scenes for normalcy, the endless arguments I only win with prepared research. Flying is all me; I spent hours doing it behind their backs. I want to prove I deserve to graduate, like the rest of them. I have only a few true friends here, the ones who know the real me, so I allow myself this small moment of happiness, knowing I will share it with them later.

"Princess Raea." With a confident smile, he taps his tablet against mine, populating my schedule. "Welcome to Sky Division." I thank him, moving to his side, quickly glancing at my schedule: Politics, Aeronautics, Study Period, Combat Training, Divisions—flight school for me. History, Intelligence, Ethnography and Cultural Anthropology, Economics, Science, Government, and Bonding. Damn, that's a lot. Classes scatter throughout the week, filling my schedule to the brim. My eyes widen, considering the workload to stay at the top. They weren't kidding; this is far more than previous Orders. I already see late nights, early mornings, and weekends catching up. No wonder they let us go to the village—it's to keep our sanity.

I look up, waiting as eighteen more students are called, none of them Kellan. I offer him a reassuring smile, hoping he gets Intel; he's a natural. The unfortunate reality sinks in as we are dismissed to our seats, all nineteen filling the two empty rows below senior Sky Division. Anders' strict rules about staying within our division mean I won't sit with Kellan during dining hours.

"Recon Division, your leader is Colton Purk." The names are called, and I breathe easy when Kellan's name isn't among them. The Recon Division primarily trains in the mountains, focusing on security and special operations—roles often filled by military or royal guards known as Regils. Though higher nobility and royalty rarely join Recon —things change.

"Intel Division, your leader is Princess Aolyn Seltn." I sigh in relief. At least he will be happy since he wasn't assigned to Veker. Anders reads the names, and sure enough, Kellan is the fourth called. We exchange a quick glance as he meets his division leader. With Kellan and I in separate divisions, we now have different classes and different schedules.

Taeolyn Hall has three classrooms based on our divisions, and we shuffle into ours next. This room is filled with long wooden tables arranged in four-tiered rows, each accompanied by swivel chairs. Between juniors and seniors, we number about forty in Sky Division.

I find a seat near the front next to a girl whose name I can't recall, though I remember her from our third year. Her parents are from the Mori Kingdom, a planet in the far reaches of the system. I pull my tablet from my bag as she starts talking. "So, who do you think will be the team leader this year?" she asks quietly.

I meet her pretty amber eyes—common for Mori citizens due to their spices and dust. "Oh, um, I don't know. I don't think they will pick until we've completed the first round of testing." I definitely do not need the job. My goal is to lay low and study; I've already agreed to take over the running club.

"I know, but you know pretty much everyone here, right?" I turn, looking around. I recognize almost every face and name, save for a few, and a beautiful blonde girl on the opposite side of the class. Tate Kinnunen, a Lord I befriended last year, walks in, his shirt untucked and combat pants loose. His black hair looks like he ran his hand through it and called it good enough. When he sees me, he grins, making his way over. Tate is easy to be friends with: hilarious and easy-going, with a don't-give-two-shits attitude. He's slender, tall, and always strolls, as if urgency isn't part of his dictionary.

"Raea," he says with his light accent and a smile on his face. His eyes are so dark they're almost black. "Lovely to see you again." I groan and roll my eyes, making him laugh; the sound is familiar and welcome. With this year's workload, I will be relying heavily on him to keep my spirits up. I grin at him and turn back to the front as his arm swings over the back of my chair casually after taking up a seat on my right.

"I do, but that has little to do with how we will rank."

"I'm Aada, by the way. We had the same dorm in Technicals." Right. Technicals, or Techs for short, is the second Order for kids who are thirteen to fifteen-years-old. The room falls silent as Trysten and Anders walk in, deep in a hushed conversation. Anders positions himself in the far corner of the room, his face pulled into a tight, no-nonsense glare.

I love flying, even though my parents wish I didn't. Kuron usually helps me sneak out of the castle for trips with Lieutenant Piori, who flies missions around our kingdom almost daily. When Kuron can manage to sneak me out, I sit with Lt. Piori on the flight deck. Ezra, my other guard, doesn't know; he's much more by the books and far less fun.

"Okay, listen up," Trysten starts, taking up a casual stance beside Anders. "As Sky Division, you learn how to launch in different weather. You learn how to not only pilot but also operate communications and navigation systems. We train you for the best possible success on a mission, should the need ever arise. Now, we all know the veil has seen areas that are weakening. The forces of the seven kingdoms push to those spots until they can be repaired."

The veil itself is nothing more than an energy barrier; the magic within shields us from others. All seventy-two planets, moons, our seven suns, and Sgya are shielded. From our direction in space, you see nothing but vast emptiness. Journals from the emperor after the veil's creation speak of days spent waiting with bated breath. Though they later breathed easier, we know it is temporary. The veil was never a permanent solution; the gods simply needed it to last long enough for us to be prepared.

And we are—or as prepared as possible when facing an unknown enemy. Factions claim the threat is gone, but I was not raised with such blind optimism. I visited colonies that were still mere shells from the first uprising; if humans cannot settle their own disagreements, what hope exists against something else? History repeats itself, and old arguments resurface. Humans are petty creatures, holding long grudges, driven by a relentless war for power, money, and control—a war that will continue until the end of days. As future queen, the safety of my people hangs heavy; I am not blind to the reality that I am part of the power those seeking to destroy it will.

"The training you receive this year may be the training that one day saves your life, or the life of others, because unless we can fix the veil, it will continue to falter, and they will notice." *At least Trysten speaks the truth.*

I relax the tension in my shoulders, thinking about what I will face as Queen. Will I be responsible for deciding where troops are sent?

Whose life means more than another? I cannot even begin to think about making that final call. The oldest history tomes in our archives recount great wars that claimed the lives of trillions of people five hundred years after creation. Other systems have known war their whole lives, but our generation sees for the first time the real possibility of death and destruction on that scale.

My hand shoots up before I can think. "Yes, Raea?" Trysten asks. I'm glad he doesn't call me princess; at school, we are all equal in a way.

"Do you know if the veil vanishing for those five minutes affected hyperjump capabilities?" Trysten looks at Anders.

Anders locks eyes with me, his attention pulling at me as he speaks. "As of right now, my knowledge is as limited as yours. I plan to rectify that once we finish here. Any more questions, or can we move on?"

How can I despise one man so much while being so undeniably pulled to him?

three

· · ·

IT'S LATE AFTERNOON, and my new black boots crunch on the gravel as I cross campus coming back early from my visit with the healers. Despite the grumpy healer, Agneta, and her typical dismissal of my pain, the healing tonic she gave me helped, and I'm determined to not let it ruin my day. My new boots are already leaving blisters—I need to break them in. Their sturdy, chunky soles add two welcome inches to my height for Executive combat training.

I skip across the wards into the dorm yard noticing the initial chaos of students has dissipated as everyone settles in for the first night. A surge of energy propels me forward, up the steps to my room.

Inside, the palatial space welcomes me home for the next two years. I take it all in: two grand beds draped in soft, neutral-colored linens, mirroring identical sleeping arrangements. Luxurious tufted headboards stretch up the wall, from which rich, velvety drapes cascade, offering privacy. The beds are adorned with cozy blankets, plush throw pillows, and sumptuous furs.

The washroom is a sanctuary. A soaking tub sits in the far corner beneath a floor-to-ceiling window, perfect for late-night stargazing. To the right, a spacious shower gleams; to my left, a deep wash basin anchors a wide counter. Though dimmable, the already lit candles cast a warm, welcoming glow throughout the space.

The spacious living area feels like a continuation of the forest outside, with soft furnishings, mood lighting, and lush potted plants adorning the space. It opens onto a private terrace draped in lush greenery, featuring thick rugs and comfortable seating. I spread my arms wide, leaning against the balustrade, inhaling the fresh scent of the forest. This back-corner room offers a level of privacy rarely afforded to princesses.

Not long after, Kellan knocks on my door, a lopsided grin on his face. He whistles low when he enters my room. I smack him playfully, leading him to the seating area where we spend the next hour reviewing our schedules. I hate that we don't have a single class together. It's only day one, and already I know I won't see him as much. I attempt to convince him to join the running club, despite his hatred for it, hoping for more time together. He gives me his standard eye roll, clearly convinced I'm being ridiculous. He has plans to join the robotics club. The afternoon fades into evening as we talk about nothing and laugh about everything.

When he finally leaves, it's time for dinner, and I can't help but frown that Aolyn still isn't here.

The dining hall is full of students at their assigned dorm tables. Sky Division's section is distinguished by rows of blue chairs adorned with Taeolyn's crest. I look around the room, finding all our divisions sitting together as ordered. Across the hall, I spot the other dorms.

Veker's chairs are made of a black velvet with a green 'V' in a honeycomb shape embroidered into the back, and Bragr with its orange and ivory crest on its chairs—a fading B with an armor helmet sitting on top. This is the only place where all three dorms mingle.

The other two dorms don't appear to be separated into divisions, but maybe that's just a Taeolyn thing—or an Anders thing. *Gah, he's annoying.*

The dining hall is an expansive space designed to comfortably accommodate more than two hundred Executive students. Rich wooden tables are strategically arranged throughout the hall, accompanied by elegant high-backed velvet chairs. The grand hearth at the opposite end of the room, the soft glow of the chandeliers, and the flickering candlelight combine to create a warm and inviting atmosphere.

Despite our advanced technology, many areas in the system still rely on candlelight for lighting and fireplaces for warmth. Our system once experienced a period of rapid technological advancement, but progress has since stalled. Some attribute this stagnation to the veil, while others believe it coincides with the disappearance of Astor and Calia.

The floors are made of dark wood, similar to those in the administration building, with rugs scattered throughout to create a cozier atmosphere and dampen noise levels. Both sides of the dining hall feature a variety of food stations. The diverse selection is prepared and arranged on individual trays adorned with fine china. According to the welcome guide, we rotate through specialties from different kingdoms on a weekly basis.

Dinner is also the only time of day when we are expected to dress as the royalty we are. I am wearing a soft pink gown adorned with shimmering Watteau trains trailing from my shoulders. I've paired it with a gold diadem and a rose-quartz lariat.

I find a seat with some other junior Sky Division students I recognize: Jakob, Ember, Britta, and Kristien. Tate joins me, finding a seat to my right, and introduces himself to the others.

He spends the full dinner hour telling jokes, and Britta fills us in on gossip from Sagchyl, a planet in the Ateria kingdom. Apparently, there are rumors that Prince Boyce is visiting brothels and still refusing to Bond, despite the duchess he should be Bonded to being sick all the time. The healers claim it's because she's unBonded. I can't help but feel a little sympathy for her. Also, King Alexi hasn't been seen for several months, and Queen Sava has been filling in. I'll have to ask Aolyn how everything is going. If her father is sick or something, maybe I can reach out to Albin, one of our healers on Kyrr. He's one of the best and strongest there is.

When our plates are cleared, Kellan finds me and asks if I want to head to the bridge with him. I nod and take his hand, standing while I say my goodbyes. As we approach the door, Kellan realizes he left his Prism at the table and rushes off to get it.

I pause at the door, taking in the room and students lost in conversation, and I smile softly. It's been a good first day. Classes begin tomorrow, and I'm ready to return to a routine. Idleness has never been something I enjoy.

"Princess," Anders' deep, velvety voice purrs before I feel a calloused palm brush against my lower back, sending a shockwave through my system. I turn and find his eyes filled with surprise. Shock renders me speechless as we both gaze into each other's eyes for a few heartbeats, while a strange energy buzzes between us. My skin feels warm and tingly beneath his palm.

By the fourth heartbeat, my breath hitches slightly as I watch his eyes, which are more silver than sapphire, swirling again like a brewing storm. I don't remember them being like this earlier. *It's probably just the lighting.* His fingers press a little more into my skin, bringing me a step closer.

The way he looks at me...it's strange. I almost think he feels the same sort of energy.

Kellan clears his throat, grasping my hand and snapping me out of whatever spell I've been under. The room rushes in, surrounding all my senses at once, making my head spin.

"Ready to go?" Kellan asks, glaring at Anders.

"Yep, yes." I feel flustered. I look between the two men, who both still have their hands on me. Kellan's squeezing my hand in silent communication while Anders possessively presses into my lower back like he's considering forcing me to follow him. The two men couldn't be more opposite; their differences don't stop with how they hold me.

Where Kellan is handsome with soft features and a boyish look that I love, Anders is all hard lines, broody, and devastatingly beautiful—it makes my insides feel fluttery.

"Anders," I say, a little breathless, bowing my head. I need some fresh air *now*. I step out of his hold and follow Kellan through the doors, my mind still hung up on what happened. I've never felt or experienced anything like it. I can still feel the heat of his palm pressed into my back.

"Raea," Anders calls out, catching up in a few graceful strides. Both Kellan and I turn, our hands still locked onto each other. Honestly, it's more a habit than anything romantic. Anders towers over me, his eyes holding me to the spot, not once looking at Kellan. His jaw clenches once, twice.

"Your parents..." he starts, running a hand through his dark locks. "Chancellor Xara has assigned me as your new escort while you're here. Unfortunately for me, this means that where you go, I go when we aren't in class." He looks pissed about the arrangement, but it's nothing compared to what I feel.

Anger, hurt, disappointment...they all tangle together, warring over which emotion will present itself first. Anger always wins. I feel my flush as I glare at my dorm leader. There's no way I'm agreeing to this. I can't believe they did this.

"They what?" I snap. "I don't need a bodyguard. This is school, Anders." I cross my arms, digging my nails into my biceps. "What is going to hurt me here?" Something similar to amusement flashes through his eyes, but it's gone before I can be sure I saw it.

"They aren't worried you'll be hurt," he huffs, locking down his emotions as he slides his hands into his trouser pockets. "You are not to be *Bonded*." His gaze swings to Kellan, and I swear the temperature drops a few degrees. Kellan doesn't let go of my hand, no, his response is much worse. He wraps a possessive arm around my waist.

I have half a mind to snap at Kellan, but not here, not in front of Anders. I could never hurt or embarrass him like that. Instead, I keep my ire on Anders. This will be the shortest assignment in history because, like hell do I agree.

"Nobody. Is. Bonding. With. Me." I jab a finger into his chest, punctuating each word. *Damn, he's solid.* Not the right time to think about that. "And you are not my bodyguard." I turn with Kellan and storm into the dark night, not daring to look back.

four

. . .

I WAKE UP GASPING, my body sweat-slicked as I fight to untangle my mind from the weird dream. Vivid flashes of a forest covered in mist, black ravens cawing unnervingly, and me...or at least she looked like me. Dressed in a daring black gown, she stood next to a creature that could only be described as evil incarnate. Her milky white hand brushed over the leathery skin and sharp spines of the beast, who bared bloody fangs at me. The girl, me, just stood there with a smile on her blood-red lips that sent a cold shiver down my spine. It was as if I were watching myself, or a version of myself. Except, her eyes weren't dark green; they were lighter and surrounded by black makeup painted like a mask over her eyes.

I shake off the uneasy feeling as I scrunch my toes in the rug, allowing my body to cool off as I rip off my nightgown, and shift my gaze out to the open balcony doors where I find Baedyn's twin moons still above the horizon. This is the only time of day that I feel like I can be truly alone. At home, this is the time of day when the palace is quiet, and I can roam the halls undisturbed or walk my mother's gardens without Kuron or Ezra at my side. They'd probably lock me away if they knew I snuck out.

The first week at school always demands adjustment. It's just a silly nightmare, I tell myself. At home, I am Princess Raea Tierson, heir to the Treon Kingdom. Handmaids, bodyguards, and a team manage my studies. I wear gowns and fine jewelry, surrounded by every comfort. My mornings are for kingdom lore, my afternoons for queenly training, brunches, and teas. Thrice a week, I also train in combat maneuvers. My mother cannot bear the thought of me fighting; my father allows it only because Kuron insisted I learn to defend myself. In the palace, I'm a reflection of my parents, a future queen.

At Drithm, it's the opposite. Here, I am simply another royal, immersed in histories, politics, and training for a battle we may never experience. Here, I run, laugh, and feel free. I get dirty, roll on the floor, take hits while sparring without a room full of assistance. Here, I am not fragile. I walk with my feet in both worlds. I am Princess Raea Tierson, daughter of King Bastian and Queen Amaya, rulers of the most powerful kingdom, and I love my gowns, my jewelry, and the views from our palace. But I am also Raea—Sky Division transport pilot for the system, the girl who runs barefoot, connecting with the land's energy without being told it's unladylike.

I feel it—the energy pulsing beneath me, around me, even in the whisper of the trees. It's always there, speaking to me, as if the planets are alive. This energy, unnoticed by anyone else, pulls at me night and day. I feel it even now with my bare feet on the plush rug. My tutor once laughed when I asked about it, dismissing it as the rumble of the waterfall. I have never told anyone else.

I find Aolyn asleep in her bed, making a mental note to ask her where she was; it seems odd I missed her all day yesterday. I dress quietly in my Xori pants, pulling a black chunky-knit sweater over my corset. These custom-made pants, a gift from Kellan's mother, are woven from a flexible, nearly impenetrable material—a rare, high-cost commodity from the Okenen Kingdom's planet Saedn. The fabric feels like a second skin, breathable and comfortable, and I wear them almost every day at the academy. I head down to the forest below.

Outside, I feel the damp soil between my toes, the soft hum of the planet exhilarating and comforting. The moons illuminate a small pathway along the forest floor. I walk until the AerBall stadium appears to my right—a massive structure in the dark. AerBall is the system's biggest sport—fast-paced and brutal. I've only been to a couple of games and never seen the appeal, though my father loves it.

I find the hidden path in the dark shadows of the trees, remembering it by heart, and follow it through the forest until I reach the secret lake. Most students don't wander this far into the woods. Kellan and I discovered it during our third year at Drithm, and it became our special spot. It's where we swam after long days of sparring and shared our deepest secrets.

Out here, there are no expectations. Just the crystal waters, a forest of trees, and boulders lining the shores, with the occasional Quelin flying overhead. Their wings mirror the ground below, but if you know what to look for, you can find them soaring on invisible winds above the trees.

I'm still angry about last night and need to clear my head. Of course, my parents wouldn't trust me. As a royal female coming of age, it's said that the closer you get to your twenty-third birthday, the more intense your emotions become. This includes not only the Bond but also the attraction to the man who could very well be your future husband.

So far, I only know of Kellan and Anders, but I still have a whole school year ahead of me, and I'm sure things will be downright awkward by next year.

I dip my toes into the lake, and the warm water envelops them like a gentle embrace—the lake is dependably warm. Beneath the shimmering surface lies a natural thermal energy pod, releasing heat that radiates up through the depths. It's always the perfect temperature, even when it's hot outside.

As I gaze at the glowing moons hanging in the sky, I realize I have at least an hour before the sun begins its ascent. I make quick work of my clothes, tossing them to a nearby rock, and with a deep breath, I dive into the water.

The moment I plunge under the surface, a sense of peace and rightness washes over me, releasing the uneasiness of my dream and the sweat on my body. As I swim through its depths, the water glides over my skin like silk, smooth and soothing.

Mixed emotions swirl within me regarding my parents' insistence on needing an escort. Their fear that I'll form the wrong Bond before The Ceremony is louder than my own doubts. They fear I might lose it, but I would never take unnecessary risks. Though the prospect of the Bonding ceremony fills me with apprehension, I refuse to jeopardize my chance at something meaningful just because of an attraction. During the end-of-year ball last year, a Lord from Lyrek tried to force a Bond while we danced. As he leaned in, an unknown energy buzzed around us, but before anything could happen, Kellan swooped in, yanking him away—a protective gesture that left my heart racing.

At that moment, I had realized how deeply I craved a genuine Bond; it was a revelation that made me acutely aware of the delicate tension lingering between Kellan and me. Even now, whenever he leans close, I hesitate, feeling an invisible barrier keeping me from closing the distance. To safeguard my Bond, I dedicated months to honing my mental shield, ensuring it remains securely tucked away, hidden from all potential men and untimely connections. I never want to find myself in that situation again. I felt so scared, so...helpless, but never again.

It's not that kissing him would give away my Bond. It's the heat of the moment that makes most women drop their mental shields, allowing their Bond to link with the wrong man. Doing so leaves you without a true match when you turn twenty-three and therefore, no magic. I can't trust myself to keep control. I'm told I feel things more intensely than others.

In an effort to quell the storm inside me, I take several calming breaths, allowing the night air to fill my lungs. I close my eyes, concentrating on the symphony of energy and sound enveloping me as the water ripples around my body, washing away my anxiety. The hum of Baedyn resonates like a low, steady heartbeat, grounding me. A soft breeze brushes against my skin, the same breeze causing the oak leaves to rustle softly. I always find solace in nature, a halting of time that allows me to rest and gather my thoughts.

Before I know it, the moons sink beyond the horizon, their silvery light fading, signaling it's time to return to the dorms. We're permitted outside, but an unspoken rule warns against wandering into the darkness. Even with Baedyn's protective wards, lurking dangers remind me that some dare to kidnap a royal for gold.

As I swim toward the shore, neon Sella fish flicker like tiny stars against the inky depths. I trail my fingers through the water, feeling their smooth, gel-like bodies brush against my skin, their curiosity matching my own. They dart playfully, illuminating the water with glowing colors.

I use my sweater to dry off, the fabric rough against my damp skin. I regret leaving my towel and swimsuit behind. My single thought at the time was to dip my toes. The brisk air wraps around me, raising goosebumps, yet the water's warmth clings to my skin, shielding me from the chill.

My black panties and bra, a gift from my best friend, Ciara, offer little warmth. She's away on her kingdom's tour, not due back until next week, but her words echo: *take more risks this year. Have fun, but don't give away your Bond.* She has somehow figured out the delicate balance of kissing boys and having fun while maintaining control. I'm a little jealous of that. I've always thought I have pretty good self-control, but when it comes to my emotions...well, I feel...a lot. My pants stick as I pull them on. I don't want Aolyn to wake to an empty room and leave before we've had a chance to catch up.

"You know, you really shouldn't sneak out." I startle and then still, covering myself with my sweater. "Chancellor Xara would have to alert your parents," Anders drawls. I can't see him, but I'd recognize his voice anywhere.

The dark, husky caress of his voice should annoy me, but I can't help the way the Bond light ripples. The sound is deep and resonates within me, melting me on the spot, but it's also laced with sarcasm and danger. I should avoid him, I know I should, but I can't...something about him elicits a sense of life. I am, however, annoyed at the way my traitorous body responds. My breathing becomes shallow, my core aches inappropriately, and I find myself wanting to spend just a few minutes testing out how I'd feel in his arms.

I look around in the fading light of the moons that will drop us into the few minutes of pitch black before the sun rises, and my skin prickles when I can't find him. How the hell can he see me?

"I could say the same about you," I snap as I fumble to get my buttons done on my pants. Anders steps out of the shadows of the tree to my right, jaw tense. He keeps his gaze locked on my face as he nears, his eyes smoldering.

"I told you, escort, remember? You don't have to like it, I sure as hell don't, but..." He tilts his head, watching me. "I won't ignore my duties either." He circles me like I'm his prey before standing in front of me, close enough that the heat radiating off his body warms me.

His eyes lock with mine, giving me time to finish the last of the buttons. Without ever tearing his eyes away, he reaches to the side, grabbing my corset.

"Get dressed," he curses. "The last thing we need is you parading around without clothes on. It's a sure way to lose your Bond, Raea." His jaw clenches, his breathing heavy despite the look of pure annoyance on his face. In this light, his eyes are definitely a darker shade of blue, but the silver stirs, reminding me of a caged cat pacing.

A pastel, iridescent light ripples toward us. He can't see it. Otherwise, I'm sure he would step back. I hold his gaze for a moment, letting the energy tickle my skin. His eyes darken with something like a warning before he brings the corset between us.

I grasp hold of it. Our fingers brush on contact, making me arch into him as emotions and power swirl through me like a gust of wind —emotions I'm not entirely sure belong to me. It's power and lust. Need and longing. Light and dark. A collision of our souls. It's the beginning of life, belonging, and something that feels a lot like home. A small, breathless moan escapes my mouth as he releases it so quickly that I nearly stumble, barely catching myself before bumping into his chest.

What the hell was that?

I take a cleansing breath to regain my thoughts. We are playing with fire. He knows it. I know it. His heavy breathing indicates he felt all of that, too. I don't know what the hell that was, but I'm not sure I want to ever feel it again. Not knowing how to make things less awkward than they are, I resort to sarcasm and attitude to hide my bewilderment.

"What? You've never seen a girl in her underwear before?" I scoff, pulling the fitted corset over my breasts as I lace up the back with practiced dexterity.

He groans almost silently, but I feel it. "It's one thing to be in underwear," he exhales. "It's entirely different to be swimming in nothing. And yes, to answer your question, I have."

Something twists in my chest. Surely not jealousy, but another part —anger—dominates every other emotion. "You were watching me?"

"Don't worry," he scoffs with a slight, arrogant tilt to his lips. My eyes drop there on their own accord. "I wasn't watching you. I was a perfect gentleman." He pauses, his eyes waiting for a reaction I won't give him. He shrugs his hands into his pants casually before continuing. "I watched you leave the dorms and followed."

"Unbelievable." I pull my sweater over my head. I don't bother letting him know I'm done before brushing past him, letting my shoulder collide with his arm. *Dammit, he's tall.* I'm angry, embarrassed, confused, and yet, all I want is to turn around, push him against the rock wall, and feel the hard lines of his body pressed against mine. To feel his hands roaming over me. To feel all of that, whatever that was, again.

"Raea." He reaches out, wrapping his hand around my wrist, yanking me back. I'm surprised at the gentleness with which he holds my wrist. It's in stark contrast with everything about him. I'm pulled against his chest in one simple move, my back to his front. My body hums delightedly as he keeps a strong arm wrapped around me, pinning my wrist to my hip.

"Please, for the sake of your Bond," he whispers against the shell of my ear, making goosebumps break out over my body. I close my eyes, and it's all I can do not to lean back into him. "Stay fully dressed. I only have so much self-control."

I can't help the small gasp that escapes my lips and the heady feeling as I breathe him in. It's warm and citrusy and something entirely unique that I haven't been able to place. Something that brings up a memory, but no matter how hard I try, I can't pull it forward into clarity.

We both held still, our breaths coming in fast, quietly trying to figure out what was next. Then, the sun burst from the horizon, shooting rays of gold and pink around us and awakening us. What the hell am I doing? I break free with what little resolve I have left and march back to the dorms, never looking back, knowing he has decided not to follow.

It's going to be a long year.

five

. . .

"WHAT DID YOU DO FOR BREAK?" Aolyn and I are getting ready for dinner. We're both in my bathroom, products spread on the counter before us. It's the first time we've been able to catch up. As we chat, I focus on braiding the thick strands of my hair into sections before pulling it up into an intricate design.

I was beginning to worry after a full day of classes and not seeing her yesterday. She assures me she is fine. Apparently, being a division leader comes with the perk of meetings with Chancellor Xara, the professors, and dorm briefings. Not to mention, she was on a call with her mother late into the night.

"Spent time at the resorts and hot springs. Things at home are..." she sighs, brushing out her long, onyx hair. Mine is the opposite: white as fresh snow, shimmering like the stars in the sky. I'm the only one I have ever met with such hair, a curious anomaly. My parents claim a dormant gene, but a whispered family tale speaks of a different truth: a gift from the gods, a touch of pure starlight, bestowed upon my mother when she was barren. As a child, I cried that I couldn't have my mother's chestnut waves or my father's darker color, but now, this bright white is a part of who I am. I could dye it, but I never will.

We've been friends for years, and every time we're pictured together, someone comments about our hair. It's annoying.

"Difficult?" I supply. "I heard..." I stop braiding, glancing over at her. Her glassy blue eyes narrow a moment, waiting on me. "I've just heard that Boyce is still not accepting the Bond?" More like refusing the Bond.

The media has consistently portrayed her brother as problematic and rebellious. His refusal to Bond with the poor duchess says as much. While most people wish for and pray for a strong Bond, including commoners who yearn for one, I find myself questioning why it is necessary at all.

Aolyn rolls her eyes and turns back toward the mirror, picking up the coal she lines her eyes with. I watch as she lines both top and bottom, never wavering, her hand so steady. The black reminds me so much of my dream, I have to look away.

Aolyn shifts her weight uncomfortably. "My brother just isn't ready to settle down. Despite my parents' protests, he still wants to party and explore his freedom. It's only temporary." She drops the coal and turns to me. "Look, I know the rumors. I've heard them, but Boyce is just being Boyce, and my father is alive and well. He's been locked away in his study, working." Her words attempt to reassure, but a cold tendril of intuition snakes down my spine.

After a long moment of silence and nodding, I offer her a tight smile as an apology and then tug her into my closet. I have a whole row of dinner gowns, and we're basically the same size. "Pick one," I tell her, gesturing to the wall of opulent silks, chiffons, and fine materials hanging delicately on fabric hangers. She rolls her eyes, but a big smile crosses her face as she reaches for my only black gown.

"If this is your version of a peace offering, I accept." We both chuckle and, minutes later, head down to the dining hall, arm in arm. As we walk, she tells me about an initiative she's working on to provide villagers with better heating systems, rather than relying solely on fireplaces. Her kingdom has ten planets, all of which are in a perpetual state of winter.

We split when we arrive at the intimately lit hall. The hall is filled with hushed voices and the clinking of silverware as she heads to the front of the room, where the other leadership members sit. I move to sit with Sky Division.

Around the room, the candlelight casts everyone in warm hues, the lighting bouncing off silk gowns and bronze buttons of the men's jackets.

I'm hit with the rich scent of spices and savory food, making my mouth water as I drop into my chair, already eager to see what is on the menu for this evening. At home, our cook rotates through foods harvested from our gardens, local forests, and waterfalls. While I enjoy the fresh, clean foods, these rich scents remind me of the deserts of Mori.

"I just don't think it's a good idea. It's too risky," Britta argues as I pull out a seat between Aada and Tate. Having classes and eating together forces us to get to know each other like I haven't done in other Orders. Kellan and I would often hang out with Ciara or by ourselves, and occasionally talk to Tate.

"That's just because you have no faith in your mental shield," he retorts before shoveling a bite of stew into his mouth, followed by a piece of flatbread that looks and smells fantastic. I drop my stuff and find the window for the flatbread and stew, bypassing the seafare window and the dessert window, which is stacked with miniature cakes and custards.

The cook slides a tray through for me, her eyes twinkling as she smiles at me.

"Is it possible to have some of the flatbread too?" Someone behind me barks out a laugh, making me smile even though I have no idea why they are laughing.

"I'm so sorry, we're out." She looks around like she can conjure a piece. "Let me go see if they're making more." I tell her to take her time as she leaves the window, pushing through another door where the food is prepared.

I lean against the cool tile, waiting for her return, when the air around me seems to change, charging with the same kind of energy you feel just before lightning strikes. I roll my shoulders uncomfortably as the energy works its way through every nerve ending. Before I have time to look around, Anders says, "You can have mine," his voice deep and warm.

Don't look. Don't look.

I look over and up, and warmth spreads through my body as I meet his eyes. *Dammit.* His gaze cascades down my body, taking in the gown I chose to wear tonight. It has an illusion neckline, sheer gossamer over my chest and arms, and a thicker, darker material bodice, allowing me to wear my corset beneath.

The navy-colored gown features a flowing skirt that sparkles when I move. It's one of my favorites, and I wear it to dinner parties frequently.

When his gaze meets mine again, his nostrils flare, and his jaw ticks like he's angry, but what in Astor's name could he be pissed about? I haven't done anything that could possibly upset him. It's not like I saw him this afternoon after classes, since he had AerBall and I had my running club meeting, but I've done nothing wrong.

"I'm good," I state, pasting on my "fuck-you-very-much" smile and turning away from the counter, annoyed. The flatbread doesn't seem so appetizing if it means I have to spend another minute in his presence.

I find my seat, still feeling flustered, when he walks by. His eyes dart to my table before focusing on the woman walking toward him. She's gorgeous. The woman is tall, with long blonde hair, tanned skin similar to his, big bright blue eyes, and a red, fitted gown that shows a lot of skin.

Her arms wrap around his neck, and he tugs her close with his free hand. She's precisely the kind of woman I picture he will Bond with. Something uncomfortable unfurls in my chest, making me rub the spot.

She giggles, leaning in and batting her long lashes. It shouldn't bother me, but I instantly dislike her.

I'm still glowering at the woman, rubbing my chest, when Jakob asks, "You okay?" His question cuts through the hum in my head, bringing me back to the conversation. Jakob raises his brows as I look around, attempting to catch up with the discussion.

"Yep," I say too quickly. "Just a little sore." The lie rolls off my tongue easily. When I glance back up to where Anders is, he's gone, already seated at the leadership table, talking to Trysten.

Professor Brendn's voice booms through the Transport Hall, instantly silencing the usual chatter. "Listen up," he commands, his gaze sweeping over the assembled Executive Sky Divisions from all three dorms. Outside, twenty different transports gleam on the launch pad, waiting to be assigned to us juniors. "Today, we're learning about weather patterns and emergency situations," he continues. "You've all mastered piloting, communication, and navigation. Flying the system is exciting, but you need to know what happens if there's an emergency and you need to land on a planet."

He surveys the room. We have class with the seniors once a week, allowing us juniors to learn from their experience. For the past few weeks, we've been reacquainting ourselves with school transports. Just yesterday, we were tested for our unit positions. I'm assigned pilot, with Tate for navigation and Ciara for communications. When we got our assignments, Ciara and I jumped around like giddy teenagers while Tate playfully groaned.

Ciara, who arrived a week after my lakeside incident with Anders, still hasn't let up on the teasing.

Lady Kaetlyn twists in her seat in front of me, craning her neck to look back at Ryker—Anders, as I stubbornly call him. Everyone else at school seems resigned to using his given name, but knowing it gets under his skin makes it all the more enjoyable for me. "Ryker," she begins, "I was hoping you could help me—"

Trysten's growl cuts her off. "Turn around, Kaetlyn." I fight the stupid smile threatening to spread across my face as Kaetlyn's red hair swings around her shoulders, her cheeks turning a dark crimson as she faces forward again.

"How many planets do not have a breathable atmosphere?" Professor Brendn asks.

Instinctively, my hand shoots up. I love learning, and frankly, my private tutors—the best in the system—ensure that school never really ends, even during breaks. It keeps me busy, which I appreciate.

"Yes, Raea?" Professor Brendn leans back against his makeshift desk of manuals and maps. He crosses one ankle over the other, his silver brows rising in a silent prompt.

"There are only four planets without a breathable atmosphere," I reply, relieved that my astronomy professor's weekly quizzes at home are paying off. "Three are in the Kadora Kingdom, but one planet is in the Ateria Kingdom."

"And how do those planets survive? We know all four are inhabited with growing populations," he presses, knowing I will continue. Students around the room turn toward me, half of them likely hoping I get it wrong. Since school started, I've already faced my share of criticism about preferential treatment. People either love or hate my parents. It seems the closer we get to graduation, the more vocal citizens—both ours and those of other kingdoms—become.

"The Kadora Kingdom created what are called Mesh units that allow each citizen to walk around in their own breathable atmosphere. A Mesh can be worn on any piece of clothing. Their colonies are also surrounded by Mesh barriers, allowing free movement without a personal Mesh. Single-Mesh units are primarily assigned to scouts and reconnaissance teams who train on their volcanoes. The planet Zinik in Ateria began trading with Kadora in UC 183, and Zinik now has its own Mesh cities."

He nods. "Well, Princess, it would seem your parents have done a great job with your education." He rubs a hand over his beard. "Bonus question: What are the Mesh units made of?"

Thankfully, during my kingdoms tour—which requires royals and nobility entering their junior year to visit all capital planets and three trade planets—I toured the facility that makes the Mesh units.

"They're made of plasma shingles meshed together. The plasma shields you from the toxic atmosphere and radiation while recycling your own oxygen, allowing you to breathe fresh air. The mesh stretches and moves with you, keeping you within its protective bubble."

I settle back in my seat as Ciara rolls her eyes next to me. "Showoff," she whispers, twisting the tablet pen she uses to sketch creatures onto her notes.

"Hey, can you help me with my planets assignment?" Tate whispers from my other side. "I can't remember which planet is which, or which kingdom it belongs to." I glance at him, noticing his black, wavy hair is once again a mess, hanging over his forehead. Still, his eagerness to learn wins me over, along with his goofy grin.

"We can study before class. I'll help you. Now, pay attention."

For the remainder of class, we learn about flying through wind, fog, rain, and blizzards. Most students here have never flown through all four, but thanks to Lt. Piori, I have. On my home planet of Kyrr, we deal with intense fog and rain, but it never snows. For snow, we have to head towards the Ateria Kingdom, where their planets have the highest and most prominent mountain regions in the system.

Our closest planet to Ateria, Gowden, experiences similar weather patterns, but its mountains aren't as high or cold. Kuron is always unhappy when we fly through there, but Lt. Piori seems unbothered by my guard's general grumpiness.

"Now, an assignment for you all," Professor Brendn announces. A resounding sigh and groans echo through the room. "By the end of the week, I want you to name every weather pattern you might experience during a typical flight. I don't want to know about planets you may never visit. Instead, focus on the planets your kingdoms trade with, and which kingdoms you'll be required to visit during Bonding ceremonies. Turn them in before class. Don't forget to check your transport assignments on your way out. You are dismissed."

I grab my bag and stand with Ciara as we head back to the dorms before lunch. It's an unusually hot day, and I pin my hair up, desperate for any breeze to cool me down. Throughout my years on Baedyn, the weather has been temperate, but this year, I seem to be struggling to stay cool. The moment I rip my corset off in my room, I feel ten degrees cooler. The Nakata material it's made of is the strongest in the system—impenetrable, fire-resistant, even supposedly safe from an asteroid chunk. My parents would put me in a full-body uniform if they could.

Between the corset, the energy shield band I wear on my wrist like jewelry, and the near-zero crime on Baedyn, I'm practically invincible. But today, I quickly change into lighter leggings and a thin black tank, happily forgoing the corset—only for today.

After lunch, we have a short break before History Class, so Ciara and Tate follow me to one of the many study spaces on the first floor. We find the first empty one: a circular glass room with a round table at the center, perfect for projections. It's the ideal spot to help with their planet assignments. After dimming the lights and shading the glass walls for privacy, I take control of the panel.

"Tate, what planet are you from again?" I'm a little embarrassed I have to ask, though he doesn't seem to mind. He's already shuffling books and his tablet from his bag across the table.

"Brinvek." I use the system simulator to project our three planets in the center. Ciara and I, of course, will no doubt have the same planets and route on a typical mission. She spends half the year in the Southern Forests of Kyrr, where her family estate is, and the other half on Kallik, a planet near the Kadora Kingdom. Kallik is renowned for its sturdy timber and is one of the most vital trade planets in our kingdom.

Ciara leans back in her chair like she's already done the assignment, and I can't help but giggle a little. I wish I could be more like her—so laid back and calm all the time. She's six months younger, but sometimes I feel ten years wiser. Her light caramel skin is still tanned from her kingdoms tour, and her long brown hair is woven into a mix of small and large braids that reach her mid-back. Her big brown eyes soften as she glances at something on her Prism before setting it down. She's the perfect blend of her parents: her father, tall with carob skin and one of the funniest people I've ever met, and her mother, beautiful, fair-skinned, loyal to a fault, and possessing a presence that makes everyone pause.

"Okay, so let's start with my kingdom so you can see how I learn and what planets I know will be along my route." Tate nods, holding his pen as if everything I'm about to say is crucial. I appreciate that about him. For all his goofiness, he still takes his studies seriously.

"So, obviously, Kyrr is near the center of the system, making it a stronghold. My kingdom has twenty-two planets in total. My instructors helped me by breaking them into smaller groups of resources and trade routes. If I bring up all the planets with essential natural resources…" I change the map, and eight planets appear.

"These eight planets have many of the resources that power the kingdoms. Resources essential for colonies and villages, and more importantly, these planets provide the materials for cleaning the water in the smaller, outlying planets." Tate is fascinated, as if he's never seen them before. This is surprising since he should have completed several hours of tours before returning to school.

"So, okay. Essential resource planets. Do you visit those?" he asks, brushing back his loose hair.

"Of course. What kind of leader would I be if I never took the time to visit and understand exactly what we're harvesting and trading? How can I rule if I don't understand how precious these planets and their resources are? The colonies there live and breathe the work they do." I swipe my hand, and the planets drop to small dots, replaced with our ten essential trade planets.

"These ten are our trading outposts, where supplies move in and out of the kingdom. For example, Rayek borders the kingdom of Thirik and is a direct shot to the kingdom of Mori, which needs timber and minerals. Do you know why Mori needs them so badly?"

Tate and Ciara both shake their heads. Gods, from here on out, I'll have to teach them. I can't help but feel that, somehow, the academy has failed them. To me, this is essential knowledge. Then again, they aren't in line to be king or queen.

"The Mori kingdom has planets full of canyons and valleys, but also dry deserts and little to no vegetation, with dried seas and very few freshwater resources. Some of their planets, like Ia and Ulen, have vegetation and water, but it's not enough to sustain the whole kingdom. So they trade with us. Feandra has spices we use in our cooking. Chyr has dyes from underground cave systems that we use for our clothing. See, every planet has something to offer another. We just have to know what it is and what they're willing to trade for."

We spend the rest of our study time going through Tate's kingdom of Thirik and categorizing its six planets. Ciara uses my notes to do the same with ours. By the time we're done, I feel more confident they will pass this class.

Before History, I run upstairs to trade out my books. Once again, I find Anders in my personal space after closing my door. Couldn't he at least stand across the hall, along the banister?

"Princess," he grunts, clearly annoyed with me, even though I haven't assigned him this ridiculous role. I ignore him, reaching to push him away, but make the mistake of laying my palms on his stomach. Gods, I can feel the mass of rippled muscles beneath my hands. I yank them away quickly and march toward the steps. He doesn't have History with me, so I'm not sure why he bothers following. Right now, he has senior intelligence, which is the opposite direction.

"You know Intel is that way?" I remind him, throwing a thumb over my shoulder without looking back.

"Well, I was going to tell you about a veil report I just received, but since you're intent on ignoring me..." I swivel so fast my head spins. I look up expectantly. His lips quirk before he pulls out his Prism. "Its thinnest spot is along Ateria with a small hole near Kadora. The weather in both places has been extreme." I nibble on my lip, thinking of all the implications. Should they be evacuating?

"And our kingdoms?" He hands me his device.

"All good," he says as I read through the report. I feel a little guilty for the sigh of relief that escapes me. "Are we doing anything to help them?"

Anders takes his Prism back, tucking it into his pocket as he nods for us to keep moving. We take the stairs together as he tells me Kadora is taking precautions with the villages near the lava fields, moving them into the colonies for now. Ateria is working with my kingdom to order more wood to stockpile as they wait and weather the unprecedented cold.

I say a quick thanks for the update as I make my way into class. He lingers a moment before heading to his own, the crowd parting for him as he goes.

History is essentially a recap of everything I have already learned. Professor Darci discusses the battle between the first great houses, which fought for planets and established the first trade agreements, all of which have been archived.

I zone out and use my time instead to map out the royal households for my Bonding ceremony. Our first Bonding Class is next week, and we'll need to know who in the royal households are of age. Plus, I like being prepared.

There are only three other princes my age, including Anders and Cole, and Prince Felix from the Oris kingdom. Even though he's technically five years older, he's still unBonded. They'll be the first to receive invites, though Bonding with another royal would probably create chaos—at least if I were to Bond with a crown-prince. If it was a second heir, I doubt anyone would bat an eye.

My hope, this is all for nothing. If I could somehow will my choice into existence, it would be Kellan.

I step into the study room the four of us use for our Government Class. While everyone else takes the standard Government I and II, Anders, Cole, Aolyn, and I have the not-so-luxurious task of taking a specialized class for ruling monarchs. Cole and Aolyn are second in line to the throne but need the same education as we do.

Professor Sukín arrives, a short, pale-skinned woman with jet-black hair and wide, dark eyes. She's worked with us individually since we were in Primms, overseeing our schedules, adjusting classes, and supplementing where needed. This is the first time I'm required to take an actual class.

I slide into a chair at the round table across from Cole and try to ignore Anders, though I can't help my eyes navigating to him of their own accord. Cole lifts a single brow at me when I don't answer Anders' question about my interview with Kelci for the school newspaper.

Last week, Kelci, the editor-in-chief of the school news distribution, asked if I'd be willing to discuss an article she wanted to write. She omitted the part about Anders and me being featured in the same article. In said article, she may have overexaggerated that Anders and I will be the two most powerful rulers in a hundred years. Funny, as I have no intention of taking the crown from my parents anytime soon. Tradition dictates that the crown passes on the ruling monarch's sixty-fifth birthday or if they become ill and unfit to rule. My father is completely healthy and has another ten years until then.

Aolyn nudges me, and I roll my eyes, sighing dramatically before turning to face Anders.

"Yes?" I ask in a saccharine-sweet voice, batting my lashes. Cole covers a laugh with a cough while Anders mutters something under his breath about me being a pain in his ass.

"I asked if you knew about the article?" He feigns indifference, though I can tell I've gotten under his skin again. It's becoming my favorite pastime despite our occasional moments of harmony. He sits back, stretching his legs out and crossing his arms over his chest, putting his whole body on display.

Aolyn kicks me under the table, knocking some sense into me. I slam my drooling mouth closed and clear my throat, hoping he didn't just catch me openly admiring him.

"I did not. It would seem Kelci kept that little fact to herself. No matter. What's done is done. She didn't say anything in there that could harm our parents or tarnish our reputations." I shrug and make a show of inspecting my nails, which definitely need some filing.

His fist slams onto the table, making the whole thing rattle. "She made my kingdom seem weak without my father."

I shrug again, but I can understand his irritation. Since King Aki went missing, there have been claims that Queen Priana's health is declining. Whether or not it's true, I have no idea. I've seen her in photos attending trade meetings and the yearly summit where all seven kingdoms gather to discuss their grievances.

"She didn't say anything that hasn't already been brought into question by other media sources. Nobody believes it anyway. Your mother is ruling just fine, and there's been no move to dethrone her. Besides, after you're Bonded, you'll be crowned king, and this will all be moot come next year." I swear the room drops about ten degrees, making my hair stand on end. He doesn't even have to tell me how he feels; it's written all over his face.

Professor Sukín finally arrives and glances between the four of us, dismissing the looks of boredom, irritation, amusement, and provocation on our faces. She sets a strange iron tube on the table before us. The iron has a weird set of markings etched into it. Anders shifts uncomfortably, and when I look up at him, I swear his eyes are pure silver. He shakes his head with a deep breath, and his eyes are back to normal. *Is he okay? Was that just the light?* I glance at Cole, but he doesn't seem to notice.

"Alright, today we have the opportunity to read one of the few ancient scrolls preserved from Einvald that was found in a library on Orcleus. Cole, would you please read aloud about the transitions of the last empire to the seven kingdoms?" She lifts the iron tube and pulls a scroll unrolling from it, the parchment marked with old ink and age.

Cole sighs as she sets it in front of him. While I lean closer to get a better look, Anders seems frozen in place, his gaze burning a hole into the scroll. I frown, catching the intensity of his stare, something more than just academic interest.

"It is with great sadness that Empress Anele has passed, her body now encased in the imperial tomb on the palace grounds. Since her death two months ago, Prince Aric has fallen ill. He's not expected to survive the week." Cole clears his throat before continuing. "Date 8,991 AC. It is with astonishment that our beloved Prince has joined his mother in the imperial tombs. With no heirs, Emperor Aren has declared the Astral Council will rule as one.

"The seven great households will be divided into seven kingdoms on the death of our last emperor. Lord Treon will oversee the twenty-two planets currently under his command. Lord Okenen, his eighteen. Lord Thirik, much to his disagreement, will remain overseeing his command of the six. Lord Mori, with his eight, and Lord Ateria with his ten. There has been much deliberation over the eight planets overseen by Lord Oris and Lord Kadora—a combination of the two sectors —but after a heated discussion and the allocation of resources defining the eight planets, it has been decided that each will remain as they are. Lord Oris with his three, Lord Kadora with five."

Cole continues reading about the first preparations for the transition of power, which was done in secret, only announced when the emperor joined his family in the tombs.

We spend the last thirty minutes of class paired up. Blessedly, I'm paired with Cole since we are both juniors, and Aolyn and Anders are seniors. We have to choose one of the first households after the Lords passed off their new crowns, to present and share what they did well, where they made mistakes, and whether we agree with the laws they implemented during those first few years as the system fell into chaos.

Cole and I immediately choose King Kàstiel, who ruled as the first true king of Treon, while Aolyn and Anders choose King Orin of Ateria.

While we research King Kàstiel, Cole murmurs a half-apology for being so rude at the beginning of the school year. I wave him off, telling him I don't hold grudges. He grins at me and glances at his brother mischievously.

Cole seems to love getting under his brother's skin as much as I do. For the remainder of class, we bump shoulders, lean into each other's space to glance at each other's tablets, and speak in hushed voices, smiling and laughing over literally nothing. By the end of class, Anders looks like he might actually burst.

"See you tonight," Cole says with a wink when he leaves, making me blush even though we had no conversation about meeting up. I know it's just a ploy to annoy Anders, so I go along with it and give him a small smile.

"Raea," Anders growls as he comes to stand beside me. Aolyn looks between the two of us and grabs my hand.

"Rae, I need some help." Then she pulls me from class, my arm tucked under hers as she shoots me a knowing smile. I don't bother looking back at Anders. I can feel his heated glare on my back. We both giggle as we make our way up to our room for a few minutes before our next classes.

six

. . .

Is ignoring Anders a bit petty? Perhaps, but I refuse to be swept away by his dark and mysterious charm. Unlike so many women around me who seem eager to vie for his attention, I hold my self-respect in high regard. For that reason, keeping my distance feels best—safe.

I don't complain when he walks me to class each morning, or when he escorts me back to my room in the evenings. Our interactions, however brief, remain polite and surface-level, avoiding any deeper connection. Yet, despite my best efforts, a small part of me knows that I can't maintain this distance indefinitely. There's an undeniable pull that tugs at my resolve, making me wonder what it would be like to let my mental shield open just a little.

I attempted to have a conversation with Chancellor Xara about my concerns, only to discover later that Anders had also approached her regarding the removal of his detail. As expected, she remained unmoved by my plight. Despite her indifference, this arrangement causes him to arrive late to class each morning and leaves me with a towering presence—a six-foot-something distraction—with an ever-rotating cast of girls batting their lashes in his direction. It feels like every time I look up from my books, there's another flirty exchange happening mere feet away from me.

I can't quite decipher his intentions with me. Perhaps he's trying to win me over? Just the other night, while I was up late studying, he unexpectedly brought me a cup of tea. Not coffee, mind you—tea. This small gesture spoke volumes, suggesting that he knows my preference for the soothing herbal liquid over the typical bean juice that most students crave. It's not that I'd outright refuse coffee; I just find that tea has a much more appealing flavor.

Underneath it all, there's an unpredictable quality to him that leaves me reeling. One moment, he presents a side that is warm and considerate, offering glimpses of someone I might genuinely enjoy getting to know. But then, there are times when he transforms into the brooding asshole everyone else knows him as. I'll walk right into a door he lets swing shut in my face, and the momentary glare he shoots my way makes me feel as though I've somehow offended him. The inconsistency is maddening, leaving me to wonder which version of him I'll encounter next.

It shouldn't matter to me...it doesn't matter. He's graduating at the end of the year and off to Bond with someone else. He won't be a problem much longer, and I will continue to pray for a release from my shadow.

It's been a few days since that awkward Government Class, but Cole has made every attempt to say hi to me whenever Anders is watching. Whatever game we are playing, I'm not enjoying it anymore. I need to talk to Cole, set some boundaries, and clarify that we can be friends for real—not because he wants to annoy his brother.

Speaking of said brother, Anders is nowhere to be found today. I have no idea where he is...nor do I care, but I'm thankful for the autonomy. How surprising that I can get myself to and from all of my classes alone, without someone attempting to Bond with me in the halls without my scary escort around.

During lunch, I find a quiet spot in the corner of the yard and tuck myself under one of the ornamental trees to read. The weather is warm today, but a light breeze keeps the heat from overwhelming me.

The fresh air carries the scent of newly fallen snow from the mountains, mixed with the smell of pine and a hint of flowers from the fall blooms. I let out a contented sigh as I lean against the brick wall, propping my tablet on my knees.

It might not be the most exciting material, but learning about the Lumos Bond and the first emperor and empress to receive it settles some of my nerves about our first class.

I scroll through the pages of *The Lumos Bond - A New Beginning* and realize that the entire court went through a Bonding ceremony after Emperor Aren did. I reread the page to make sure I have it right.

Hours after the first Lumos Bond was completed, members of the court, both married and unmarried, participated in what is now known as The Ceremony. At that time, the process was archaic and painful, as they had yet to discover the serum that would later help identify Bonded partners. Many remained Bonded to their spouses, but for a select few, their connections turned out to be much stronger with different partners.

It was not until UC 05 that we learned the significance of the Bond on the twenty-third birthday of the female partner. However, males typically exhibit a more substantial Bond before the age of twenty-eight.

My jaw drops as shock and outrage stir in my chest. Married couples were forced to Bond with others? Anger stirs in my chest. How the gods think this is fair, this is right....*ugh...* it's not. I scroll further, bypassing the rest of the section, landing upon a section on the Bond itself.

Light, colors, minor zaps of energy—it's everything I've been feeling with Kellan and Anders. The connection I share with Kellan is unlike anything else. It's gentle and soothing, like a soft caress or a gentle breeze that wraps around me, enveloping me in a lulling warmth.

It's a stark contrast to the potential Bond with Anders, which ignites a very different kind of fire within me. It's intense and electrifying, and makes my skin feel ablaze and my body hum with energy. It feels like raw energy, filled with passion and urgency, every interaction leaving shockwaves reverberating through me. While Kellan's presence brings tranquility, Anders awakens me in a way I can't ignore.

The lunch bell sounds, softly ringing out three times, signaling that I need to head inside. I groan and shuffle the tablet back into my linen bag, taking a long pull of water before shoving the bottle in next. My body aches from sitting in one position for so long as I head back toward Taeolyn.

I don't make it past Veker before three men, who I believe are seniors, approach me, their faces all masked in irritation. The one at the center, the tallest of the group, has a hawkish nose and is a little round at the stomach. I keep my focus on him as he approaches ahead of the other two, his hands clenched at his sides.

"There ya' are, Princess," he says with a thick accent I recognize from one of the smaller colonies on Dionek. "We've been looking fer ya." The other two huff behind him. It's only then that I realize I'm being herded as I step back and find myself against the backside of Veker, away from all witnesses.

Now would probably be a good time to sprint—or I don't know, call someone—maybe. These three seem pretty pissed, and I'm positive I don't have a clue who they are except that I've seen them around.

The three of them are wearing Bragr Recon colors, and I take a few seconds to analyze them, looking for weaknesses. If I ran, I'd outpace at least two of them, but the third looks like he could catch me in two strides.

I need to distract them if I have a hope of getting away. For the first time since school started, I realize that I may very well be in danger. "Ah, well, I'm going to be late for class, and I'm meeting with Ryker, so I should really get going," I ramble as calmly as possible. I inhale slowly, trying to slow my racing heart. Adrenaline pumps through my system as the man at the center steps closer, now only four feet away.

"How very interestin'," the one on the left starts. "One." He holds up a finger. "Yer dark prince isn't here. He's on Kyrr with yer father." *What?* Anders is on Kyrr? Why, and why didn't he tell me? "And two..." Another finger. "Yer father 'tis responsible fer my father no longer having a job and is currently bein' stripped of his title." My stomach bottoms out. *Oh shit.* It's rare for nobility to lose their titles, which means one thing: he is responsible for illegal activity. My father would never strip anyone unless there was undeniable evidence.

The other two flank me, giving me nowhere to run. The one to my right is a man with auburn hair tied back in two war braids, and the look he's giving me promises retribution. The one to my left is tall, his black coils shaved short, and his smirk says he's enjoying this.

Focus. I need to focus.

"I'm so sorry to hear that. Maybe I can call my father and ask if it was a mistake?"

The one to my left chuckles darkly. "Tis no mistake," he hums. "Our families are as corrupt as they come." He steps closer, three feet. "All yer father had to do was turn a blind eye. We aren't hurtin' anyone who didn't already deserve it, and yer *daddy* had to go sticking his nose where it doesn't belong."

The other two shuffle closer, and they're all so big that I don't stand a chance. All the training in the world won't help me when I'm not armed. I discreetly tap my energy shield on, the cool metal of the bracelet humming to life at my touch. At least if they attack, they'll have to move at the right speed to pierce through it.

"Let's go," the one on my right snaps. "They'll be here soon. Bind her hands and gag her." He reaches for me in one heartbeat, rebounding and growling. The second heartbeat, the one in front of me, boxes me in, a purple material in his hands that I'm assuming he plans to use for the gag.

I knee him where it hurts, and in his anger, his head slams down against mine, causing my vision to splinter as pain radiates across my head. Nausea swirls in my stomach, but I don't think I'm concussed.

I feel my hands being yanked in front of me and wrapped tightly as my energy shield is ripped from my wrist.

"Please," I beg, my vision finally clearing. I can feel my heartbeat throughout my entire body. My head throbs with every pulse. Here I was, thinking I didn't need Anders. The one freaking time. "What are you going to do with me? Kidnapping a royal is an immediate thirty-year sentence, if not banishment to work on one of the moons."

"Just gag her already," the one to my left says, ripping the purple material from the one in front of me, who's on his knees, seething through his pain.

I should scream, but it gets lodged in my throat. When I try, it's a sob that rips through my lips before the material is shoved into my mouth, making me gag. My feet aren't tied, and I know they'll take me if I don't run.

I've never been in so much danger, and right now, all that training I've been doing my whole life is telling me to fight back. I shove my boot at the man in front of me and leap over his kneeling frame, launching into a sprint as soon as I land. If I can just get beyond this wall, I'm sure there will be students still leaving the dining hall who will see me.

The two men behind me roar as they chase after me. I don't dare look over my shoulder to see how close they are. I use every ounce of energy and focus to get into the central courtyard.

Thirty feet. I run faster than I have before, thankful I've been running every day, and even more thankful I'm wearing pants and not a dress. My boots barely make a sound as I fly across the packed dirt toward the brick paths.

Twenty feet. An arm snaps out, wrapping around my waist and hauling me to him.

It happens so fast, I can't even process how, but I scream through the material, kicking and flailing as fat tears stream down my cheeks. If they plan to take me, it will not be without a fight. I throw my head back and meet a hard chest.

"Dammit, calm down, Raea," a male voice barks—and...and...I pause, my body going completely stiff. *Wait*, I recognize that voice. "What the hell is going on here?" he roars, letting me go and pulling the fabric out of my mouth, but he's talking to the men behind me. As I turn, I see all three of my attackers now flanked by Cole's friends. Cole's hands are so gentle as he unbinds mine despite the lethal glare sketched across his features.

His blue eyes simmer with icy, unchecked rage as he keeps me close to his side. I inhale his woodsy scent and nearly sob as my adrenaline comes to a screeching halt.

"That bitch deserves to be spaced," the redhead snarls as he's shoved to his knees. My breath hitches, but my head is swimming from the hit, and now my thoughts are stuck on being spaced. It's a practice that has been outlawed for over three centuries. The imperial guard used to take prisoners who couldn't be forced into work and dump them in space. It was an immediate death sentence.

Cole just cracks his knuckles like he's imagining cracking their bones. "Take them to the chancellor and tell her to call the Protos to escort them to Treon. She can alert King Bastian—"

"No!" I beg. "No, please. If my parents find out." I look up into Cole's bright blue eyes and find how intensely they're staring back at me. "Please, Cole. They'll pull me out." His jaw ticks, reminding me so much of Anders.

An ache settles in my chest, and there's an unwarranted desire for Anders to be here, which is so damn irrational. But it's probably because I know this wouldn't have happened if my grumpy shadow had been here.

Cole's nostrils flare. "Fine." He looks up to his friends. "I'll call Rhoan. He'll know what to do." Something in my gut tells me that whatever it is, it won't be good. The kinder punishment might be sending them to my father.

One of Cole's friends, I think his name is Luca, slams his fist into the temple of the redhead, knocking him out with a single strike. The one holding the dark-haired one sends him flying with a kick to his temple. I grimace and bury my face in Cole's side. We might not be friends, but I do feel safe around him.

"Don't let your friends kill them," I whimper.

Cole chuckles as he wraps an arm around my shoulders, turning me around so my back is to them. "They won't. Just need to keep them quiet until Rhoan gets here."

"And who is Rhoan?" I let him lead me around the corner. To my surprise, the courtyard is empty of all students and staff. *Dammit.* That means I'm late for class. Not that I should go. My hands are trembling, and my head is still throbbing.

"You don't want to know. Trust me. For now," he responds, turning us left and leading me out of the Executive Yard. "We are going to the healers because you tripped and hit your head on the brickwork." I see his cover for what it is, and I almost let out a sob of relief.

So the asshole's brother is actually kind and sweet. I nod and let Cole lead me there, not daring to look back or think of who Rhoan is and what he will do to the three students.

seven

. . .

The relentless pounding on my door reverberates through the air, jarring me from my thoughts as I step out of the steam-filled bathroom. My hair clings to my shoulders, and the warm scent of forest blooms still lingers on my skin from the shower. Thankfully, I managed to slip into a flowing gown moments ago, dressing for the first Bonding class. Yet, despite my outward appearance, my mind is a whirlpool, still reeling from the day's events.

After my apprehensive visit to the healer—a young woman who fussed over me despite Agneta's constant glare—Cole had escorted me back to Taeolyn. His voice carried a mixture of reassurance and finality when he informed me that Chancellor Xara had been made aware of my unfortunate *fall* and that I was permitted to spend the afternoon resting. As if to reinforce his words, he urged me not to dwell on the men or utter the name Rhoan ever again, remarking, "This is what you wanted," before abandoning me at the foot of Taeolyn's grand steps. He walked away casually, hands buried deep in his pockets as if taking a leisurely stroll rather than departing with a now heavy secret between us.

Once inside my room, I crumbled with the weight of it all,

spending what felt like an eternity in the shower, the water mingling with my tears as I surrendered to a wave of nausea, releasing the contents of my stomach until I was nothing more than a pathetic mess on the tiled shower floor. But in the end, I arose determined. I wouldn't let fear or helplessness define me any longer. That moment of weakness had ignited a fire within; I was determined to find my strength and never feel that way again. I made a promise to myself—I'd rather bleed standing than live on my knees.

I need to start taking my combat classes more seriously and dedicate more time to the gym. Perhaps Cole and his friends would be willing to help me out with that? I never honestly considered the possibility of growing close with the second Rykerson brother, but after today, I'll admit it wouldn't be so bad. We don't have a Bond, which I'm thankful for, but maybe we could be friends in secret.

Another loud, insistent pound on the door jolts me from my thoughts. The urgency in the knocking suggests that if I don't open it within moments, whoever is on the other side might just tear the door down. Whoever it is should also be in class, but clearly isn't.

I rip open the door, ready to reprimand whoever is standing on the other side about patience and manners, but words become ash on my tongue. Time seems to slow around me, and I struggle to reclaim my breath as I take in the tall, handsome man towering over me.

Anders frames the doorway with his strong arms, his head bowing slightly as he fights for air, like he just ran the whole way here. The familiar scent of sandalwood, mixed with citrus, drifts toward me, enveloping my senses alongside the iridescent light of our Bond, cocooning me in an overwhelming sense of warmth and safety. I feel my whole body relax as I drink in his presence.

He's dressed impeccably in tailored trousers and a fitted button-down shirt that accentuates his toned body. His dark hair seems out of place, tousled and falling into his eyes as though he's been dragging his hands through it nonstop. His sapphire eyes are storming, the silver within restless.

I barely have a moment to process that he's actually here before I feel the strength of his hand gently curling around my hip, his long fingers spanning the small of my back. The warmth from his touch radiates through me, alongside a jolt that flares to life at my hip as he guides me backward, smoothly stepping into my room and kicking the door shut with a soft thud.

A flash of anger alters his features as he gazes at me before swiftly softening into something that resembles concern. Worry flickers through his eyes, likely stemming from the fact that what happened today would reflect poorly on him as my escort. That's what this is all about, right? It's just an obligation.

He shouldn't have to worry. He wasn't even on planet when it happened. Still, his intensity is a palpable, relentless wave filling the silence between us, the weight of all that is unsaid hanging in the air.

"I'm going to guess your brother blabbed?" I cross my arms in front of me, concealing how my body responds to him being so near. I can't ignore the way his chest rises and falls with labored breaths, as if each inhale is a struggle. The hard lines of his body remind me that he isn't about to let this slide. "I'm fine, thanks for asking," I add, my voice steady despite the sob threatening to break free.

"Godsdammit, Raea," he growls, his voice low and edged with danger. His piercing gaze roams over me, assessing every inch, searching for hidden injuries. Only then do I become acutely aware of the warmth of his hand still resting on my hip, his thumb moving in slow, lazy circles as if he, too, has forgotten. I instinctively step back, creating space between us, and try to ignore the unexpected ache of missing his hand.

Nausea rises in my throat, unwelcome, just like the emotions swirling inside of me. I wish I could throw my arms around him and tell him how much I wish he were there today. He'd probably push me away and tell me to grow up. Inhaling deeply to steady my racing heart, I try to focus on his scent, allowing it to ground me as the anxiety begins to ebb with my exhale.

"My father may have revoked their parents' titles for some illegal activities." I cast my gaze down, unable to look him in the eyes any longer. "I don't know their exact plan, but they intended to take me and..." I hesitate, the weight of my words heavy. "They may have mentioned spacing me." His hands clench at his sides, and a fury like I've never seen washes over his features.

He doesn't raise his voice. That's what makes it worse. "I'll end them," he promises, abruptly turning away from me, his words sucking the life out of the room. As he raises his laced fingers to the crown of his head, the hem of his dark blue shirt pulls up slightly, revealing a tantalizing sliver of sun-kissed skin just above his waistband. My gaze is drawn to the curve of his lower back, where the edge of a tattoo peeks out on his hip.

My cheeks flush as my gaze is drawn to the black ink etched into his skin that stirs my endless curiosity, especially when it comes to him. I find myself longing to peel away his shirt and reveal all that lies beneath.

He pivots to face me again, arms still positioned above his head, showcasing his toned body. His stomach is a canvas of muscle that is hard to ignore. Despite knowing I shouldn't, my eyes wander down, captivated by the trail of dark hair that vanishes into his waistband, accentuated by the sharp contours of his hips. My hand instinctively rises, somewhere deep within me, begging to reach out and trace those deep lines. Just as I begin to reach, I hesitate and let it drop, scolding myself for forgetting I am nothing to him.

Nothing more than a job.

Anders remains oblivious to the shame now flooding me. "I'll make sure it's taken care of," he says in a deep, rumbling voice filled with promise and threat. "Nobody touches what's mine. For now," he continues, "get ready. I'll send Cole to escort you to class."

I don't think he even realizes the slip. *His?* "Not yours," I whisper. "I belong to no one." Even as I mutter those words, my heart seems to be performing some impossible routine, my stomach clenching tight.

He chuckles, the sound cascading over my nerves like an awakening. "We'll see about that."

The truth of those words slams into me, tumbling down, down, down, burying itself so deep inside me I know I'll never dig them out.

The air between us thickens. Instead, I focus on the latter part of what he said.

"I don't need Cole—" I start to protest, but then I see his composure shatter in an instant. His features become a mask of icy fury, and his stormy blue eyes ignite with a rage so cold it sends a tremor through my whole body as I fight not to recoil.

His voice drops to a low, dangerous whisper as he warns, "Stop. Whatever you were about to say, just don't. Until we're certain there aren't any remaining threats, consider yourself fortunate. When I'm not around, someone *I* trust will be. Your life will not be at risk again, not under my watch."

In the blink of an eye, he vanishes from my sight, leaving only the echo of the slamming door to jolt me out of my stupor, my heart still thundering in his absence.

Butterflies flutter in my stomach that have nothing to do with the day's events. Instead, it comes from the anticipation of sitting in Bonding class. I have a general idea of what the Bonding ceremony entails—at least as much as any outsider can understand—but I suspect that this class will delve into the complexities of The Ceremony far beyond the brief overview I received over break. My tutor had been too embarrassed to elaborate, claiming she had never witnessed a Ceremony firsthand. Only seers, a security detail, and the potential Bonds are permitted inside during such a sacred event.

"I just don't understand why we have to Bond at all. Can't we just choose whoever we want and move on?" Sienna, the new girl, questions Gunnar. Her voice grates on my nerves. Both are recent transfers from Coriat Academy in the Okenen Kingdom, and I can't help but feel intrigued by their friendship with Anders. I haven't yet had the opportunity to really get to know either of them, but I'm aware that she's a senior in Sky Division, the same woman who was so *friendly* with Anders.

"Sienna, just sit your ass down and keep quiet. You know it doesn't work like that," Gunnar challenges, arms crossed and a teasing grin on his face. "Who would you even pick? Choose one person right now."

"Ryker, duh," she replies, rolling her eyes and picking at her obnoxiously long, perfectly manicured nails. I can't help but wonder how she manages to fight with those claws. Gunnar laughs deeply, practically folding over his desk. It's hard not to notice he's another one of those strikingly handsome guys, which only reinforces my belief that good looks are a prerequisite for being part of Anders' tightly-knit crew.

Anders always seems to draw a crowd wherever he goes. He attracts women like a magnet and carries that distinct aura of indifference, paired with a palpable "don't-talk-to-me" vibe. I've watched several women approach him over the past few weeks, attempting small talk, only to be met with his blank stare. Sienna is particularly irritating. Something about her is different from the other women. There's some connection between her and Anders that I haven't been able to pinpoint.

On the other hand, Gunnar appears to thrive on the attention from the women around him, wrapping his arms around the ladies Anders is so quick to dismiss.

I'm desperately trying not to eavesdrop, but I find myself curious why she would choose Anders over anyone. A ridiculous surge of jealousy grips me, twisting my insides. He isn't mine, and I don't even want him, yet here I am, fighting the urge to lash out at the blonde sitting behind me.

I try to dismiss my moment of jealousy as a product of my nerves from the day's events. Strangely, I see Anders as my current refuge, a temporary escape from the chaos surrounding me. That's all it is, nothing more. I remind myself that it has nothing to do with the fact that Sienna embodies the kind of girl Anders is likely drawn to. Tall, with cascading blonde curls that brush her hips, honeyed skin from endless days at the beach, large breasts, and large, doe-like brown eyes that are somehow both inviting and mischievous. Everything about her radiates confidence, sensuality, and a playful spirit.

"Pray, do tell why Ryker is your choice," Gunnar muses, his laughter bubbling up again, clearly amused by her declaration.

Sienna leans back in her chair, a mischievous grin spreading across her face. "Well, they want me to Bond with Cole, but I've always thought Ryker was the hotter of the two. I mean, he's going to be king someday. Why would I settle for Bonding with a prince when I could bag a king?"

As she speaks, Gunnar's jaw drops in mock disbelief. With a flick, she resumes tapping her ridiculously long nails against her tablet. "Trust me, Ryker wouldn't mind at all. I've seen that man every summer for the past six years, and every summer, he's more than willing to...flirt back."

A soft huff escapes my lips as I turn towards the dais, and a wave of frustration washes over me. I find myself increasingly reluctant to listen to her drivel about snagging Anders as if he's a trophy, not an actual person.

The tension wrapping around my chest surprises me. I've started feeling a strange attachment towards Cole, which troubles me. The last thing I want is to develop any connection with the Rykerson brothers. Yet, an inexplicable pull within me makes me believe they somehow belong to me. The thought is amusing in its absurdity. I must have really taken a hit if I'm entertaining such ideas.

Kellan settles into the chair next to me with his usual relaxed demeanor, and I feel an immediate comfort in Ciara's presence on my other side. A slight pang of guilt tightens in my chest at not telling them about my near-kidnapping. After all, did anything significant really happen? I've always prided myself on my honesty with them, yet this secret feels alarmingly close to deception.

I gently shove thoughts of today's events into a corner of my mind, locking them away for now. Right now, I want to focus on the present. Those emotions can simmer in their box until I'm ready to face them —later...or never.

The hall is alive with the chatter of students and barely contained excitement from all three dorms. As I glance around the room, I notice how everyone scans the crowd, each searching for their potential future spouse among the sea of faces.

The atmosphere shifts suddenly, charged with an electric energy that prickles the back of my neck. I sense him before I even see him. There's a captivating mix of blues, purples, pinks, and golds from the Bond that spiral around me, signaling Anders' arrival, *finally*. There's an undeniable warmth in the connection between us.

Over the past six weeks, my Bond with Anders has deepened in ways I never expected. It's become so significant that ignoring it feels impossible. I catch a glimpse of him taking a seat directly behind me, a breath away from Sienna.

Jealousy is an irrational emotion, and I despise how it twists within me. I take a deep breath to steady myself, trying to calm the flood of feelings that threaten to overwhelm my thoughts. It's not as if I expected him to actually greet me and say hello. His earlier outburst in my room only stemmed from a place of frustration, not genuine concern for me. Yet, even with that quiet reprimand, the knot of longing and hurt remains.

Professor Becca enters the room, struggling with a large box, her chestnut hair framing her face as it sways gently, obscuring her vision. "Everyone, may I have your attention, please?" she calls out. Leaning against the table at the front of the Executive Hall, she beams with warmth. Behind her, the sun dips below the horizon, casting a palette of pinks and oranges across the sky. "I can sense your excitement! Good. For the seniors here, you're familiar with a version of this class from last year, but I'm thrilled to share that it will be a bit different this time around. Over the break, I took the time to completely revise the curriculum to ensure you feel fully prepared for what lies ahead."

"Excuse me, sorry!" a new student exclaims as he rushes in. "Chancellor Xara sent me. I'm transferring from Traven Academy." I catch a glimpse of him from my spot. He's cute, with short black hair, a tall frame, and mocha skin complemented by striking chocolate-brown eyes. When he turns to face the room, his gaze meets mine, and a charming smile spreads across his face.

"Please take a seat, Lord Jensn," Professor Becca instructs softly.

My heart races as Jensn navigates the stairs to the Taeolyn section, stopping right in front of me and offering a respectful bow. *Gods, allow the floor to swallow me whole.* Kellan shifts uncomfortably beside me.

"I'm Jensn Vigor from Ateria." He meets my gaze while some students around us stifle their laughter. His accent is distinctly from Soren in Mori. The color of hazy blue swirls between us. I can feel my cheeks flush as almost everyone's attention is focused on us, so I nod quickly, caught between unease and embarrassment.

"Princess Raea from—" I start to say.

"I know," he replies with a bright grin before finding his seat in the Veker row across from me.

Ciara nudges me playfully with a twinkle in her eye. I can practically feel the burn of Anders' gaze behind me along with the waves of jealousy emanating from Kellan beside me.

"All right, everyone," Professor Becca continues, her attention sweeping across the room. She calls up senior representatives from each dorm, inviting the women to the front to distribute crisp white folders to the senior women. She then hands out sage-colored folders to us junior ladies.

"The goal of this class," she explains earnestly, "is to deepen your understanding of the Bond. We will explore the purpose of The Ceremony, all that the Bond entails, how it can be lost, and the powers that may be received. Most importantly, we'll discuss the emotions you're already likely experiencing." She scans the room thoughtfully, her gaze drifting over the sea of juniors and seniors.

"How many of you have felt a hint of your Bond? Maybe a gentle tug or a brief spark? If you haven't sensed anything yet, don't worry. I assure you, you will."

About half of the hands in the room rise, including mine, and I can feel the heat radiating from my neck and cheeks. I can feel Kellan's gaze on me, and from behind, Anders' glare burns into my back, adding to the stifling atmosphere. Once again, I find myself hot and uncomfortable. I brush back a loose strand of hair and pretend not to notice either of them.

"Good. Duchess Eryn, would you be willing to share what you've been experiencing? Remember, you don't have to reveal any names." The class responds with a light chuckle, easing the tension. "Just explain how you recognize it's the Bond."

All eyes shift to the young woman from Bragr as she hesitates for a moment. "Sometimes, it's just a single zap. It feels like a pinch," she shares, her cheeks flushing a deep crimson, betraying her embarrassment. I can't help but feel a sense of relief that Anders isn't the one pinching me. I would get very annoyed very quickly.

"Excellent. And what about you, Lady Yessenia?" The junior from Veker, who is always smiling, takes a moment before responding. "Sometimes I feel like my skin is hot." Kellan snorts beside me.

"That can happen," Professor Becca acknowledges with a nod. "Now, gentlemen, how many of you have experienced your Bond?"

To my surprise, only about thirty hands shoot up in unison. I had not anticipated such a low response from the roughly one hundred men in this room. What truly surprises me is that Kellan's hand remains firmly at his side, as does Tate's. I scan the faces around me, my curiosity piqued, and spot Cole at the back of the room with his hand raised high. Behind me, I can see both Trysten and Anders also have their hands raised.

When Anders' intense stare catches mine and holds for a fleeting moment, it sends ripples of light coursing through me, stronger than before, jolting straight to my core. I have to summon all my willpower to maintain my composure and look away. Still, there's a deep, undeniable ache blossoming somewhere inside me, a sensation I can't quite place.

I catch a glimpse of the faint smirk that tilts Anders' lips as I whirl around so quickly that my head spins. I turn my attention to Kellan, hoping for a similar response, but all I detect is a gentle trickle of green light with soft ripples originating from him.

I face forward, determined to focus on the lesson for the rest of class. We delve into the history behind the Bonds bestowed upon royal households by the gods. It's said that after the veil was summoned and Astor and Calia withdrew from our world, the empire understood this Bond as a divine gift—a way for the gods to remind us that they were still with us, even in some small, mystic capacity. Each Bond is a potent force, entwining the essence of each individual, reflecting their true selves and the duties expected of them.

Generations have since been Bonded, inheriting powers that dictate their fates, with the stipulation that neither royals nor nobles may marry for love. We must *submit* to the Bond.

The second king of Ateria attempted to marry for love, resulting in near catastrophe for both him and his would-be Bond. I have always been curious about stories of Bonded couples, tales of passion and devotion, yet something about the Bond feels unsettling and almost forced. There's a sense of loss within the Bonds that makes me question how anyone can love their match and still feel free within it.

As I carefully sift through the papers within the folder, I discover resources centered on the necessity of protecting our Bonds. Thankfully, I'm familiar with most of the techniques that my tutors taught me over break.

Among the materials, I find extensive notes on how to nurture strong connections with those we feel a Bond to, alongside important reminders about the potential traps of losing ourselves and, therefore, our Bonds. Another flush warms my cheeks when I stumble across the section focusing on pregnancy precautions, a topic considered taboo among most noble families.

Being part of the royal family, I am strictly prohibited from taking pregnancy prevention serums—a rule designed to preserve our lineage. However, it's common knowledge that lower members of nobility often ignore these regulations. The royal houses frown upon it, but that doesn't stop them.

As I absorb Professor Becca's lecture, I make a concerted effort to remain focused despite the uncomfortable weight in the air. While Kellan inches closer, his protectiveness and attention pull at me, but the biggest distraction of all is Anders. His unrelenting gaze penetrates right through me, boiling me from the inside out.

Each moment in this class becomes a challenge, and by the time the lecture wraps up, I find myself flushed, beads of sweat trailing down my neck and back. I can't help but wish I had chosen to braid my hair into a crown instead of tying the thick layers back in a long, wavy ponytail.

As soon as the bell signals the end of class, I rush for the door, needing to escape the heat. I need to feel the fresh air on my face to cool my heated skin. I push through the crowd, ignoring the calls from my friends, and don't stop until I'm free.

eight

• • •

I DON'T SLOW my pace until I step out of the heavy doors of the Executive Hall, the weight of the Bonds finally lifting off my shoulders. As I step into the open air, a refreshing breeze sweeps over me, cooling my skin after an hour of stifling heat.

For the first time in what feels like an eternity, I draw in a deep breath, filling my lungs with the crisp scent of the surrounding trees and rich soil. Out here, the chaos of the hall fades away; there are no ripples of light, no pulsing energies, and no men. Instead, there is the comforting, familiar hum of the planet and the lush forest.

I kick off my shoes and carefully navigate a small trail I know winds past the Executive Yard and toward the river beyond the Specialist's Yard. Glancing over my shoulder to ensure nobody is watching, I slip between the tall trunks, weaving through the dense foliage while remaining cloaked in the shadows. The soft rustling of leaves accompanies my steps until I finally reach the rocky edge of the riverbank.

The ground slopes gently toward the flowing water, and I can feel the dampness seeping between my toes with each step. Grass obscures hidden boulders beneath the tall blades. As I tread carefully,

I lose my footing a few times, but each time I regain my balance before slipping down the slope into the icy river.

The ice-cold water is runoff from the Delormere Mountains to the west, where snow still clings to the peaks. In the coming weeks, the snow will thicken as Baedyn travels further from the sun. Beyond those rugged mountains lie the villages and colonies of the planet.

I find a smooth rock jutting out from the bank and sink onto it, grateful for the cool air brushing my skin. When I dip my toes into the frigid water, the sharp bite steals my breath, soothing the fire still burning in my veins. The sensation brings a renewed clarity. Above, the night sky is painted in deep navy hues, the moons rising, their soft light already illuminating the darkness. Stars twinkle into existence one by one, like little lanterns.

I close my eyes, shutting out the world, and take a moment to connect with the energy of the planet around me. I focus on the rhythmic sound of the water flowing, the whisper of the breeze through the trees, and the quiet pulse of life that courses beneath my skin. I attempt to clear the tangled thoughts in my mind from today's events. I feel weighed down by it all.

In the stillness of the night, I hear the call of an Aticat, a sound that makes me feel uneasy. The fascinating creature is a vibrant teal with orange feathers and soft, pink, petal-like ears that twitch with every noise, details I find both charming and cute. While they possess incredible intelligence and a bite that carries a venomous risk, they wisely choose to keep their distance from humans.

Above me, the rustle of wings creates a gentle flapping noise that echoes through the night. The sound is too deep to belong to a Dilly-Bird. I look up and see nothing but the twinkling stars resembling gems scattered across an endless black canvas. Three planets stand out brightly among them—Demeter, Sedgesea, and Cerus.

Cerus holds a special place in my heart. As the largest of the three visible planets, it commands attention in the night sky. Its pale blue surface is framed by thin white rings that cast a soft glow in the darkness.

Sitting here, I feel a profound connection to the magic around me, like a tangible string I might pluck from the air if I could only see it. It's a reminder of the wonder that exists and the adventures still waiting for me beyond school.

I long to be up there right now, exploring the vastness of space, a place filled with endless possibilities. With seven kingdoms and seventy-two planets in our system, I could go anywhere. But something up there calls to me, beyond our borders, beyond the veil.

If I had a transport, I could journey to Mori and get lost in the endless sand dunes under a murky red sky perpetually choked with dust, or I could find myself in Kadora, hiking toward one of the many glaciers that dot their planets.

I might venture to the Oris Kingdom and walk for miles through rich mineral mountains shrouded in thick trees and dotted with caves, never encountering another person. However, above all the kingdoms, including my own, I would love to take a transport to the Okenen Kingdom and lose myself among the water planets. I wouldn't even need to enter their atmosphere to hear the calming roar of their oceans or smell the salt and brine in the air.

I know those sounds and smells by heart, just as well as I know the sounds of rain and wildlife from my own kingdom, along with the thick clouds of mist and the scents of pine and blossoms.

The sound of shuffling feet pulls me from the depths of my thoughts and back to reality. I glance over my shoulder to see Anders sauntering toward me.

He looks so at ease, so confident with his hands tucked into his pockets. It's a stark contrast to the hurricane of emotions and confusion within me. Never have I wanted to plunge into the water and vanish more than now.

"I want to be alone," I snap, turning my gaze back to the water, where the quiet flow reflects the shimmering silver of the moonlight. I realize he can most likely sense my unease in the deliberate slowness of his approach. This year, school has left me feeling more confined than ever. I was so excited to be an Executive, but this Bond...it's so consuming.

Anders chuckles lightly, breaking the silence. "Come on," he drawls. "You know I can't just leave you here alone by the river in the dark." He settles himself beside me on the cool rock, positioning himself with a casualness that both comforts and irritates me. "Besides," he continues, the teasing note in his voice sharper, "I made a promise to ensure you're not alone until we know if any other students feel like making a move to see you punished for your father's actions." His words make me cringe. He must notice my reaction because he shifts a fraction closer, closing the distance between us.

"Can't you pick your own rock?" I retort, a groan escaping my lips before I can rein it in. My petulant attitude is beginning to annoy even me. It's not like I own this rock, but I just need to escape the feelings he stirs within me.

"I prefer this one." He makes a show of getting comfortable. I roll my eyes in response, but there's no denying the warmth his playfulness radiates, easing some of the tension in my chest. Despite my best efforts to maintain my distance, I can't help but feel a slight reprieve from the weight of everything when he's near.

"Are you trying to annoy me so we can return to the dorms?" I'm about to pull away when I notice the blood splattered on his forearm beneath his rolled-up sleeve. "What happened?" I gasp, reaching for his arm before thinking better of it.

Anders looks down and shrugs. "Not mine."

"Then whose?" I can't seem to look away from the dark speckles, noticing he doesn't have a single injury, at least none I can see. Not even bruises on his knuckles.

He waits a moment before responding, "Rhoan let me do some questioning before he dealt with them. Guess I missed a spot."

My stomach turns, and I force my gaze to the tree across the river.

Why would he have questioned them? My heart races in rhythm with my thoughts.

"It had to be done." He crosses his arms. "I needed to make sure they were operating alone."

I swallow the bile working its way up my throat. "Are they alive?" I ask, barely a whisper above the sound of the water.

"They are, but not if I had my way. Rhoan thought it best to not start a war." He huffs as if the restraint annoys him. "They crossed a line, Raea. You could have died." When I glance back at him, his jaw ticks with barely contained rage. An exhilarating current courses through me. "Does it bother you?"

I look down at my fumbling hands and search for words. Does it bother me? I don't know. It's not how I would handle it, but I do understand the need for a king to be strong, to be feared. And Anders will be king…soon. I shake my head, letting my eyes find his once more. "No. I don't—" I swallow.

"I promised to protect you, and I failed."

"It's not your job," I say quickly, too quickly. His guilt hits me square in the chest, and suddenly I hate myself for not seeing it sooner. "It wasn't fair—saddling you with me, making you my escort. You were never supposed to be my guard."

The truth burns. I've been awful to him, snapping and snarling while he's done nothing but give me what I want. He didn't choose this. He never asked to trail after me, to shadow every step I take. And still…he does. Without complaint. Without hesitation.

He runs a hand through his hair. "Well, I'm promising you now. Nobody touches you. Whether some dumbass attempts to Bond with you or tries to kill you… I'll make sure they don't get close enough to even breathe the same air." His words settle over me like a comforting blanket, and I believe him. Whatever resolve I see in those sapphire depths communicates the truth of it.

"Thank you," I sigh.

We're both quiet for long minutes. A mixture of emotions dances within me, a part of me yearning to reach out and take his hand, while another part screams to pull away. If I had known what was waiting for me this year, I might have chosen a private tutor and stayed home to avoid all of this, but then again, I can't run from everything. Sooner or later, I'm going to need to step up. I don't want to be a princess locked away in a tower.

"I met your father today," he says as if reading where my thoughts have drifted. His words land like a crack of lightning. I had forgotten about that, too concerned with the men trying to kidnap me. "He approached me directly as I entered the palace with Trysten and Ashton." He brushes his hand through his hair nervously. "He wrapped me in a hug as if we were old friends and then told me about our childhood."

I am momentarily stunned.

First of all, why was he at my palace? And second, my father isn't the hugging type by any stretch of the imagination. He shows affection to my mother and me, but that's the extent of it. Kellan and Ciara, who practically live at the palace, have never even received an ounce of physical affection from him.

"What?" I exclaim, quickly turning my head. His features soften in the gentle light of the moons. When I manage to set aside the constant impulse to find reasons to dislike him, it becomes increasingly difficult to overlook just how beautiful he is—the kind of beauty that demands a careful study of every detail, every curve and line defining him. It hardly seems fair how effortlessly attractive he appears, which undoubtedly explains why women are constantly swooning over him.

His dark hair glistens under the moonlight, streaks of silver highlighting certain strands. The sharp lines of his jaw are accentuated, while the soft light makes the fullness of his lips and the gentleness in his eyes even more pronounced. I can't help but feel a strong urge to lean in just a little closer and see for myself just how soft those lips really are.

"My Politics assignment was to sit in on a trade agreement with Kyrr. Your father mentioned that our families were best friends and even shared that you spent a lot of time on Malaya when you were little." He refuses to meet my questioning stare and, instead, absent-mindedly tosses a small stone into the water, the splash momentarily drawing my attention before I return it to his face, trying and failing to read him.

The thought of our parents being close friends tugs at something deep within me. A memory, perhaps? I have a few more questions as well. "That's a lot to unpack," I murmur softly, half to myself, as my mind searches for anything to remind me of ever knowing him before I came to the academy.

My words grab his attention as he shifts to face me. A flicker of curiosity, or maybe hurt, crosses his face before he quickly masks it behind his usual indifference.

These precious moments of vulnerability remind me that there is more to him than meets the eye, like a small voice pushing me toward him.

"He mentioned that we were friends when we were toddlers until you all stopped visiting around the time you were five or six. I suppose our parents kept in touch, but they stopped traveling to Malaya. He didn't go into detail as to why. I never realized how intertwined our childhoods were. I can't remember anything from then. Odd." He shrugs casually, tossing another rock into the flowing water.

"So we've known each other our whole lives without even realizing it?" I feel a spark of curiosity as I sit a little straighter next to him. The moment I move, our shoulders brush, and the same energy I felt when our fingertips touched comes flooding back. Clearing my throat, I instinctively grab a stick to keep my hands busy and subtly shift away.

"Why do you do that?" he asks, his tone gentle and free of judgment.

I sigh, contemplating for a moment, feeling generous with my honesty. After all, if we were friends once, maybe we can be again. I mean, I'm open to the idea of being friends with his brother, so why not with him?

But what would our friendship look like? We don't seem to share much in common aside from our shared love of flying off into space and the weight of being heirs to our crowns.

He's the mysterious, broody, popular type, while I prefer to retreat and hide, or attempt to blend in the best I can. As I meditate over it, I realize how much I want to feel normal in a world filled with expectations of who I am and who I should be. Anders—Ryker, whatever name he deigns to go by—seems indifferent to the opinions of others.

I wish.

Shaking off my thoughts, I respond, "Do you feel it? If you do, what does it feel like?" I toss the branch into the water, watching it drift away on a current.

"Are you talking about the light or the energy?" He holds my gaze, making my heart beat faster. I hate that he answers with questions, but I refuse to be the one to break the trend, so I ask another question of my own.

"Are they different?" I curl my knees to my chest and rest my head on my folded arms.

His eyes crinkle a moment as if he's studying me. "They're definitely different." He runs a hand through his disheveled hair, and his piercing gaze seems to search the depths of my soul.

I shift my weight nervously, feeling momentarily exposed, before looking at the water. "I think the Bond between us is the light. Can you see that?" He catches my gaze again, and I nod and watch as he closes his eyes. I allow my walls to crumble.

Magic washes over me like ripples of light. It's then that I realize the difference. The Bond explodes around us, the iridescent colors flowing like a gentle breeze, reaching out in every direction and weaving between us, burrowing deep within us.

"It's beautiful," I whisper, keeping my eyes closed and absorbing the colors that shift and sway, wrapping around us, intertwining our energies. This connection—whatever it is—fills me with a hope I can't quite comprehend.

"Can I have your hand?" I blink and meet his gaze. I don't know why, but Sienna's words echo in my mind. I don't want to just be another girl on his long list of potential suitors.

He lets out a gentle sigh. "Raea, this is simply to demonstrate the difference. Holding your hand won't change anything between us."

My cheeks flush.

"I know that. It's just..." I pause, feeling the subtle energy flickering around us. *What is that?* There's an undeniable pull encouraging me to trust him, to let him in. It feels overwhelming, so consuming, like I'm losing a piece of myself every time I acknowledge it.

I take a deep breath. If the Bond between us didn't exist, and it was just us, who would I be to him?

"Before we go further," I tuck my hands into my lap, needing a distraction, "I need to understand—you have such a busy life. Why did you agree to be my escort? You have friends, your brother, and a lot of responsibility as a dorm leader. What made you say yes?" I realize I've spoken more forcefully than intended, but I need to know the truth. Holding someone's hand isn't something I take lightly. It means something to me.

His eyes shift to the river, his body so preternaturally still. I wonder whether he's on the verge of walking away or if he might share his thoughts with me. I've been tortured over the past few weeks, wondering what prompted him to say yes.

"Remember when we were in Techs?" he begins. "I was in Valik's dorm, and you were in Kaera's. There was that big Recon assignment where we were tasked with finding our way back to the dorms after being dropped off six miles away." His eyes seem to lighten, and at the same time, the memory flashes vividly in my mind. "The boys were buzzing with excitement, all of us ready to prove how big and tough we were. Some of the girls were excited about the adventure. But then there was you, standing there, looking as if you were moments away from breaking down and crying."

I groan into my palms. I remember that moment, how I had felt like I was teetering on the edge of panic. It had been one of my most humiliating public breakdowns, and one I don't care to revisit.

Anders lets out a good-natured chuckle and encourages me to listen. I nod, settling in for the story. "I'll never forget how Kellan pulled you into a hug and whispered something in your ear." He leans back on his elbows, a sad smile playing on his lips. "I never found out what it was he said to you, but the way you smiled afterward lit up the entire room. I'll admit, it was the first time I ever felt a twinge of jealousy toward Kellan Hyston, Raea Tierson's best friend."

A flutter of warmth blooms in my chest at his confession, making my heart beat erratically. I press a hand to my chest to make sure I'm okay. I had no clue that Anders ever noticed me back then, let alone felt envy toward Kellan.

I can vividly recall that moment as if it were only yesterday. I was so afraid of getting lost or hurt, but Kellan's incessant teasing helped.

"He said the Azeban would steal all my snacks if I didn't walk fast enough," I giggle softly at the memory. "He always joked about strange, mythical creatures coming to get me or eat me, and somehow, his humor could transform the terrifying unknown into something less scary." *Oh, Kellan.*

A painful burn is lodged in my throat, and a pang of guilt squeezes my heart. Kellan has no clue where I am, and I took off so quickly. Kellan, the one who's always had my back, who's been my rock through every hardship, deserves so much more than the secrets and the half-truths I've been giving him.

Guilt slams into me, a knife twisting in my heart. I need to tell him the truth. He deserves that much. "I have to go." I gather my bag as I rise.

"Raea," Anders says, his voice a tangle of pleading brokenness. He reaches for my wrist, but our fingers brush together, the contact sending a wild sort of energy through me. Emotions I don't quite understand fill my mind, and I sink to my knees before him.

nine

. . .

L IFE IS full of moments that shape us in unforgettable ways, those pivotal experiences that change us irrevocably. When I was seven, during a game of hide and seek with Kellan and a few members of our palace staff, I managed to lock myself in the basement supply room. The door wouldn't budge despite my best efforts. Surrounded by darkness, I felt fear wash over me, spiraling into thoughts of never being found, of wasting away and dying alone. I sobbed on the floor, succumbing to those irrational thoughts.

But after nearly an hour, relief arrived as the door swung open, spilling light into the room. One of the court's handmaids knelt beside me, gently lifting me up from the floor and wiping away my tears. She reassured me that I wasn't alone and that they'd never stop searching. At that moment, I learned how easily fear could overpower clarity. Even today, when I encounter dark, confined spaces, I have to remind myself that I am safe and not in danger of being trapped.

When I was eight, I went out to explore the forest. I thought I had been blessed by Calia herself when I came across a chittering Phranik —the creature was no larger than a shoe. With its pitch-black body spattered by glowing speckles reminiscent of stars, this little being captured my attention. It had delicate tendrils sprouting from its head, adorned with tiny lights, and magnificently oversized ears that made me giggle. Its ears shimmered with those twinkling flecks. Its long tail and stunning wings had a pearlescent hue of pink and green that took my breath away.

To my delight, it perched atop a log instead of fleeing. We shared a long moment of curiosity before it scurried away at the sound of another animal. It's said that Phraniks are becoming increasingly rare, so encountering one felt like a gift.

When I was sixteen, I had the opportunity to take control of a transport flight to Trao, thanks to Kuron's trust in Lieutenant Piori. In that moment of guiding the transport through the emptiness of space, I knew my life had permanently changed. Flying ignited a passion within me that I could never take back.

And now, I find myself in another life-altering moment. With a simple touch, a small brush of his fingers, I have been forever changed. Regardless of what may come next, this experience has left a mark on my heart. My soul feels an ache for him that is both new and old, nearly as essential as the very act of breathing.

Within me, there is a deep well filled with an energy that wasn't there before, but also an emptiness that feels cold and foreign.

"Raea," Anders breathes softly, the touch resonating with him too. There's an undeniable depth of sympathy lacing his voice. "Raea, please, look at me."

I can't seem to meet his gaze right now. Maybe it's the tears rolling down my cheeks that I can't quite understand, or perhaps it's the profound energy I felt coursing through me with a simple brush of his hand. It might also be the realization that he felt it too. What we share is much more than just a connection or Bond—it's something else entirely.

"Please," I whisper with a soft exhale. "Give me a minute." He nods, leaning back on the rock and waiting, with only the sound of the rushing water surrounding us. Deep within my soul, I sense this is far greater than I can comprehend. Our Bond feels different, subtle, and gentle, while this sensation is overwhelming and exhilarating. It is raw and unfettered power, unlike anything I've ever experienced.

When I finally regain my composure, I muster the courage to look at him. His body is relaxed, and his eyes are closed. More than anything, my curiosity compels me to know—no, to understand—what's going on in his mind.

"Anders," I whisper, breaking the long silence between us. His eyes flutter open, locking onto mine, revealing the longing and confusion mirrored in each other's gazes.

"I'm so sorry, I didn't mean—" he starts.

"It's okay," I interrupt gently. "Honestly, I think it's better that it happened here than..." I wave my hand around us, gesturing to 'anywhere else'.

He nods, leaning on his elbow and turning to face me fully. "What exactly was that?" I ask.

"I can't say for certain." He pauses for a long moment. "It's the energy I mentioned earlier. I thought I felt it by the lake, but I was unsure whether it was just my imagination. Then I realized it's the same sensation each time I touch you, though much weaker. I didn't want to ask until I knew you felt it too."

I wipe away another tear, feeling a mix of vulnerability and trepidation. We're both about to cross a line we can't come back from by being honest and admitting some strong feelings I've been so desperate to ignore. "What exactly do you feel?" I inquire, keeping my voice low yet audible amidst the relaxing sounds of the river.

He lets out a soft chuckle, dropping his head back to gaze at the sky as if it might hold the answers we both seek.

"I can't quite put it into words. It's just this surge of energy. I feel electrified, as if my emotions are bursting at the seams. It's simple to explain when it's just your wrist or a hand on your back. It's like I've just downed a strong cup of coffee. I feel vibrant and full of life—honestly, it's almost addictive." He grins at me, and my breath rushes out of me. I've seen him smile plenty, but this...this is new, and damn, that dimple is the absolute worst. "Your turn! Since we're being honest and all." His eyebrows raise with playful expectation.

"Honestly, it's pretty similar." I shrug, but I know it's so much more than that deep down.

"Soraea." He gently tilts my chin with his finger, forcing me to meet his gaze. His touch radiates a subtle energy and warmth, igniting an inappropriate want that travels down my core, making my toes curl. Hearing my full name sends me reeling. Only my parents call me Soraea. Kellan, Ciara, and a few trusted acquaintances know my full name. I chose to go by Raea ages ago, and it's been years since I was called Soraea.

"Promise me you will never hide the truth from me. It's the one thing I ask of you." His words somehow sober me. I can't help but gasp at the intensity as if he's speaking to the depths of my soul. I quickly push those feelings aside, retreating to my familiar defense mechanism—sassy humor.

"It's not really a lie." I shrug. "'Pretty much' is such a vague term. But if you really want to know the whole story..." I cross my legs and pull them close, instinctively shielding myself with my gown. "Oh gods, you're going to think I'm crazy," I murmur, half-laughing.

I am crazy.

As I look up at him, he's wearing an authentic smile that softens my anxiety. It makes me want to see more of them. I can't help but notice how his eyes crinkle at the corners and how his annoyingly adorable dimple pops on his right cheek. It's utterly disarming. I can't even remember what made me dislike him in the first place.

Oh, gods, no...I can't let myself fall for dimples. But his smile? It seems capable of warming the entire universe.

"Yes?" he encourages, a playful smirk dancing on his lips as he notices my gaze lingering on his mouth.

I can't help but roll my eyes before looking up at the stars above. Perhaps they're the better audience for my confession.

I muster up the honesty before saying, "It's hard to put into words. It feels like throwing open the windows after being in the dark for so long. Suddenly, there's light and color everywhere, and a whole world just waiting to be explored. There's an incredible blend of warmth and cold, with the deepest shadows contrasting against the brightest lights. It's power and comfort all at once." I glance back down at him, finding him relaxed against the rock, and I can't help but frown a little.

"It's different," he exhales. "Raea, that power…I think it's coming from you." He turns his head, watching my reaction that doesn't come. I think I'm too stunned. "What else?" he asks, his fingertips nearly brushing against my hand on the rock. It sends a prickling awareness through me, and I wonder if he even notices. It would only take a slight movement to reignite everything we've been dancing around.

"It's just… right," I manage, pushing back the lump in my throat. "Being with you feels like an answer to a question I didn't know I needed to ask, and wrapped up in that feeling is this whirlwind of desire. Ugh, I can't believe I'm saying all of this!" With an exasperated huff of disbelief, I glance back at the stars as if they're far better at receiving confessions than he is.

"Soraea," he whispers, snagging my attention. "I understand," he continues, his voice dropping to a deeper timbre. "Just hear me out before you run off." His sapphire eyes lock onto mine. "We're stuck together for the rest of the year, and we both know it. So, instead of having another little moment—" He makes air quotes with his fingers. "In front of everyone else, let's explore this and see how deep it goes. Maybe we can figure out a way to manage it so we don't react at a simple touch." He sits up, our eyes level, his gaze glowing with an almost irresistible light.

"I'm scared," I admit, squaring my shoulders and holding his stare, feeling lost in the depths of his eyes as I watch the silver swirl quietly. It's terrifying to strip back the layers and admit how strong my feelings have grown so quickly.

"I understand. We can keep this between us until we truly figure it out, and we won't know until we take that leap. Just you and me. All you have to do is take my hand." I find myself captivated by his sincerity. It's hard to believe how we've become an *us*.

My heart races at the thought, and I hesitate, biting my lip, trying to keep from saying yes. He's so hard to think clearly around. Even if every part of me wants to stay, I shouldn't be here. I need to check in with Kellan and Ciara. They're probably wondering where I've disappeared to.

"I can't. Not tonight. My friends are likely worried about me," I blurt out, my body acting before my mind can catch up. I stand quickly, taking my bag in hand and glancing back to see him still sitting there. "Thanks for chatting with me." I offer a wavering smile despite the ache it leaves behind. I need to distance myself while I still feel in control and keep everything from unraveling.

"Where have you been?" Kellan rushes to my side as I step into the softly lit Taeolyn dorms. "We looked everywhere for you! You vanished and didn't answer your Prism." The relief and concern merge into exhaustion in his eyes.

"I know, it felt like you were right beside me, then suddenly...poof!" Ciara adds, her face reflecting the same stress.

"Told you she's okay," Tate chimes in from his cozy spot in what we affectionately call the tube, a circular nook filled with cushions. It's the perfect place to relax or dive into a good book.

"I'm really sorry," I reply sincerely, hoping they know I didn't mean to worry them.

"You missed dinner, but don't worry, I saved you a plate. It's in your room. I'll let you catch up since it's clear she's not been kidnapped," Tate says with a smirk, throwing an amused glare at Ciara as if that could ever be a real worry.

Little do they know how close I was to danger today. The pang of guilt settles in, making me feel uneasy. With a wave and a goodnight, Tate heads up the stairs, leaving me with my two best friends.

"Rae?" Ciara asks, her brows furrowing with concern. I hesitate to admit where I've been and with whom. Everyone knows that Anders has been assigned to me, so I don't need to deceive them about his presence, but I just can't fully explain our time together. It's not that we did anything wrong—far from it. It's just that the experience was intimate in a way that's hard to articulate.

"Sorry! After class, I felt overwhelmed and really needed to step away. Did you guys notice how intense that room felt?" I glance between them, hoping to find some understanding. But as they exchange uncertain looks and shake their heads, I realize today just needs to wrap up. I pinch the bridge of my nose, wishing for a hot shower and my bed. "Anyway, I ran out of the hall to gather my thoughts, and Ryker followed to ensure I was okay. I wound up getting lost in my thoughts, and I genuinely lost track of time. It felt like only thirty minutes had passed."

I realize I'm rambling, a hazard of being a talkative, nervous person. But by the expressions on their faces, it's clear they've heard enough.

"Wait, you and Ryker were in the forest for the past two hours?" Kellan asks, and I can see a hint of disappointment in his eyes. I want to reassure him, but I also need to be honest.

"Yep. We were just talking. Interestingly, he met my father today since he had to fly to Kyrr for a politics assignment. I didn't mean to cause any concern for you both," I explain.

Ciara shares a playful wink and a cheeky smile before saying she needs to catch up on her beauty sleep, joking that she'll turn me over to the Dhabur, a mythical monster parents use to scare their kids into behaving.

"Come here," Kellan says, and I gladly wrap my arms around him. His hug feels like home to me, so different from what I experience with Anders. I cling to him, resting my head against his chest and inhaling his scent. I'm so thankful to have him. Even if there's a lot we need to talk about, I know Kellan will always be here for me.

I'm feeling really overwhelmed right now, as if a good night's sleep might not be enough to lift this weight. Today has brought a mix of emotions: longing, anger, confusion, you name it, I've experienced it all.

"I'm so sorry I worried you," I say softly.

Kellan kisses the top of my head, a gesture he's done so many times, yet today, it feels different. I can feel the shift of energy in the air as Kellan's embrace tightens around me. I close my eyes, trying to gather my thoughts. As much as I appreciate Kellan's protective presence, I'm just not sure I'm ready to face both of them.

"You could have brought her back instead of leaving her out in the cold," Kellan remarks sharply. I draw back from his embrace and capture Kellan's attention.

Behind me, I can feel a strange energy emanating from Anders, our Bond stills, as if the invisible breeze it usually floats on has disappeared, freezing the colors in place.

"Kellan, it wasn't his fault at all. I chose to stay out there; that was my decision. He spent his evening waiting on me," I assert. I'm not entirely sure why I'm defending Anders, but it feels important to stand up for him when Kellan's being unfair. I turn to face Anders, crossing my arms, hating being between the two of them.

"Princess," Anders drawls, his mask already in place; yet, the tone betrays his disappointment. Catching a fleeting look of hurt on his face before he masks it, I can't help but feel the tension hanging in the air. He clenches his jaw as he glances between Kellan and me. "Thank you for that...enlightening conversation. Let's have another one soon."

A rush of warmth floods my cheeks. I can tell he knows I understand the underlying message, and thankfully, the shadows here shield my blush from Kellan's view.

Anders shifts his weight as he slides his hands into his pockets, and the devilish gleam in his eyes makes me wary. He winks at me before taking the stairs with a smirk plastered across his face. He doesn't look back as I watch his shadowy figure retreat up the stairs. A surge of frustration bubbles up within me, and I fight the urge to stomp up the stairs after him and physically wipe that smirk off his face.

"Goodnight, Raea," Kellan says coolly as he backs away with confusion written in his gaze. He looks up to where Anders is on the stairs and then back to me.

Shit.

ten

. . .

With thirty minutes before our next class, this is the perfect opportunity to get some valuable practice in. Professor Ainslyn clears me for the simulator, and just as I'm about to step through the door, I almost get bowled over by a rather imposing figure.

He growls, clearly startled, but as soon as he sees me, his surprise shifts to an apology. "Shit, sorry." I raise an eyebrow at him, scowling, and he quickly turns away, mumbling a silent curse to himself. As he walks off, students part like waves for their *dark prince*. His toned muscles ripple beneath his shirt with every step, and I can't help but watch with amusement as he dismisses a tall blonde from Bragr, shrugging her off effortlessly without a single glance before he vanishes into the men's locker room.

Feeling slightly flustered, I head straight into the simulator room and strap on my vest of daggers with determination. *I will not be weak.* It's become my mantra, my driving force. Never again. With three sheathed on each side of my ribs and one on my thigh, I take my position on the center platform as the room dims and the green holographic attackers materialize around me.

While I've practiced throwing daggers at targets and creatures before, the thought of facing off against men is a new challenge. Yet, with the recent attack still fresh in my mind, I know I have to prepare myself. I need to be ready for anything. When I confided in Professor Ainslyn about wanting to train against opponents much larger than myself, he didn't hesitate—he simply nodded and instructed the simulator operator to pull up test twenty-seven.

I jump from foot to foot, hyping myself up. I can do this, I need to do this. The first hologram runs at me, and I don't hesitate to throw the dagger. Trusting my instinct and years of practice, I sink the dagger into the mark right into the hologram's heart. For a moment, my breath catches in my throat.

As the assailant vanishes, the dagger drops to the floor with the pull of a magnet. I barely have time to turn before the second threat is upon me. With what feels like slow motion, I bring up another dagger, slicing across his throat, fighting against the urge to close my eyes. One by one, from every angle, they charge at me, and one by one, they disappear after a dagger takes them out.

Keeping my focus on the situation, I turn, striking them with fatal accuracy. *Now, if I just had a dagger or three the other day.*

Out of nowhere, an eighth challenger bursts from behind a boulder, clearly ready to face me now that I'm out of daggers. Without a moment's hesitation, I spring into action. I charge forward, sliding onto my knees to grab the nearest dagger—just in time. As he closes in on me, I slice the tendons behind his knee, turning as he falls before pouncing, shoving the dagger into his neck.

Oh gods. I take a deep breath and swallow down the bile, threatening to come up, and I remind myself that this is just a simulation. I'm not entirely sure what just happened. It's like something within me snapped, and some instinct took over. I barely remember driving that blade into his neck.

I inhale sharply, my adrenaline flushing through me as the lights lift and I hear the sound of applause. I turn and see Professor Ainslyn clapping, standing with Anders just beyond the glass.

What the hell is he doing back here?

The expression on Anders' face should scare me—the intensity of his gaze pinning me to the spot—but it's the way his eyes heat that has my breasts swelling with arousal. His gaze cascades down to my toes and back up, his thumb tracing his bottom lip, his arm crossed over his chest.

I take a moment to wipe the sweat from my brow, the moisture beading in my hairline already. I grab the daggers, sheathing them once more, ignoring the wave of embarrassment that washes over me. I should not be responding to Anders the way I do. I push it aside and head back out to reset the simulation.

"That's exactly what we want to see," Professor Ainslyn praises.

I can't help but smile as I take a refreshing sip of cool water before storing my bottle back in my bag. The professor exchanges an approving nod with Anders, "Well, I guess we can discuss it more this evening. Meet me on the sparring mat later." Anders makes some non-committal grunting noise before strolling past me.

As the backs of his fingers delicately brush against my palm, an exhilarating warmth surges through me, awakening every nerve ending. My whole body flushes with energy and emotions, and it takes every ounce of determination to maintain my composure, aware of his undeniable effect on me.

He leans in, no more than a subtle pause, and I swear I hear the words "Damn, that was hot" leave his mouth, but I can't be sure. The thrill of it sends my heart racing. I clear my throat as he continues to the door, holding steady so as not to watch him go. I shake off the whirlwind of emotions swirling within me and summon my confidence to go another round. This time, I ask for hand-to-hand combat, needing to bury my feelings deep, deep down and lock them away for good measure.

"The imperial bloodline came to a sudden end after their beloved heir tragically succumbed to an unknown illness, following closely after the Empress's death, which came as a result of her formidable powers.

She was an incredible healer, but even the most gifted among us have limitations," Professor Darci explains passionately.

I've heard this piece of our history before. Still, as I glance around, it's clear my classmates are listening as if it's their first encounter with this story.

"Following their deaths, we entered the era known as the dawn of the kingdoms…" I stifle the urge to roll my eyes. *Yes*, the 'dawn of the kingdoms', a phrase that has become a pretty euphemism for a time of great unrest. While we tend to shy away from the harsh truths of this period, it's essential to acknowledge the reality of what happened. Beneath our glorified and simplistic recollections of those years, the reality is much darker.

Millions of lives were lost, villages were reduced to ashes, and warlords wreaked havoc across colonies, leading to devastating famines when crucial supply routes were blown up before reaching their destinations. "An entire accounting of history and knowledge was lost in the chaos. Countless libraries and schools were destroyed," she continues, her eyes scanning the sea of faces before her.

"We now wrestle with key questions such as: How did the empire coexist alongside the gods? What caused a decline in technological progress? How did our ancestors flourish without trade from other planets? What kind of magic did they have, and was it gifted or were they born with it? There are so many questions awaiting answers," she prompts, surveying the room with an inviting expression. "Now, let's open the floor to questions."

I find myself drifting off, my thoughts wandering toward Anders. It's been two long weeks since that night by the river, and my heart is still torn. I struggle to move past what happened between us, but it's even harder to admit how willing I am to jump. Then he winked at me as if I had been lying about just talking. It felt intimate and infuriating all at once. It took days to reassure Kellan that nothing inappropriate took place, and it stung to feel that hint of distrust from my best friend.

The way Anders spoke to me today, whispering things in my ear, only added fuel to my frustration. His words are tantalizing, a promise of what would happen if I let him in. He's so maddeningly arrogant yet incredibly enchanting, leaving me feeling drawn to him while simultaneously exasperated by his every word and action.

"Have all the trade agreements always been in the common language, or have they been drafted in various languages across the system?" Aada's question sparks my interest, and I eagerly raise my hand, ready to move on from my incessant thoughts.

"Raea, care to share your insights?" Professor Darci asks. I nod as I sit up a little straighter.

"According to our earliest records, each planet once had its own unique language—many even had multiple dialects. However, during the era of the Ryverian Empire, when hyperjump technology enabled us to traverse our system and great distances, they unified the systems with what was then known as Kaelish. It was primarily spoken by the elite, but a law was enacted requiring every child to learn it as the common language.

"Over time, Kaelish became the common tongue across the planets, gradually overshadowing many of the older tongues that eventually faded with each generation. Yet, if you journey to the remotest corners of our system, you may encounter small villages where dialects akin to those of their ancestors are still spoken. Fortunately, we have recorded many of these original tongues in our digital archives. Sadly, many cultures have been lost in accepting Kaelish and our ability to travel."

It's a bittersweet reality. While I recognize the necessity of unification, it saddens me to think of all the cultures that have been lost. It makes me ponder what else we may have sacrificed along the way.

"And what lies beyond that loss?" Professor Darci prompts, crossing her arms gracefully over her navy blue jacket worn over black fitted trousers and a black blouse.

"Interestingly, the establishment of a common language significantly improved trade relations. In the past, conflicts and misunderstandings were common among planets, but with the adoption of a shared language, everyone gained access to trading opportunities. As a result, all planets can now enjoy essentials such as clean water, supplies, and a variety of foods. This also opens doors for villagers seeking better opportunities; they can now explore jobs across different planets. Many of the larger colonies have become melting pots, bustling with people from all walks of life, and in some areas, preserving elements of their original cultures."

"And this is why, Raea, you're destined to be an extraordinary queen one day," Professor Darci praises, as her bobbed black hair dances with her movement.

The rest of History passes in a blur, and with the almost sick feeling I have over the constant confusion and intensity of my Bond— how it consumes virtually every thought—I decide to speak with Professor Becca.

After class, I reassure my friends with an enthusiastic smile that I'll join them for our study group before dinner, then race toward Professor Becca's office.

With a light knock, I hear her voice inviting me in. She looks up from her papers, and her warm smile instantly puts me at ease. Professor Becca is unique among the faculty since she has been in my shoes. The other professors here have all married for love.

"Hi, do you have a moment to talk?" My stomach flutters, and I notice my palms are slightly clammy as I take a seat in the plush chair facing her desk. The color reminds me vividly of Anders' eyes, bringing a torrent of emotions—confusion, frustration, hope. *Gods.* I almost want to sob from how tired I feel. I'm usually such a stable person, but now I feel like I'm losing my mind. I use my shirt to fan myself. My body feels so dang hot.

I take a moment to look around the room. Natural light pours in through large windows, and a hearth blazing to my right casts a warm glow on the dark wood desk.

Behind Professor Becca, the bookshelves are packed with ancient tomes whose spines are worn from heavy use. As my gaze wanders, I spot a photo of her and what I assume is her husband, their smiles radiating undeniable love and joy.

Scattered among the books are trinkets collected from various corners of the kingdom—there's a finely carved figurine that looks like it hails from Kao, a neighboring planet in my kingdom, and a crystal hand sculpture from the villages of Ateria that I've had the pleasure of visiting. Each detail in her office tells me more about her, making the space feel both inviting and imbued with wisdom.

"What's on your mind?" she inquires, leaning back in her chair, fingers steepled in thought, her Bond marking a direct contrast against her white blouse.

"I've been contemplating why royals aren't free to choose their partners. It feels like my own emotions are slipping away from me as if this Bond is controlling every aspect of my life." I close my eyes, fighting back the sting of tears I don't understand.

"I can see why you'd feel that way." She shifts in her seat and crosses her legs. "Let's unpack this feeling of being overwhelmed by the Bond. It's important to note that, at this stage, the Bond isn't the source of your emotions." She pauses, allowing me to digest her words. "Your feelings should be uniquely yours until an actual Bond forms. If you're drawn to someone, it's likely because you already feel a connection to them.

"While the gods play a significant role in the Bonding process, your own inclinations are also part of it. For instance, a Bond is likely to develop if you're genuinely interested in a guy and he feels the same way. However, the Bond might not even develop if you're indifferent towards someone. Could you share more about your feelings towards this person?"

I hesitate, unsure of how much to divulge. What if Anders was right? What if we should keep this between us?

"I'm overwhelmed, honestly. It's as if he's all I can think about, and yet I don't want to feel this way. It's just so overwhelming. When I'm around him, which seems to happen often, it's hard to breathe, yet everything feels off without him," I admit, looking down at my clothes, picking at an imaginary thread. "It frustrates me, and I'm just exhausted."

She hums, a knowing look in her eyes that makes me question if she knows it's Anders I'm talking about. "Instead of resisting it, perhaps consider spending time with him to unravel what draws you to him. There might be so much more to discover about this man, and he may be the right fit for you. Destiny has a funny way of showing up when we least expect it."

A gnawing discomfort grows in my stomach. Destiny is just a beautiful word for a cage. "But what if I don't want this? It feels so...oppressive." The familiar burn of unshed tears threatens to surface again.

"I understand it feels confusing, but this is where faith in the gods comes into play. It might seem odd, but a strong Bond is truly a blessing, Raea. A Bond like this indicates immense potential—you and he could harness great powers together."

I've always viewed the gifts of power with a twinge of unease. Power can feel like both a burden and a blessing. I think of my father, who tires so easily when he has to protect new territories. Healing abilities draw attention, and those who possess them are often sought after, especially when illnesses arise within our village or new royals are born. It's a hefty responsibility, and I've carried the weight of that expectation my entire life. It's not something that particularly excites me.

Professor Becca's words linger, and maybe, just maybe, it's time for me to embrace this journey and see where it leads. *Should I let Anders in? Can we be friends, or possibly more?* It's thoughts like these that keep me up late at night.

"Raea, I completely understand that this feels really unfair. Let me share a little story that might resonate with you." She rises, her heels clicking on the hardwood floors as she tucks her hands into her pockets. "When I was around your age, I attended Coldwell Academy, and I felt a connection with so many men around me. I had a huge crush on one particular guy, but I later discovered there was no Bond between us.

"As I reached my senior year, frustration built up inside me, similar to what you're experiencing, and I started acting out. I kissed that guy, and we became more involved. However, as my graduation approached, things shifted, and it became clear he wasn't the right person for me. I still had feelings for him, but something just felt...off.

"During that time, my husband—with whom I knew I had a Bond —became my closest friend. He supported me through some challenging moments, like when I lost my mother, and we shared late-night walks that cleared my mind. Over time, I fell in love with him well before The Ceremony. When Bonding day came, I silently prayed it would be him, and the gods answered my prayer.

"I often wonder if I would have experienced this love if I hadn't taken the chance to truly get to know him. I feel incredibly grateful that I had the opportunity to love him before the Bond confirmed everything for us." She gently places her hand over mine with a warm smile. "Sometimes, it's all about taking that leap."

I nod, appreciating her perspective, but I still feel a bit lost. How could anyone feel what I do and think it's a gift? After thanking her for her time, I rise and make my way back to my room. I need to meet my friends for our study group and possibly rethink exploring whatever it is between Anders and me.

"My father just messaged me and said he's coming to visit this weekend," Aolyn sighs, dropping back onto her bed. "I guess he's coming for the AerBall game."

Glancing up from my Cultural Anthropology assignment, I notice she's already slipped into her cozy pajamas and started her nightly routine of searching The Link for the system's juiciest gossip.

"Why don't you sound happy about that?" I ask.

She blows out a breath, turning to face me with a slight frown. "Things at home are...complicated." I've only met King Alexi once, and he never struck me as a friendly man. "My father...keep this between us?"

I nod and wait.

"Well, something is going on that he's not telling us. He's always tired, he's angry, and over break, well...we had a lot of strange visitors to the palace, but they never dined with us. I don't know, I just wish I knew how to help."

"I can understand that," I reply, letting my empathy shine through. She hums, and I realize there must be more she isn't telling me. "How is your mother?" Queen Sava has a formidable presence, though she's always been kind during our encounters. Plus, Aolyn absolutely adores her.

With her long black hair and pale complexion, Aolyn is almost a carbon copy of her mother. Queen Sava's features are sharper, often set in a serious, no-nonsense expression that has the ability to make you feel tiny. She's attended many of my mother's events over the years.

Aolyn lights up as she shares stories about her mother and the ice sculptures they've been working on. Her mother is an ice wielder, so it makes sense that it would be a hobby. It's an incredible power, but I can't imagine living with that endless bone-chilling cold.

Their palace feels like a majestic fortress perched high in the Halgan Peaks, one of the tallest ranges on their beautiful capital planet, Cryos. Nestled against the mountain's side, it experiences a fresh blanket of snow daily.

As we discuss the dynamics within her family and the fear surrounding the royal succession if Boyce doesn't Bond, the conversation soon shifts to her love for AerBall. I know very little, but we exchange thoughts about our favorite pro players.

By the time I drift off to sleep, my mind is flooded with thoughts of AerBall and Anders—a playful, muddy smirk he might shoot me that would make me feel like I might mean something special to him.

Even in my sleep, there's no escaping him.

eleven

. . .

"H ey, have you heard about Micah and Alec's breakup?" Ciara asks, a week later, as she drops into the seat beside me. Her braids are unbound today in long black waves.

Tate chuckles, lounging back in his chair. "I heard it was an epic fight. Shame I missed it," he sighs. "Honestly, we could use some more excitement around here. It's been a little dull lately."

The two of them share a conspiratorial glance before she leans in, filling me in on the juicy details of the latest scandal. "You won't believe it! Turns out Micah was involved with another guy from Specials. Plot twist!" Her face lights up with amusement that I don't share. *Yikes.*

"Alright, everyone, let's settle down," Professor Maleka calls out, her voice strained as she strolls in, looking like she didn't sleep a wink last night. Her tall frame is wrapped in a cozy brown sweater. Purple smudges frame her usually bright green eyes, now dull and almost gray. Her typically curly hair looks untamed and wild, pulled back into a knot at the top of her head.

"Today, we are discussing the Ancestor Isles on Demeter. Which, for those of you who don't know your planets..." She frowns around the room as if to tell everyone how disappointed she is. "It's one of

Okenen's, a planet rich with history and culture." With a flick of her hand, she activates a fresh projection on the board behind her, illuminating images and maps of the Isles. The vibrant colors and intricate details of the illustrations ignite my curiosity.

Professor Maleka tries to stifle a yawn before continuing, "The Ancestor Isles claim to be one of the oldest cultures in our system, with a bloodline that traces back to the original people with a pure genetic line. To this day," she pulls up a map of the islands, "no outsiders can reside on the Isles, but they're open to trading and visiting Benek, the nearest city in the Opus Colony, to share their culture."

I pull out my tablet and begin taking notes. I've heard whispers about the Isles, but I've never been allowed to study them until now. The knowledge of these Isles is safeguarded, and even the Isles themselves are shielded from boats due to the turbulent currents surrounding them like a magical barrier.

The islanders have a unique way of navigating the waters using a water creature about the size of a small transport pod. What I find truly fascinating is that only the locals can communicate with this animal, leaving scientists stumped as they attempt to study it.

The projection changes to a photo of the main island. "The main island, Elingra, serves as the hub for their small governing body," Professor Maleka shares.

"Have you ever seen them?" Tate leans in, eyes wide with curiosity.

I shake my head, keeping my eyes trained on the board. Throughout our Ethnography lecture, we learn that every islander speaks their native language, while only a handful of their mini-government officials understand the common tongue. This communication barrier presents its own challenges for the crown, especially since the common language and technology are prohibited on the islands.

The hairs on my arms rise as old photos of the islanders pop up. They aren't what I expected. The islanders are taller than all the visitors, with their skin in various shades of bronze and deep brown, long, wavy hair for both men and women, and dressed in makeshift clothes made from leaves and hides. Their faces are all painted with white paint in symbols that nobody has been able to translate.

They remind me of the symbols and inscriptions carved into the stone in Ayallenora—an ancient village on my home planet. *This place, these people, hold secrets.*

By the end of class, we are given an assignment to investigate one of the customs on the Ancestor Isles and present it to the class next week. As we shuffle out of class, Beric, a boy who's been harassing me and starting rumors, corners me.

When he grips my wrist, I turn, pushing against his chest. "Don't touch me," I hiss, attempting not to make a scene and failing.

He chuckles. "My boys and I were talking—why don't you come to a party we're having in the woods this weekend? We'll have some fun." His grimy eyes slide over me. I'm about to shove him off when Anders' hand wraps around Beric's wrist, twisting it with a sickening crunch.

Beric shrieks in protest, but Anders leans in and, in a murderously calm voice, says, "I suggest you remove your hand." Beric is glaring at Anders, surely about to spew something when Anders says, "If I ever see you lay a hand on her again, I'll have you stripped of your titles, sent to a moon. Your family will be sent to live with the commoners, and that will be the kindest punishment I'm willing to consider." The color drains from Beric's face. I'd really like to get out from between them, but Anders has me trapped, his front pressed into my back.

Beric glances down at me and mutters an apology before storming out of the now-empty classroom. "Was that necessary?" I spin to face Anders.

He shrugs. "He shouldn't touch what isn't his."

I scoff, rolling my eyes, but I'll never admit that I kind of like this side of him. Something about him playing the role of dark prince has my toes curling, especially when those piercing blue eyes meet mine.

"We need to talk," he says quietly as I approach him.

I nod and continue toward my next class, ignoring how I long to throw myself into his arms and forgive him. I'm lying to myself that I don't desire to feel his arms wrap around me while I bury my face into his chest and breathe in the scent that drowns me in feelings of need and want.

"Sure. After class?" He deposits me safely into the combat class, lingering at the door like he wants to say more, but when I lift a brow, he sighs and disappears without another word, leaving me feeling a little breathless and off-kilter.

I'm thrilled when Professor Ainslyn sends me to the simulator for Hallo gun practice. I see it as an outlet to calm my racing thoughts and sharpen my focus—something I desperately need right now.

After checking out a practice gun from the attendant, I head into the simulator. The weapon has a sleek design and is lightweight, even for me. The cool grip fits perfectly into my hands. I make my way to the center of the spacious, dimly lit room, letting the anticipation build within me. The projection rays embedded in the walls flicker to life, casting an ethereal glow that sets my first simulation in motion.

On my left, a long, glass wall darkens and is blessedly vacant. To my right, a cushioned wall provides a soft barrier should I need it. Behind me, the operator's voice breaks through my thoughts, preparing me for the start of the trial. I take a moment to nod. Inhaling deeply, I close my eyes and center myself.

Kuron and Ezra have always told me during training that my emotions could get me killed. They've been relentless in honing not only my skills with my daggers but also my mind. They've taught me how to harness and channel my emotions for whatever situation.

With my mind blissfully empty of doubts and emotions, I open my eyes with a clear determination. Holographic opponents and creatures spring to life from projected walls, trees, and buildings surrounding me in the landscape. It takes a moment to gather my bearings, but once I do, I make quick work of taking down the human simulations first, thankful they're masked. Next, the system's predatory creatures.

I find myself holding my breath when the onyx leopard leaps into view, its sea green eyes and shimmering, iridescent scales adorning its head, shoulders, and parts of its face, illuminating in the dark. I never know whether I'm terrified or amazed by these creatures.

Despite their lethal intelligence, they're beautiful. Their scales resemble glitter, with vibrant hues of emerald green, sapphire blue, and amethyst purple, catching the light like a constellation of tiny jewels embedded in their fur. It's always a part of my simulations and one of the hardest to take down. The creature pacing before me is an exact replica of the animal found on Neptyn and Kyrr.

Above me, it growls, baring terrifying rows of razor-sharp teeth that could shred anyone or anything in an instant. It reminds me to calm my racing heart and pay attention.

I focus on the leopard as it confidently prowls back and forth atop a towering boulder. The way it watches me draws up more adrenaline as I lie in wait, watching for the subtle moment just before it will take the leap. In one heartbeat, the cat pauses; the next, he launches into the air, claws out, and ready for an attack. I fire off two shots directly to his heart just before throwing my arms over my head, waiting for a weight that will never come.

I learned that the hard way, the first time I was attacked by an onyx leopard, the only way to kill it is to go for the heart. The last time I was attacked, I fell to my back and screamed like I was actually about to be eaten alive just before pulling the trigger. That same adrenaline pulses through my body even now. No matter how many times I run a simulation with it, I can't convince my body it's just a hologram.

The lights flash, signaling the conclusion of the simulation, but remain dimmed, casting the room in shadows. The hairs on my neck rise, and something tells me I have an audience in the darkened observation room.

Professor Ainslyn had alerted me earlier that I had been chosen to demonstrate the weapon to juniors taking the test. I take a moment to hydrate and gather my breath before heading back toward the platform.

The following simulation will be interstellar, pushing my knowledge and skills to the limit. Space training is packed with challenges that require me to think quickly and adapt to the unfamiliar environment. As I strap on the vest and waistband designed to mimic the sensation of antigravity, I can't help but feel a surge of excitement.

The room darkens even further, creating a sense of vastness that makes me aware of how small I truly am. I embrace the weightlessness that blurs the line between standing on the platform and floating freely. It's part of the magic of this place. I spin, awash in the cold darkness dotted with twinkling stars, beautiful planets, and a golden sun peeking out from behind a moon, offering me a glimmer of light on the set before me.

I inhale deeply, and then I hear the familiar clacking associated with enemies filing out of their shuttle, their magboots grounding them to the ship's hull as they run for me. I fire a warning shot, but I'm too far off, not accounting for the lack of gravity—a rookie mistake.

With a grunt, I grab the tether that will pull me back to my ship, securing it to my waist with one hand. Three figures, clad in shining black suits, stand before me, each poised and ready. I quickly assess the situation, noting that the plasma won't hit its mark from this distance.

I can't help but appreciate Professor Ainslyn's effort to incorporate real opponents into my training. Previously, they were just faceless shapes, but now, as I peer through the glass of their helmets, I catch a glimpse of their hate-filled expressions—two men and one woman—before the glass transitions into a dark, reflective amber.

My attention shifts to my own suit. I'm dressed in a white space suit that resembles my flight gear but with thick shields. Padding enhances my defenses, and the gold belt at my hips holds my weapons. I blink, and my helmet appears, already locked in place, displaying information such as distance, temperature, and the rate of my heartbeat.

The holograms feel so tangible, but as I reach out, my hand slices right through the projection. A sudden clank of metal pulls me back into focus. This is the pivotal moment where I decide to fight.

With a surge of adrenaline and determination, I throw my hand back, activating a small jet of air that propels me forward. I land solidly with a thud, my boots magnetizing to the hull of their ship. I don't waste a second, throwing myself forward as I race toward them.

Each step is heavy with the weight of the magnet's pull, and I know I'll need to practice running in these.

The first assailant charges me, and I manage to get one shot off. He disappears, leaving the two others still running toward me. My gun throws an error at me, probably intended, but I'm out of time. I'll have to do hand-to-hand.

I slide across the surface on my knees, hearing the screech of metal on metal, keeping the edge of one boot attached to the hull so I stay anchored. With a swift movement, I kick out the knee of the second soldier, but before I realize it, he tumbles onto me, and we become locked in a rolling wrestle. Out here, he feels almost weightless. The energy shield I rely on when on planet doesn't protect me here. Every hit I take feels like a physical blow, leaving me breathless.

In a moment of focus, I reach for their helmet. While they throw punches at my sides, I manage to dislodge it, and he vanishes from the simulation, leaving me one more opponent. She doesn't hesitate, lifting me effortlessly—I guess antigravity helps with that. She screams, hurling me from the ship, but follows after me, colliding mid-air. With a firm grasp on me, the battle begins.

A cracking sound alerts me to the splintering glass of my helmet as my head snaps back. I gasp as the screens inside my helmet glitch and then disappear, leaving me staring into the dark form of my attacker. These suits are designed to withstand extreme temperatures and are lightweight enough that I can move with ease, but if the glass breaks, I'm dead in a single heartbeat.

The third hit almost splinters the glass, and I realize she has a chunk of something in her hand. I throw my hand into her stomach, blasting a quick stream of air at her, but she doesn't let go, her grip tightening around my neck. Fear tries to lodge itself in my throat, but I shove it into a box quickly before it overtakes all logical thought.

I will not be weak.

My Hallo gun is finally ready, and with another loud, splintering crack to my helmet, I fire off a shot to her side, hitting her just below the plate of armor. She disappears instantly, becoming nothing more than a blur of colors as the simulation lifts along with the lights.

I find myself on the floor, gasping for air, and it takes a second for me to come back to reality. I'm still at school...in the simulator...not in space. I pat my face, finding no helmet there. I gasp for another breath while gazing at the black domed ceiling now filled with bright lights.

The sound of clapping and laughter fills the air. I turn my head to find the entire class behind the glass wall already snapping photos of me on my back having a minor anxiety attack over a dumb simulation. My gaze shifts to the two men taking up too much space.

Really?

Anders and Trysten are also there discussing something when Anders and I lock eyes. He flashes me a warm, genuine smile—dimple and all. I groan internally. He has a knack for always showing up when I'd rather he not.

We hold eye contact for a moment, and it's enough to feel and see the ripple of light between us. My core heats, and not from embarrassment that I almost got my ass handed to me. I hold his gaze for another heartbeat before glancing back up at the dome.

Who cares why he's here?

"Well done, Princess Raea," Professor Ainslyn says over the speaker. "That's a senior-level simulation, and you just passed with flying colors."

I close my eyes, still coming down from the adrenaline coursing through me. I have some choice words for the professor right now, but I swallow them down, letting oxygen flood my system and chase away the jitters and nausea that are now threatening me.

Anders and I find a small alcove not far from the simulation room, where we can talk. I can see that he's stressed about whatever it is he wants to talk about, as he continuously shoves his hand through his hair. I'm not even sure he's aware he's pacing.

"Something is wrong." His hand brushes through his dark locks.

"Please just hear me out. You're the only one who might understand." My face scrunches in confusion. "The veil...I..." He looks down the hall both ways, assuring we're alone. "I think I can feel its power, and something is draining it."

I grab his wrist, halting him in place and flinch, swallowing the surge that threatens to consume me. "How?" I bite out. "How do you know?" I take a deep breath and relax back into the pillows. Anders sits across from me, elbows resting on his knees with his hands clasped in a prayer.

"For the past year, I've been able to feel the magic around me. When I'm around Bonded couples, it's like they have a certain aura around them. It started as a feeling..." He shakes his head, groaning.

"And now?" I whisper.

"I can see strands of light; not like the Bond itself; it's different. I haven't been able to figure out which colors are associated with what, but today, the colors vanished for forty minutes. While you were in the simulator, they came back. And you..." His sapphire eyes meet mine. "Raea, you have magic."

I swallow, my throat feeling dry as my heartbeat quickens. "What do you mean I have magic? I haven't Bonded, I swear."

"I know that," he assures me. "But, Raea, whatever magic you have, it's flowing through you now, and I don't know why I know this, but it's a different kind of magic. It feels...old."

"What you're saying is ridiculous!" Voices silence me as we both wait for them to fade again. "Anders, I don't have magic."

"You do. But I need to know...do you believe me about the veil? Something is going on. I should be getting reports on behalf of my mother, and I've heard nothing." He pauses, looking both ways again. "Which means either nobody knows, or someone is intercepting the Proto reports."

My heart stammers.

The reports from our space military, Protos, are the only thing keeping the crowns informed. What he's suggesting is treason. "You can't know that." The look he gives me suggests that I need to wake up. "But who would stop the reports? Our kingdoms need those."

"I don't know. But I need to find out. In the meantime, will you help me? I can't trust anyone else."

I scoff and bury my face in my hands. Why me? I'm not trained for this. I'm not taking the crown anytime soon. I have years.

"Soraea," he whispers, prying my fingers away, making my skin pebble with the energy flowing through me. "Please. You're the smartest person I know and the only other person who has magic that isn't Bonded."

"You have magic," I say. It's not a question. "Oh, gods." I let the truth of it settle over me. Memories rush forward, our connection, strange sensations…strange urges. *Magic.* "Okay," I whisper. "I'll help. But nobody can find out. Where do you want to start?"

The edge of his mouth tips up in the beginnings of a smirk, just enough for the shadow of his dimple to appear.

"You're the smarty pants, you tell me." I nibble on my lip, leaning back and letting the cool stone seep through the material of my shirt. "What do you know about the Ancestor Isles?" I play with an invisible thread. "They're as untouched as can be. Maybe they have ancient texts or scrolls? We need to find out more about the veil and how Astor and Calia powered it."

"Really?" he deadpans. "That's where you want to look? That's almost impossible. They only allow ten visitors a year. I'm not even sure we can play the royal card."

"You can ask," I say sweetly, lifting a shoulder. He makes a grunting noise. "And you should see if you can get reports from the Protos. Maybe have them deliver them directly to the palace?"

"Yeah," he mumbles, his gaze drifting eons away.

"I'll see what I can find on the Nexus."

His face drains of color as his gaze returns to mine—the muscles of his jaw locked. "You can't! Raea, you could get in serious trouble."

He's right; the Nexus is an illegal platform for selling black-market information. If you're caught selling or trading, you can be sentenced to a full year on the moons. "Well, where do you suggest we look? We can't exactly search for unBonded magic manifestations, or veil-magic, without it being flagged."

The bell rings to signal the end of classes. He stands quickly, leaning close so only I can hear. "Find books, Soraea. They aren't traceable, and I don't believe for a second they've all been destroyed."

Before I can answer, he shifts in front of me, his body a shield against curious eyes. "In the meantime, I'll get us a pass to the Isles."

With an hour to spare before Bonding class, a few of us gather in our favorite study room, the one with the projector. Aolyn and Kamden have joined, along with Tate and Ciara, all of whom seem to think I have the answers to everything.

Our politics assignment is due in two days, and we need to propose solutions for challenges faced by three different trade planets from three various kingdoms. I glance at Aolyn and whisper my thanks. She had this assignment last year and is only here for moral support.

Kamden, one of the junior Recon division students, is quick to jump in and help. It seems he is one of the only students I've met who took his tour seriously. He's smart, but easy going, and when I catch him staring at Aolyn, she tells me how they met over break when he was in Ateria skiing.

It was a week that her father sent her away from Cryos, so she spent an insane amount of money renting out half of the fanciest resort on Ashum, inviting her friends and their friends to join, and spent a week partying.

She giggles when she says her father didn't even bat an eye when he got the bill. He tossed it aside and muttered that he had more important things to deal with, and to talk to their treasurer to pay it.

My jaw drops. If my father had received a bill like that, I'm pretty sure he'd send me to one of the labor camps for a month just to teach me a lesson.

"Let's go to the village," Kamden says, dropping his tablet on the table. He grins, revealing perfectly white teeth. His bright green eyes light up when Tate shoots to his feet.

"Yes. Right after class," Tate agrees, shoving a hand through his black locks.

"I'll go," Ciara says, head resting on the table, her brown hair splayed out around her like a blanket. It's down to Aolyn and me. We both look at each other and shrug.

"Okay, let's go. Let me put my books away. I'll meet all of you after class by the doors?" Aolyn asks. We all nod and head to our rooms before we need to be in the hall for class.

After switching into a gown and cleaning up, I find Cole waiting outside my door with a satisfied smirk. "You look stunning," he comments, holding out his arm like he's going to physically escort me. I snort and turn down the hall.

"I find Bonding to be rather dull, wouldn't you agree?" he asks, coming to walk beside me. "Not that you care, but my brother said he'll see you after class. He was pulled into a palace meeting."

Well, that was quick.

I glance up at Cole and shrug. "I think I'll be just fine."

He chuckles and opens the door to the bridge. "This is why I like you, Raea." He doesn't say more as we enter the hall of students filing into their dorm sections and finding seats.

During class, Professor Becca teaches us about the point of The Ceremony. According to the text in *A Seer's Didactic on Lumos Cere-monies*, without the Lumos Bond, magic would disappear completely. The magic gifted to Bonded couples comes from the gods, allowing the Bonded to help our system in ways the gods no longer can. Essentially, it's now up to us to protect the system.

Something gnaws at me as I read and read the passage about the gods gifting us the power in their place. After a few minutes, I give up. My head hurts, and I need to be done thinking for now. In fact, the village sounds like the perfect distraction.

twelve

. . .

W HEN A OLYN and I return to our room, I instantly feel lighter. We throw our bags down and change quickly into simple gowns, complete with thick cloaks to conceal us. I let my hair down to fit in with the commoners and use a quick color spray to attempt to conceal the recognizable white strands. The brown covers the white easily enough, but the hints of blue still shimmer through, albeit in a duller hue now. We both use the masking clay to cover our family crest tattoos.

As Baedyn transitions into the season of waning light, there's a noticeable chill in the air. The temperature will gradually drop for the next five rotations, but true winter will never impact Baedyn, one of Calia's designs of our system, and each planet's individual weather systems.

After checking out at the front desk, we make our way to the storage buildings that house the transport pods. The pods are egg-shaped, glass transports that can seat up to ten people, five on either side. We hop into the assigned pod, excitement becoming a tangible thing around us as we head to the village for the first time. The soft chime of the pod fills the air as the lights dim to a soft green emanating from the control panel at the front. Aolyn taps the pre-populated navigation button as it navigates out of the garage and across campus. While the hologram professor goes on a spiel about remaining seated through the ride, Kamden and Tate scroll through the list of music.

As we leave campus, I realize I should have left a note or message for both Anders and Kellan. I left my Prism behind, opting for a technology-free evening with my friends. I'm sure they'll both be worried about my absence at dinner.

The guilt knots in my stomach when I remember I was supposed to meet with Anders before bed. I'll have to find him in the morning and explain. Plus, it's not like I've had any time to research.

During the ride to the village, the five of us snap selfies on Ciara's Prism, and I beg her to send me some of them to post on The Link. Cassia has been hounding me again about posting. The four of them power off their devices, tucking them away safely in their cloaks.

Tate and Ciara's off-key singing fills the air as the pod glides through the snowy mountain pass. The tall granite walls are adorned with a blanket of snow. Unlike the larger transports, this pod hovers just above the ground, giving us a panoramic view of the landscape.

Tiny animal tracks weave through the sparkling snow. It's interesting to think that on this vast and largely uninhabited planet, few choose to call the snowy mountains home over the endless warmth of the forest.

As we step out of the pod, I'm greeted by the tantalizing aroma of exotic spice and the delightful sounds of laughter and music from somewhere deep within the village.

The village is surprisingly larger than I expected, not that I knew what to expect, as I've never been here. Cobblestoned streets and alleyways wind between buildings that vary in both size and shape. Some of the structures appear dilapidated, as if they've stood for ages and are entering their final stages, with mismatched, overlaid boards holding them together.

Others outshine their neighbors with modern touches of stone and glass, reminiscent of colonial architecture. The blend of old and new speaks about the community here and their willingness to live side by side, rather than creating districts or factions based on wealth and status.

I love it.

"This way," Tate orders, leading the way down an alleyway with clotheslines overhead.

Linking his arm through Ciara's, he tugs her into the first shop we stumble upon at the other end of the alleyway, which spills into a vibrant market. The delicious aroma of freshly baked bread fills the air, making my mouth water. Aolyn and Kamden follow, sharing smiles of their own.

We meander from shop to shop, sampling delectable treats and trying on various outfits, playfully modeling them for one another. I even wander into a bookstore, dutifully hunting for anything ancient, but I come up empty-handed. I needed this escape to feel free from worries about the future and the weight of the Bond, to focus on my friendships, and to allow myself to genuinely relax.

With the evening still young and in the spirit of being twenty-one, I find a stand peddling a fruity drink, deciding to treat everyone. A blend of strawberries, lemon, and honey hits my tongue at the first sip.

While waiting, I notice the woman behind the counter looks dead on her feet, as if she's been awake for days. My heart clenches when she spins to fill a bottle with another liquor, and I see the baby secured on her back. I struggle with emotions, only able to imagine the challenges she's facing. I wish I could offer her support, but I'm not allowed to intervene as a princess. Something about handouts, bad optics, and favoritism.

Instead, I leave the remaining coins I have in a pouch with her and walk away, hoping they will assist her in some way. It should be enough to pay her rent for a month or hire a sitter.

As dusk settles in and the moons cast a silvery glow over the tents and buildings of the market, we wander toward the bustling square, filled with music and dancing. When Aolyn shakes her head at Kamden, I push him onto the makeshift dance floor, letting myself get lost in the music as the crowd around us brushes past, lost in their own worlds.

After several songs, I find Aolyn on the edge of the dance floor, and I know it's time to call it a night and head back.

"Let's go," I squeal as Tate lifts me over his shoulders and spins me.

He chuckles, holding me tightly as he takes off running. My laughter drowns out the music as he runs toward an alleyway to shortcut the walk back.

"Do we have to go back?" Ciara pouts, running after us. Her caramel face is flushed but looks beautiful, even with her sweat-slicked hair.

"We do," Aolyn chimes in playfully, wrapping her arm around Kamden's waist. He turns even more crimson than he already is from dancing. Tate drops me back to my feet as we reach the pod.

It's late when we make our way back to Taeolyn, and the gentle illumination of the hall lights casts a warm glow around us. With my sweat-cooled skin, a chill dances across my bare arms.

Kamden hoists Aolyn onto his back, ready to carry her upstairs. Meanwhile, Tate bends low, shooting me a grin over his shoulder with a questioning challenge in his eyes.

"Ready for a ride?" he asks, wiggling his brows.

I groan. "Gods, you're insufferable." I leap onto his back, and everyone attempts to contain their laughter.

"So eager," Tate chuckles, just before I smack his shoulder. He grips my thighs over my gown as I toss my cloak to Ciara. She'd never be caught on anyone's back—her pride wouldn't allow it.

Our voices are a symphony of hushed whispers that echo through the hall as we ascend to the top floor. We shush each other, attempting to stifle the flow of laughter.

Kamden and Tate bring us to our door, and with a shared glance, Aolyn and I slide down from their backs. Both men pause, the air thick with an unspoken tension that makes them hesitate. I push past Tate and halt, guilt pinning me to the spot.

"Let's go, now," Anders demands, his voice firm and unyielding.

His withering glare would make anyone crumble, but I muster the strength to stand firm, although a tremor wracks through my body, betraying my emotions.

The others glance at each other, a silent understanding passing among them, and one by one, they slowly retreat from my side, leaving me facing the angry dorm leader alone.

"Thanks, guys." I scowl as I witness them all take another step away from me. A part of me wishes for one of them to stay, but Anders looks terrifying shrouded in darkness.

"Do you want—" Aolyn starts, throwing a thumb over her shoulder, gesturing towards the group, attempting to assist my escape. She pauses mid-sentence, flinching as if sensing the weight of Anders' glare landing on her.

"Just Raea. The rest of you better find your rooms," he snaps, turning away with a briskness that leaves no room for argument. He marches down the hall, leaving me reeling with my thoughts. I've never witnessed him so worked up before. His anger is like a tangible, living thing, radiating off him like a storm, waiting to swallow me up.

Drawing in a deep breath, I brace myself and follow him.

"Good luck," Kamden whispers, and my shoulders tense with apprehension as I round the corner, disappearing from their view. I should have been more open with Anders to at least alert him that I was leaving. It was a shitty move, and I'll own the mistake.

When Anders finally turns to face me, I can see the storm raging in his eyes—a whirlwind of anger and longing that is both terrifying and strangely...intoxicating. My body reacts without permission, going on high alert for all the wrong reasons.

"In. Now," he demands, his voice a rough growl as he holds open the door to his dorm room, the dim light spilling out in the hallway. The air between us crackles with tension, though our Bond is thankfully hidden.

I cross my arms tightly over my chest, determined to stand my ground, even more unwilling to give away my inappropriate thoughts at the first sight of his room.

His room is tucked away down its own secluded hall, away from any prying eyes. When it finally sinks in that I won't be stepping inside, he clenches his jaw, working the muscle in his cheek, and with a sharp exhale, lets the door close.

"Where were you?" he snaps, his voice cutting through the thick silence. He towers over me, his frame casting a long shadow as I tilt my head back to meet his stormy gaze. There's something about the dimness of the hallway, the strong scent of sandalwood and citrus, but the urge to wrap my arms around him and pull him close, somehow bridging the distance between us, overwhelms me and drowns out my anger. Right now, I just want to reach out and beg for forgiveness.

Instead, I bury those emotions deep within me. "The village," I reply, with a slight shrug. "I'm sorry. I should have told you."

"Why didn't you?" His question is laced with fear I'm not ready to acknowledge. It would only further my guilt, but I promised myself I wouldn't be one of those women.

"Can we not do this? Look, I'm sorry. I messed up. I'm not used to having to check in with you. It won't happen again. But I'm tired and now is not the right time to argue." I say, as I watch his jaw tighten again, along with his whole body. The fabric of his black shirt stretches taut over his muscles as he stands silent for a moment, his eyes swirling, the only emotion that gives away the war within. His hands swipe through his hair in exasperation as his features crack.

Abruptly, he closes the gap between us, his palm pressing against the wall beside my head, effectively boxing me in. He takes several ragged breaths, squeezing his eyes shut as if to stave off the brewing storm within. After a heartbeat, they pop open again, and I'm met with a silvery gaze, a mix of fury and something deeper...maybe...fear.

My throat feels thick as I try to swallow down the emotions bubbling to the surface. Just as I'm about to apologize *again*, he speaks first.

"Raea, gods, I was worried sick about you and—" He reaches for me, but instinctively, I step back, hitting the wall. Suddenly, this hallway is too small and too intimate.

"And what, Anders?" It comes out a little breathless. I was aiming for stern, but it seems I've lost all ability to talk. "I was fine. I'm allowed to do things with my friends. I just want to be normal while I can. You have to understand that."

He looks genuinely distressed, his hair tousled as if he's spent the entire evening running his hands through it, and with the faint scent of mead wafting off him, I know he's been drinking.

"I do," he sighs. "Gods, I do, Raea."

His large, calloused hand gently grips my elbow, drawing me closer until we're nearly touching. I attempt to take another step away, but he follows, eliminating the distance between us.

His hands find my waist, fingers pressing into my hips. His sudden proximity makes my heart race even as my mind shouts reminders to pull away. He bends down so close that we share air, the energy between us humming in delight, taut like a physical string pulling us together.

His gaze flickers to my lips, and my core liquifies, pooling in my stomach. I bite down on my lip to suppress the whimper that threatens to betray me. I desperately need air—fresh air—to gather myself because if I don't leave, I don't trust myself not to close the final distance and find out for myself exactly how soft his lips are.

My mind lingers on how it would feel to kiss him while my eyes lock on his mouth. If I kissed him, would it be tender and gentle? Or would he possess me, devouring me and taking control, leaving me craving more? I find myself leaning more toward the latter. The thought is almost as intoxicating as if our lips were to actually collide.

I don't know who moves, him or me, but the space between our mouths dwindles until our bodies are flush, his warmth stealing every thought from me as I bring my palms to his chest. Beneath my hand, his heart thumps erratically.

Time has slowed around me, the world falling away as he rests his forehead against mine, the rapid rise and fall of our breaths the only sound I hear. If his touch is a spark, his kiss will be an inferno.

Dorm leader. Not yours. Don't be that girl. My mind almost screams the words at me, even though my heart is begging me to stay. In a moment of clarity, I gently push, retreating quickly before I turn back.

Oh gods. I almost just kissed Anders Rykerson.

thirteen

. . .

I BEND OVER, feeling the delicious burn in my hamstring as I lead the others in pre-run stretches while a girl from Specialists counts out to thirty. After going to the village the other night, my body yearns for a good run to shake off the lingering aches and tightness that have settled in. Running has always been my sanctuary—a chance to unplug from the chaos, elevate my heart rate, and embrace the freedom that comes from putting distance between you and your starting point. Plus, there's something about the forest, or nature in general, that sings to my soul, immediately boosting my energy.

Unfortunately, amidst the stretching and anticipation of our run, my mind keeps slipping back to that almost kiss. Being near Anders has become nearly impossible. I replay the scene in my mind over and over again. The soft brush of his body against mine, his intoxicating scent wrapping around me, and those deep, hungry eyes locked onto mine as his lips parted, dropping so close to mine that they nearly touched.

I swallow down the thoughts, shifting my focus back to the warm-up. I glance around and notice everyone else is antsy to get started. Once Mallory finishes counting, I draw everyone closer to explain our run today. If I'm going to be tormented by thoughts of him, then I'll return the damn favor.

"We're running stairs today." I look around the group gathered here. There are eighteen of us in total. Thirteen Executives and five Specialists. "We'll start with a light jog through campus, and then when we get to the AerBall stadium, we'll run the whole stadium."

There's a chorus of groans and shocked expressions as reality sets in. The AerBall stadium is no small feat. It can accommodate twelve thousand people.

"C'mon, no time for excuses!" I encourage them with a bright smile, spurring them on as I lead the way, winding around the different dorm yards. As we set off toward the arena, a slight smile pulls on my lips.

Anxious energy settles over me as I catch sight of the circular arena. Its architecture glitters against the landscape, commanding attention, and I know that inside, Anders and his team are nearing the end of their practice.

I can't help that my mind is already thinking about seeing Anders soaked and sweaty and looking absolutely sinful. Desire floods my system, leaving my breasts full and my core throbbing.

I clear my throat and come to a stop. "Melody, lead the way. Everyone, single file." The gate creaks when I pull it open. Melody bounds up the steps first, her red hair catching the light, looking like a fire in the afternoon sun.

I round the corner to follow them, coming to a screeching halt when Trysten steps out in front of me. His eyes go wide, surprise illuminating his features as he glances back and forth between me and the rest of my team, who are already halfway up the steps of the first section.

"Well, that was a disas—" Anders curses, coming around the corner and halting at my appearance. Their imposing height and built frames block my way. I'm about to complain when my mouth goes dry, the words getting lodged in my throat. Anders uses the hem of his shirt to wipe his face, displaying miles of warm, tan skin stretched taut over the dips and curves of his hard muscles. The defined V of his hips points straight down to where his shorts hang low; *it should be illegal to look that good.*

"What did you say?" Trysten asks, his brows knitting together as he pulls me back into the moment. The intensity in his gaze makes me acutely aware of my surroundings. I tilt my head in confusion, realizing I inadvertently voiced my thoughts out loud. *Shit.* Embarrassment flushes my body.

"I really should go." I gesture toward the arena where my team members are gearing up for their third ascent. My eyes linger on Trysten, who raises an eyebrow, his expression curious as he shifts his focus to Anders, silently inquiring about my slip-up. A million thoughts race through my mind as I pray they didn't hear me.

Anders stands with his arms crossed over his broad chest, accentuating his arms and tall stature as he surveys me. His eyes sweep over my bare skin, and I can't help but notice the way a playful smirk tugs at the corners of his lips. It's precisely the kind of reaction I was hoping for. I want him to feel just a hint of the agonizing desire I've been avoiding for the past two days.

The atmosphere around us crackles with energy. As Anders' gaze heats, I am hyper-aware that I am clad only in a sports bra and short running shorts. The fabric clings to my skin, and I can feel the unspoken desire in the air around us.

"Do you plan on holding me hostage?" I tilt my head to the side and cross my arms under my breasts, lifting them just enough for his eyes to drop to my chest. A strangled noise comes from the back of Anders' throat, making Trysten chuckle and pat him on the shoulder.

"Our apologies," Trysten muses. "Have fun." He steps aside, gesturing for me to run ahead. I drop my arms and begin my jog. I look over my shoulder once to see Anders' eyes on my ass as he runs a hand through his hair. A genuine grin spreads across my face. *I win.*

The following week, during divisions class, it's impossible to ignore Anders. I can't seem to keep visions of his bare stomach from making appearances in my thoughts and dreams. I know I shouldn't indulge in these thoughts; it's a dangerous edge I'm walking, but, frankly, every free moment in my mind seems hooked on him. The anticipation I feel knowing he'll be at my door each morning should irritate me, and yet, he's like an addiction I can't seem to satisfy. I only want more.

Anders and I agreed to meet up after dinner to discuss what we've found so far. I'm hoping he found us a way to the Isles because finding an ancient text with the knowledge of the magic fueling the veil seems impossible. I haven't tried the Nexus yet, but it's still not off the table.

As I settle into my seat beside Ciara, a palpable sense of excitement fills the classroom. It's the long-awaited day when Professor Brendn will announce the details of the upcoming test. The flutter of nerves dances in my stomach, and a brief sense of exhilaration courses through me at the thought of flying unassisted for long stretches.

Just then, Jensn plops down in the chair beside me with casual confidence. His black coils have grown out, cascading over his forehead. "Princess," he purrs with a glint in his eye.

I make a conscious effort to keep my irritation at bay. He shouldn't even be here; he should be in Intel right now. "Jensn," I respond with a fake smile.

"I was wondering...I've heard you have quite the wealth of knowledge regarding history and planets." His features soften with genuine curiosity. "I was hoping you'd be willing to tutor me; I promise to make it worth your while." His words come out smoothly, and his eyes flick down to my lips, sending a surge of irritation through me.

Is he really flirting with me?

The thought is a little unnerving, especially when a rush of blue light fills the space between us.

"What are we talking about over here?" Tate interjects, leaning in closer while sitting on the edge of my desk. I can't help but roll my eyes at his painfully obvious attempts to gather information to most likely tease me with later.

"Raea here is making me beg," Jensn remarks with a wink.

I scoff at the exact moment I feel the heavy weight of Anders' gaze and the charged energy in the air, sending the fine hairs on my neck standing on end. A warm heat envelops me, and I know that if I were to turn and look, Anders would be seething. The thought makes me pause. Instead of pushing away the strange flow of energy between us, I let it in. *Anders is barely holding it together.*

A flicker of sadness stirs within me, but I'm pulled back to reality.

"Oh, she likes to make them beg," Tate purrs, eyeing me from head to toe playfully with a wild grin.

"I appreciate you asking, but I'm busy," I respond quickly, attempting to keep my tone light. "I believe Aada also has a study group, and she's brilliant. I'm sure she could help."

Jensn's grin falls, masking his disappointment with a quick shrug. Ciara nudges me gently, still engrossed in the phony conversation with Britta, who appears equally entertained by Jensn's attempts to get close to me.

"Raea," Trysten interjects as he settles behind me. "Can we step outside?" When I glance back, I read his expression and see the lifeline he's offering.

With a grateful nod, I quickly apologize to Jensn before my gaze shifts to Tate. His grin widens, making me wonder if I'm escaping some sort of hell he was bound to trap me in. I throw a withering glare his way that makes him chuckle as I push out of my seat, side-stepping Jensn.

As we make our way out of the transport hall, the atmosphere shifts, and I'm met with a rush of cool, pine-scented air that fills my lungs alongside the scent of fresh snow from the mountains.

My attention snaps to Trysten, who stands a few steps away, looking a little hesitant and cupping his nape. "Yes?" My directness disarms him, causing him to raise his hands, palms out, backing away in surrender.

His eyes lighten with amusement as I lean against the opposite wall.

My eyes roam over him, taking him in without the distraction of

Anders, who is usually plastered to his side. His tanned skin is covered in ink, one piece of art fading into the next, and beneath it, an athletic physique, toned and strong but different from the bulk on Anders.

I sigh with relief when I realize there's no Bond, no flickering light, no zaps...absolutely nothing between us. He must sense the same thing as I watch his shoulders visibly relax.

Trysten crosses his arms first, then his ankles. "I was rescuing you. Or maybe them. You looked seconds away from eating them alive." There's a spirited glint in his eyes, daring me to challenge him.

I let my false swagger rise as I take a step toward him. "I didn't need saving," I chuckle. "Maybe..." I take another step. "I just wanted to watch him beg." *Lies.* The words taste like ash on my tongue.

Trysten studies me intently for a moment, his gaze unwavering, before he responds, "Unlikely." He lifts a brow in response, waiting for me to argue. Instead of rising to the bait, I find something curious about his demeanor—an openness I've never seen before. His features soften. "Come sit with me. I'll fill you in on all you need to know for the test."

I crumble, revealing the swirling storm of emotions. His eyes gleam with genuine empathy, and I can't help but reflect on how different he is. Then again, I've made the same mistake judging Anders, too.

I'm so tired of this game, the tumult of hormones, and the intensity of all these Bonds. What I wouldn't give to go back to the time when school consisted of learning and easy friendships.

"Okay," I reply quietly. A small but genuine smile tugs at the corners of his lips. He opens the door, the quiet calm instantly dissipating in the loud chatter filling the hall. He gestures for me to enter first, and I mutter a quick, "Thanks."

I hesitate inside the doors, half-expecting him to lead us to the open seats beside Anders. Instead, he guides me up the steps to the top of the hall, to a pair of secluded seats away from prying eyes.

My friends exchange puzzled glances as their eyes bounce between Trysten and me. I can feel their curiosity even from up here. Though

Trysten and I haven't had many conversations, I'm glad he's my division leader. He shares a brief, meaningful look with Anders, a silent communication of intent, before settling in beside me.

The classroom door swings open, allowing Professor Brendn to stride in. He's one of my favorite professors despite his lack of practiced manners. Trysten fills in any gaps with his insights and experience as Professor Brendn explains that we are expected to fly to other planets, racing against transport teams.

There are twenty-one teams among the juniors, and each team will be assigned a senior to assist and guide us throughout the test.

Trysten doesn't hold back when it comes to gloating about his team's victory last year.

Over the next few weeks, we'll engage in rigorous training sessions focusing on launching and landing, alongside logging hours in the simulator, which will allow us to practice in various weather scenarios.

We'll receive our senior assignments a day before the mission. For now, Ciara, Tate, and I need to hone our skills because I plan on winning.

We have one month between me and my first off-planet mission, and the bubbling excitement feels like I am going to burst. By the end of class, I've warmed up to the division leader and given him my gratitude before rushing down the steps to meet with Ciara and Tate.

"Let's go, Raea. Right now," Anders demands, his voice cutting through the background chatter, pulling me from my thoughts as I finish the last bite of my stew. The energy in the air pricks the edges of my senses.

Gods, what now?

Here we go with his demands. I take a deep breath and set my spoon down, carefully patting my lips with the linen napkin. "Excuse me, are you speaking to me?" I reply with a playful lilt, my eyes drifting across the table to Ciara, who's stifling her laughter behind her hand. It's a struggle not to smile, especially when the banter between us gives me a rush.

"Raea," he growls, his voice dropping to a low, rich timbre that sends a delicious heat blooming along my spine.

I feel my posture tense for a fraction of a second, my heart skipping a beat, before I compose myself. With determination, I rise from the table, deliberately avoiding his piercing gaze.

I turn toward Ciara once more, saying my goodbyes, and catch her studying us both. There's a hint of concern etched onto her face, and I can't quite figure out whether it's for my well-being or his. My lips tilt in amusement, making her features soften.

With a deep inhale, I turn to face the prince, crossing my arms and giving him a questioning look as I wait. He gently places a hand on the small of my back, shifting the atmosphere and sending my world sideways for a moment. He leads the way back to the dorms, the cool evening air brushing against my heated skin as we cross the bridge.

When we arrive at the basement gym, I almost chuckle. The space is open and, at this hour, is wonderfully deserted. The soft hum of the lights overhead fills the silence. Recently, I've taken to establishing a routine in the early mornings, learning how to use every single machine here. If Anders knows, I'm unaware.

"Seriously?" I chuckle. "We're having our meeting here?"

His responding chuckle feels dark. "Oh, no. That's later. No, you're going to show me you know how to defend yourself. One attacker— me."

My stomach knots. "I just ate?" I respond like a question because, honestly, I'm just grasping for an excuse. And I don't mention that I'm wearing a low-plunging gown. The thought of him touching me anywhere in this gown has my skin heating. The luxurious green fabric caresses my skin, and I can't help but smile at how well it shows off my figure, even if it's entirely impractical for whatever he has planned.

He snorts, his eyes glinting with mischief, unfazed by both my attire and the recent dinner still making its way to my stomach. He rolls up the sleeves of his fitted shirt, revealing strong forearms.

"Then I guess we will see if you can hold it down or if you'll be running for the can in the corner of the room." His challenge hangs in the air.

Part of me wants to push him on his sorry ass and storm out of here. But as I stand here, a heavy tension builds between us, something far more dangerous than anger.

Without warning, he grips my wrist. The sudden touch sends a rush of energy through me as he activates my energy shield from the gold band on my wrist. The sensation envelops me in a whirlwind of emotions. My knees feel wobbly as I lean into him.

"Is this some sort of punishment because of the other night?" I argue, gaining my stability.

He doesn't answer, his attention shifting as he strides toward the wall lined with various weapons. As he saunters past the weapons rack, he pauses before a wall lined with shelves. My breath catches at the sight of him reaching for something on the high shelf, muscles taut and on display. He turns, catching my wandering gaze, and smirks.

"Are you going to keep staring at my ass, or are you going to follow?" he questions from across the room.

My eyes narrow into slits as I groan and follow after him. He turns toward me, brandishing a roll of black wrap.

"I can wrap your hands, or you can do it yourself," he challenges, stirring something very inappropriate deep within me.

What the hell is wrong with me?

Suddenly, the air feels thick with desire, and it dawns on me that we're both teetering on the edge, waiting to see who will break first.

My mouth feels as dry as the deserts of Mori. There's a part of me that almost wants to let him wrap my hands. I want to experience that rush, that exhilaration of feeling alive, to feel his warm hands on me. But my rational side reminds me just how lightheaded he makes me feel. I quickly snatch the binding from his grip, cautiously avoiding his touch.

"In need of letting off some steam?" I taunt, wrapping my knuckles just as Ezra taught me. When I glance back up at Anders, the intense glare he's giving me could rival the heat of the seven suns—and not in a good way.

Shit. He's really pissed.

Without a single word, he yanks the roll of tape from my hands, putting it back on the shelf, all while keeping his eyes locked on me. I carefully tug at the material of my gown, feeling so damn hot. Silently, he strides over to the mat.

"We're going to see how much of your training you can put to use. I'm not going to hold back. You're going to fight me off. Got it? Since you're so godsdamned determined to ignore me and my help, and there's more men trying to get into your skirts everyday, show me you can protect yourself."

Oh. That's what this is about, then? "Is this about divisions with Jensn or my, what did you call them? Enemies?"

He falls silent for a moment, letting the tension between us build to an all-time high. With a sharp intake of air, he closes the gap between us, his height towering over me, forcing me to tilt my head back to maintain eye contact, our gazes locked.

"All of the above, Raea," he snaps, his composure shattering like glass, revealing a rush of fierce emotion. "Your father has upset some people. There are plenty of people who'd rather see you pay for your father's actions. And do not think for a single second that I do not notice how many men have let their eyes wander."

To make his point, his eyes cascade down my chest, down the entire length of my body, and back up, heating before his eyes return to mine.

He swallows thickly before muttering with strain, "I see how they look at you. Like you're theirs for the taking. Like they've already imagined you beneath them, your hair tangled in their hands." My breath catches, and my thighs clench together. Nobody—and I mean nobody—has ever made me feel so desired while also punishing me over it.

The gap between us closes until our bodies are flush. His scent envelops me like a warm blanket, filling the air with the aroma of a cool breeze rushing off the raging seas, freshly squeezed citrus, and masculinity. My mouth waters, my body betraying me, the undeniable need between my thighs pulsing like a heartbeat of its own. I passed on my Nakata corset again, so my full breasts brush against the soft material, hardening my nipples. The air is alive with our Bond, the vibrant hues almost palpable, the room a kaleidoscope of colors that dance around us, making my heart beat in perfect rhythm.

"You can't save me from everyone," I say harshly.

"Then stop making it look so damn tempting."

My heart threatens to beat right out of my chest. He leans in close enough that I can feel the rough scrape of his stubbled chin lightly brush against my cheek, sending another wave of shivers through my overly sensitized body.

His voice is a soft whisper, the air brushing my ear intimately. "And do not think for a single second you don't need to know how to fight a guy off." His nose drags along my cheek as he stands to his full height, his sapphire eyes settling on me again. "The least of your worries is your Bond at this point."

I look down at my gown, brushing my hands down the material. "Do you see what I'm wearing? I can't do anything in this dress," I argue back, gesturing to my gown, but it falls flat, my voice softer and breathless and nothing like mine.

He smirks knowingly, his gaze relaying just how happy he is about my clothing. He sucks in his bottom lip, his gaze snagging on my breasts. I let my eyes wander, taking in all of him, including his tattoo peeking over the collar of his shirt, and a presence that demands every last bit of my attention.

"You need to learn to defend yourself, even dressed like this," he instructs, his tone shifting to sober. "Fight me off, Raea."

Before I can process what he's saying, his arms wrap around me. The warmth of his body engulfs me at the exact moment a burst of energy explodes between us. The Bond kindles a storm of confusion, excitement, vulnerability, and something more profound, almost primal. He must sense it as he pauses. We both stand there, chests heaving, breaths mingling, all while the world fades away.

Despite my mental alarms ringing, there's an undeniable rightness to being in his arms. For a brief moment, I feel weightless, as if gravity no longer exists, as I lean into his hold. His arms gently embrace me as if he, too, has forgotten what we're doing.

After a few seconds, minutes, hours, who knows, the shock begins to settle, and clarity returns, reality slamming into me like a slap to the face. With resolve, I attempt to push him away, focusing on the goal and not the fact that I miss the tenderness with which he held me.

He snaps out of whatever moment we just had, and his arms grip me tighter. "C'mon, Raea," he taunts, clicking his tongue. "Stop playing."

Any lingering emotions dissolve instantly. My training rushes back to me. I hear Ezra's voice in my head, repeating instructions from a similar lesson. I had been on the training mats on the palace grounds, and a member of our royal guard had agreed to train with me for this specific exercise.

"Don't let them get their arms around you," Ezra had said. "But if they do, bring your knee up...hard. Don't hesitate, Raea." The memory fades as I struggle with Anders' arms still wrapped around me. *Knee him where it hurts.*

I force back a giggle and wrap my arms around his neck, toying with his hair. When he's distracted, his eyes studying me, I bring up my knee while pulling myself up on his neck, needing to use him for leverage.

Shock flashes across his features before he chuckles, brushing my knee away just in time. My leg hooks around him, causing him to stumble as I throw myself back, pulling him off balance.

He grunts at the sudden shift, throwing out his arms to catch our fall, easing my body to the ground beneath him with surprising gentleness. I half expected to be crushed under his weight.

He grins, glancing between us, studying how I've managed to pin myself beneath him. Embarrassment floods my body as I cover my face with my hands.

I've read enough romance novels to fill my head with sinful thoughts, and boy, are those visions flashing through my mind right now. His weight settles between my legs, my skirts sliding up my thighs, making me gasp as I shift my hips.

I gently place my hands on his shoulders, trying to create some space, though I'm not entirely sure if I want to push him away or draw him closer.

"Come on, Raea. It feels like you're inviting me to take it from you. Set your defenses now," he asserts.

I close my eyes, going to my mental shield. In my mind, I visualize a tall, white iron gate closing off the source of our Bond. With Anders, it's becoming increasingly apparent that a gate isn't going to hold back our Bond. An iridescent light radiates from him on one side and from me on the other, flowing along the winding path through the lush forest of my thoughts. It's a reminder of just how strong our Bond really is.

He chuckles darkly, and dammit, if that doesn't turn my core molten. "That's a sorry excuse for a shield," he throws back. His breath tickles my neck. So many images of how I'd like his hands to run down my sides, the feel of his mouth on my neck, how he feels settled between my legs, the safety and comfort of his weight pinning me to the mat. It's all too much and not enough.

Get control of yourself, I chide myself. *Focus.*

Taking a deep breath, I push again, yelling for him to get off me. He chuckles, wrapping his calloused hands around my wrists and pinning them above my head. He smirks, challenging me with a lifted brow.

"You got us into this mess. Get us out," he responds with a devilish spark in his eyes as he leans back slightly, a teasing smile dancing on his lips. My heart races between annoyance and determination. My frustration is mainly directed at myself for letting us end up in this situation in the first place.

"And since we're here," he pauses. "I got us a pass to the Isles. We can go whenever."

I stop fighting immediately. "What? How?"

He grins, his dimple making a very distracting appearance. "I have my ways. I'm very good at negotiating and getting what I want." I swear I feel his hips shift. I gulp down the desire burning me alive.

With an exasperated sigh, I thrust my arms up as I wrap my legs around him, throwing my weight, attempting to get out from under him. His quiet chuckle fuels my frustration over this whole thing.

"What was the point of turning on my energy shield if you were just planning on lying on me?" I grumble, yanking on my wrists with another feeble attempt to break free.

"To protect you, but it seems like you prefer to distract your enemies...in other ways." His eyes dip to my chest, where my gown has shifted, exposing the swells of my breasts.

The energy shields never help with slow attacks. They block fast and brutal attacks, but nothing about this is fast. I'm not even sure this is an attack or even training.

Whatever *this* is, it's slow, and sensual, and *dammit*.

I struggle, wrapping my legs around his, attempting to buck under him, and gods, I can't think. Everything feels sexual, and the way the friction rubs at just the right spot has me curling my toes. He groans when my legs wrap around his waist as I thrust up again, still pathetically telling myself we're supposed to be training. I'm breathless, and I'm hot, and quite frankly, way too turned on for this to actually work. We both know that it's all a front at this point.

Accepting the truth and defeat, I relax under him, my body going soft and pliant. "Nobody is getting this close. Not when I have you, remember?" I smile with all the practiced sweet patience possible. "I promised to be a good girl."

He huffs, a groan hidden in his breath, muttering what sounds like a curse.

"Now be a good little prince and get off me."

He chuckles and shifts over me, making me gasp when I feel his growing erection against my thigh. I let my legs fall to the side, the cool air of the gym informing me of how exposed I truly am.

He releases his grip on my wrists, his fingers lingering for just a moment longer as if he's reluctant to let me go. Supporting himself on his forearms, he leans closer, whispering another challenge, "Make me."

A soft huff of air leaves me as his gaze lingers on my lips.

We inch closer, the distance closing ever so slowly. Every heartbeat is a challenge and a question lingering between us, urging us to close the distance, seeing who's brave enough to move first. My tongue brushes over my bottom lip, wetting it in anticipation. My head is screaming at me that he's supposed to be my rival, but somewhere deep inside, my soul is screaming something else—my destiny. The war between them feels like it's tearing me apart. For now, just for this moment, I silence everything and focus only on the present. Destiny can wait.

His hand gently glides down my arm, causing my skin to erupt in goosebumps. My white locks cascade out around me, framing my face. He picks up a single strand of hair, allowing his fingers to brush through it tenderly. His touch travels down over my ribs and along my back, bringing us closer.

As we lean in, so close we're sharing air, the world around us fades to a distant blur as if time itself has been suspended. Just as our mouths are about to meet, the sound of voices echoing in the hallway shatters the spell between us. My heart sinks.

I catch his gaze, both of us sharing a fleeting moment of unspoken longing before his jaw ticks, and his mask snaps back into place. In an instant, he pulls away, both physically and emotionally. He stands quickly, adjusting his clothes.

The swift shift sends a chill coursing through me, leaving me acutely aware of his absence, both his body and vulnerability. My breath whooshes out of me as tears threaten to spill over.

"Lesson over," he states, his voice steady, yet tinged with an unnameable emotion, turning as he avoids my gaze. His body language suggests he's struggling to walk away, but his mask of indifference is firmly in place, and behind it lurks the distant, arrogant prick.

"Don't go," I plead, my thoughts becoming words on my breath.

His eyes shudder closed, his fists clenching at his sides, before he shakes his head, walking away from me. "I have to, Raea. Trysten will be training you from here on out." His voice grows distant and cold. "I'll tell him to connect with you. Training starts tomorrow. We can talk tomorrow at breakfast."

I watch him disappear, something in my heart cracking. The absence of his warmth is a sudden, sharp ache, leaving me trembling in the cavernous silence of the gym.

fourteen

. . .

I'm up before dawn, inwardly groaning from the pounding in my head. Outside, the sky is still a deep shade of indigo. I quietly change into my running gear, handle my business in the bathroom, and slip out the door, taking painstaking measures not to wake Aolyn.

Aolyn, Ciara, and I had spent hours last night talking about boys and crushes, the latest drama circulating between dorms, and my complex and all-consuming Bond with Anders. Much to their delight, I recounted the basics of what happened in the gym. They both pestered me, insisting that Anders and I needed to sort out our differences—preferably in the bedroom. Just as Aolyn was about to dig deeper into my "experience" in that area, Ciara swooped in, changing the topic to my Bond with Kellan.

As I step outside into the crisp morning air, I feel...alive, as if every cell in my body is awake and charged with energy. I need a solid run to kickstart my day. Last night, my dreams were a relentless blend of Anders pinning me down, followed closely by visions of Kellan holding me, and then Jensn leaning in like he was about to kiss me. Each dreamscape was a torturous hell I couldn't wake from.

The air hums around me as I stretch and warm up my muscles. I bend low, laying my cheek against my knee, the tight pull in my hamstring reminding me I need to stretch more. Last night, I skipped it, opting for a long, cold shower.

I groan when I feel the distinct shift in the atmosphere. It's different from the familiar energy of Baedyn. I turn and see Anders stalking toward me, his gaze fixed on me, clad in nothing but athletic shorts and running shoes. My pulse quickens as I stand straight, rolling out my ankles.

"Why?" I whine. "I just want to be alone."

I don't mention that I also need to process everything that happened between us last night. He walked away. I begged him to stay, and he just walked away and left me on the damn floor. I'm not sure if it's embarrassment or hurt that upsets me more.

He shrugs, coming to stand beside me. "I need a run. And I wanted to apologize for my behavior last night. It won't happen again."

His words cut deeper than they should. Tears prick the back of my eyes as a fresh wave of hurt crashes into me, leaving me utterly confused. I should be happy we didn't kiss. I keep telling myself that I don't want this, and I certainly don't want him. I swallow my feelings and shove them into another mental box, a skill that's becoming far too easy lately.

"You look at me as if you're deciding whether to kiss me or kill me."

I roll my eyes and mutter, "The thought has crossed my mind."

Then, to myself, I add, "Both of them."

I swear he hears me by the way his eyes light up. Needing some distance to gather myself, I say over my shoulder, "Don't keep up," as I race down the steps of Taeolyn.

The courtyard is empty this early in the morning; the only sound is the crunch of gravel beneath my shoes. I push myself into a punishing pace, desperately trying and failing to outpace Anders. In all the years I have attended this academy, I have never once seen him run, yet here he is, annoyingly keeping up with me, stride for stride.

At least he's quiet. It seems we both get lost in our own thoughts, with only the rhythm of our breathing breaking the stillness. I navigate through the trails that I know as well as my own heartbeat, having spent eleven years familiarizing myself with every twist and turn. The silence between us gives me time to process the events from last night.

As I replay each moment with astonishing clarity, my confusing emotions only grow. The way his intense gaze seared every inch of me, the unspoken tension building between us, and the way our mouths hovered just within reach. He wanted me just as much as I wanted him. If those students hadn't interrupted, we would have kissed. So why did he treat me like that? It doesn't make any sense. The more I think about whatever emotion he's hiding, whatever keeps him locked away behind a mask of indifference, the more it fuels my desire to draw it out of him.

It might be hypocritical of me, but it's maddening. I know I'm doing the same thing; hiding my feelings and pretending to hate him when I'm just annoyed at him…at myself, but I'll admit there's something between us, something far beyond a typical Bond. Whatever it is, it's intense and all-consuming. Something that keeps drawing us together, no matter how hard we push away.

One of these days, neither of us will be able to ignore it anymore. The constant back and forth, the facades of hatred and annoyance, and the boundaries we've built between us will all come crashing down. And I think that day is coming sooner than either of us is prepared for.

The cool breeze kisses my skin as I work myself into a sweat, my sports bra doing little to soak up the sweat beading up and sliding down my spine. Still, I push myself harder, faster, willing each of my pounding steps to drive away the unrelenting, tiresome thoughts.

We run past all the other dorms on our left, and just beyond the wards, I know there's a trail that leads around the backside of the lake. I don't bother alerting Anders to my plan to leave the protection of the school grounds. He can follow me or not.

I feel the wards cling to me as I run through, as if checking my identity, before releasing me. I shudder, shaking off the sticky feeling as I keep going, continuing along the hidden trail.

Our footsteps feel louder out here as I find the rocky footpath to the lake, slowing down only so I don't roll my ankle on the uneven ground. I miss running at home. The forest floors on Kyrr are spongy from constant rainfall. Here, the ground is packed and dry, and my joints rebel against me.

It's a good thing Aolyn and I have separate bathing chambers, because the amount of time I spend soaking my muscles at night would never give her time to shower.

The path veers right, shrinking to the width of my shoulders. Large boulders line each side, winding up a hillside to overlook the lake below. I don't bother looking back—not here. It's too risky.

I reduce my pace to a slow jog. I can feel the heat of Anders behind me, but he remains silent nonetheless. I shouldn't be scared out here, but running in the gray light of dawn isn't the safest idea either.

Baedyn not only has Aticats, but several other creatures that could find me high on the food chain, especially with my height. White lions with wings and beaks were also said to roam here once upon a time, although I don't believe in folklore. Nevertheless, most stories contain some element of truth.

Ahead of me, a shadow of a creature on all fours sulks off the path, its form momentarily coalescing before turning to fix a large pair of yellow eyes on me. My heart hammers as fear grips me, and I let out a piercing scream that echoes off the boulders. In a split second, my feet lose their grip, sliding helplessly on the gravel as I flail backward. Just as I brace for impact, a slick, solid stomach breaks my fall.

Holy shit.

Anders chuckles softly above me. "Scared of foxes?" he teases, his eyes sparkling as he looks down at me, my body braced awkwardly against him.

A fox? My mind struggles to reconcile the creature I thought I saw with a measly fox.

As Anders helps me regain my footing, his hands glide over my bare skin, trailing a current of warmth and emotions that sends a jolt through me. I take a moment to steady my breath, glancing back along the path, searching for the animal.

I swear it wasn't a fox. I shake my head, blaming my lack of sleep.

Surely, I would recognize a fox. I often see them in the forest near my home. I draw in another shaky breath as my disbelief claws at me. It couldn't have been.

"Want me to check?" he offers, placing a hand on my shoulder. My shoulder instinctively rises, shaking him off as I nod. Our bodies brush against each other as we switch places on the path. I extend my hands, awkwardly attempting to flatten my body as we pivot.

Once we're both back on the path, Anders faces me with an annoying smirk playing on his lips. He tsks. "Who knew she was scared of foxes?" he muses. "I thought it was just—"

Before he can finish, he stumbles backward. In a reflexive attempt to catch him, I reach out only to find myself pulled down atop him. We both emit a grunting noise as Anders falls, and I land squarely onto his solid frame.

"Oh my gods." I press my palms into his very bare, well-defined chest. "Are you okay?" My voice comes out strained with concern as I search him for signs of injury.

"There's a...boulder...there," he groans between gritted teeth. His strong hands wrap around my hips, his fingers pressing into my lower back, holding me in place. "Are you okay? Sorry, I didn't mean to pull you down."

I nod, feeling a rush of embarrassment as I attempt to shift my knee to ease myself off him. Instead, I accidentally nail him squarely between the legs. He curses softly, his grip only tightening on my hips as a pained expression deepens his features. My hand slips on his slick, warm chest, bringing us flush once more. The closeness sets my heart racing for all the wrong reasons.

"Shit. Sorry." My cheeks flush in embarrassment as I fumble for the right words. "That was totally an accident." He has his eyes tightly shut, one hand draped over his mouth as he groans, yet somehow, he maintains a steady grip on me. "Sorry," I whisper, hoping to reassure him amidst the awkwardness.

"Just give me—" he groans. "A minute."

I nod, unwilling to detach our bodies and make another mistake. It would be comical if it were anyone else, but of course, it had to be us. And my dumb luck, I kneed him in his manhood.

Gods. Is this karma paying me back for being a jerk? Well, I guess it would be his karma, too. It's been less than a day, and he's been on top of me, and now I'm on top of him.

A soft giggle slips past my lips, but I quickly bite my lower lip to stifle it as memories of last night collide with the present. One sapphire eye pops open.

"Are you laughing?" He looks at me incredulously, his breath low and raspy, still tinted with pain. At least he can manage a few words. Unable to suppress the urge any longer, another giggle bubbles up, and I surrender to the moment, allowing my laughter to build and flow freely. I bury my face in his chest because where the heck else can I hide?

A moment later, I feel a deep rumble of laughter resonating from him, the sound tumbling through me before I lift my gaze to meet his. He's looking at me as if he's seeing me for the first time. Everything shifts, reality rushes in, and suddenly I'm aware of every inch of our bodies and where they're touching.

"Sorry," I whisper, my voice barely rising above the sounds of nature waking up.

"You're burning up." His hands mold around my waist, effortlessly lifting me as I push against his shoulders until I stand above him. Gods, he's breathtaking. Early dawn sunlight streams through the trees, illuminating miles of golden skin stretched over packed muscles.

I can't help but think that the gods must be enjoying a good laugh right now. It seems that fate has a wicked sense of humor, continually drawing us back into questionable situations. I groan inwardly, thinking of the girls' suggestion that Anders and I take each other to bed, hiding my flushed cheeks as I turn away. I take a clarifying breath before turning back toward him.

"I'm just hot from the run."

"No, this isn't the first time. Your skin feels hot to the touch."

I look down at myself as if I can see the heat rising from my skin. "I feel fine." I shrug. I reach out as Anders' gaze flickers between me and my outstretched hand. A frisson of delight traces my spine when his massive, calloused fingers wrap around my wrist. He easily pulls himself up, gripping the boulder that caused this chaos, leaving me to balance my weight as he rises.

My chest tightens with guilt while a heavy knot forms in the pit of my stomach. I remind myself that it wasn't my fault he fell. "Thanks."

"Turn around, let me see." I say, twirling my finger.

He shoots me a teasing smirk before complying. "Never would've thought you were an ass kinda girl, but sure." His tone is annoyingly playful.

I'm about to scoff when his back comes into view. Beyond the smear of dirt and gravel, there are a few superficial cuts scattered across his skin, but what grabs my attention is the deep gash just beneath his shoulder blade. Blood oozes from the wound, tracing a path of crimson through the grime.

"You're bleeding," I mutter, horror and concern lacing my voice.

He looks over his shoulder as if he can assess the damage himself and shrugs. I can't tear my gaze away. Blood doesn't make me squeamish, but seeing him hurt has more guilt settling in my stomach like a weighted rock.

"I'll be fine."

Despite my rising anxiety, I shake my head and gently brush away the dirt and leaves. If I had more fabric to work with, I could use my shirt to patch him up, but considering he's shirtless and I'm in a sports bra and running shorts, there's very little material to go around.

"We need to get back. I'll patch it myself if you want." My fingers linger over tender spots. If we don't go soon, we'll probably miss breakfast. It was reckless to drag him out here, and for what?

He shivers when my thumb brushes over another tattoo on his back I've never noticed, probably because I haven't been close enough to him while he's shirtless to really take in the details. The tattoo is a series of waves, each line a swirling pattern of thick black ink. My fingers instinctively follow the curves and lines, tracing the artwork that spans over his left shoulder and part of his spine as the waves crest.

As my fingertips drift down, they pause over another tattoo that caught my eye before. This one is even more expansive, extending up his whole right side. It combines bold lines and swirling shapes, creating a collage of elements that appear to be distinct. Dancing swirls at the bottom represent flames, followed by flowing waves symbolizing water above, and finally, the airy swirls at the top look like gusts of wind.

His skin prickles as I continue to trace the thick, dark lines, moving from his hip up towards his ribs, feeling the warmth of his skin beneath my touch. A question escapes my lips before I can stop myself.

"Do they hurt?" My voice comes out breathless. I've always thought tattoos were beautiful pieces of art, but I don't know if I'm brave enough to get one. And where would I put it? One day soon, I'll have the Lumos Bond mark, but I won't have a say in the magical design. The only thing I know for sure is that it will start on my left hand and wind up my wrist, just like every Lumos marking.

"You're going to have to be more specific than that, Princess." His voice is low and teasing. Our eyes lock. He's been studying me over his shoulder. I instinctively drop my hands, tucking loose strands of hair behind my ears like I've just been caught touching something I shouldn't be.

"The tattoos," I clarify, feeling mildly flustered. I hold my wrist out toward him, showcasing the crest marked on my wrist. He turns to face me fully now, clearly unfazed by our proximity. He cradles my hand in his, brushing his thumb over my inked skin. "I don't remember getting this one," I say.

"They can if you don't take the elixir."

A moment passes before he's gripping my biceps, gentle yet firm. His expression shifts to one of concern, and he scans me as though searching for clues that I might have sustained an injury. "You didn't hit your head, did you?" His gaze scrutinizes every inch of my body before finally returning to meet my eyes, revealing his annoying dimple at the corner of his mouth as his lips tilt up in a playful smile.

"Nope." The sound of the 'P' popping annoys me. "Not a scratch. Just had to check since you're being so sweet."

With a roll of my eyes, I step out of his grasp. I thank the gods our little moment is over.

It's closer to the dorms to continue on the path than head back the way we came. Unfortunately, there's a very large, very arrogant human in front of me.

"Can you move?" I prop my hands on my hips. "I'd like to get to class on time."

He gives me that cocky grin I'm annoyingly familiar with before turning from me and striding away. I groan and follow him, carefully avoiding the boulder hidden beneath the brush.

We make it back in time for breakfast, both of us hustling to grab something before running upstairs to change. Our lack of clothing makes us quite the spectacle for the students gathered in the dining hall, but I don't have time to explain. Besides, everyone should know at this point he's my escort. I clearly went for a run, and he followed. Simple enough.

After showering and dressing for the day in my usual all-black attire, I quickly braid my hair back into four thick strips, bringing them together at the back in a ponytail. I roll my eyes at myself when I smear some blush and rose color on my lips before misting myself with my favorite scent: frost blooms. Checking myself in the mirror, I remind myself it's not for Anders. I just feel like looking nicer today, that's all. It takes all of a minute before I'm knocking on his door. He opens it, combat pants hanging low on his hips, boots on, and shirt missing. My mouth waters as I take in his bare stomach, as if I haven't seen him shirtless already this morning. With a deep breath, I push into his room.

"Let's get that shoulder cleaned up." I hold up the gauze and cleaner I brought. He turns, and my breath catches. "It's healed."

He strides across the room, turning to see his back in the mirror. He hums, "Guess it wasn't that bad after all."

My head spins with the truth. *Magic. Magic. Magic.* It's the only explanation. He had a deep cut.

"Anders," I start. "How often do you heal quickly?"

"Hey, RaeRae," Kellan calls out, jogging toward me after History later that day. My lips curve up into a genuine smile as he slows his pace to match mine. I can't help but notice the way his brow furrows slightly. I lift a questioning one back at him. Readjusting the straps on his bag, he sighs. "I feel like I never see you anymore."

I pull him to a stop, the crowd flowing around us like a river parting around a rock. I take his hand, playfully squeezing. "Kellan, you see me every day," I tease, but my heart squeezes at how distant we have grown.

I never expected to get to our last Order of the academy and find us drifting apart, especially when all I have ever wanted was to curl up into his arms and promise him we'd be together forever. Somehow, in the past few weeks, all of that has changed. Or, maybe it's just me who has.

His frown disappears as his features relax. I feel guilty for not being a good friend, so I say, "I happen to have a study period right now. How about you skip Modern Science, and we catch up instead?" Kellan loves school and classes as much as I do, but he loves the rules and order of it all even more.

He pauses for a moment, considering my offer, then nods eagerly. A breath of relief rushes out of me. He wraps an arm around my shoulders as we ascend the stairs to his room to drop off his books and change before heading to mine.

We have the whole hour to talk before Bonding class, and I plan to take full advantage of it, giving him all of my undivided attention. Once we're in my room, the open space feels instantly cozier with him there. After I slip into my gown, Kellan launches into an animated update about his studies, his Division class, and his current projects.

"I'm flying to Mori next week for two days!" he exclaims, dropping down on the sofa. "A few of us were chosen to observe their intelligence command center, which is supposed to be state-of-the-art." With every word, his grin broadens, his shoulders relax, and something about his enthusiasm brightens his whole countenance.

I gently bump my shoulder against his, mirroring his excitement. "That sounds incredible. I'm happy for you, Kel. It seems like you love working with Intel." I tilt my head back, soaking up the warm, golden sunshine streaming through the open doors.

"I think I've discovered my thing, you know? Like my passion and place in society. Do you think your father might consider me for a role in intelligence at the palace?" I glance over at him, and I can't help but grin. Not because of the Bond, a shimmer of green wrapping around us like tendrils of smoke, but because of his palpable joy.

The sunlight filters through the leaves above, casting a warm glow on his brown curls and highlighting the freckles scattered across his cheekbones and nose. I've counted every single freckle—there are seventeen of them, to be exact.

"You're smart and dedicated, Kel. You can achieve anything you set your mind to, and you're like family. I'm sure my father would love to have you working at the palace." I feel a rush of love swell within me, fortified by our history, our friendship, and our familiarity; at this moment, it feels unbreakable. He pulls me close, enveloping me in his comforting scent of cinnamon and pine, reminding me so much of home that my chest aches.

We both fall silent, allowing the gentle rustling of leaves in the breeze to wrap around us. He leans back on the armrest, bringing me with him until I'm settled against his chest.

After several long minutes of silence, I recount my time in the simulator last week. He chuckles and encourages me to keep training. He playfully complains that they need a new simulation for sword fighters. I laugh and jokingly offer to submit a formal complaint on his behalf. The shaking rumble of his chest is his only response. In moments like these, I remind myself this is why he's my best friend.

I can't lose him.

"Are you going home for break?" Kellan asks.

We have a week-long break next month, a time for students to unwind and recharge before returning for the rest of the school year. Some of our friends plan to vacation on beaches in Okenen, while others have decided to take the opportunity to see new planets. Meanwhile, I'll use the six days away to spend quality time with my family.

On Kyrr, the entire week is spent celebrating and honoring the gods, the festivities transforming cities and villages into swaths of color and life. Origin Day is the one occasion celebrated throughout the entire system. Each kingdom celebrates in its own way, weaving its own traditions into the festivities. Every capital city holds towering statues of the gods. Yet the faithful travel farther, making pilgrimages to their kingdoms' capitals for the great celebrations at the sacred temples. There, gratitude is given, offerings are left, and blessings are sought for protection.

I can't help but chuckle while rolling my eyes. "You know I don't get to choose." My features soften as I think about the rest of our plans. "Besides, my mother is planning a trip to Kliax for two days of diving with Moonrays."

The mesmerizing creatures are nothing short of magical, with their shimmering, translucent bodies gliding through the clear water and bioluminescent tails illuminating the dark when they dive into the depths. They also have a charming quirk of cuddling with people.

"What about you?"

"My father has organized a trip for us to the capital on Gowden," he says with a shrug of disinterest. "After that, we'll spend a few days skiing in Ateria. We haven't decided on which resort to stay at."

"You should totally go to Ziofrost!" I exclaim, unable to contain my enthusiasm. "Their hot springs are the absolute best after a long day on the slopes. Just picture yourself soaking in bubbling warm waters, steam rising up all around you, and views of the snow-capped mountains at sunset. It's the most beautiful experience. Promise me you'll go."

Kellan sits us up, retrieving his Prism from his pocket, and after a few moments, projects colorful holograms of Ziofrost above the device.

Resort layouts, images of the hot springs at sunset, photos of customers on the snowy slopes. We lose ourselves in the details of planning his trip, discussing which slopes to hit first and where to eat. We're so lost in planning that we almost forget we're supposed to be headed to Bonding class.

In a flurry to get to class on time, we grab our tablets and rush toward the door. I swing it open and collide with Anders' solid chest. I silently curse him as he steadies me, his grip firm around my upper arms. As I regain my balance, I catch a glimpse of his emotions flashing across his features. First amusement, then fury, as he glances over my shoulder, most likely finding Kellan coming out of my room. He masks it quickly, a broad, smug smile transforming his face as he slips an arm around my shoulders, tucking me in tight.

"Running late again, Princess?" he teases.

For a brief second, I feel a rush of gratitude for his decision to keep our little incident this morning to himself. I reluctantly pull away from him, already missing the warmth and stability of his body beside mine.

What the hell is wrong with me? I shake my head, clearing my thoughts and mustering some defiance.

"I seem to recall this question from the first day of school, and my answer is still the same," I reply with as much sass as I can throw his way. He casually leans a shoulder against the wall, blocking Kellan in the process, his hands tucked comfortably in his pockets, looking very much the part of an arrogant prince. His lips tilt up slightly, clearly enjoying this back-and-forth banter between us.

"Could you at least stand somewhere else so I'm not always running into you? Perhaps against the railing?" I let out my frustration, gesturing to the railing for emphasis. His smirk widens, the look only antagonizing me more.

"Oh, but I love it when you run into me," he purrs, his eyes darkening with desire.

Memories of this morning dance in my mind. Lying across his sweat-slicked body in the middle of the woods was a little more than 'running into him.' A blush rises to my cheeks. There's an undeniable truth to his words in his eyes that makes our little...okay, obscenely large, impossible-to-miss Bond shimmer even more.

Before I can dwell on it, I roll my eyes and pivot on my heel, determined to put distance between us. It's a familiar dance the two of us seem to repeat over and over again. Much to my dismay, or enjoyment, before I can reach the end of the hall, Anders is beside me, keeping pace and effortlessly blocking Kellan, who is trying to reach my side. I shoot Anders an annoyed glance, silently pleading for a moment's peace.

Before I can slip into class, a ripple of happiness at our constant banter rushes through me. "Bye, Prince," I say over my shoulder, earning a hint of that annoyingly adorable smirk.

I settle into my usual seat, with Ciara on one side and Kellan on the other. Right behind me, Anders drops into his seat with Trysten and Sienna at his sides. I don't know what it is about her, but something deep inside me dislikes her with an intensity I usually reserve for my enemies.

Professor Becca makes her way up to the dais, looking out over us with excitement. She's dressed in a black long-sleeve gown, belted at her waist with knee-high boots, her Bond mark flowing seamlessly with the lace sleeves of her dress. She looks radiant—and hot. I wonder if she is headed home after this. Maybe she has a date with her husband.

"Alright, everyone," she begins, placing her hands on her hips with a knowing smile, like she's about to spill some secret. "Today, we are diving into the topic of the magic of the Bond!" Professor Becca clasps her hands excitedly as whispers ripple through the hall.

Professor Becca takes a moment, allowing the murmurs to settle before continuing. "The Bond itself is a mystery as to how it chooses your partner, but we know that there's one perfect match for you. When you go through The Ceremony, you will Bond with someone who has the perfect match in energies. Once the connection is complete, a Bond marking appears, solidifying it."

"Yay, a forced tattoo," I mutter, earning a small smile from both of my friends. Tate leans forward, shooting a disappointed glance my way.

"So grumpy," he grumbles. "I want a Bonding mark."

Ciara stifles a laugh, hiding her face in her palms. I wiggle my brows and smirk at him.

"Didn't know you were such a romantic," I tease.

He mumbles something about true love and being lucky enough to find a soul mate.

In front of us, a projection of different Bonding marks appears. Women's marks appear on their left hands, while men receive a small mark on their chest over their heart.

"Settle down, everyone," Professor Becca declares as an excited hum travels through the crowd. "Now, after The Ceremony, you'll need to go through what we call a Bonding phase." Kellan, not so subtly, puts an arm over the back of my chair, earning what sounds like a growl from Anders. "The Bond needs time to strengthen before your magic will appear."

An unsettling feeling twists in my stomach as I contemplate the implications that Anders and I are already experiencing magic, though I still have no idea what mine is.

My tablet chimes as a variety of articles and scans populate my screen. As I look around, others are now browsing their screens as well. I glance back at the folder, tapping it open to find scans from ancient tomes I've never heard of.

One document in particular catches my eye: "The Veil and The Bonds." It dates back to an era long before our current unified calendar. Is this what we need? Do our professors have access that we don't? I can't deny it's a possibility. I reluctantly set my tablet down, some deep part of me stirring to life. I quickly message Anders.

> Raea Tierson: We need to discuss our project later.

I hear his chuckle just as the message pops up.

> Anders Rykerson: Forgiven already?

Raea Tierson: You're insufferable.

"While the Lumos Bond undoubtedly holds strength, there's some folklore out there suggesting an even deeper Bond that exists on an entirely different plane." She pauses her pacing to lean against the table and take a moment to look around the room. When she speaks again, her voice is filled with awe and admiration: "It's said that when this mating Bond snapped into place, it knitted their hearts, their souls, and their minds together. These documents also state that if your mate were sick or hurt, you'd be able to feel it and know exactly what they needed.

"One such ancient text claims that once the Bond is established after passing some sort of test, a different magical marking would appear, becoming a permanent fixture along their spine, symbolizing a union with eternity in mind, binding them not just for this life, but in every life to follow."

My body hums with energy as a cold sweat coats my skin. With a shaky hand, I lift my tablet again, scanning the folder frantically, looking for anything to help us while ignoring the idea of a deeper Bond.

Because that's what we need.

She continues to talk, discussing the differences between the Bonds, but my erratic heartbeat fills my head with a whooshing noise, drowning out the world around me. As much as I'd love to deny its existence, what if she's right?

What if there is a deeper Bond?

And if so, why don't we see them anymore?

fifteen

. . .

Aolyn and Kamden were practically vibrating with excitement after our Bonding Class last night. Their enthusiastic pleas to join them for today's much-anticipated AerBall game against Wildwood, one of Ateria's academies, had me reluctantly agreeing.

I had mentally scrambled for an excuse to get out of it first thing this morning, but Tate and Ciara, who know me all too well, quickly caught on. They declared they would literally drag me to the game, even if it meant hauling me over Tate's shoulder, kicking and screaming.

So here I am, Aolyn and I both dressed in school colors: hues of vibrant blues and gold, and little 'D's stamped on our cheeks. As we find our seats among the chaotic crowd already chanting our team's name and waving signs, I admit to Kamden that I don't know much about the game. My father has tried for years to get me into AerBall, but the brutality of it has always made me a little queasy; this game is not for the faint of heart.

Kamden practically gleams as he leans over. "The rules are simple," he begins. "The team with the most goals wins, and scoring with the AerBall earns you five points."

I recall the small AerBall my father has stored in his personal study in the palace, signed by one of his favorite pro players. The AerBall is small, no bigger than a man's palm, and the soft outer layer conceals a solid core.

"Oh, and don't forget the groundball," he continues enthusiastically. "That's worth one point." Aolyn nudges him playfully as she chimes in with her own insights about strategies for the game.

"The game is played over the course of an hour, divided into three twenty-minute periods," she explains. "Each team is composed of eight players: one goalie, two defenders, a guardian, three attackers, and a spy."

Tate raises his brows. "Which position is the safest? I've heard this game can be a little..." he glances toward the empty rings, "bloody."

Kamden chuckles softly. He takes a moment to break down the various positions for us. "Let's start with the goalie! That player needs to be both large and agile, as they are responsible for defending not only a goal open in the ground but also a net looming ten feet above them. Whoever plays this position needs to have quick reflexes and a dominating presence to fend off the attackers whose sole goal is to score points."

Aolyn interjects again, "Now, as for the defenders, they have to be strong and fast. Their role is to stop the attackers. Here's the kicker: the opposing team's spy is constantly watching and calling out plays, exposing any weaknesses in their defense." She grins, tossing her hair over her shoulder. "There's even a chance that the spy can be captured for a brief span during each period. If that happens, they'll find themselves suspended twenty feet above the water until the end of the period." I notice Tate swallowing with a grimace, but Aolyn continues to elaborate.

"Meanwhile, the attackers...well, as the name suggests, they attack. They're the offensive position, doing whatever they can to get the two balls into their goals. The guardian's role is equally critical. They defend the bunker from their post on the island, though at any moment an opposing attacker could send them crashing into the water." It becomes abundantly clear that there's no "safe" position at all.

Ciara's brows furrow, and she asks, "But wait, aren't sticks involved?"

It's Kamden who responds. "Yep, but only the center attacker and goalie have one." He points to the field where the five rings are located. "At the center of the arena, there's an island where the spy and the center attacker start the game. They will sprint to free our balls from the opposing team's bunker, which starts off unguarded." His devilish smile makes my lips pull up. "Once the horn sounds, it's an all-out race against time to snatch them before the rival team can get to them. After freeing the balls, the spy takes on the role of scouting the field ahead."

He continues to explain the point of the icy water surrounding the island, explicitly designed to shock the players' systems, drastically slowing down their movements. Surrounding that water ring is another ring of land dotted with obstacles and traps to test the agility and strength of the attackers. Everything from rugged stone structures meant for climbing to muddy pits potentially hiding snares that require the attackers to carefully navigate, only to reach the fourth ring, which is also filled with water.

"The next stretch of water is home to bladefish," he adds. "Their small bodies sting when you brush against them, but thankfully, the cuts are not lethal. However, that doesn't make it any less daunting. The fifth and outermost ring is where the goals are positioned at either end of the arena. If we fail to score, the ball is unceremoniously tossed into a chute and sent back to the opposing team's bunker, meaning one or two attackers must navigate their way back to the island. But, if we score, the ball returns to our bunker, where our guardian protects it until the attacker returns."

Aolyn jumps in again, "If the ball is in the opposing team's bunker, the attacker will have to fight the guardian to win their ball back. It slows them down and makes them tired. But, if we make the goal, the attackers are given a break and are allowed to scale the ladders and take the skywalk," she points to the iron walkways over the rings, "back to the island. It rewards the attackers, allowing them to catch their breath instead of retracing their steps and returning to the bunker to start all over again.

"The AerBall itself is lightweight and propelled into the nets using the stick, which has its own net at the tip, designed to slingshot the ball upwards toward the goal. The groundball is the opposite. It's heavier, measuring about fourteen inches across, and players need to get up close and personal to either shove or toss it into the goal located in the ground at the goalie's feet."

As their explanations end, I'm pulled back to the present, where spectators have filled the entire arena. I've been on this campus for half my life, and I've never been to a single game here. The thought makes me cringe slightly.

Memories of the first time I stepped foot in this arena two weeks ago, and seeing Anders in his gear, make my stomach flutter.

Our seats are located a few rows up from the team's box. The spectators buzz with anticipation. The scent of sweet rolls and excitement floats on a breeze, and as the players make their way out of the locker rooms and into the box, the crowd goes ballistic.

On our side of the arena, the fans proudly wear a sea of blue and gold, waving flags and roaring with excitement as our players take their seats on the bench in front of the coach. The energy rises infectiously as chants of encouragement ripple through the crowd behind me. On the opposite side, the crowd cheers for their players, clad in white and black, with black W's on shirts and jerseys.

"That's Vori McDanielson," Aolyn says, leaning in from my right. "He's the center attacker—Ryker's direct rival." She points him out, and I can't help but gawk at his size. Even from across the arena, he's massive, and his dark hair is tightly bound in a single war braid—he's terrifying. "And over there," she gestures, directing my gaze to another player, "is Polk Dexen, their star defender, Trysten's opposite."

Our side of the arena goes wild when our players stand, huddling together like they're expecting a motivational speech from their coach. Our players wear protective pads and blue jerseys with their names and numbers in shimmering gold. I catch sight of Anders almost instantly, as if my body is drawn to him by some innate power. He looks incredible in his navy blue jersey, the number seven displayed on his back beneath the thick block letters of his last name, "Rykerson," which makes my heart race for some odd reason. Standing beside him is Cole, sporting the same name but wearing the number eleven, and looking quite charming.

As my gaze sweeps across the team, I'm surprised to see four women in their ranks. They're as tall as the men and athletic enough to match them in strength. The coach stands at the center, addressing the players, but our team appears bored, as if they'd rather be studying than here.

Their demeanors shift when Anders replaces the coach, taking a spot in the center of the huddle. "Is Anders, I mean Ryker, the team captain?" I murmur to nobody in particular as my gaze is fixed on the man animatedly rallying his team. It's impossible to look away. His magnetism is infectious, even from up here.

Each player nods enthusiastically, smiles spreading across their faces at whatever Anders says to them. I desperately wish I could hear what he's saying. Whatever it is, it's like a spark in kindling, igniting a flame within the team. He lifts his stick triumphantly into the air, and Aolyn, standing beside me, confirms that he is their captain.

Around him, the team forms a tight-knit circle as they wrap their arms around each other's shoulders. They sway left, then right, then back again, in a synchronized movement.

"What will we do?" Anders bellows, his voice booming over the roar of the crowd.

Aolyn cups her hands around her mouth, joining in as she chants along with the team, "We will fight!"

Anders responds a breath later to the roar, "What is pain?"

"Temporary!" The crowd responds in unison, their voices thunderously echoing the team. The thrill is palpable on Anders' face. He's clearly alive in his element and loving every second of this.

"And what are we here for?" he shouts again. His rallying cry sparks something within the crowd and, surprisingly, even within me. The arena's noise levels become deafening as feet stomp, creating a resonating pulse in the stadium.

I can't help but laugh and join in when Aolyn quickly tells me the response. "The W! We are Drithm!" we all shout back.

Anders smiles as the team erupts, jumping up and down, energy radiating off them as they feed off the crowd. The beautiful man in the center genuinely smiles, his lips pulled up high, and his dimple fully on display, every feature soft as he looks around. Trysten moves to stand beside Anders, giving him a slap on the shoulder as they exchange a wild grin. I feel like I should look away, like I'm an unwelcome spectator in their private moment.

Moments later, an iron bridge swings open from both sides of the arena, meeting at the center and connecting to the skywalk over the island, forming a cross over the field. Anders, Trysten, and our coach, Coach Beck, walk out to meet the opposing team, exchanging handshakes and words.

After the greetings are through, Anders turns toward our section of the stands, now eye level with our row, raising his arms high above his head. The crowd erupts in another thunderous roar. Witnessing this side of Anders—with his charisma and ability to rally his teammates and the audience—fills me with an unexpected joy that I can hardly contain. The energy building within me makes me feel like I'm going to burst, my body too small to contain it. I bite my lip to suppress an involuntary grin.

Alright, I'll admit that perhaps I've developed a small crush. Just a smidge. It's enough to explain away the ridiculous flutter in my chest, yet not enough to overlook his attitude that drives me crazy most days.

In the section beside us, one row up, six young women I don't recognize are decked out in cropped blue shirts that expose bare stomachs, with "RYKER7" spelled across them in bold blue ink. They wave dumb signs proclaiming things like BOND WITH ME, MARRY ME, CHOOSE ME, I LOVE YOU, NUMBER 7 IS MINE, and the most ridiculous of them all, BE MY BABY DADDY. I can't help but feel a flare of annoyance, at least until I catch Anders rolling his eyes when Trysten points out the signs, teasing him.

Before I can react, Ciara shouts, "Go Seven!"

I slap my hand over her mouth while my friends double over, laughter bubbling up from the four of them. Both Anders and Trysten fix their attention on our group, their expressions shifting from surprise to amusement. But when Anders' gaze locks onto mine, for a split second, it feels like time stands still. The crowd falls away, the arena with it, and there's only him. His sapphire eyes deepen with something like hope, taking me off guard and leaving me breathless, before his gaze snaps away to Coach Beck, who's passing off some instructions.

"Why would you do that?" I ask incredulously, dropping to my seat with a groan and burying my face in my hands.

Ciara cackles and wraps a hand around me. "C'mon, you can't hide from me. I see the way you two keep sharing heated glances." I want to protest vehemently, to deny her accusation, but deep down, I know it's a futile endeavor. She's right. And those glances are becoming more and more frequent.

With a sigh, I redirect my attention back to the field, my mind desperately attempting to push away the acknowledgment I just made. She must be able to read my emotions, because she pulls me to stand with her. "It's not life or death, Raea. Enjoy the ride." She winks, hollering as our team moves into position.

Eight of our team members position themselves on the various rings around the arena. Anders and one of the females move to the island at the center. Anders catches my eye, winking as a playful smirk crosses his features when my cheeks heat. I roll my eyes, feigning annoyance, but can't resist the grin growing on my face.

"Kill me?" I teasingly beg Ciara, but instead of responding, she plants a loud, smacking kiss on my cheek, wrapping her arms around my neck.

"Can I be in your wedding?" she finally answers, dodging my elbow as she backs into Tate. The horn blares, and the game begins.

Just ten minutes in, and I'm addicted to the high of the game, or maybe it's watching Anders seamlessly dominate the game as he moves through the rings with ease.

Our team moves like they've had years to practice together. Cole and another player, Kamden, called Orion, are focused on driving the groundball, maneuvering through the maze of obstacles. Meanwhile, Anders and the spy, whose name I now know is Savenne, maintain their attention on the AerBall.

As Anders scales one of the larger boulders, there's a resounding gasp as an opposing attacker sneaks in from the other side and tackles him.

The opposing attacker should be on the opposite side of the arena, not hiding among the obstacles, right?

"Is that allowed?" I ask.

Ciara breathes, her grip on my hand tightening. I hold my breath as both men plunge into the icy water below. Moments later, they both resurface, and with a swing, Anders lands a powerful blow directly on the attacker's nose. I don't have to hear the crunch to know it's broken. Rivulets of crimson splash into the water. Anders doesn't waste a moment, already evading another attack as he pulls himself to shore.

"Yep," Kamden says. "Totally legal."

Anders makes quick work of navigating the boulder and a series of obstacles before diving straight into the water ring filled with blade-fish. I wince, watching the fish surround him, but he doesn't slow.

Meanwhile, Cole and Orion keep their defenders occupied, each move calculated as they maneuver closer to the groundball goal. The opposing team's goalie stands oblivious to Anders' approach.

Anders slips quietly from the water while the goalie's back is turned and sprints toward the goal. He's nowhere near close enough when he winds back his arm and, with a release, sends the AerBall slingshotting through the air.

Somewhere in the back of my mind, I know I'm squeezing Ciara's hand so tightly my knuckles are most likely white, but she doesn't flinch or complain. The next heartbeat propels me to my feet as I leap up and down in unadulterated joy, squealing like a silly schoolgirl as the AerBall hits the back of the net.

"Oh my gods," I laugh, brushing my hands through my wild hair. "This is incredible!"

Aolyn raises an eyebrow at me, a knowing smile crossing her lips as if she knows who, not what, has my heartbeat thumping erratically.

Come the third period, our team looks so exhausted; I fear all it would take is a single gust of wind to bring them down. This game was supposed to be an easy win, or so I've been told. Unfortunately, Wildwood Academy appears to have traded its players for larger opponents. Our team has been pushed to their limits, both physically and mentally, and I'm not sure they have another twenty minutes in them.

As I scan the player's box, every team member is sprawled out across benches or the floor in various states of recovery—a few with lesser injuries are leaning heavily on the railings. Others use equipment bags as pillows while nursing a type of energizing drink. Coach Beck stands by, trying his best to revitalize the team and rally them back into the rings, but even his motivational words can't rouse them.

I nibble anxiously on my lip, my leg bouncing wildly as I watch Anders wrap his bleeding arm. I just learned that the healers aren't allowed to touch the players until the end of the game or unless they're being pulled from the game due to an injury.

"Who's on defense this period?" Kamden asks Aolyn, studying our team just as intensely. The music echoing through the arena keeps a positive energy flowing, but I can't help but feel exhausted for them.

With only two minutes until they're back out in the arena, eight players begin to rise, their movements sluggish.

"Mac was injured last period, but they wrapped his ankle. He should be good to go," Aolyn responds. Ciara and Tate return to our row with refreshments and snacks. My mouth waters at the scent of honey rolls.

"No, I have a feeling they'll put him as a guardian. My guess is Brecken and Trysten will remain on defense, Morris in goal. They're our best hope," Kamden volleys back.

Tate leans forward, looking past Ciara and me. "What about the guy with the birthmark on his cheek?" he asks. "He looks like he could even take down Ryker."

All of our heads swivel his way, Aolyn and Kamden nodding their agreement, but I have to swallow down my words, for some reason feeling the need to defend Anders.

"That's Elis," Kamden responds with a grin. "He's got great potential, but he's new talent. Morris and Brecken have the experience we need right now."

The loud buzz of the horn cuts through the air, charging the atmosphere once again as enthusiastic fans erupt in cheers. Anders' little fangirl group even has a stupid chant of their own, grating on every nerve ending I have.

"Ryker, Ryker, he's our guy. He's the one who makes you cry."

Standing on the island, Anders exchanges a brief glance with Kalli, the spy for this period, before his gaze moves to mine.

My heart threatens to stop when I finally take in the bruise blooming over his eye and the split lip. *Gods, how does he do this?* Something passes between us, my worry for him bringing a small smile to his lips just before he refocuses in time for the horn to signal the start of the match.

Anders springs into action, retrieving both balls from the bunker in a swift movement, quickly sprinting back towards Cole and Orion, who look like they're using every ounce of energy just to remain standing.

Anders dives into the ice water ring, swimming for the obstacle ring when one of Wildwood's players lunges forward, tackling Cole from behind just as Anders pulls himself from the water. There's a collective gasp in the crowd, all of us holding our breath as the arena falls silent, watching and waiting for Cole to resurface.

Moments stretch into what feels like minutes, each building the anxiety in the air. Anders dives back into the water when Cole doesn't resurface, diving deep and disappearing from sight. I can feel Aolyn's reassuring grip on my right hand, clutching me tightly. Ciara's hand anchors me around the waist as we wait, our breaths becoming shallower every second.

It's a small eternity before Anders resurfaces; his expression is a mixture of urgency and worry. He's clutching an unconscious Cole in his arms, and time seems to freeze as I gasp, the world around me blurring as I fight a flurry of tears.

"Please be alright," I whisper to myself, repeating the prayer over and over. I may not be close with Cole, but I care about him. A single tear brims, tracking down my cheek.

Orion and Anders pull Cole from the water, laying him on the shore. The game is paused as the medical bridge extends slowly toward the center of the arena.

Anders kneels beside Cole, his fingers probing for a pulse. A moment later, he slaps Cole's face, urging him to wake up as his eyes grow frantic. A stream of crimson spills across Cole's forehead from a deep gash, making my heart plummet and sending a chill through me.

Finally, the bridge connects with a resonant thud, and in an instant, the healers rush forward, bags and a stretcher being thrown to the ground as they drop down beside Anders.

Around me, I hear the cacophony of outrage erupting from the other team while our spectators cheer, but I can't seem to pull my eyes from the brothers on the field.

As Cole is carefully lifted to the bridge, his position is replaced with a woman. Next to the blood and chaos, she looks too fragile. I want to scream for the game to stop—to beg for the game to be called—but my concern won't make a difference.

Ciara squeezes me, pulling my frozen body to my seat while she declares something about the player being thrown from the game as if that will help my frayed nerves.

"What the hell?" Tate growls, throwing his arm forward and gesturing toward the female player. "They're putting Katerina out there?"

I quickly glance at him, noting the tightness in his jaw and the fury in his eyes. Aolyn remains quiet, wrapping her hands around her waist in worry, as Kamden shrugs, falling back into his seat with a nervous sigh.

With a point docked from Wildwood, we now lead 26–25. Anders raises his stick like he did at the start of the game, but this time, he bellows, "For Cole!" just before he dives back into the water. Kalli takes the lead, guiding Anders through the maze of obstacles. Meanwhile, Katerina and Orion are behind him.

Kalli swiftly scales a tree, disappearing among the thick branches. Anders follows her up, while Katerina and Orion push forward toward the ring of bladefish. My leg bounces nervously, my heart racing—for Cole, for Anders, for the entire team.

A few tense moments stretch out before I finally spot Anders perched on a branch above the fourth ring, his stick gripped tightly in one hand as he clings to the branch overhead with the other. From my vantage point, only a few home-team sections have a clear view of him. My stomach tightens at the thought of him falling. I try to remind myself it's only water, but still…

Below, on the fifth ring near the goals, Orion and Katerina fight to inch the groundball closer to the goal, but their attempts seem more of a distraction than anything. Katerina dances on her feet, dodging the massive defenders and running them in circles.

"Is that allowed?" Kamden asks Aolyn, his eyes wide, as Anders leans further out from his perch. Anders angles his stick, preparing to throw, but the distance across the water seems impossible, not even taking into account that he's balancing thirty feet above the surface.

"Not sure," Aolyn replies, her voice a low whisper as she waits.

Anders hesitates, and the whole section seems to hold its breath as he swings the stick, roaring as he releases. The AerBall springs free from the net, launching into the air and silencing the arena as it soars over the water.

sixteen

. . .

I HOLD my breath with the rest of the crowd as Anders releases the AerBall. It sails over the ring of water below, over the groundball goal, and lands in the net. It's an unbelievable, should-be-impossible move. The Drithm crowd goes wild, all of us jumping to our feet and screaming.

The Wildwood players look around, bewildered. Our two other attackers are still running in circles and dashing away from Wildwood's defense. Their goalie looks around and then up to the scoreboard, where Drithm's score shifts to thirty-one. We are now six points ahead with six minutes left on the clock.

Their coach is on the other side of the arena, arguing with the refs, but with the coach's sound barriers in place, the teams have no idea what just happened. Something similar to pride fills my body as I watch Anders drop back to the ground with Kalli, both of them high-fiving each other.

Trysten is on the other side of the arena, still fighting off the opposing attacker. The attacker throws the ball, but it misses the net by mere inches just before he's thrown to the ground by Trysten. Their groundball is stolen by our other defender, and both balls are placed in the chute, where they appear back on the island with our guardian.

Our AerBall is there too, and the guy guarding the bunker, whose name I think is Mason, only attempts to guard the Wildwood AerBall.

Anders and Kalli make it back to the island using the skywalk just before our other attackers join them. They all take a moment to celebrate as the clock runs down to one minute. Anders scoops up our AerBall and turns to face me, pointing the stick in my direction, before his team surrounds him as the final buzzer sounds off.

"Oh my gods," Ciara cackles from beside me. "Did he just dedicate his win to you?" She keels over, laughing as if it's the most amusing thing ever.

"No," I argue. "He was pointing it at his little fan club."

The group of girls is all swooning over him and going on and on about how hot he is. I want to shove a honey roll in all their mouths and shut them up.

"He definitely d—" Kamden chimes in before Aolyn slaps him playfully on the chest. "Ouch," he mutters.

"I'm sure he was just pointing to the crowd in general," Aolyn supplies.

"Yeah, right," Tate mutters, dodging my glare. I gather my things and start to follow the crowd down the steps of the arena finding myself biting my lip, lost in thought about Cole. I can't get the picture of him bleeding and unconscious out of my head. Today's game was a whirlwind of emotions, and I felt like I was holding my breath for what seemed like an eternity, only to burst into cheers alongside the crowd during the most nail-biting moments.

Each time Anders and Trysten took a hit or executed a tackle, I winced, my stomach churning. I silently offered prayers on their behalf, though I'm not sure Astor and Calia would care to listen.

As we navigate the mass of spectators leaving the arena, I tuck a loose strand of hair behind my ear. I shift my cloak from one arm to the other and link my free arm with Ciara's, laying my head on her shoulder as we continue toward the gates.

"Raea," Trysten calls out, his voice laced with urgency and desperation as he weaves through a crowd all singing his praises. He's still caked with mud and splattered in blood. I pause and wait for him to reach me. The crowd continues to chant his name, offering praise as he rushes by, but he seems completely oblivious.

"The healer is asking for you. I need you to come with me."

My face scrunches in confusion, but I nod and follow, quickly saying goodbye to my friends before following Trysten. He doesn't spare a glance or provide any further explanation, leading me down the worn stone steps into the team area. The hallway branches out in front of us: the right leads to the locker rooms and the left toward the arena.

As I follow Trysten through the door into the team box, I'm greeted by a sight that makes my heart sink. Several Drithm team members are strewn about the private room, each nursing various injuries. A few faces are twisted in pain. Trysten disappears into a small door at the far side of the room, and I hesitate, feeling like an intruder.

"Princess Raea," the elderly healer greets me. He's the best the school has to offer, possibly the best on the whole planet. Cole lies unconscious on the table, his face pale but free of blood, a bandage wrapped around his head looking like it could rip open at any moment. Anders stands on the opposite side, deep in conversation with someone on his Prism. Another healer stands near Cole's head, monitoring the wound with a wand that displays the thickness of the tissue and swelling on her tablet.

This might be the first time I've ever seen Anders rattled; his usual calm composure has shattered. He's always so strong, collected, and... arrogant. None of those words fit the description of the man pacing in front of me, running a hand through his matted, wet hair, covered in mud, with panic-stricken eyes that seem to swirl with silver. When his gaze meets mine, a cloud of light surrounds me, and I find myself attempting to shrink into the shadows.

"I was wondering if you could call your mother?" the healer asks, grabbing my attention.

"My mother?" I'm unsure if I heard him correctly.

"Yes," the healer confirms. "She has a rare plant in her garden that only grows on Kyrr. Our stores have been depleted, and, well, it might be the only thing that helps Cole regain consciousness. He hit his head at just the right angle, and his brain is swelling. The plant is known for reducing swelling and mending serious injuries." He continues, letting me know Cole isn't stable enough to be moved to the main Healer's Center, so she'll need to bring it here.

A wave of nausea slams into my stomach as the reality of the situation sinks in. I don't ask what happens if he doesn't wake. I had no idea he hit his head that hard. I'd been too focused on the fact that he disappeared into the water.

Swallowing hard, I nod and pull out my Prism with shaky hands. The room is already cramped, and with the four extra bodies, there's no such thing as privacy. I make myself as small as possible in the corner as I call my mother. Thanks to recent advancements in satellite links, the call connects in just a few rings.

"Mother, we need your help."

Getting a royal visit to the academy is rare. Getting two royal visits on the same day is unheard of. I make my way over to the Administration Building, where my parents' transport is set to land any minute now, with my mother and the plant in tow. Queen Priana is also expected to land within the hour.

I stand off to the side of the launch pad as our transport enters Baedyn's atmosphere. The air around me charges with an energy I've come to know as Anders. I turn to see him stalking toward me, still covered in blood, sweat, and a thick layer of mud from the game. His cheek and eye are healed, and I can't seem to find any lingering injuries. Despite it all, he looks handsome, just a bit more rugged than the polished prince I'm used to seeing.

"Hey," I manage to say, a little breathless. "I thought you were staying with Cole?"

He steps closer, towering over me. I catch his gaze and notice the swirling in his eyes has started again. For a fleeting moment, fear flickers across his features before being masked behind a stoic expression. I don't know why it bugs me so much that he's unwilling to be open with me.

"I'll be bringing the plant back. I need to get it to the healers as soon as possible. The longer the swelling persists, the more damage he'll suffer." My heart sinks. They've had enough heartache in their family. I reach out, wrapping my hand around his forearm, wanting to comfort him. The moment our skin touches, a spark of energy surges between us, leaving me breathless. It was an unconscious move, driven by instinct rather than intention. I find myself leaning into him as my body adjusts to his. The well within me fills as my soul settles, and feelings of rightness and longing flood the space between us.

I gasp when Anders' hand wraps around my hip, molding perfectly and tugging me closer until our bodies are nearly flush. My body instantly heats. I know Anders can tell because he flips his hand to my head, checking my temperature before dismissing it.

"I'm sorry," I say, my voice barely above a whisper as I wrestle to suppress my emotions. "For your brother." He nods solemnly, his other hand brushing down my arm, igniting a flurry of goosebumps across my body.

"You're hot," he states. Not a question. It's my turn to nod in response. He looks like he's about to pull me closer, but then glances down at his muddy uniform and my gown, and clearly thinks better of it. I'm reluctant to admit that I wouldn't have fought him, even if it destroyed my outfit.

The muffled roar of thrusters catches my attention as the transport begins its descent. I withdraw my hand from his arm, tucking it awkwardly against my side. His brow furrows slightly, and then he releases me, stepping back as if to give me space. I hold his gaze a moment longer, hoping to convey the confusing mix of emotions, but Anders shifts his gaze to the transport.

My parents' transport descends, a sleek, flattened disc of shimmering forest green, its central shaft equipped with subtly recessed weapons. Multiple smaller thrusters glow with a warm amber, giving the vessel a powerful, yet controlled presence. The disc-shaped main body features a subtle upward curve in the center, crafted from an advanced composite alloy that gleams, subtly shifting in hue from deep emerald in shadow to brighter green in direct light.

The Treon royal crest is elegantly etched onto its surface. Multiple, smaller, highly articulate thrusters positioned symmetrically around the disc's rim, provide fine maneuverability, rapid acceleration, and quick braking. The weapons, usually housed within flush-mounted bays along the underside shaft, remain unseen.

As the large vessel settles into its hover, back ramps unfold with a low hiss, and illuminated steps stretch to the ground.

A cadre of my mother's guards takes positions around the transport as she descends. My emotions drown me, and my composure shatters as soon as I see her carrying the plant.

Without a second thought, I take off running across the launch pad until I crash into her, wrapping my arms around her tightly. "Oh, Raea, my darling," she responds, her free arm holding me close. The familiar floral scent of my mother envelops me, calming my frayed nerves. Pulling away, I can feel my tears flowing down my face. I didn't realize until now how much I've missed her and how difficult this school year has been, taking a toll on my emotional state.

"Queen Amaya," Anders interjects. I turn in time to see him bow. "If you don't mind, I'd like to run this ahead to the healers."

"Of course," my mother replies. She passes the plant to him, and without a second thought, he races back to his brother.

The hissing of the ramp closing behind us fills the air as I walk arm-in-arm with my mother, leading her toward the arena. She's dressed in a stunning layered gown of soft creams and delicate pinks, her chestnut brown hair pinned up and woven with ribbons. Our family crest glints around her neck, and a simple, yet regal, crown is nestled atop her head—ever the picture-perfect queen.

My mother must sense my emotions because she kisses the top of my head and says, "Let's walk and talk, my dear. Tell me everything."

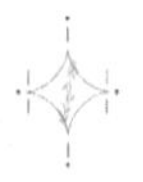

I fall into bed both exhausted and wired. I excused myself from the healing center once Cole was moved. I left my mother with Anders while Trysten walked me back to the dorms. Queen Priana was landing when we left, and Cole was awake and talking. I offered to bring clean clothes back for Anders, but Trysten stepped in and said he'd do it so I could rest.

My friends brought food up to my room, and the five of us ate around the coffee table. We had invited Trysten to join us, but he was planning to stay with Anders at the Center.

I had explained what happened with Cole and shared all the details. They all realized the severity of it before changing the topics to our upcoming break. While my friends talked about their vacations, Ciara and I scrolled through The Link, finding photos and posts from today and our team's win.

There was a video of Cole getting tackled. Watching it again somehow made it even worse than it was in person. Maybe it was because I knew what happened. His head clipped the edge of the water ring. The soft-shell helmet didn't protect his forehead.

Ciara had chuckled when we came across a photo of Anders pointing his stick at me. You couldn't see who he was pointing it at, but he had that classic smirk pasted on his face, his eyes alight with amusement, and his high from the win. Annoyingly, I couldn't stop the laugh and smile that tumbled out of me. My friends left soon after we were done scrolling, allowing Aolyn and me to get ready for bed.

Now, lying here in the dark, I secure my music patches on, turning on a playlist I use when I'm stressed. Even the calming melody can't soothe my racing thoughts. Glaring at the shadows playing across the ceiling, I beg the gods to let me sleep. Unfortunately, no matter how much I try, I can't.

My mind floods with a relentless barrage of tasks yet to be completed. Next week marks the deadline for my final assignments, and I can't shake the excitement of heading home. More than anything, I just need a reset. I'll have to beg Lieutenant Piori for more flight lessons when I'm home.

Despite the skills I've already mastered flying the school transports, I can't shake the thought of making a mistake and causing a fatal disaster. It's a ridiculous fear; the transport's autopilot is designed to kick in long before an error like that can happen, yet flashes of the console screaming errors at me keep playing in my head.

After what feels like an eternity of grasping and clawing for rest, I decide I just need to move. I slip into my swimsuit and tie my Nakata corset in place before layering my loungewear and cloak around me.

The rugs dampen the sound of my footsteps as I navigate the dimly lit dorm corridors. Soft, ambient lights guide me until I reach the glass doors at the entrance, their slicing noise piercing the quiet. A rush of cool evening air greets me.

I wind my way through the dense forest, following the hidden trail to the lake. In front of me, my breath is visible in little puffs of white. The canopy overhead makes the trail shadowed, only occasionally illuminated by the silvery glow from the moons high above. Once I reach the water's edge, I undress quickly, feeling the bite of the breeze, and dive into the warm water.

The water soothes the last of my nerves and restless thoughts as I swim slowly toward the center of the lake. Around me, the pulsing hum of the planet resonates through me, synchronizing with the rhythm of my own heartbeat. The small island emerges like a shadow as I reach the shoreline. It's easy to find the shallow ledge acting as a natural seat.

"Can't sleep?" Anders asks, his voice conveying how tired he is, the words cutting through the stillness of the night. I startle momentarily before regaining my composure. It feels like he's a shadow, always lingering nearby, sneaking up on me.

Even in the dead of night, here he is. I keep my gaze fixed on the calm water, unwilling to turn and acknowledge him. Not because I'm upset with him, but because whatever is going on between us feels—big. Like it has the opportunity to change my entire life, and I still haven't come to terms with it.

"I just needed to clear my head. Swimming helps," I reply, drawing in a deep breath and centering myself. "Is Cole okay?" He is silent for a long minute.

"My mother had to leave," he finally says, his voice detached but laced with an underlying pain. It's intentional—him letting me see this side of him. "But Cole won't be returning to school after break." I can hear him shuffling, then feel the water ripple beside me as he drops in, creating a small splash.

Maybe it's the magic of the moonlight, or the fact it's the middle of the night and this feels like another dream—or perhaps I've lost my damn mind—but I have to fight the urge to reach out and hold him.

He sighs and leans back, closing his eyes to the world, and for a moment, I'm struck by the emotions playing on his face, so openly available to me. We sit in silence, the minutes stretching into what feels like hours, neither of us moving or speaking, simply being. The warm water laps against our bodies, shielding us from the crisp air.

Overhead, a flapping bird's wings distracts me, and I follow its path until it vanishes into the dense forest on the opposite shore. My body begins to surrender to the pull of sleep, and drowsiness pulls me down. With a yawn, I turn to face Anders, whose features are finally relaxed.

His eyes remain closed; dark lashes fanned out against his cheekbones, the image of serenity that almost makes me want to reach out and brush his hair back. I'd almost believe he was asleep if it weren't for the hint of a smile that pulls at his lips.

"What?" he asks, still in a dreamy haze, his eyes sealed shut.

"I'm going to bed," I announce softly. Exhaustion tugs at me, begging me to surrender right here. Anders hums in response, crossing his arms over his chest.

"Okay, see you tomorrow," he murmurs lazily. I almost ask why he's going to let me leave in the dark, but decide against it. He needs the quiet, not another burden.

As I prepare to rise from the natural stone shelf that we've been using as our seats, I feel a gentle pressure on my wrist. I look down to find his fingers wrapped around me, igniting a peculiar sense of belonging that I can't quite explain. Perhaps it's just familiarity since we're together so frequently.

"Thanks for today." His blue eyes finally meet mine. The muted glow of the moonlight catches the flecks of silver in his irises, and I can't help but lose myself briefly in them.

His thumb brushes lightly against the sensitive skin on the inside of my wrist, sending a delightful, soothing warmth flooding through my body. "What for?"

"For coming to the game. For helping Cole."

I can't help but chuckle, rolling my eyes dramatically. "I didn't come for you," I tease. His lips quirk up as his gaze settles on me, with amusement dancing in his eyes.

"Sure. Whatever you need to tell yourself."

I roll my eyes again, breaking free from his grasp, and fall into the water. "You're insufferable." I swim in place. "Don't fall asleep out here. Your drowning would really bring down the calming vibe of this place."

His laughter resonates through me, pausing my backward momentum.

Gods, I love that sound.

With a sigh, he slips into the water beside me, the darkness enveloping us as we both tread water. The minimal distance between us allows me to feel the warmth radiating from his body. Our silence is louder than cannon fire, filled with every word we're too afraid to say. I can't bring myself to swim away. How long until one of us breaks? How long will we play this game, letting this tension build between us?

After what feels like a small eternity, he reaches out, his hand cradling my face with a tenderness that gives me butterflies. I hold his gaze as his thumb glides softly across my cheek.

"Why are you looking at me like that?" My voice is barely audible over the soft lapping of the water.

"I—" he pauses, gulping. "Sleep well, Raea."

Disappointment crashes into me. I'm not even sure why. I don't know what I want from him. Needing to feel something other than the lingering hurt, I close the distance between us, my hand settling on his shoulder as I lean in and place a soft kiss against his stubbled cheek. For a moment, I'm pretty sure he stops breathing. I pull away slowly, watching him, before turning and swimming away.

I dress quickly, acutely aware of his gaze following me as he makes his way to the shore, but he remains in the water, allowing me the space to compose myself. Just before I slip into the shadows of the forest, I glance back, locking eyes with him once more.

In that fleeting moment, an entire world of unsaid words passes between us.

seventeen

. . .

I SPENT most of yesterday in my room, needing a quiet space to catch up on my assignments and rest. Sleep had been intermittent, plagued by restlessness and tormenting dreams.

Preparing for another school day, I meticulously braid my hair, weaving the white strands into two neat plaits. Feeling overwhelmed by the amount of assignments I still need to submit, I grab my bag and pray I'll have enough time to grab something to go before submitting my Aeronautics report.

I open my door, attempting to slip out unnoticed. Instead, I do a double-take, finding Anders leaning casually against the balustrade across the hall.

"I see you chose not to invade my personal space today," I grumble, turning toward the stairs.

"And I see that you're as cheery as ever," he shoots back with amusement. "You really are a grumpy thing in the morning." He extends a hand toward me, and I glance down to see a steaming cup of tea being thrust into mine.

"You brought me tea?" I refuse to allow the weird lump in my throat to mean anything. My feelings for him keep growing without my approval.

"Don't worry," he replies nonchalantly, falling into step next to me as we descend the stairs together. "It's more for me than for you. This way, your mouth is busy consuming your first caffeine hit instead of firing off snarky comments before I've had my breakfast."

I feel a smile tugging at my lips despite my resolve to remain grumpy. I take a tentative sip of the tea as we reach the bottom of the stairs, discovering it's the perfect blend of honey and green tea.

"About our little trip to the Isles," he starts, pulling me into an alcove. "I never got to finish explaining. We can go next month. Their chief is unavailable until then." I nod, taking another sip.

"I haven't been able to find any texts, but I'm not giving up on that. Last week in Bonding, that Seer's book Professor Becca uploaded —I want to see the whole thing."

"It's a good idea."

Students pass us, unaware of us as they take the covered walkway to the dining hall. "If you need help, just let me know." His hand moves to my lower back as we slide into the flow of students.

When we enter the rush of the dining hall, I swear I feel a gentle squeeze of his hand on my hip, guiding me through the throng of students. By the time the crowd thins for him, Anders has already made his way across the room, taking a seat with Trysten and Elex, leaving me reeling.

"Rae," Kellan calls out as he quickens his pace to catch up to me. A bright smile spreads across his face. "Hey! Didn't see you yesterday. Aolyn mentioned you weren't feeling well?" We step into the line for simple fare.

"I'm okay now," I reply, attempting to shake off the lingering fatigue. "I just didn't sleep well. How was Mori?" As we inch closer to the breakfast window, his eyes light up as he begins sharing every detail about his recent visit to the intelligence room. His words tumble out in a stream of consciousness, and I mentally note to discuss the possibility of Kellan visiting the one at the palace.

When he turns the conversation to my weekend, I hesitate before admitting I had gone to the game. I keep it vague, not wanting to delve into details. I'm not ready to share how I actually enjoyed watching Anders or dish out details about Cole. I'm not sure how we've ended up here. I usually tell Kellan everything, but this year, things feel different between us.

As we finally reach the window, I grab a plate with an assortment of fruit and a berry muffin to take back to the dorm while I submit my work. I glance over to find Kellan grabbing the same.

"Why are you eating this? They have protein dishes over there." I gesture to the far side of the dining hall, where heaping plates of sausages and browned potatoes wait in the windows.

He shrugs with a faint blush tinging his cheeks. "I don't know. I just wanted to talk to you." I roll my eyes playfully and tell him to go get what he wants, and promise to talk more later.

Just as I'm about to head back to Taeolyn, Trysten corners me with a nervous smile. "Morning, Raea." He fidgets, glancing at Anders, and then back to me. I wait, wondering what he needs before he admits he's finally ready to take over my training. On days when I don't run, I meet him in the gym. I don't know what prompted the discussion, or what Anders said to convince him, but I agree, thankful that he even offered.

Classes drag today as most involve discussing random events, how to clean a transport, and so on, with everyone's focus—even the professors—clearly on our upcoming break. I walk with Ciara and Tate to lunch, sitting with our typical group. Kamden waves to us from where he's sitting with the junior Recons. At the next table over, Kellan looks up and does the same, and I can't help but notice the hint of sadness in his expression. He's really taking this whole divisions arrangement poorly. I offer him a sad smile before plopping down into my seat.

"Looks like Anders has another admirer," Ciara teases as she gestures across the hall.

I glance up and catch sight of a girl reaching out toward Anders, her fingers almost brushing against his arm. I can't help but stifle a laugh as he jerks away, nearly elbowing the guy standing in line beside him.

The girl seems unfazed as she twirls her long, brown hair around her finger, biting her bottom lip in a far too exaggerated manner. She leans in a little closer, her eyes sparkling with hope—but Anders' expression quickly shifts from mildly annoyed to uncomfortable.

He mutters something I can only assume is a curt dismissal as I watch her flirtatious, doe-eyed gaze shift to hatred. She crosses her arms tightly across her chest, her cheeks turning a shade similar to strawberries. Everyone in the hall can hear her shriek of annoyance when she retorts, "It's Laci, not Kara!"

She storms off, leaving Anders visibly relieved, yet amused by the encounter. Tate, Ciara, and I share a chuckle over the drama. It's a familiar scene—Anders and the determined flirt attempting to win him over when nobody else has managed.

"I'd tap that," Tate remarks beside me. "Seriously, what do all these women see in him anyway?"

I feel a hint of a blush as I avert my gaze to my plate. I can't speak for anyone else, but the truth is, Anders is…Anders. His confidence, which often borders on arrogance, has a strange charm that is growing on me. And dare I say it, but kindness lurks beneath that broody exterior which I've come to love. I doubt many people ever get to see that side of him. Plus, his looks. I can't even pick just one thing—the man is the embodiment of every fantasy I have.

"How did you do on the Aeronautics exam?" Ciara interjects, pulling me from my thoughts.

A grin spreads across my face as I tell her I scored a hundred percent. My body hums, a tingling sensation sliding down my spine, both infuriating and exhilarating at the same time. I don't have to turn to know who's behind me.

I feel his hot breath tickling my neck as he leans down to whisper in my ear. His presence is borderline intoxicating, and it's a struggle not to lean back into him. "Care to join me by the river for lunch?" he asks, keeping his voice low and inviting.

I gasp softly, caught off guard as his fingers graze my arm ever so slightly. *What is he doing?* This is too bold, too intimate, especially in front of…everyone.

It takes a moment to gather my thoughts, but I respond, "I'm quite happy here, but enjoy." I feign indifference even though the idea of joining him is more than tempting. The last thing either of us needs is the gossip that will spread like wildfire if someone sees us. Instead, I offer him a playful smile, hoping to mask my internal conflict, then redirect my attention back to Tate, who is now deep in conversation with a few others.

"I swear Professor Trygg hates me," Tate snaps in frustration. "How the hell was I supposed to know that the thinner the atmosphere, the harder it is for the pods?" I'm all too aware of Anders lingering behind me like he has more to say before making his way across the dining hall.

Deep down, I know I shouldn't care that I turned him down, but I do, and shame fills me. Another realization that surprises me. I don't want to hurt his feelings, and that thought unsettles me more than it should. He seems so nonchalant in rejecting women, yet the idea of doing the same to him fills me with a strange sense of guilt. I watch his retreating form as he strides through the door, his mask firmly intact, yet I notice the subtle way his free hand is clenched tightly at his side.

As if he can sense my gaze lingering on him, he pauses and turns, locking eyes with me. The world around us fades, and for a heartbeat, it's just the two of us, the moment charged with possibilities and maybe something more.

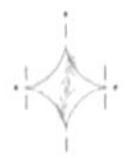

I sit in Modern Science, and all I can think about is leaving Anders to eat alone. I don't know why the guilt is eating me up so much, but it is. After classes, I'll have to make it up to him somehow. With our running club scheduled for this evening, I can probably make a detour to turn things around.

Professor Mathison, a short, frail man, stands behind his worktable and projects a holographic image of our system—the seven suns, seventy-two planets, and hundreds of moons—springing to life in vivid colors. "Who here can tell me why it's impossible for all seventy-two planets to rotate, keeping time with each other? And why is it even more impossible that our planets orbit the seven suns as they do?"

Paxton's hand shoots up. "Even though all seventy-two planets have a similar core and composition, the variance in mass between them is significant. Moreover, each planet's distance from its sun is fundamental to understanding gravitational pull, and this isn't factoring in the gravity from Sgya and the suns' own orbits around it. We should also consider tidal drag from surrounding moons, angular momentum, and the spin of the protoplanetary disk. Even if every planet were an exact replica of the other with identical mass, orbits, and moons, it would still be impossible."

"Excellent, Duke Leighton!" Professor Mathison praises, "And why is it that our planets have exact rotations and orbits despite all of these factors?"

I glance over to Tate, sharing a reassuring nod. We've had extensive discussions on this topic recently, and I know he could use the participation points to bolster his grade.

"Magic?" Tate ventures hesitantly. Professor Mathison nods, a slight frown on his lips.

"Yes, magic, Lord Kinnunen," he acknowledges, crossing his arms. "But let's remember to raise our hands next time, yes?"

Tate huffs in annoyance, sitting back.

"It's okay," I whisper. "He'll still give you points."

"As Lord Kinnunen pointed out," Professor Mathison continues, his glasses falling down his snub nose, "magic. We don't yet fully understand why the gods chose to impart these particularities on our system, but we know that prior to the veil, the planets operated independently on their own calendars. Now," he declares, moving back to change the hologram. "Today, we will learn about telling time when you don't have a clock."

By the end of the day, I'm scrambling to get dressed for running club. I reach for my lilac sports bra, featuring delicate straps that criss-cross elegantly across my back. It's a favorite of mine, and I pair it with lace-trimmed shorts. Am I dressing up for him? Maybe… fine, yes. Still, I feel the strange need for him to notice me. Once dressed, I rebraid my hair and finish with a quick dab of blush on my cheeks.

As expected, the students grumble about us rerunning the arena stairs, but I remind them how good it will feel when we're done. It isn't long before we arrive at the arena, and I spot Anders making his way into practice. He's dressed in athletic shorts, his torso gloriously bare, and a shirt hanging haphazardly out of the waistband of his shorts. My heart skips a beat at the sight of him.

I inhale deeply, reminding myself not to be a coward. Waving my team forward, I jog to catch up with him. "Hey," I call out. "Can I talk to you for a second?"

He nods, a slight smile playing on his lips as we step away from the flow of runners.

As he tugs me closer, his palms molding around my hips, a surge of energy pulses between us. The warmth of his calloused hands on my body sends my mind racing with thoughts of where else those hands could wander. I almost forget what I came here to say.

Clearing my throat to regain my thoughts, I muster up the courage to just ask. "So, I wanted to say thank you for the invite at lunch. It was really kind of you." I step back, putting some distance between us, which I desperately need to gather my thoughts or potentially sprint away if things don't go well. "Maybe tomorrow?"

He raises his brows, a teasing glint in his sapphire eyes, waiting for me to elaborate. His thumbs hook casually into the waistband of his shorts, and I can't help but admire the deep grooves of that delicious 'V' at his hips. Gods, why does he have to be so…so…distracting? "Eyes up here, Princess," he crows, and my cheeks flush as I realize I've been staring.

I glance up, crossing my arms. "Do you always have to be shirtless?"

"Do you always have to dress like that?" he counters, gesturing to my outfit with an appreciative gaze. I shrug, delighting in the way his gaze cascades down my body.

"What about tomorrow?" he probes, his expression shifting to something dangerous.

"Maybe tomorrow we can have lunch down by the river?" I attempt to play it cool despite my racing heart. *Please say yes.* He studies me for what feels like forever, then tugs me closer, our bodies colliding with a surge of heat.

He leans down, dragging his nose along my neck, sending a pulse of power through my whole body. "A whole lunch hour with you sounds like a dream," he purrs into my ear, his voice deep. My body responds instinctively, leaning closer until my chest brushes against his. My breath quickens as I wrap my hands around his biceps, feeling the muscles and strength below.

"Is that a yes?" I tilt my head up to look into his eyes, suddenly aware of how close our faces are.

His eyes dip to my lips, the moment thick with desire, just as someone clears their throat behind us. I jolt away from him, feeling like I've been caught doing something scandalous. Turning around, we find Trysten, who's doing a poor job of hiding what looks like a smile.

"Want me to start with warmups?" His gaze shifts between Anders and me. Anders clenches his jaw, grinding his molars, clearly annoyed at the interruption. I can't blame him.

"I'll be there in a minute. We're all training on defense today." Trysten nods and takes off at a run, probably to give us some sense of privacy. "I'll grab the food," Anders says, brushing a hand through his hair. Our charged moment vanishes. Looking to where Trysten has retreated, he sighs. "See you later, Princess." He saunters away, hands tucked into his pockets.

And just like that, I'm left with a mix of excitement for tomorrow and disappointment that, once again, we didn't kiss.

"Keep your head up," Trysten barks, launching at me after instructing me to watch for weaknesses and where he keeps himself unguarded.

Moments later, his bō staff connects with my side, sending me tumbling to the ground.

I let out a groan as I rise again, "I'm exhausted." Running the stadium seemed like a good idea initially, but after practice, Trysten found me and said to meet him in the Taeolyn gym. I had begun to protest about it being a running day, but he just shot me a terrifying grin. I didn't have it in me to argue. By then, I could barely stand, and now every breath, every wobbly step, hurts.

"Exactly." He circles me, the staff swirling in his hands. "I want you to be tired so you can learn how to push through, how to think. You think an opponent will pause to check if you're well-rested?" Though nausea churns in my stomach from over-exertion, I push through my weariness, reminding myself I need this. Trysten has been relentless in our training this week, even now, despite my exhaustion.

I can't argue with Anders' and Trysten's assessment that I haven't been trained as I should be. Maybe I should have asked Kuron to train me when I was home instead of Melaina, one of the female Regils.

I barely have the energy to remain standing, but memories of the three men surrounding me and capturing me makes my spine straighten as I circle Trysten. When I consider how I almost lost my Bond last year and how helpless I felt both times, I take up my stance. *I will not be weak.* It's become my mantra every time I want to give up.

Squaring my shoulders, I give my approval to start again, watching Trysten's movements as he advances. I block the first strike, my arms shaking with fatigue as he presses down on our crossed staffs. How he has energy after practice, I have no idea. I go on the offense, spinning away from him to disorient his next attack and bring my staff down upon his back with a loud thwack.

Over the next hour, our bodies dance in exhausted movement as we train. He proves to me, over and over again, how badly I need this. He doesn't even have to try to break through my defenses. I have none.

We continue the training until Anders comes to collect me, stepping in and declaring that I've had enough for today. I don't fight him

when he offers me an arm to lean on as he guides me to the elevator,
knowing I'd never make it up the stairs.

eighteen

• • •

MY EYES FEEL like they're about to bleed from my head, and no matter how hard I try, I can't stop yawning. After showering off from my run and sparring session, I came to the common space to work so Aolyn could sleep. Not long after, Anders found me and took a seat beside me, engrossed in a book written in an intricate script I have never seen before. The letters dance across the page so elegantly, all flowing together as if the words are a piece of music.

I need to finish my midterm paper for History, but my brain seems to have lost its ability to function. The words on the page blur together, and I have to refocus to understand what it is I'm reading. My attention keeps drifting to Anders and his book, particularly how his leg grazes mine under the table, sending sparks of energy through me.

"The temple is built entirely of glass—" I yawn, my voice trailing off mid-sentence.

Anders snorts beside me as he sets his book flat on the table. "Why don't you go to bed?" he suggests, a hint of concern in his voice. Usually, I'd reply with a sassy comment, but I'm just too damn tired to think.

"I really need to finish this." I frown, realizing I've lost my place yet again. "I've never procrastinated like this before." I yawn again, feeling like a weight is dragging me down, and he mumbles something about stubbornness before sliding back in his chair. He leaves his book beside me and disappears across the common space.

After blinking a few times to sharpen my focus, I stand up, shaking off the weariness clinging to me. I give my cheeks a few light slaps, hoping to shock some life into me. The air shifts as warm arms wrap around me from behind, his body pressing into mine. It takes the rest of my energy reserves not to lean into him and close my eyes.

"Don't sneak up on people," I grumble.

He whispers an apology in my ear while handing me a steaming cup of tea. I groan in relief and accept his offering. I don't know when or how touching like this has become commonplace, but right now, I'm not arguing—especially when he's taking care of me.

I retake my seat, savoring the warmth of the tea, and hear the rustling of paper. When I turn around, I watch him settle onto one of the couches nearby, one long leg propped up against the cushions while the other dangles off the edge.

Even though it's late, and the rest of the dorm has gone to sleep, he's still here. For once, I don't mind having my handsome shadow around. As much as I love this dorm, it can feel a little creepy when you're alone at night.

The dorm is dark, with only a few dim lights illuminating the walkways. I'm sitting at a desk in the center of the common space with a lamp on. Anders also has a lamp beside him, but that's the extent of our lighting.

I'm not typically afraid of the dark, but on nights like this, when there's a strong wind from the north, I dislike the groaning and creaking of the windows and doors.

I look down at my paper and grumble softly to myself out of pure frustration. I'm so close to finishing—I just need to write this last section, and then I can be done. My paper is about the formation of the largest temple dedicated to Astor and Calia on Ista, of all places.

Ista lies within the Oris Kingdom and is relatively remote, being one of the least populated planets in the system. Its primary industry is mining, which poses significant hazards. With the advancement of technology, many traditional mining jobs have become obsolete, leaving only a few specialized and dangerous roles. It only makes me question why anyone would construct such a monumental temple in a place so unsuitable for attracting visitors.

The capital of Ista houses fewer than a million residents, and due to the planet's notoriously harsh weather—its winds and ice-cold rain—most of the population spends a considerable portion of the year indoors. They navigate through a complex network of tunnels carved into the mountains, which serve as passageways. Their oceans are filled with extreme currents and icebergs, making the few smaller landmasses within them uninhabitable.

Historians suggest that the original temple was built around ten thousand years ago, but they lack evidence to support their claims. All they have are samples recently collected, dating back to the planet's creation era. I've read their notes and analyses, but I remain skeptical. Placing the origins of the first temple still feels more like speculation than fact.

The original temple showed no signs of deterioration, but a new temple was constructed over it, effectively burying the original for "preservation purposes." The new temple is five times larger than the original. As I continue reading, I learn that because Ista doesn't have much to offer in terms of tourism, its leaders focused instead on the faithful, using pilgrimages as income.

Creative, I'll give them that.

Today, the current temple attracts over fourteen million visitors to Oris' capital each year, transforming their little colony into one of the largest travel destinations and essentially doubling their population each month. I've had the opportunity to visit it myself, which makes this assignment even more engaging. Now, if I can just get my brain to form coherent sentences.

I drop my head into my arms and yawn again before turning back to look at Anders, finding him asleep. I shut off my tablet, pack my bag, and turn off the light before approaching him. There's no sense in staying up any longer. It would be better to get some sleep and finish the assignment in the morning.

Kneeling beside Anders, I hesitate to wake him. It's only the second time I've seen him unguarded, his features so at ease. Dark hair tumbles over his forehead, lashes black as ink resting against high cheekbones. But it's his lips that undo me... What is it about them that drives me insane?

Gods, how did I get here? So drawn to the one man I should never want. The truth is, I crave him with a desperation that feels almost primal—as urgent as my next breath. I can't pinpoint where this feeling comes from; I just know it's there, and I'm tired of fighting it.

He inhales deeply, and my eyes are drawn to his tattoo. The design is so clean and detailed. I sigh and place my hand on his, which rests over his chest. If I sit here any longer, I will become a certified creep.

"Hey," I whisper, my voice barely audible. An explosion of longing and desire swells within me. I wonder if this feeling will ever stop, lessen, or become easier to ignore. My hand tingles where it rests against his, but I can't pull my eyes away from his face. I shake him lightly again, and he grumbles, slowly opening his eyes.

Some emotion flashes across the sapphire depths as he links his warm, calloused hand with mine. Neither of us moves as we hold each other's gaze. If I had to guess, my body is too shocked to continue breathing—every breath feels futile.

His brows furrow before he releases my hand, allowing me to breathe again.

"I'm going to bed," I say, my voice shaking. "I just didn't want to leave you down here." His eyes bounce between mine as if he's studying me or searching for something. His hand, still wrapped around his book, releases the older tome and moves to cup my face, his thumb brushing a strand of hair back.

"Do you even realize the effect you have on me? You're breathtaking," he mutters before dropping his hand and standing up. He reaches out, offering me his hand. I take it, standing beside him in stunned silence. He can't just say things like that—it's not fair.

"C'mon, sleepyhead," he rumbles, his voice deep and laced with sleep. "Get out of your head." Somehow, I will my feet to move until I'm in my room, still reeling from the past few minutes.

The sound of trickling water fills the air as I descend the grassy slope toward the river. The trees are nearing the end of their life cycle for the year, their leaves turning a dull green. Soon, they will shed their leaves, and new buds will grow in their place. We refer to this period as the turn of the season, as we approach the point in our orbit that is farthest from the sun.

The grass is long, its tips taking on a soft shade of gold as it sways in the breeze. Pink and white flowers are scattered across the ground around me, their sweet scent now faded and replaced by the fragrance of frost-pine blooms from the surrounding forest. I haven't spoken to Anders today, but I intend to keep my promise to have lunch with him.

I set my bag beside me, watching the canvas sag as I settle onto the boulder. The sound of gentle waves lapping at the shore fills the air as I pull out my Prism, sending a quick message to my father about our upcoming trip to Kliax. He's been counting down the days and is just as excited as my mother is for three luxurious days in the warm water.

I feel Anders approaching by the way my skin tingles, and I turn to see him making his way down to me. He's balancing two dishes in his hands, and I notice his tablet peeking out from the back of his pants. I bite down on my lip to suppress a smile.

For once, I feel relaxed and excited to spend time with him. Now that I've stopped denying the pull between us, I want to get to know him. If anything, it's less exhausting than what felt like trying to swim against an unrelenting current.

"Princess," he purrs as he plops down beside me, handing me one of the dishes. I accept the container, then allow him to pull his tablet free.

"Here," I reach out to take it. "I'll stick it in my bag. Do you need it for Intel today?"

He shakes his head, a brief flicker of appreciation lighting up his eyes. I offer to return it to him during Government.

I open the box to find one of the Treon dishes: a vibrant salad filled with fresh fruits and colorful vegetables, topped with flaky white fish that live at the base of most of our waterfalls. The vinaigrette is already mixed in, and when I take my first bite, I moan in delight. I've missed fresh food like this; the heavy, rich dishes from the other kingdoms can't compare.

Anders snorts, ruining my moment of indulgence, and pulls two wrappers from his pocket. "I didn't know which one you wanted," he says, holding them out for me to choose from. One is a mint and chocolate stick, the other is a pack of chocolate and sea salt-covered berries. I grin and snatch the chocolate-covered berries, ripping them open and popping one in my mouth. He watches, and a small, amused smile spreads across his face.

Clearing his throat, he asks, "So what are you doing for break?"

I hold up my finger, savoring another bite of my lunch, then lick my lips clean after swallowing. I guess he's not going to bring up last night, which is great. I don't need to talk about it. Those words can just go in the same box as all the other confusing things he's said to me, alongside the box of emotions that's at risk of overflowing. "We are headed to the capital on Kyrr for the ceremony and then to Kliax for diving. My mother is obsessed with the Moonrays and hasn't stopped talking about them for the past year. What about you?"

He swallows thickly, and I watch as his throat bobs. He takes a sip of the water packed in our lunch boxes, pausing as if weighing his words. "I'll probably hang around the palace. Maybe FinSurf if I can get away." There's something somber in his tone. It's strange—his casual demeanor contrasts sharply with the heaviness in his voice. I remember him mentioning Cole isn't returning to school, but I didn't think they were that close.

"You could crash our vacation if you want," I tease softly, trying to lighten the mood as I take another bite of my lunch. Anders offers me a tight smile, his gaze drifting before he changes the subject. I can't help but feel there's a story there he's not ready to share.

The sun warms my skin as I lean back and listen to Anders talk about the languages he's learning in class. It honestly sounds interesting. I'd love to know one of the ancient languages one day. You must apply to take the Dead Languages class, and only a select few seniors are chosen each year.

"How's the Powers Class with Professor Becca?" I ask, savoring the last of the chocolate-covered berries.

"Interesting," he replies. He stretches his arms and leans back on his palms, basking in the sunlight. "But honestly, I think the whole thing is a joke. We don't even know what powers we'll be gifted with. Take your father, for example; there hasn't been another ward builder like him in a century. Studying the most basic types of powers seems pointless."

I nod, my gaze drifting to a branch floating by. I want to ask him about his father's power since it's classified, but I know I shouldn't. I know that my father can build wards without the use of technology, and my mother can grow and nurture plants. His mother's power has something to do with emotions, but I'm unsure of the details.

Around the seven kingdoms, the royals wield an array of abilities. King Alexi from Ateria can create illusions, and Queen Sava is an ice wielder. In Thirik, King Urik and Queen Mara harness the element of air, which is helpful during the big storms that hit their ranches. King Hunter from Oris can detect lies, while his wife, Queen Isobel, can amplify magic.

King Garrek from Kadora wields fire, which is fitting given that he rules over volcanic planets. His wife, Queen Nalana, can redirect water, and Queen Meganna from Mori can detect water from miles away. King Osiris can sense storms before they hit, which can be deadly out in the middle of the desert.

Anders notices my silence and nudges me gently. "Talk. What's going on up there?" He gestures towards my head with an inquisitive expression. I hesitate, nibbling on my bottom lip while I contemplate just asking.

"Will you hate me if I ask what your father's power is?" I hesitantly look up at him, expecting to find annoyance, but instead, he snorts.

"First off, I can't hate you," he chuckles. "And secondly, no, I can't tell you. But who knows, maybe one day you'll find out."

Thought so.

Changing subjects, I say, "I found something. I think we need to go to Ista. The temple, to be exact. They buried the old one, but what if we can get in?"

He sits thoughtfully for a moment before nodding. "We go before break. I can get us a pass. Day after tomorrow."

I nearly jump out of my skin when my Prism alerts me to a message from Tate.

"Shit," I gasp, jumping to my feet, bag in hand. Anders glances at his watch and mutters a curse, quickly standing at my side.

"You can blame being late on me," he offers. I stare at him for a moment trying to figure out if he's joking or not. I can never tell. When the dimple appears, I roll my eyes playfully and start the trek back up the slope, my trash from lunch in hand.

Once we're both at the top, he challenges me. "Race you back to Taeolyn?"

I'm the runner, not him, so I don't hesitate to break into a sprint, giggling when I leave him behind. I glance back as I cross the threshold into the Executive Yard, slowing only for a moment, but he's right there, nearly knocking me over. His arms wrap around me, preventing me from colliding with the stones, pulling me back firmly against his chest. Our laughs fill the quiet, bouncing off the three dorm buildings.

"Sorry about that," he chuckles, his breath warm against my ear. My body tingles everywhere we are connected. I can't help but giggle as I step out of his arms, cheeks warming.

"Thanks." I regain my balance and head up the steps to Taeolyn. I'm going to be late. Anders walks me to the door of my History class, peeking inside with a satisfied grin when he realizes we made it just in time. With a quick wave, he heads off to his own class, leaving me feeling high from our lunch date.

I'm still thinking about his arms around me when I drop into my seat and find Kellan waiting for me. "Hey, RaeRae," he says with a grin. "Great news." I look up to see him approaching, completely distracted by my thoughts. "I get to go to Kliax with you. Your mother asked mine if you could take me along."

"Really?" I squeal, standing up and nearly knocking over my desk.

"Really." He hugs me tighter and then sets me back on my feet. "See you later," he says before disappearing from the classroom.

Professor Darci clears her throat as she approaches the door, and I quickly drop into my seat beside Aada and Tate. I pull my tablet out of my bag, only to realize it belongs to Anders. His background is a photo of him and Trysten after a game. They're both shirtless, covered in mud, and sporting huge grins on their faces.

I wish I could see him smile like that. What would it take? Sure, Anders has smiled at me, but it's never been genuine—not like this one.

"Why do you have Anders' tablet?" Tate whispers in my ear. "Or is that your new background?" I slam it face down a bit too hard, drawing the attention of a few students as I glare at Tate. I quickly swap out the tablets and open my History paper, submitting it to Professor Darci's box.

Tate gives me a playful shoulder bump and raises his brows in question. Ciara tilts her head on the other side of Tate, clearly curious, as she looks between the two of us.

"Um, I'm just holding it for him until Government." Tate narrows his eyes but then shrugs, letting it go. I settle back in my seat and take a much-needed sip of water.

"Today, we will be learning about the history of our magic," Professor Darci begins. I nearly choke on my water. This is exactly what Anders and I were just talking about. Tate pats me on the back as I try to regain my composure. The annoyed glares from my classmates return, and Professor Darci shoots me a disapproving look before continuing. "It may surprise you to learn that magic was once also gifted to commoners. After the veil went up, the gods only had enough power to grant it through the Lumos Bond."

I open the class notes on my tablet and read through the articles she has pulled from the archives. Some state that the old magic flowed freely and that most people had some form of magic. Although they don't explain how or why, they mention that because of magic, many of our colonies were built as they are today.

As Professor Darci starts discussing the architecture found throughout the system, I zone out, pulling open a notepad of questions I want answered. After class, I rush to Government, eager to see a certain prince, realizing that I'm the first one to arrive.

I sink into the cushioned seat at the round table and lean back, letting the sunlight streaming in through the glass exterior walls warm my skin. This is one of my favorite classrooms. The floor is made of frosted glass, and the rounded walls are also made of glass, half facing the forest outside and half looking into the dorm's interior from the second level.

There are more crescent-shaped tables for the other students around the room. Beyond Professor Zdravn's desk—he's the Government teacher for the nobility—hanging in boxes along the wall are several trees and plants.

The scent in this room reminds me of citrus, which brings to mind how Anders smells. I hear a chair roll next to me, and Anders slips into my field of vision. I inhale deeply, breathing in the sweet scent of the room mixed with his heady aroma, while ignoring the warmth I feel from his gaze. Aolyn and Professor Sukín walk in, discussing her brother wanting to break his Bond with his match and what that might mean for Ateria and Thirik if such a thing were possible.

I finally turn to find Anders still watching me. He has his arms crossed on the table before us, resting his head on them. I force myself to act unaffected as I return his tablet. He flashes me a brief smile of thanks.

For the next hour, we both are on our best behavior, pretending that the charged atmosphere between us doesn't exist, even as our every exchange feels loaded with unspoken words.

Without Cole here to lighten the mood with his usual banter, I find myself struggling to concentrate with Anders as my partner. We must collaborate on how to position our military if the veil were to rip along the borders of our kingdom.

My stomach sinks as I grapple with the reality that this could very well be our future. Each scenario feels impossible, accentuated by the knowledge that no matter what, people's lives will be lost. The clock ticks slowly, and by the end of class, I'm feeling restless.

I'm not sure who needs a break from the unbearable tension and heavy topic more: me or him.

nineteen

. . .

I DROP into the pilot seat before Anders can and grin. "I'm flying, you can be my co-pilot." He playfully scoffs but drops down into the seat beside me anyway. Internally, I do a little dance that I got my way. I thought for sure he'd attempt to pull rank on me.

"I trust you," he says, sliding on his headset. "But if you need help or have questions, please just ask." I nod and radio in for takeoff. When we get the all-clear, I launch us into space, my stomach fluttering with excitement.

We escape Baedyn's atmosphere only to be greeted with an unending blanket of black. Anders charts a path to Ista, noting it will only be an hour and a half using hyperjump. I engage the reactors and let the autopilot take over.

"So, Prince." I swing my chair to face him. "What are you looking forward to most after graduation? Becoming king? Bonding?" I attempt to keep a straight face. His chair swivels to match mine.

"I'm looking forward to being home and spending time with my sister. Clara is one of my best friends, and I miss her." I roll my eyes.

"Okay, well...that was just sweet." He chuckles. "What else, besides being the best big brother?" He's contemplative for a while as I let my gaze settle on our tracker. We're speeding past Okenen. With hyperjump, the planets and suns are nothing more than a flash of light in the endless emptiness.

"Nobody has ever asked me that." He swipes a hand through his hair. "I don't feel ready to be king, and definitely don't feel ready to be someone's husband." His gaze bores into the side of my face. "You may not believe me, but I'd like my choice of bride."

I swallow thickly, ignoring his gaze. "I heard your friends, Sienna and Gunnar, talking one day. She'd pick you."

He snorts, pulling my attention to him as he drags his palms down his face. "Ignore her. I do. She's nothing more than a flirt who's working every angle hoping to put herself at some advantage. She's just like her mother. She craves power." I hum in response, fiddling with the hem of my shirt.

"And who would you pick?" I swallow the weird lump in my throat. "If you could, that is." *Why the hell did I just ask that?*

"Soraea," he says too gently. "Look at me."

I look up, meeting his gaze. "Why are you asking? Do you want the truth?"

I bite my lip, ignoring the way my chest tightens uncomfortably. The sting of tears pricks my eyes, sharp and unwarranted. *Why am I about to cry over this? The truth. The truth from him. It could change every-thing. It could break me.*

I shake my head. "No," I whisper. "Never mind. Don't tell me."

His features soften, a flicker of something unreadable—disappoint-ment? understanding?—crossing his face. He doesn't push. Instead, he shifts the subject, asking about my upcoming break, my family's trip to Kliax. I try to listen, to respond, but his gaze, though no longer direct, feels like a physical weight, a warmth lingering on my cheek where his breath had almost kissed me.

Even as we talk about FinSurfing and bioluminescent beaches, a potent current still hums between us, a silent language we both understand but refuse to speak. The casual facade we try to adopt feels thin, stretched taut. By the time we arrive at the temple, the surface of our conversation is smooth, but the undercurrent is a raging torrent of unspoken words and simmering desire.

The familiar, shimmering glass of the system's largest temple comes into view as I lower us onto the visitors' launchpad. Anders insisted we didn't tell anyone aside from Professor Ainslyn, as we'd both be missing combat, and the Chancellor. Neither seemed to ask questions; maybe they didn't want to know, or perhaps they trust us enough. Either way, we're alone, without our guards, and without anyone's knowledge, we're here.

If we had alerted King Hunter and Queen Isobel that we were coming, there would have been considerable fanfare, guards, and all the other things. We need to slip in and out before anyone notices. I tap my energy shield on, watching him do the same as he pulls my cloak over my disguised hair. We're both dressed in all black, unassuming clothing, with black cloaks. When we step out into the wind, Anders tugs me close, wrapping a hand around my billowing cloak and shielding me with his body.

Inside the temple, it is quiet today, with only a few prayerful visitors moving between different stations to offer prayers to both Astor and Calia, as well as their parents, the Primordials. This is the only temple I know of that has offering tables for them.

We make our way across the rich wine-colored marble floors, illuminated with an orange glow from the thousands of sconces. The glass building allows for ample natural light. However, due to the constant cloud cover, the need for artificial lighting still persists. We pass patrons murmuring their prayers, and find an information screen along the back wall.

Anders moves quickly, pulling up a map and the history of how the new temple was built. Looking over the maps again, he nods silently, urging me to go through the door on my right. We find ourselves alone in a long hallway with only a few doors labeled storage, candles, and holograms.

We slip into the last door, labeled archives. The door, thankfully, is unlocked. We begin our search. He takes the far side of the room, while I stay close to the shelving of books near the door. I run my fingers over the new leather-bound books, knowing that what we're looking for is much older. When I find nothing, I groan. Anders does the same, running a hand through his hair.

"Well, shit," he mutters. "There has to be somewhere else—" His voice drifts off as the hair on my neck stands with a prickling sensation. An eerie "I'm here" is like a whisper on an invisible wind. I turn, focusing, and he falls silent. Another call to me pulls me out of the door.

On the other side, we're met with another long hall, this one illuminated with bright white walls and offices. I nearly collide with him when I back up. "Keep your hood up, but walk to the end of the hall. Act like we belong here." I'm about to tell him about the voice when a door to our left opens up, and two men exit, lost in conversation.

We both turn, walking quickly but not quickly enough to catch attention. I'm just thankful it's normal to be found in cloaks here.

Anders holds me back a moment, looking both ways. For some reason, he doesn't question me. He just lets me lead, following, staying close. I follow the sound, like it's drifting and leading me down the hall, then another, and another. I've lost my surroundings, but I keep going. The last turn we take leads us to an old hallway that appears to have been unused for years.

A door sits alone in the old stonework. The voice drifts behind it, disappearing. With a shaky voice, I say, "I think—I think it's through here." He studies me a moment before nodding. Without questioning, he tries the handle. When it doesn't budge, he looks around just before his hand connects—hard, breaking the handle and lock off completely. My mouth falls open as I stare at him.

"I'll leave a donation to fix it," is all he says. I don't bother asking before the door swings open, revealing stone steps that descend into the dark. Anders urges me forward, and the clang of the heavy door behind us swallows the last flicker of light, plunging us into absolute, suffocating darkness. It presses in, thick and cold, stealing the air from my lungs.

My hands instinctively fly out, hitting rough, damp stone, while my breath comes in ragged gasps. Despite the unending darkness, my vision swims.

My fingers continue to scrape along the wall as I take a step. The only sound down here is the sound of the rushing noise of my blood pumping through me, and the thump of my heart that feels like it's attempting to escape my chest. A sharp breath comes out just before I ask, "Is this a bad time to tell you I don't like dark, enclosed spaces?" Instantly, his hands find mine. They're warm and steady, and despite the energy that exchanges between us, I feel my heart begin to slow, my breath becoming even.

"Breathe with me." His voice is no more than a whisper against my cheek. He inhales for a few seconds and then out for a few. I follow him, letting him guide me. We do this a few times, and after a while, I stand straight. "I'm here. I won't let anything happen to you."

I sense his gaze on me, steady and unwavering, as if the darkness doesn't exist for him. Maybe it doesn't. He's not normal. I know it in my bones. He leads me down and down uneven, slick steps, the passage feeling as if it narrows with every step. He keeps hold of my hand, whispering if there's a big step or a short one, his soft words echoing off stone walls.

We keep descending, further and further, the air growing heavier, colder, and damper. It gets so cold that I can almost see the cloud of my breath in front of me. We keep going, though.

Down. Down. Down.

When he tells me there's a turn in the steps, I notice that the air is somehow thinner, tasting of ancient dust and forgotten stone. We continue then in silence for another few minutes.

"I can see the bottom." His voice echoes off the stone. "Almost there." The cold down here seeps into my bones with a creeping chill that echoes my mounting panic. We're so far down, and nobody knows we're here. As if knowing where my thoughts have gone, he says, "You're safe with me. I'm here. I won't let anything happen." Panic claws at my throat, threatening to choke me. My other hand flies to his arm, gripping it with white-knuckled desperation. His fingers, which are still interlaced with my other hand, tighten, solid and warm, a lifeline.

"I'm here,'" he murmurs, his voice a low thrum against the suffocating silence. "Always." He tugs, pulling me against his solid warmth, wrapping an arm around me. I nod, squeezing him, breathing through my nose, out through my mouth, just like I was taught. "Good girl," he whispers, running a hand over the back of my cloak. "You're doing well."

When we finally reach the last step, Anders pulls an old sconce from the wall, using a lighter he has stored in his pocket to light the flame. I don't even bother asking as my jaw drops.

Walls of impossibly smooth, jet-black obsidian rise around us, scarred with ancient, glowing carvings that pulse faintly, like a sleeping heartbeat. The ceiling soars, lost in shadows. The floor, an expanse of polished, dark marble, reflects the torchlight like still water, broken only by a single, massive carving at its center.

A monolithic altar of dark, unpolished stone dominates the chamber's heart, stained with time, bearing faint, faded etchings of symbols I don't recognize, yet feel hauntingly familiar. Colossal statues, easily double Anders' height, tower around the edges. They depict figures with elongated limbs and eyes carved from luminous crystal, their expressions serene yet unnerving. The air here is heavy with the scent of forgotten magic, buzzing faintly against my skin.

I don't know what I expected to find, but my breath hitches. This is more than something. This is *everything*.

"There," Anders murmurs, pointing to a hidden door on the far wall, almost invisible against the obsidian. He holds the torch in his right hand, my hand clutched in his left. When we push it open, a cloud of ancient, stale air washes over us. I nearly sob with relief, not just from escaping the cold, but from the sight before us. There's a long room filled with dusty shelves that looks abandoned and hasn't been touched for half a century since the new temple was constructed. Candles, dishes, cleaning supplies... We continue along the wall, Anders sticking to my side.

I swipe my finger over one of the wooden shelves, and it comes away with a thick coating of dust. We find another section of vases and altar cloths, and then beside it, a massive painting of the gods. It looks old, the paint peeling from the canvas. I sigh and turn to him.

"Nothing." He steps closer, as I step back. There's that same look in his eye that makes me want to surge up onto my toes and lay claim to his mouth. Another step back makes my shoulders connect with the painting, and it shifts. The way he's looking at me makes my mouth water, but then a breeze hits the back of my neck.

I turn, just as he says, "It's a passage." My head swings back to him, then to the wooden door just behind the painting. Behind it, I can feel a strong pulse of energy, just like I do on all the planets—yet it feels more concentrated.

I inhale sharply. "Anders, I feel—"

"Yeah. Me too." He's at my side in an instant, removing the painting from the wall. The thing has to be heavy; it's at least twelve feet tall, and the frame is pure oak. He doesn't even grunt or break a sweat.

My gaze falls back to the handle, which is a small iron ring. I notice the slight tremble of my hand as I reach for it, the flow of energy getting stronger. I lift the ring, turning it slightly, and the door pops open with a rush of dusty air and an eerie howl.

Anders and I both cough, waving away the dust, and when it clears, I can't fight the grin that spreads across my face. Inside the doorway is a vast, circular room, its walls lined floor-to-ceiling with row upon row of dusty, ancient shelves. This isn't a storage closet. This is an archive. I spin, taking in the room. There are so many books. Books, books, and more books. And then tubes of scrolls. I huff out a laugh and turn to Anders.

"Is it wrong to say I want to take them all home?" He shakes his head.

"They have to stay, but we have the whole day if we need it."

Hours and more than half the books later, I sit back on a wobbly stool and sigh. So far, we've found lineage books, writing in languages even Anders hasn't seen, books on medicines and weather patterns, temple practices, priestess accounts, a journal, and a log of visitors. I give up on the books and search through the tubes of scrolls. Some are standing upright, while others are on their sides. I begin pulling them out, feeling a little overwhelmed by how many there are, but when I find a mysterious-looking one wrapped in some sort of casing, Anders is immediately at my side.

I pause, looking around, half expecting soldiers to come rushing in. "What?"

He studies the scroll in my hands before reaching for it. "May I?" he asks. I nod and hand it over. He returns to the desk we've been huddled over at the center of the room and clears a space to unroll it. My breath lodges in my throat, and my head spins when the parchment begins to unravel, revealing an old text. But it's the way a wind sweeps through the room—completely unnatural and impossible— that has me stepping closer to Anders.

Anders runs his fingers over the text with pure awe. "I can read this," he claims, his voice rough with disbelief. "Raea, listen."

I step closer, studying the weird markings etched into the leather. The words he reads are not in the common language; they're ancient, breathy, and make the hairs on my arms stand, and at the same time, feel a weight settle in my bones. As he reads, my body tingles, like my blood has been replaced with bubbly water. My shoulders roll uncomfortably before the words transition, filling my mind with understanding. I hear them, understand them, not in the way I'd expect—but directly in my head. They start bleeding into my mind, bypassing sense. They settle in the hollow of me like a truth I never asked for.

"The veil was insufficiently empowered, prompting each family to take action as time diminished. Males and females, alongside their children, voluntarily relinquished their lifeforce to enhance the veil, thereby sacrificing their immortal existence to ensure the continuity of their bloodlines. The youth aged rapidly, with some disintegrating entirely, transitioning instantaneously into the aether. All participants offered their contributions willingly."

Anders' voice trails off, the last word hanging heavy in the cold air of the chamber. A strange nausea slams into me, forcing my head to hang, my mouth watering. It feels as if I've just taken a blow to the stomach. I muffle a cry as my stomach grips tighter.

He keeps reading, "Upon the departure of the last immortals, the gods entered the veil, forfeiting their own mortality and corporeal forms, thus leaving humanity as the sole representatives of the three councils."

Anders makes a low sound next to me, a sound of staggered surprise. He grips his head. "The empire remained the last of its kind within the system, as all trade and travel to Auralan had ceased..."

The words keep coming. I can't breathe.

"When the moment arrived for the transition into individual kingdoms, the emperor entered the veil, uniting with his family in the aether. Consequently, Einvald would be sealed, safeguarding everything that remained..."

I choke on a breath. My vision narrows.

"Only the heirs of the restored lifeblood may return to this realm once more."

Silence.

The words fade. But the weight of them doesn't. I gasp, bent at the waist, eyes stinging with tears I don't remember forming.

Anders groans, grabbing his head, fighting something as he leans over the table. The knowledge burns into me, a profound hum deep in my core. Seconds pass, but it feels like an eternity.

When the nausea subsides, all traces of pain vanish. I remain panting over the scroll, trying to regain myself. Anders' hand runs up my spine. "You okay?" he asks, breathless.

I nod, my mouth still watering, but I stand to look at him, scrubbing at my eyes. All around me, in me, under me, life and power exist. I see an invisible power like lines drifting out of the room. When I glance back at the scroll, an invisible current hums through my veins.

"Anders!" My hands tremble against the cool table. "I can read it." *Elvisiah*—I feel the words more than hear them.

He studies me, then the scroll, still rubbing at his temples. "Your magic." His eyes go wide. "Your aura, it's...different." My face scrunches as I look him over; he doesn't look well. His typically tanned skin now appears pale.

"What's wrong?" He shakes his head, taking a seat and breathing deeply. After a moment, he opens his eyes, scanning the room. I've never seen him look so unnerved before.

"Can you hear it?" he asks, his voice tight. "The hum. It's...the veil. It's screaming." He stands, walking to the wall behind me, where several old artifacts lie scattered. I've already looked them over and found nothing of importance.

"A book on the gods..." He pulls an old tome from the very bottom shelf, its cover old and tattered, with a deep hole in the center. "Grab this." He holds out the book.

I rush to his side, grabbing the hefty tome and set it on the table beside the scroll. I still can't believe I can read the scroll, and now I want to check every book here. The book's cover is soft, dark green leather, and around the edge of the hole, tarnished bronze vines and a tree stump design wind around the hole at the center.

Behind me, he's searching shelves again, then moves out to the other room, searching the shelves full of artifacts. I hear clanking and shuffling, my mind spinning, then he's coming back through the door with hurried steps, holding what looks like an oval paperweight. It's a milk-white disk. I almost ask how he knows it belongs, but when he places the disc into the hole, the book transforms.

The disc glows with a vibrant blue and sinks, settling into place as the edges close the gaps, holding it in place. The disk illuminates, as if looking through a window, to another place, another time. There's a sky with a different set of moons, but it's the radiant trees glowing to the left that tell me this place isn't in our system. The locks on the book I hadn't noticed before spring open with a click. My heart races as Anders turns to me.

"Are you sure you want the answers? Because I'm positive we're about to get a lot more than we asked for." I nod, even though deep down, I don't know.

208

twenty

. . .

THE BOOK FLIES open of its own accord, pages flipping until it settles. Lines of gold script ripple into being. The letters shift and pulse, as though alive, before resolving into readable form. Gold ink shimmers across the pages, forming words I shouldn't understand— but somehow do. Unease continues to prickle at my skin. This book— it shouldn't exist.

Anders reads the illuminated passage. "The Fae were born of sky and storm. The Elven, of root and stars. Their magic flows not through will but memory. They do not cast. They become. Their souls remember the world's first name."

A chill rips through me. I look at Anders. "What does that mean?"

He shakes his head slowly. "I don't know. But it's beautiful."

The page flips, of its own accord, to a new section. "The Codex of Origin," Anders murmurs, reading the title. Below it, a picture: five sibling gods, and beneath them, three distinct groups of people. He scans the text, then the image.

"Before the councils were formed, before the gods rose from the breath of the Primordials, there was harmony in separation. The Elven remembered the roots of the world, and the Fae sang to the sky's first winds. The humans—newer, more fleeting—were born of will and fire. Their potential drew the gaze of the divine."

My gaze drops to the image. The first council: the Elven. Tall, beautiful beings with pointed ears and eyes of wisdom. The second council: the Fae. Similar to the Elven, but harder, more cunning. The third: the humans. We are silent as we study the image, something stirring in me, a deep hum that feels both ancient and utterly new. It pulses behind my ribs, a strange ache of recognition for a memory I don't possess.

After a few silent minutes, the pages flip of their own accord, like the book wants us to read specific passages. Anders shakes his head. I clutch his side, not amazed but scared. He reads the new illuminated passage:

"Astor and Calia, firstborn of the Primordials, forged the veil with their immortal councils, sealing what could not be destroyed. Kane and Ravana, their middle siblings, hungered for what was never theirs. Jealousy burned them hollow. Rage gave them shape. In shadow, they wait. Though they were not the first heirs to the Primordials, ancient gods whose names are lost to mortal tongues, they pursued the dark, ignoring the commands of their creators. For from their breath came sky, sea, and flame. Their children shaped their own worlds, but even the gods fear what they cannot control. For darkness awaits until the time of the two to unlock and make anew. The veil holds. But not forever."

"They had parents." I already knew that, but my head spins with knowledge. "The gods...are born?"

Anders stands, pacing. "Which means they can die. And be replaced."

Something in the chamber shifts. Anders flips a few pages.

"From the Primordials came five: Astor and Calia, bearers of light and time, knowledge and creativity, and Kane and Ravana, shadow-born twins, seeded with unrest. They were not evil by nature but unruly, insatiable, bound by no law but their own will. They sought to undo the veil of life and death, to lift the chains of mortality from themselves and others. What they created instead was corruption:

twisted immortality, a hunger that devoured time and memory alike. The youngest, Caelus, the most contemplative, always watching, always learning."

A gust of cold air curls into the chamber. Another page flips. The light from the disc dims, turning bluish-white.

"When the two awaken, the veil will stir. The gods will whisper again. Seek the place where roots meet sky. There, the first song may be heard once more. And in song, remembrance. In remembrance, power. But beware: not all who remain in shadow have forgotten their hunger."

The light dims. The book closes with a soft, final click.

Anders exhales, running a hand through his hair; his earlier paleness has been replaced by a subtle flush of exertion. "This isn't mythology."

"No," I whisper. "It's a warning." The air feels heavier now. The disc still pulses, like it's waiting for someone to ask the next question.

"Raea, I think we need to go before our magic shifts again." He's right. I feel something coiled inside me, not a voice exactly, but something older. A presence. A pressure. Something waiting.

My knees feel shaky. "Okay, just for now."

Anders nods. "We'll come back."

"But we can't just leave this here. What if we don't make it back?" He reaches for the book, tucking it carefully into his bag. "And a few of the scrolls, too. Just in case." He rolls his eyes, but shoves those in as well.

I don't know what we've stepped into. I only know this: nothing is the same anymore. Not in this room. Not in me. And I'm not sure if I'm terrified...or ready.

And I swear—for just one breathless second—I hear a voice behind the veil. Low. Cold. Whispering my name.

I don't know who I am anymore. But I think something else does.

And it's waking up.

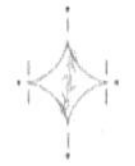

"I'm so freaking excited," Ciara shrieks as she throws her arm around me as we make our way to my transport the next day. She, Kellan, and a few other students are taking the palace transport back to Kyrr before dispersing to their planets.

Ciara's parents have agreed to let her and Tate head to Brov, to the Fountains, where there will be a three-day celebration for the holiday. It's really one big party with lots of dancing, drinking, and bands from around the system coming to play.

During the day, vendors and shops sell paraphernalia featuring pictures of the gods, often printed or engraved on items. There are even parades and pop-up temples for offerings.

"It's going to be so dope. Sorry you can't come," Tate teases from my other side. I give him a dramatic eye roll because we've been over this. I have zero desire to be in that kind of environment—it's like my own personal brand of torture.

"We're going to have so much more fun than you," Kellan claims. I look over at him beyond Ciara and smile. His brown hair flops over his forehead as he offers me a knowing look. He is like me; we would both rather be alone, holed up with books or exploring a forest or swimming, than surrounded by a bunch of strangers.

Our bags are loaded, and the other students coming with us file onto the transport ahead of us. They all offer their thanks as they find their seats in the common space.

"You are going to tell us what happened on your trip, right?" Ciara asks, changing the subject. I'm grateful for the distraction before Kellan starts throwing longing looks my way, and I have to come up with an excuse as to why it's starting to feel suffocating. I never thought I'd find myself attracted to two very different men.

"We need all the deets...was it steamy?" Tate asks around a mouthful of water just before he chokes, spewing the liquid everywhere. Kellan slaps him on the back while Ciara and I just laugh.

"Serves you right," I tease.

"Raea," Anders yells breathlessly from behind me just as we get to the ramp. I look back to find him running across the launch pad from where his transport is. Cole is being helped up the steps by two healers. He looks a lot better, but they said it would be another week before his strength returns.

My friends all pause at the base of the ramp and look at me questioningly. I tell them I'll meet them up there, and Anders and I wait until they're inside and out of earshot. I'm still shaken up about what we found.

We ended up sneaking out whatever we could carry. I feel a little guilty about it, but we couldn't just leave them there. When we got back to the transport, the tower grounded us without providing any information. It was Anders who told me he could feel the veil acting up again.

With nothing to do but wait, we studied more of the books and scrolls, and when my body was flushed with unexplained heat again, he promised to help me search for answers. We were stuck on the launch pad for five hours. It was late by the time we got back to school.

We both agreed that for now, they'll stay locked up in his room here at school, and when we get back from break, we're going to spend more time going over them. He was right down in that chamber —the knowledge has changed our lives, and now I can't look back. It's like my eyes have been opened, and I'm still not sure how I can pretend. But I have to. We agreed. People would kill for that information, and I'm not sure even a crown could protect us.

"I just wanted to say have a good break," he says, swiping a hand through his hair nervously, the movement lifting his shirt and baring a sliver of tanned flesh above his waistband. "Kliax should be amazing this time of year. There's FinSurfing too if you want something else to do. Or there's an aquarium on the main island. Or the Bubble Village is always fun to walk through." He's stalling even though he's been at my side for the majority of today, finding excuses to see me between classes.

I dip my chin and hide my smile. He's kinda cute like this.

"Thank you," I reply. "I hope you have a good break too. I hope you can get out of the palace. The invite still stands if you want to join us in Kliax. Maybe you can show me the Bubble Village." He smiles, like really smiles with his dimple and everything, and I'm knocked breathless. Gods, he's got an amazing smile. We hold each other's gaze for long moments until I remember that I'm holding everyone up.

"Well," I clear my throat and hold out my hand like an idiot. Am I really going to shake his hand? Anders glances down at it and then snorts.

"A handshake, really?" he drawls. And his cockiness is back. I roll my eyes and pull my hand back with a shrug.

"Guess not. See ya later," I say, and turn with a smirk. His hand yanks me back until I find myself stumbling into his chest. I'm a little reluctant to admit this is exactly where I want to be. My hands slide up his chest, my right settling over his heart, feeling the erratic beat beneath.

He just tsks and bends down, his mouth hovering over my ear as he whispers, "Feel free to miss me, Princess." I don't know what I expected him to say, but that wasn't it. My whole body shakes with laughter.

I pat him on the chest, not bothering to admit that I will, and turn up the ramp, refusing to look back even though I know he's watching me. The ramp begins to lift as I reach the top. Once the doors are closed, I fall back against them with a smile, my heart doing some sort of flip routine, and for the life of me, I can't figure out why I'm so high from that interaction.

The pilot announces we are cleared for takeoff, and I feel the engines turn on as I make my way up the stairs to the royal family suite, where my friends are waiting. They already have drinks in hand when I get there, and I drop into one of the sofas as we lift off.

twenty-one

. . .

I WALK BESIDE MY PARENTS, surrounded by the royal guards, the
Regils, on all sides. Their pristine white uniforms, adorned with intricate silver trim and polished silver breastplates, stand out among the
shades of deep, rich purples and brilliant golds worn by those gathered here to pay homage.

Ahead, the temple towers majestically over everything on the edge
of the capital city, and the sense of reverence and anticipation feels
like a buzz against my skin. People from every corner of our kingdom
have converged on Kyrr's capital city to offer prayers and express gratitude for the divine protection that Astor and Calia have bestowed
upon us. This gathering marks the commencement of a week-long
festival filled with feasting, music, and celebration.

The temple's ornate stone doors, traditionally sealed to the public
for the year, will open to the public today, allowing the faithful to
enter the sacred chamber that houses an altar for prayers and
offerings.

Although I've never felt particularly drawn to the temple's prayer
room, whenever I step inside, I'm enveloped by an overwhelming
sense of rightness. I often ponder what it would have been like to walk
alongside the gods, to converse with them, and learn from them.

As we make our way through the crowd, the sea of faces erupts in cheers, their voices blending into a symphony of excitement. Hands stretch out, reaching for my parents as we pass, seeking just a moment, or a single touch of their beloved rulers.

As I look out among the masses roped off on either side of us, the crowd is clothed in robes of shimmering golds, each intricately embroidered with various designs. Calia was beautiful, and her mind and creativity, even more so. Without her vision, who knows what our planets would look like? Would our economy and kingdoms thrive if she hadn't created them as they are? It's said that she meticulously designed every planet and moon, breathing her very essence into them. Among the gold are robes and tunics of deep indigo, a tribute to Astor, the god of wisdom and knowledge.

As we near the temple, I take in its beauty. The temple is shrouded in moss and vines, as though nature has claimed it as its own, despite its location in the city. I can hardly see the ivory sandstone beneath the lush greenery. Two intricate columns stand guard on either side of the grand arched entrance. They reach skyward, supporting the domed roof that appears to be draped in similar layers of green flora.

The frenzied energy of the crowd calling out for my parents and the chatter crescendos to a deafening level as we approach the temple, where a large podium has been set up for my father's speech. Kuron guides me up the wide stone steps, Ezra directly behind me, as we find a place behind my parents. My heart beats in rhythm to the excited crowd, and the smile on my face is not forced, but genuine. I love our people, and seeing them happy and celebrating together brings a warmth to my chest I'm not familiar with.

Growing up, knowing I would one day be responsible for trillions of lives was just a task for me. However, as I grow older and approach the age of maturity, the enormity of this role resonates more deeply within my soul. I have become increasingly aware of the significance of my duty and the true value of each individual's life. Their status, occupations, skin colors, and titles all fade into irrelevance—not that each shouldn't be celebrated, but because they're *all* my people to protect. The gravity of my future title hangs heavy on my shoulders.

Aside from my temple trips twice a year, I hardly ever visit the capital city. I've always found it a little overwhelming. I never know where to settle my eyes. Should I look at the towering stone buildings, the holographic signs, and advertisements? Or maybe the crowds always walking to work or out to run their errands?

Though our palace is only a thirty-minute flight from here, it's a world away. The palace island is peaceful and quiet, suspended above and surrounded by waterfalls and forests below. It's definitely a stark contrast to the hundreds of thousands gathered here. Standing here now, with our people gathered before us, I find myself longing to come more often.

"Thank you, citizens of Treon," my father starts, the crowd growing silent as his voice echoes off the tall buildings. "Today, we celebrate the nine hundred and ninety-ninth year of the protection given to us by Astor and Calia. We have gathered here to give thanks and offerings as we conclude the celebrations here in the capital on Origin Day."

The sun beats down on us from above in the light blue, cloudless sky, wrapping me in a heat that feels almost suffocating. My outfit doesn't help. My gown is an exquisite creation of indigo silk that cascades in sumptuous layers, each fold intricately designed to catch the light. The golden trains drape elegantly from my shoulders. My designer outdid herself yet again.

My diadem, a circlet of delicate jewels and metalwork, rests atop my head. It feels oddly foreign and somewhat uncomfortable, only made worse by the fact that I've been away at school.

Having been briefed on the day's movements and the sacred rituals we are to partake in, a sense of anticipation thrums within me. It won't be long before we are ushered into the temple, where we will present our offerings to the gods, honoring the traditions of genera-tions of royals who have come before us. I slide my hand into the pocket of my dress, finding that my offering is still there.

"I first want to quote our dear goddess, Calia, if I may." My father clears his throat before continuing. "It is with unfailing love that we must take our leave from you, but with our departure, our hope is that many generations shall live on until the end of the age. May you never stop dreaming, and may you always see the good in those around you. Remember to love your differences and uniqueness, and know that together, you are stronger."

My mother bows her head, bringing her fingertips to her forehead, to the statue of Calia that stands stoically to the left of our group. As my mother does this, the crowd follows suit, solemnity passing through those gathered in a moment of respect.

Meanwhile, my father's voice resonates through the square, commanding attention as he continues his speech. He highlights Astor's profound knowledge and emphasizes our commitment to protecting our kingdom. He speaks of our family's promise for a better future as we endeavor to learn from our people and meet their needs.

"Citizens, let us put aside our differences and embrace the beauty of our neighbors and all that they are. Let this new year be a fresh start as we aim to be more compassionate and loving." My father's arm stretches out, embracing my mother in a side hug.

"And we hope the celebrations this week have filled your hearts and minds. We wish you all safe travels home." The crowd erupts in joyful cheers as launchers fill the air with sparkling confetti that falls over the crowd. Music starts up just as the Regils guide us into the temple.

The carved temple doors open, exposing the dark interior, while a cool breeze flows out, carrying the faint scent of incense and age-old stone. A long, tiled walkway stretches before us, flanked by towering columns that rise like sentinels to the gilded dome above us.

At the base of each column, a single flame flickers in a bowl, casting a warm glow that dances over the intricate carvings of Astor and Calia's life. The soft candlelight adds to the ethereal ambiance. Each step we take echoes softly, disrupting the stillness as we progress toward the altar.

Standing on either side of the wine-colored marble altar adorned with golden bowls and candles, soft-white holograms of Astor and Calia open their arms in a welcoming greeting. A resounding thud reverberates through the air as the heavy doors seal shut behind us, muffling the sound of the crowd and plunging us into a realm of reverence.

My thoughts return to the temple in Ista, but I push them away. I can't think about it right now—especially not here. There's no secret chamber here hiding more artifacts and ancient texts. I know because I've been given a tour by the head priestess herself.

My parents take the lead, kneeling before the altar, and I follow suit, feeling the cool, dark, polished marble graze my knee. Something similar to a hum resonates through my core—a sensation so powerful that I almost gasp. It's as if the very essence of the temple itself is drawing me in. And maybe it is. I don't know anymore.

Warmth washes over me, accompanied by an unexplainable tingling sensation that spreads through my whole body, blurring the line between past and present. It isn't until the priestess glides through a doorway to my left, her flowing white robes sweeping softly across the ground, that I regain my focus. She stands before us, her face set in a serene expression as she closes her eyes and begins to chant her prayers. Her voice is a beautiful melody that weaves through the space and wraps around me.

With her arms outstretched above, her melody lifts like a spring breeze as she thanks the gods for their martyrdom and unwavering protection. I find myself caught between the ethereal melody and the vibrant energy enveloping me, feeling as if I am levitating behind my parents instead of kneeling on the hard marble.

The song shifts seamlessly from the common tongue to an ancient dialect I feel like I've heard whispered before. *Elvisiah.* Though the words are unknown to me—I can read them, but not speak them— they bring forth something within my soul. Tears cascade down my cheeks as I sink further into the unfamiliar words.

Suddenly, visions explode in my mind—a clash of ethereal light and cold, empty darkness sweeps through me, followed by a sensation of being ripped in two. The feeling is washed away by a warmth and love, knitting me back together. Once again, I'm a baby cradled in my mother's arms, her gaze filled with hope and a love so deep my chest feels like it might crack open from the intensity.

Images flash by with dizzying speed. I see my young self asleep in a dimly lit room, cocooned in warmth by another child asleep beside me, whose face remains obscured by shadows. Around us, a shield of familiar iridescent colors swirls with a blinding white light that resembles pure starlight, embodying the very essence of the melody, as if the colors are dancing in harmony with the priestess' song. More memories, each confusing and cloaked in shadow, but I feel the love—the safety of those moments.

As the last notes resonate, I'm jolted back to the present. I find myself hunched over on all fours, my hands pressing against the cool, glowing marble as tears splash onto its reflective surface. An ancient voice, neither male nor female, rich in wisdom and filled with the echoes of creation, pierces my mind as the rest of the world falls away once again.

"Daughter of the Forest. Harbinger of light. Gift of the forgotten line and balancer of evil. The time draws near when the barrier is shattered, and the scales tilted. Embrace the truth, and all will be revealed." My skin prickles as the voice fades, and I'm back beside my parents.

What the heck just happened?

I gasp, hastily wiping my eyes, and rise to see my mother and father placing a radiant emerald jewel on the altar, completely unaware of me. The priestess's emotionless gaze is directed solely at me, though. The solid gold circlet on her brow glimmers in the flickering candlelight. Her dark eyes seem to delve deep into my soul, and the weight of her gaze sends a cold shiver down my spine. Does she know the visions summoned by her song? Was it the gods? Does she know the truth? Is she even human?

I wipe my eyes once more, summoning my composure as I approach the altar. My skirts swish around me as I place a golden necklace with a rare diamond into the offering bowl.

"May *your* truth be revealed, and the gift of offspring come swiftly," the priestess intones, her voice unnervingly clear as if speaking into my mind. I blink, and she vanishes through a door, leaving me reeling in her wake.

"Are you okay?" my mother asks, startling me as she wraps an arm around me in a comforting embrace. The guards step forward to make their own offerings as I nod, sinking further into her, attempting to shake off the weight of the last few minutes and quiet all the questions now swirling in my mind.

For the next several hours, our entourage explores the marketplace, adorned with delicate ribbons and illuminated buildings. Many of the shopkeepers and citizens wait patiently, offering heartfelt conversations and gratitude. Only one citizen makes a snide remark about the ostentatious celebration disrupting his sales. As the sun begins to set, we are ushered into a pod, returning to the glowing palace islands still shrouded in buttery, golden sunlight and puffy white clouds.

When the shimmering, glass-and-stone palace comes into view, I feel the weight from all that transpired in the temple melt away. There will be time to grapple with the experience later, but for now, I want nothing more than to focus on our trip to Kliax tomorrow.

"Oh my gods, that was fun!" I giggle, throwing my arms, still dusted with salt and sand, around Kellan and pulling him in for a hug. He grins, wrapping his arm around my waist before we turn to find my parents walking out from the water where we just finished part one of our dive. Tomorrow, we'll take a boat out and dive around a small cluster of islands.

My mother's long, rich brown hair is braided and soaked, but she looks radiant. This vacation has brought out a light in her that I haven't seen for a while. The way my father gazes at her, his face breaking into an endearing grin, makes my heart swell with emotion and longing. I can't help but wish for a love as deep as theirs.

Behind them, the crystalline water is so clear you can see straight to the white sandy bottom. Swimming alongside the rays was an unforgettable experience I'll not soon forget. Their glass-like bodies glided through the water, brushing softly against our skin with a surprising chill that contrasted with the warmth of the water. Their oversized eyes gave them an aura of cute and cuddly, while the gentle pulsing of their bioluminescence cast a soft light around us.

"Hey kiddos, let's head back to our rooms and change," my father calls out, breaking my reverie. "Once we freshen up, we can grab some lunch before we head out on the boat." After lunch, we plan to explore the coast. We all agree as the four of us walk the sandy shore back to the resort.

As we approach the entrance to the resort, I take it all in. It's a luxurious haven reserved for royals and dignitaries, its pristine beaches surrounded by guards, and I can't help but feel a sense of enchantment. This place feels like a dream, and with my family, it almost feels perfect.

The long, winding pier, which houses over-the-water bungalows the size of small homes, comes into view. The bungalows are spaced out, allowing for privacy on the decks and the outdoor soaking tubs. The guards bow at our appearance before letting us through the azure iron gates displaying the Okenen crest in shimmering silver.

The boards clack beneath our feet as we recount our dive and the amazing sea life we encountered. Seeing my mother beam with joy has made the whole trip worthwhile. As we near the first row of rooms, Kellan waves to us before breaking off to the right to take the section of the boardwalk that leads to his designated bungalow.

My parents are staying in the largest of the rooms at the end of the pier, so I leave them, taking the winding path on the left. The resort houses twenty-one bungalows, three per kingdom, but not all seven kingdoms have ever stayed here at once. In fact, no more than two of the royal households ever travel to the same location unless it is for the yearly summit or a mandatory meeting.

Once upon a time, the Astral Council was made up of the seven kingdoms. Before they were kings, they were representatives of their districts and council members of the empire. Back then, it was common for the seven households to travel together, and they often stayed on Einvald, one of Sgya's three moons, though now it's nothing more than myths and whispers. It was there that the Imperial family lived and ruled.

After the demise of the last Imperial family, powerful magic surrounded the moon, sealing it off from everyone. The moon now sits alongside the planet of the gods, a ghost of what it once was. The ancient halls are now most likely buried in a thick layer of dust. Sad, really. I've seen the sketches of the beautiful palace.

As a young girl, I would find myself lost in daydreams, imagining what it would be like to roam the halls and ancient corridors of the Unending Palace, or Ael'drien, as it's called. I used to imagine grand halls adorned with intricate and beautiful tapestries, rooms gilded with finery and draped in lush linens, and gardens that stretched as far as the eye could see. What wonders might still linger in the throne room or tucked away in the vaults? A longing still lingers within me to see them for myself.

I find my room at the end of the pier and push open the large wooden door. My open-air bungalow consists of two bedrooms, one at each end, with a living space at the center, a small kitchen, and a soaking tub that overlooks the water. The back wall is entirely open to the elements and the glittering cerulean water.

Off the main living space, an outdoor seating area features a few steps leading down to a platform hovering over the water, adorned with low, comfortable seating, an umbrella, and lanterns that glow endlessly.

I shower off the salt water, the scent reminding me of Anders. It makes me wonder if he swims in the ocean every day when he's home, or if the scent is just who he is—if it's in his blood.

I'm toweling off my hair and dressed in a cobalt linen maxi skirt and a matching cropped tank that shows a sliver of my stomach when there's a knock on the door. Kellan must have finished getting ready early.

He came over last night, and we spent the evening playing games and laughing until we were both in tears. I never thought that school would be the place where we felt the most distance between us. Last night, I remembered why I had developed my feelings for him in the first place.

His easygoing personality and goofy smiles do something funny to my insides, turning them to goo and leaving me acting like a child. I swear, I made an ass out of myself last night, stumbling over my words and awkwardly smiling. Kellan had just wrapped me in his arms at the end of the night before kissing the top of my head goodnight.

As I pull open the door saying, "Hey, ready to—" I pause, blinking once, twice, and then looking around like maybe I've lost my damn mind. I open my mouth to respond, but close it again when nothing comes to mind.

The deep rumble of his chuckle sends butterflies fluttering in my chest, confirming he is, in fact, at my door. I open and close my mouth again, forgetting how to form a sentence.

"Hi," he says with a slight smirk from where he's leaning against the frame, hands tucked into his pockets. "Can I come in?"

Without responding, I hold the door open and step aside. The scent of roaring seas, warm sandalwood, and fresh citrus floats toward me on a breeze, and I feel my whole traitorous body relax. I close the door and fall against it, realizing just how much I've missed him.

twenty-two

· · ·

"How?" I ask ever so smoothly. Anders lifts a brow, tilting his lips slightly. Glad he finds me amusing.

"You invited me, remember? I'm here to take you to the Bubble Village." He slides his hands back into his shorts pockets and looks around the open-air space, waiting for my response. When I had invited him, I had meant it, but I never thought he would actually show up. That was also before I found out Kellan was coming.

"I have plans," I start, gesturing behind me like that is an answer. I'm still trying to process that Anders freaking Rykerson has just walked into my room...at a resort on Kliax...looking like a damn god himself.

He looks utterly divine in dark cerulean shorts and a crisp white shirt, his octopus tattoo a stark contrast against the fabric. The humid air gives his dark hair soft, loose waves, and his skin is a sun-kissed tan that highlights his chiseled features. Here, amidst the ocean, he seems entirely in his element—a prince among the waters, more relaxed, happier than I've ever seen. He looks fully alive.

He chews on his bottom lip. My eyes track the movement before my gaze returns to his.

"I spoke with your parents. They're taking my sister with them and said they hope you have fun. They'll see us at dinner. We should get going so I have time to show you everything I want."

I cock my head, unsure whether to be pissed at him for going behind my back or impressed he planned it out. Something akin to happiness stirs within me.

"Wait," I take a step toward him. "Your sister?"

He hums softly to himself, a grin spreading across his face as he nods in my direction. "I brought her along. She didn't want to go to the village, so your parents offered to take her with them." A flurry of questions swirls in my mind, each one more pressing than the last, but I know they will have to wait. My gaze drifts down to my outfit, and I can't help but frown. It's not as though he hasn't seen me in less —running or swimming at the lake—but today feels different, and I feel a flush in my cheeks. The sliver of my exposed stomach feels intimate.

"You're perfect," he states confidently, as if he can somehow hear my inner turmoil. "Let's go," he adds, brushing past me with an air of confidence, heading toward the door. "I promised you'd be back for dinner."

"But—" I start to protest, feeling a mix of uncertainty and excitement.

"Soraea, you look beautiful. Let's go," he insists, his eyes making a deliberate sweep over every inch of me, lingering on my hair cascading down my shoulders in natural waves, still damp and glistening in the light. The warmth of his gaze ignites a flutter of nerves in my stomach, and I decide against arguing any further.

With a resigned sigh, I grab my woven bag and slip into a pair of rope sandals. Taking a deep breath, I follow him outside, anxious yet excited to spend the day with him. There seems to be a fine line between the two emotions.

"This is the best way to the village," Anders declares, holding up a sleek barrier disk, its metallic surface gleaming under the sunlight, before placing it gently on my temple. We stand side by side in front of two hoverboards, their black polished surfaces reflecting the azure sky. I have only attempted to ride one once before, and the memory of it still makes me cringe. The barrier disk is intended to act as my energy shield, protecting me from injury should I fall. Yet, taking no chances with me, he also activates my energy shield at my wrist, the delicate gold band warm from sitting against my skin.

His touch feels infuriatingly comfortable as he grips my arm, as though our bodies have grown accustomed to touching. I swallow hard to suppress the storm of emotions within me. When I lift my gaze to meet his, I'm struck by the fact that his deep sapphire eyes are nearly devoid of the silver flecks, as if they, too, have relaxed. He brushes his thumb softly over the pulse point in my wrist, which races under his touch, and he arches a brow with an amused expression before stepping back and releasing my arm.

He leaps onto his hoverboard in one fluid motion, a grin like I've never seen before spreading across his face like sunlight breaking through the clouds. I stand there, mouth agape, unsure how to move. He accelerates, lifting no more than two feet off the ground, gliding forward with ease. My nerves flutter as I'm pulled back to the task at hand. Gripping the controllers tightly, my palms already slick, I take a deep breath, steeling myself and reminding myself I can do this.

Slowly, I allow the board to rise from the ground. It wobbles beneath me for the briefest moment, but I pull my core tight and breathe. I lean forward slightly, urging the board forward just as Anders circles back to me, his laughter ringing out through the calm silence. I roll my eyes, determined not to let him witness me fall. With a playful gesture, I signal for him to lead the way, feigning impatience.

He responds with a wink, that ridiculous dimple deepening on his cheek, and then he flies ahead, leaving me behind. With another breath, I move forward, gradually finding my balance and footing as I follow after him.

Brine-scented wind brushes against my skin, lifting my entire mood. It's impossible to feel anything but hopeful and full of life when you're on a beach, the soft, melodic roaring of the waves at your side, and a handsome prince showing off in front of you. Because that's definitely what he's doing as he spins and moves with the board like he's on a wave.

We cross the sandy beaches and soon find the cobblestone streets of the byway heading east along the shore. There is nothing for miles except for the sound of the waves and the rustling of the tall, broad-leaved trees. On this side of the island, there aren't many people, but there's a bustling city on the opposite side with crowded streets and stacked townhomes.

Anders slows his pace several times, hovering beside me as we approach the Bubble Village. With a gleam in his eyes, he shares stories about Kliax and the community we are headed to. For years, I had labeled Anders as a self-centered, entitled prick, too caught up in my own preconceived notions to see the truth. But now, witnessing him in this light—relaxed, filled with energy, and truly himself—reveals a side I never knew existed. There's a sincerity in how he speaks about his home and its inhabitants that captivates my attention and challenges my earlier judgments about him.

Before I realize it, we find ourselves gliding to the edge of the village, the cobblestones beneath us worn and covered in moss. I'm struck by a completely unexpected sight as we meander through the quiet streets. Enormous glass domes rise up around us, resembling colossal bubbles that a giant has scattered across the landscape.

Each dome is unique; some are transparent, allowing natural light to enter, while others are frosted, ensuring privacy. Some of the glass structures rest atop towering, organic formations that mimic the shapes of trees. Others nestle snugly into the earth, their rooftops adorned with lush moss and vibrant grasses that blend seamlessly into the surrounding nature, as if the hillsides are in the process of claiming them.

A sparkling river meanders through the heart of the village, its crystal-clear waters flowing toward the ocean beyond. Bridges arch over the river at intervals, as though the village had been crafted around the waterway.

The entire village embodies harmony with nature. Every surface is alive with plant life, and fragrant flowers spill from pots and window boxes while vines crawl up the sides of the domes, even weaving their way inside. As we continue our journey along the cobblestone paths, I can't help but smile and wave at the villagers we pass. Some greet Anders with warm recognition, while others look puzzled, seemingly unsure of who he is. I sense he prefers anonymity.

As we draw closer to the river, a boat resembling a hollowed-out tree trunk captures my attention. It glides over the peaceful ripples of the water, carrying a family within. A tinge of warmth filters through me as I watch a little girl nuzzle into her father's lap, her small frame curling up contentedly against him while the mother passes apples around to the other children.

Anders continues to lead me deeper into the village until we reach an impressive glass dome at the center—the largest of all the structures here. I can't help but feel a sense of awe.

We park the hoverboards, tucking the controllers into my bag. The village's energy surrounds us as people enter and exit the large dome, and the scent of food wafts through the air each time the doors open.

"Do you trust me?" Anders asks as he extends his hand toward me. I gaze down at his outstretched hand, a whirlwind of thoughts stirring in my mind. I momentarily weigh the implications of taking it, but something tugs at me, urging me to, and I realize, I do trust him with my life. Without overthinking it, I slide my fingers into his, and a sharp gasp escapes my lips at the intensity of the energy that rushes through me.

I feel my magic rise in response as tears prick my eyes. *Not here. Please, not here.*

He grips my hand, steadying me with his other hand braced on my arm as I stumble forward. We hold each other there, in the middle of the village, our gazes locked. He knows this secret, this deep, scary secret, and yet it doesn't change how he looks at me—like I'm the answer to everything. My emotions blend into a complex explosion of longing and rightness, something deep within me claiming him as mine. I take a steadying breath, inhaling the humid air. He brushes a hand down my heated arms, and I feel his magic rise in response.

"You figured it out?"

His mouth quirks. "Just a little. I'm still working on it. It helps when you're around."

After a few heartbeats, a warmth spreads across my cheeks, and although I can't help but feel shy, Anders remains focused on me, his free hand moving up and down my arm, gently caressing me as I regain control. The slide of his cool hands along my arm sends a wave of goosebumps over my skin. He tightens his grip, interlacing our fingers in a way that feels utterly natural as he turns for the door, ignoring the fact that we both just called on magic we shouldn't possess—not yet anyway.

"Ready?" he murmurs, his breath brushing against my ear like a summer breeze. I nod, enthralled as he tugs me closer to his side, our bodies fitting together perfectly.

A carved sign on the glass door reads "Welcome to Seamark Shallows." I stall for all of a heartbeat before my head falls back as I laugh. Anders seems to stall, entirely unsure of what is happening. Through my giggles, I breathlessly point out that I believed the village was, in fact, named the Bubble Village.

A mischievous grin spreads across his face as he shrugs. "It is in my mind. Ever since I was little, I've called it that. I sometimes forget that its true name is Seamark Shallows." After a minute, my giggles calm, but a few chuckles still rattle me as he brushes my hair back. "Besides, I like my version better." I allow myself to live in the moment, leaning against him, my neck arched as I gaze up at him with abandon, my smile genuine and free.

His free hand slides to the nape of my neck, bringing his forehead to mine as he breathes me in. "Keep smiling at me like that, and I'll never let you go." Before I can respond, he pulls away and opens the door, tugging me inside.

All my protests and questions die the instant my gaze settles on the room. Inside, the marketplace buzzes with life, showcasing four levels of shops, each brimming with a diverse array of wares. Lush plants from around the kingdom are draped elegantly throughout the space. At the heart of the dome lies a gathering area filled with rustic wooden tables, mismatched chairs, and stools, where villagers share meals and engage in lively discussions.

"This is the heart of the village," Anders says, his voice filled with pride. "This is where they eat, where they hold their meetings. All of their shopping is conducted here and often done in trade." We take the weathered wooden steps, the creak of the boards noting our ascent. The air is fragrant with scents of various cuisines, making my mouth water and my stomach grumble.

While one shop we pass offers an array of prepared meals, another showcases crates brimming with vibrant fruits and vegetables. My senses are immediately captivated by a bakery, where the aroma of freshly baked croissants and honey rolls wafts through the air, making my stomach rumble loud enough that Anders' gaze snaps to me. I offer him a slight shrug back. Just beside it, another shop is dedicated to sweet treats, all neatly displayed in glass cases: muffins, cakes, and tarts.

"Thank you for bringing me here." My voice is tinged with wonder as I take in the sights. As we stroll along, our hands still interlaced, Anders gently pulls me closer, releasing my hand only to drape his arm over my shoulder, keeping me from overheating. He approaches one of the counters to place an order for two dishes, and as he reaches for his coins, the shopkeepers and patrons begin to notice us, recognition flickering on their faces.

Feeling their gazes land on me, I attempt to pull back, but Anders' grip tightens reassuringly, holding me close and tucked into his side. A nervousness spreads through me as I look around and see the gentle smiles on people's faces as they glance between us. Friends can hold hands and each other, right?

"My Prince," one of the villagers says, dropping to a knee. Others follow as whispers carry through the dome; before we know it, everyone has bowed. Anders gestures with his free hand to rise. I watch as his shoulders rise and fall. I know how it feels to be surrounded by people who've placed their faith and trust in you when you feel so undeserving and incapable of the job.

"Thank you for coming," one of the men says, his voice shaky as he stretches out a weathered hand. It almost startles me that he would be thanked. Perhaps it's because King Aki has been missing, and there are fewer visits? Most royals try to get to their different planets at least once a year to see their people. My guess is Queen Priana is probably overwhelmed running the kingdom herself.

Intertwining our fingers again, we are ushered to the center of the dome, where we are placed at the head table, and two large, comfortable chairs are brought over. I thank them kindly as another man, this one young, most likely still in his teenage years, delivers our food. Moments later, an older woman, short and thick, her hair gray and pulled into a tight bun, sets bubble-shaped glasses filled with a blue liquid and covered in some sort of cream before us.

"For you." She offers us a soft smile and gestures for us to try it. It is only then that Anders releases my hand, and I instantly ache for his touch. I take a tentative sip, the chilled liquid coating my tongue as my taste buds explode with the flavor of coconut and berries.

"Thank you," I say with genuine gratitude as I take another eager sip from the glass. The vibrant, refreshing concoction dances on my taste buds, and I can already tell it has claimed the title of my new favorite drink. I lean in toward Anders. "Do you think we could recreate this at school?"

He maintains steady eye contact, a playful glint in his eyes, as he lowers his mouth over my straw, drawing up the last remnants of the blue liquid. My heart races at the sight of his lips enveloping the straw where mine just were, sending a warm rush through me, igniting a wholly different and inappropriate heat that spreads throughout my body, straight to the apex of my thighs. I can hardly focus on anything else as I become acutely aware of the moment, the closeness between us, and the building tension that lingers in the air.

His lips quirk into a subtle smile as he pulls away from me. "Delicious." I nearly choke on my own spit.

The atmosphere around us buzzes as guests filter in, each one pausing to greet us with friendly smiles or to present us with thoughtful gifts. Most of the offerings are handcrafted treasures made from rich, polished wood, reflecting the skill of local artisans. Others bring forth enticing food dishes, eager to share their creations. My heart swells with delight when a fresh, warm roll is placed on the table, the steam still rising from its perfectly golden crust.

As we eat, the flavors explode in my mouth. The seafood is tender, the fluffy rice has been soaked in rich broths, and the vegetables are perfectly roasted, all harvested from the fields surrounding the village. I might have let out an involuntary moan of pleasure, much to Anders' amusement, who raises an eyebrow at my shameless enjoyment.

A young girl, draped in soft pink, her golden brown hair braided with little bows, approaches our table with a large basket of trinkets she is selling. When her horrified mother comes rushing forward, we wave her off. Inside the basket are woven bags crafted with intricate patterns, alongside bubble-shaped terrariums that house a glowing aquamarine and peach-colored flowers resembling a large raspberry, which Anders explains are Etlingera Elatior.

I purchase a few items, including all the flowers, deciding to gift them to my friends and staff. I tip generously, thanking the young girl. After lunch, we wander through the stalls, some inspiring me with their sustainable practices. Nothing here goes to waste; everything has a purpose or use.

As we move throughout the marketplace, I purchase a light summer dress, spun from local Haka trees—a material similar to bamboo, yet as sturdy as cotton. When I model it for Anders, his gaze never leaves my accentuated hips. Anders buys a seagrass doll, dressed in a handmade patchwork dress, alongside a large, pink, pearlescent conch shell. I discover a spyglass made from recycled glass, deciding to gift it to my father, a medicinal book filled with local herbs and healing practices for my mother, and an old scabbard paired with an intricately crafted dagger for Kellan. Before we know it, our arms and my bag are laden with gifts.

"So, Princess," Anders says as we stroll over one of the many bridges. "How has the Bubble Village lived up to your expectations?" The world around us fades into a blur, and for once, I hate that every time we attempt a kiss, it's interrupted. All I'd have to do is lean up on my toes and press my mouth to his, but with prying eyes all around us, it's too risky.

Instead of telling him to kiss me, I say, "Thank you for bringing me here. It's a lovely place. If you ever come to Kyrr, I'll have to show you my favorite village." He squeezes my hand but doesn't say anything further. The water beneath the bridge sparkles in the late afternoon sunlight. Anders shifts, and as I glance up, I notice a man approaching, eyeing us both. Anders not so subtly swaps sides with me, taking my left hand as we continue across the bridge.

A chill sweeps up my spine, and I notice Anders' slight movement as he positions himself in front of me.

As the man nears, I notice his worn, thin cloak covering wrinkled, ashen skin, but his violet eyes give me pause. He stops before us, his eyes locked solely on me behind Anders' shoulder. "The birth of the new dawn is coming, Light-bringer," the man rasps.

The man bows before us both, and Anders tenses. The weird interaction is over before we can say anything, and the man continues on in the opposite direction.

"What does that mean?" I look over my shoulder, recalling the exact words from the temple. But as I look back, the man has already vanished. Anders shakes his head, displeased with the interaction, and mutters about strange people before protectively wrapping an arm around my shoulders as we continue to the other side.

"Alright, Princess, it's time to head back." He turns his gaze toward the horizon where the sun is beginning to set, casting a golden hue across the landscape. "I have a promise to keep to the King and Queen, and I don't think they'd be too pleased with me if I broke it." As he speaks, the sun highlights the light brown and gold streaks in his effortlessly perfect tousled hair. I let him lead us back to the hoverboards, his arm still draped around me.

I can't help but tease him, "So you actually want my parents to like you?" The words escape my lips with a playful lilt, but I notice a flicker of something darker in his eyes. For just a brief moment, the playful mask he usually wears slips away, revealing a glimpse of the secrets buried within. But as quickly as it appears, he regains his composure, sliding his mask back into place with practiced ease.

That sudden shift unsettles me, creating a knot of unease in the pit of my stomach. "I want everyone to like me," he replies, his tone light, though the faint tremor in his voice hints at something more lurking beneath the surface.

A thousand questions rush to my mind, but it's not my place to push, and we've shared a lovely day together that I don't want to ruin. He's not obligated to divulge his secrets to me. I am, after all, just a momentary blip in his life. By the time he graduates, he'll be ushered into Bonding ceremonies where he'll find a wife and then be crowned king. This is all temporary. So why does his shutting me out hurt so badly?

Instead of pressing him for answers, I swallow my disappointment, trying to keep my emotions in check. I roll my eyes in a feigned expression of annoyance and march ahead.

"You're truly insufferable, Prince," I tease when we finally reach the hoverboards, my sarcasm tinged with some truth. He merely chuckles in response. I struggle to shake off the sadness and heaviness in my heart that he feels obligated to hide a part of himself from me. I wish he would let me in—if only just a little.

He loads all of our purchases into a seagrass bag and straps it to his back while I fish out the hand controls from my own overstuffed bag. As if sensing the change in mood, he steps closer, tilting my chin up.

"What's going on in that head of yours?" he asks quietly, his eyes searching my face for answers.

I bite into my lip and shrug as nonchalantly as possible, begging the burn in the back of my throat and my eyes to go away. By some miracle, my eyes don't fill with unshed tears. He studies my face a moment before I wrap my arms around him, burying my face into his chest. If he won't let me in, I'll just be here in whatever capacity he allows.

"I don't want today to end," I admit, my voice betraying me as it wobbles.

He wraps his arms around me, tucking my head into his arm as he presses his mouth to the top of my head. For long moments, he doesn't say anything; he just holds me, and that unsettled feeling leaves me in the form of a few tears, but once they're shed, I feel so much better.

I step back and tuck my hair behind my ears, wiping my eyes before looking up at him with a small, closed-mouthed smile. He studies me again, brushing my hair back before placing a soft kiss on my forehead. After a short pause, he pulls back, nodding like he's accepting whatever just happened between us. I exhale and turn to get on my board. The sun will set soon, and I want to be back before it gets dark. Plus, I really want to meet Princess Clara.

Anders' hands wrap around my waist from behind me. His grip tightens, his thumbs brushing the bare skin on my lower back until my feet are strapped in.

His hands leave my waist, and he walks in front of me, cupping the side of my cheek while his other hand places the barrier back on my temple. "Thank you."

His thumb brushes so close to my lips while we maintain eye contact. He dips his head, and just when I think he might actually kiss me, he whispers a response of "My pleasure" back.

I hear him sigh and, at the same time, get a lungful of his scent. In a moment of desperation, I'm gripping his shirt, holding him in place. A raucous laughter breaks whatever spell we've been in, and he pulls away, placing his own barrier on his temple.

"Keep up, Princess," he teases before jumping on his board. His one-eighty in his emotions has me confused for a moment before I laugh and follow after him.

twenty-three

. . .

During the ride back to the resort, I replay how Anders leaned in repeatedly in my head. Was he going to kiss me? Did I want him to? The whole day with him felt so unexpected and so...perfect. I wasn't worried about the Bond, even though it was there the entire time, and I didn't worry about the future. With him, I felt completely at ease and normal.

We are both silent the whole way, taking in the landscape. Over the open ocean, pastels of pink and purple paint the skies, and the water glows a dark cerulean. The waves are smooth as they creep toward the sandy shores before the tide sucks them back out. Fishing boats worn with age and salt bob near the shore, their colors faded from the sun, and a few larger vessels are anchored further out.

Anders studies me several times, his gaze lingering, yet I choose not to lift my eyes to meet his. A sense of contentment has settled between us that feels like it's balancing precariously on a ledge as we near the resort. The world we've shared, so blissfully separate from reality, is about to collide with the outside.

As the resort comes into view, the flickering torches lining the path cast a warm glow, illuminating the shadows around us. Anders decelerates, coming to a stop at the front desk. We return the hoverboards and barrier disks, and when Anders extends his hand to me once more, I shake my head, feeling a knot of insecurity as we approach the gate.

Anders falls into step beside me, adjusting his long strides to match my own pace. It's a subtle gesture, one he has repeated throughout the day, always anticipating my rhythm without needing to be asked. There's a comfort in the way we move together, even as we approach reality.

"Today was really special." I cling to my bag to give my hands somewhere to be.

"I'm glad we could make it work," he responds, his voice hinting at confusion over our sudden distance. Our feet shuffle along the boards as we pass the first path.

"Where are you staying?" I ask. He gestures toward the room down the path to the right, close to mine.

"Clara and I leave tomorrow. I promised her I would take her to see the aquarium before we leave for Malaya." I nod, offering a tight smile as I push open the door to my room, allowing him to follow me inside.

"I just need to change for dinner."

It's now chilly outside, and I want something warmer than the skirt and top I'm currently wearing. He settles down on the deck below while I slip into a long summer dress and pull a soft, thin cardigan over my shoulders. I brush my hair, leaving it down and weaving in a small diadem. I add some lip stain and slip my feet back into my sandals.

I head down the steps to the platform where Anders is waiting, gazing out over the water. The wind tousles his hair, and from behind, he looks absolutely divine. He spins around, his eyes scanning over me twice before he reaches out and gently tugs on my waist, pulling me closer until I have to tilt my head back to meet his gaze.

"I truly enjoyed spending the day with you. I wouldn't mind doing it again," he confesses, his voice soft yet edged with uncertainty.

I nod, unsure of how to respond.

He must sense my walls being erected because he lets out a long sigh before saying, "Soraea, please don't push me away."

The raw vulnerability in his tone makes my heart crack while also threatening to beat out of my chest at the enormity of his words. In truth, I wouldn't mind spending all my days like this with him, losing track of time wrapped in our own little world, sharing stolen glances and genuine smiles.

My palms move instinctively up his chest, feeling the strength and warmth that radiates from his body beneath my fingers. His eyes flutter closed, and I watch him swallow hard as if trying to steady himself before opening them again. The intensity of his gaze holds so much heat that I feel like I could melt right in front of him. My thighs clench together, desire coursing through me as my eyes dart to where our lips are so wonderfully close.

It feels like a standoff at this point, and one of us is bound to give in. Looking braver than I feel, I slide my arms around his neck, my fingers tangling in the hair at the nape of his neck, and pull him closer. His head dips toward mine, tantalizingly slow. His nose grazes mine, and his lips just barely brush against my own, but the contact sends enough energy through me that it could light up the whole universe. The simple brush of his lips is enough to draw a breathy gasp from me.

I surge up on my toes just as he grips me tighter, our mouths locking over each other's. Just as the moment begins to deepen, his lips pressing to mine, firmer as if ready to finally, truly kiss me, a sharp knock at my door shatters the spell and jolts me back to reality. Despite the interruption, I grip Anders firmly in place, unwilling to let this moment slip away.

"Please," I whisper, almost pleadingly, my eyes locked onto him.

Anders lets out a heavy sigh, raking a hand through his hair, and another knock reverberates through the room. He looks torn between desire and duty, and just as I reluctantly release him, allowing him to step back, I can see the regret in his expression.

"It's probably Clara," he mentions with a hint of guilt. "I messaged her that I was here."

My heart leaps at the thought. I can wait for that kiss if it means I finally get to meet his sister. I feel a rush of excitement as I race after him, my heart pounding, and catch up to him just as he opens the door. In a swift motion, he slides an arm around my waist, drawing me closer to him.

But the moment of intimacy is abruptly interrupted when we find a furious Kellan standing on the other side. My stomach drops as the realization washes over me. It isn't a little blonde girl searching for her big brother, but rather my best friend. He's still that…right?

Kellan doesn't even bother glancing in Anders' direction. All the fire of his anger is directed at me, and I wince as guilt twists uncomfortably in my stomach. Once again, I remember neglecting to inform my best friend about where I was headed. The truth is, it completely slipped my mind. Every time I'm around Anders, the world seems to fade away, leaving just the two of us.

"Where have you been, Rae?" Kellan all but growls, his voice a low rumble as he pushes into my room. As I reach for his hand, he pulls it away.

"I was in the village," I reply, my voice growing quiet with remorse. "I know I should have messaged you, but it slipped my mind."

He lets out a deep sigh and walks to the edge of the sitting area, realizing that Anders is right beside me as if he hadn't seen him before.

"You were with him?" Kellan's voice rises as he points an accusatory finger at Anders.

Anders spins on his heel, once again positioning himself protectively at my side. His posture straightens, making him taller and his shoulders broader. I try not to roll my eyes at the alpha male display— not helpful.

"Duke Hyston," Anders drawls in an exaggeratedly cordial tone, as if welcoming Kellan into his home rather than a confrontation. Kellan offers Anders nothing more than a glare before shifting his focus back to me.

"Let's go, Rae. I told your parents we would meet them at dinner. And I'm furious because I told your parents I would stay back. I came here, fully aware that you weren't with them, and now I find out you ditched me for him! My Prism cracked when I dropped it earlier, so it's not like I had a way to reach you."

"I'm really sorry." I say, feeling small as I reach for him again. This time, he doesn't pull away, letting the warmth of his hand encase mine. "I didn't mean to worry you or ditch you. Anders and I made a plan before we left school. I wasn't sure he was—"

"You just left!" Kellan cuts me off, his voice straining with anger.

Cringing again, I step back, finding comfort in Anders' solid chest. Protective as ever, Anders wraps his arms around my waist, tugging me back to his side just as Kellan yanks me forward like I'm a ragdoll in a game of tug-of-war.

Anders stiffens behind me. "Let her go," he says, punctuating each word in a dangerously calm voice.

I swear the room around me drops twenty degrees, my skin prickling with the sudden cold. When I glance between the two men, I see Anders' gaze filled with an icy rage while Kellan's fury burns hot.

"You let her go, asshole. I don't care who the hell you are. She isn't yours," Kellan hisses back, pulling my hand again, causing me to stumble, my body colliding with his. Anger radiates through me, heating my skin and igniting a weird energy that buzzes beneath the surface.

"Both of you let me go," I demand, managing to free myself from their grasp, my voice firm. "I'm not either of yours, so stop it." My gaze flickers between them, both glaring daggers at each other. "In fact, I would like to have dinner alone with my parents. Please figure out other arrangements for dinner—both of you."

With that, I turn on my heel, leaving them in the living room, mouths agape in shock. I slam the door behind me, the sound echoing off the other buildings.

As I step into the outside dining space, I find my parents already seated, the table set for six with lights draped overhead. Disappointment settles on my chest when I realize they're alone. My mother explains that Clara was just sent to dress for dinner.

No doubt, Anders will be arranging dinner for both of them.

When my parents ask what happened, I angrily swipe away a tear and simply respond that we'll be eating alone. They exchange a brief glance but continue on as if nothing is amiss. I push my food around, half-listening to them recount their day as I process how quickly my day has turned to shit.

twenty-four

. . .

I CURL up in my bed, tears streaming down my face as Aolyn sits beside me, gently running her hand along my back. We've been back at school for a week, and I already miss my mother. I wish she were here with me right now. The pain from my cycle is unbearable, and the school's healers seem to be too busy to help me.

When I arrived at the Center, doubled over in pain after classes, Agneta merely tsked and suggested that a heating pack would suffice. It's amusing, really—I've had one wrapped around my lower abdomen and back for the past two hours. It hasn't provided any relief from the searing pain that feels like it's branding my ovaries.

It feels as if my insides are being shredded and burned from within, and I'm now at a point where I'm almost numb because I don't think I can bear any more pain. My breath shudders as I look up at Aolyn, sweat dripping down my temple. Her black hair is perfectly straight, and her gown sparkles in the dim light. As I take in her attire, I remember it's dinner hour. Guilt twists alongside the pain in my stomach; she should be downstairs, not here taking care of me, especially when I know there's no relief in sight.

"You should go." I attempt to soften my features. "I'll be okay. Nothing is going to change. Can you bring me back something?"

Her lips press together, and she examines me from head to toe, her crystalline blue eyes filled with so much sympathy that I want to hug her and remind her she's a great friend. I almost laugh at myself; I always feel vulnerable and emotional during my cycle.

"Are you sure?" she asks, her voice tinged with doubt. Her hand continues to stroke my back in comforting, sweeping motions.

A soft knock at the door startles us both. Her gaze shifts to the door and then back to me, uncertain if she should answer it. I try to roll my eyes and reassure her that I'm fine as she crosses the room to open it. I can't hear who it is, but I bury my face in the pillows, muffling a half-sob, half-shriek that escapes me as a fresh wave of pain hits my ovary. I just want my mom or my dad...someone.

Tears soak my pillow, and my hair clings to my cheeks as I turn my head and attempt to catch my breath. A moment later, the air charges around me. I'm too tired to fight with him tonight, and somewhere deep within me, I want him here. I crave his presence, his attention, despite the endless apologies he's offered over the past week—apologies that have grated on my nerves to the point of screaming. I forgave him the first day, realizing that he was just being protective. Which was unneeded, but Kellan had crossed a line. Kellan's apologies, however, have not won me over as easily. I've never seen Kellan act like that.

I've come to realize that being around Anders brings a sense of safety and calm that I desperately need and want. And, well, if I can't have my parents, he's the next best thing. At least for tonight, anyway.

"Hey," he whispers soothingly as the bed dips gently under his weight, and his warm hand brushes over my trembling arm.

The moment his fingers make contact, comfort blankets my senses. My body begins to relax under his touch. My muscles finally begin to ease, allowing me to take a deep, shaky breath. I open my tear-stained eyes, wiping away the blurriness, before letting my eyes settle on him.

I find him seated at my back, his dark hair neatly swept to the side and his eyes glistening like sapphire pools flecked with shimmering silver. He always seems to look effortlessly handsome, and even now, in the low light of the room, I can't help but drool. I'm not sure the man knows how to have a bad hair day.

"Hi," I croak out softly, wiping away my tears with the back of my hand, smudging my mascara further as I tug the blankets higher.

I take in the concern etched into his features as he takes in my appearance. I'm sure my eyes are red and swollen, my face a disaster, and well, I know that I look pale, hence the makeup I wore today. My heart aches a little more as we sit in silence, taking each other in, reminding me how much I truly need him here with me.

"Are you okay if I head down?" Aolyn asks quietly from the foot of my bed, her eyes darting between us. "I can bring my food back up if you'd prefer."

I shake my head slowly, feeling a flicker of relief wash over me just by having Anders here by my side. As much as I appreciate Aolyn's friendship, her presence doesn't offer the same level of calm that Anders does. "Go eat. Just make sure to bring something back later, okay?" I add, attempting to inject a note of reassurance into my voice.

She hesitates for a brief moment, uncertainty flickering across her features as if she's gauging whether I truly am all right. Eventually, she nods, her shoulders relaxing slightly. Without casting another glance in my direction, she exits the room, leaving Anders and me in silence.

"Why are you here?" I ask. I'm not mad, or even upset that he is; in fact, I'm grateful.

He doesn't answer me right away, looking me over first. "Would you believe me if I said I felt like something was off with you? I don't —" he pauses, swiping a hand through his hair, "I just needed to come check on you. Why haven't you gone to the healers?" His jaw tenses in frustration. "I haven't seen it this bad."

My gaze lifts to meet his. I haven't revealed the unfortunate reality of my monthly cycle to him; it's not exactly the kind of topic one brings up casually, even with someone you trust. Only a few people know about the extent of my pain, and even they often shy away from discussing it openly.

Anders must sense the confusion clouding my expression because he continues gently, "I know you're always in pain about every four weeks or so. I'm not blind, Raea."

The way his voice trails off into a whisper sends a piercing ache through my chest. It makes me acutely aware of how vulnerable I've allowed myself to become in front of him. I can't help but feel unworthy of him. How did I get so lucky to have him as a friend? Or maybe more?

"It's my cycle," I manage to say. "The healers don't exactly believe me, and right now, they're busy."

Another wave of pain hits, making it feel like my ovary is about to burst. I grip the bed sheet tightly, my fingers digging into the fabric, and squeeze my eyes shut, desperately trying to push the agony to the back of my mind. I don't want to break in front of him.

"We have to go," he demands. "If they won't see you, I'll take you home." There's a determination in his tone and in his features now as if he's already made up his mind. "They can't let you just sit here in this kind of pain."

A whimper escapes my lips before I bury my face in my pillow again.

I feel the shift of weight on the bed beside me just before I feel the warmth of his palm resting gently over my side, under the layers of the blanket. He lies beside me, moving closer as if understanding that that small contact might ease my pain. The intimacy of it crumbles what little defenses I have around my emotions, and soon, my body is wracked with unchecked sobs.

With such tenderness, he brushes my hair away with his hand, and I find myself wanting to just curl up into him and never let go.

"We have to fly tomorrow," I sob. "I'm scared I won't be able to go." I can feel the tension in his body as he lets out a heavy, exasperated sigh. He pulls me closer until I'm tucked into his side.

He's quiet for a minute. "Let me take you to the healers," he pleads quietly. "If they won't see you, we'll fly to Kyrr or Malaya. Whatever it takes."

The mention of Malaya, Anders' home, sends a strange rush of nausea through me; the thought of traveling to a place I haven't visited since childhood, especially with him, fills me with a strange mix of anxiety and longing.

The truth feels heavy. Somehow, we've become close enough that he's lying in bed with me. He knows the deepest secret I have, and he is the sole owner of that knowledge. Somewhere along the way, even if we haven't talked about it, I know...deep down I know, in some small way, we're in this together. But are we together, together? It's a question I keep asking myself and keep coming up short.

"Did you eat dinner?" I force the words out as I try to distract myself from the emotions clawing at my insides.

"Trysten is leaving something in my room. Raea," he breathes out, a deep sigh escaping his lips. "Please, don't do that."

With a shaky breath, I reach out, my fingers trembling slightly as I find his hand. The warmth of his skin against mine steadies me for a moment, grounding me amidst the chaos swirling inside. I look up when he laces our fingers together, catching his gaze. At that moment, I realize he's looking at me in a way that no one ever has. It's a blend of concern, tenderness, and something more profound that makes my heart race. I swallow hard.

"Please," he pleads softly.

I squeeze my eyes shut and nod, surrendering, before opening my eyes just in time to see the tension drain from his shoulders as he stands, carefully pulling back the blankets. He carefully helps me out of bed, one hand resting on my hip while the other wraps around my arm, steadying me. Only then do I remember I'm dressed in a thin nightgown.

Once I feel stable enough to walk alone, he rushes into my closet, his movements quick as I hear drawers slamming closed. He emerges moments later, holding my cloak and a pair of fuzzy socks. With a gentle touch that is at odds with who he is, he drapes the cloak around my shoulders, fastening the three buttons before dropping to his knees before me.

He grips my ankle, allowing me to steady myself on his shoulder as he slips on the socks for me, his fingers brushing against my skin with a delicate touch. I might enjoy this moment more if I wasn't in so much pain. I'm not sure Anders, the arrogant, dark prince, would kneel before anyone.

"I need shoes," I sniffle, trying to regain some dignity. He shakes his head decisively.

"No, I'm carrying you," he states firmly, his voice leaving no room for argument.

"What? No—" I start to protest, but he scoops me effortlessly into his arms before I can finish. The sudden motion takes me by surprise, eliciting a release of unexpected tears as I instinctively wrap my arms around his neck.

"Did I hurt you?" he asks, searching my face.

I shake my head, my heart swelling with gratitude and something more. I let my head rest against his shoulder, surrendering to the moment. For a fleeting instant, I inhale deeply, breathing him in. His scent and familiarity feel like a balm to my soul. I allow myself to pretend, just for a moment, that he's mine and this is normal, to forget everything else, and to just allow myself to be held.

I must have drifted off because when I open my eyes again, I find myself in a bed at the healer's Center. Anders is sitting in a chair beside me, his hand wrapped in mine, sleeping with his head resting on a pillow at the edge of the bed. Above us, the two moons are halfway across the sky. It's late.

I shift in the bed and realize, for the first time, that there's no pain. I sigh in relief, letting my head fall to the side to take him in. What is it between us that keeps forcing us together? And why is he still here? He could have dropped me off and returned to the dorms to eat and sleep. I'm not the only one who has to fly tomorrow, and guilt settles in my stomach, making me uneasy.

"Anders," I whisper, brushing my thumb across the back of his hand. He stirs but doesn't wake. I try again, and this time, his head shoots up from the pillow. Pillow creases line his face, and he looks so tired. "Go back to the dorms. Get some sleep."

He stands, scrubbing his hands down his face before forcing one hand to tame his hair. He sits on the edge of the bed, retaking my hand, and I blush when he does. What I said or did in pain was one thing, but now...

"Really?" he asks, chuckling, a slight grin pulling at his lips. "Let's get you back. They said you were free to go when you woke up. Also, they won't be sending you away next time you come."

Something flickers in his expression, but he doesn't explain further as he helps me into a sitting position. He stands, wrapping my cloak around me, and it suddenly hits me that he carried me the whole way.

Gods...why?

"I can walk," I blurt out. He snorts and crosses his arms over his chest, the simple move making his chest seem like a wall of muscle and emphasizing just how capable his arms are of holding me.

"You don't have shoes. I'm not letting you walk across campus in socks."

"Well, I do remember asking you for shoes, which you didn't grab, so excuse me, but this is your fault. I'll walk." I stand, testing my legs and twisting to find there's nothing left of the pain.

I take a few steps toward the door when Anders scoops me into his arms. I let out a yelp as he cradles me to his chest.

"Put me down, you big oaf!" I squawk, slapping his chest. He chuckles darkly in response and squeezes me tighter. I'm aware of every point of contact. This is humiliating, and gods, I passed out the last time. "Anders, I can walk."

"I know, but then I'd have to listen to you complain for the next week about you hurting your feet on rocks and then blaming me. So I think I'll just skip that fun and carry you," he says.

I groan and cross my arms like a child throwing a tantrum. The idea of wrapping my arms around his neck and being close to him feels overwhelming, especially now that I'm thinking clearly.

"Gods, Raea," he groans. "Just say thank you and move on."

The door slides open as we approach, and he steps out into the dark night. It's freezing out here, and I find myself leaning just a little more into him. He's so warm and comforting. It's difficult not to wrap myself around him.

"Thank you," I mutter.

"See? Was it that hard?" he teases as we cross over the bridge back to our side of campus. The boards clack beneath his steady feet. Feeling a bit guilty that he's carrying dead weight right now, I relent and wrap my arms around his neck.

"Painful," I reply, relaxing a bit into him.

I can't help but notice that his arms aren't trembling under my weight—they feel steady and strong like I weigh nothing to him. Beneath his dress shirt, I can feel how broad and strong he really is. Thank the gods it's dark outside because my cheeks flush.

"I'm sorry for keeping you up," I say quietly. He just shakes his head, looking down at me.

"Anytime, Princess," he replies.

Something passes between us, and I'm not ready for it, so I look away, laying my head on his shoulder. We continue in silence, and when we return to Taeolyn, even though I'm safe to walk now, he insists on carrying me all the way up to the fifth floor, only setting me down when we reach my door.

"Good night," I whisper, stepping back until my back is pressed against my door. He follows, bringing our bodies flush again, and he tilts my chin up so that I'm forced to meet his gaze.

"Sleep well, Soraea." The way he says my name feels like a caress, lighting up my nerve endings.

I realize he wants to say more, but he holds my gaze for a heartbeat, and then he's gone, already disappearing down the hall to his room.

Today, we've been excused from our usual classes for our Divisions test, and I can barely contain my excitement. After returning from the Center last night, I crawled back into bed, and the moment my head hit the pillow, I fell into a deep sleep. I suspect that the exhaustion was a result of all the energy I poured into coping with the pain. I'm still unsure about what exactly Anders said to the healers that prompted them to come to my aid, but I am deeply grateful he arrived when he did.

As I settle into my seat for the briefing, Professor Brendn stands at the front of the room, leaning against his table and looking over the sea of excited students. "You'll be flying with your assigned seniors for this trip. You'll fly down, land on the launch pad, and two of you may exit the transport to retrieve a token. After completing the entire course, you'll fly back here. The first transport to finish the course wins. Any questions?"

Kami, a junior from Staxver in Ateria, shoots her hand up.

"Yes, Lady Kamryn?" Professor Brendn addresses her, using her full name. Kami gives him an exasperated look, eyes narrowed slightly, before she continues.

"What happens if we encounter civilians?"

Professor Brendn's expression turns serious. "You know the rules, and so do the towers. Energy shields will activate the moment you land. Hoods up, use your Colony names. The towers will recognize the transports as flight school transports from an academy on Dionek. Only upper officials are privy to your real identities. Ensure that whoever is on comms reports any suspicious activity, and don't forget to activate the live feed before takeoff. Now, you all have your trackers, yes?" he asks, scanning the room. Our Colony names are considered our alternate identities meant to keep us safe and hopefully unrecognized.

A low murmur of conversation spreads like wildfire through the classroom as we each pull out the jewelry trackers we've been given. While our school trackers are embedded within us, these additional ones are necessary, especially since our school trackers weren't designed for interplanetary travel. I fidget with the gold band that sits uncomfortably on my pointer finger. It feels heavy and clunky, the cool metal smooth against my skin as I unconsciously run my thumb back and forth along its surface.

I was told that last year, the professors accompanied the juniors instead of the seniors during these missions. As I glance back a few rows, I catch sight of Anders, who is also nervously toying with his own ring. His gaze remains on his hand, but I can't help but notice the way his mouth curls into a smirk, a silent acknowledgment that he knows I'm watching him. It's a thing we apparently do now—dance around our true feelings and the truth of our magic, but hey, who am I to change?

I wish Anders were our assigned senior; I'd definitely feel safer if he were. The tug I feel to always be around him is only getting stronger every day, and when I touch him, gods, it's the only time I feel relief from the growing charge in the air. Even the hum of Baedyn and the other planets feels stronger.

"For those of you who have checked out your weapons, please keep them in their holsters unless absolutely necessary. Transport teams, you may exit to the launch pads to begin your takeoff inspections. When your assigned senior arrives, you may load up. Your time begins when you radio in for takeoff."

Students stand, and excitement fills the air as we shuffle to the aisles and down the steps. All fliers take this astral test in their junior year, which will be combined with our final grade.

Trysten catches up with Ciara, Tate, and me as we make our way to our transport. The shiny onyx body of the space transport glimmers in the early morning sun. I can't believe I get to fly around the system today.

I'm not paying attention when I feel a surge of energy coursing through my entire body. It's so powerful that I let out a sharp gasp as my knees threaten to buckle beneath me. I feel like a live wire sparking to life. Irritation surges through me. He should know better than to touch me when I'm not paying attention.

"Don't do that," I hiss, keeping my voice low enough for his ears only. "Others will see."

"Gods, calm down," he responds, releasing his hold on me. Even through the fabric that separates us, I can feel the lingering remnants of energy, dampened, but still strong enough to send a jolt of excitement shooting through me. "I was going to warn you about Naelik. The volcanoes are active today. And when you get to Klea, steer clear of the big guy with the scar on his face. He will recognize you, and let's just say he keeps questionable company. Send Tate instead and tell him not to look him in the eye."

I catch a flicker of something akin to fear in his eyes, which displaces my irritation, replacing it with a warm, tingly sensation. I hesitate, my instincts battling between maintaining my composure and reaching out for him. Touching him wins out as I wrap my hands around his biceps. As he steps closer, I feel a rush of warmth radiating from him as his hand briefly brushes my hip, as though he was considering holding me and thought better of it. A small smile pulls at my lips, and I find myself swaying slightly, leaning into him as the world around us blurs.

After a few heartbeats, the sound of boots on metal snaps me back to reality, and our moment fades. The gravity of our surroundings rushes back to me with clarity. Students around us are watching, pretending to be busy, but I can feel their eyes on us.

"Thank you, Prince," I respond, a smirk forming on my face as I shoot him a playful wink. "Oh, and Anders," I pause as I take a step back, a mischievous grin spreading across my face. "Don't keep up." I swiftly turn, whipping my head back toward my friends, and feel my hair hit him. Behind me, I hear him chuckle softly, the tension dissolving between us.

I don't acknowledge the strange tinge of fear I feel from walking away from him.

twenty-five

. . .

"Great job, team," Ciara cheers over the headsets.

We've successfully navigated seven planets in record time, all before our scheduled dinner break. Before we can head back to campus, we have five more destinations: Cresnigan in the Ateria Kingdom, Cidal in my kingdom, Ista in the Oris Kingdom, Naelik in Kadora, and finally, Saedn in Okenen. "We're so winning this," she adds.

"Hell yes," Tate responds as he pulls up the holographic display, mapping our course to Cresnigan. "Yo, Rae, the weather is shit on this next one. I kinda want to live, so maybe, like, I don't know, don't kill us."

"Don't be such a baby, Tate," I retort, unable to suppress a grin. "Is that what's beneath that cocky exterior of yours? A little fear of dying? Hate to break it to you," I click my tongue and grin, "but we're already dying. Every minute of every day."

Ciara bursts into laughter, and I can't help but join in; even Trysten coughs to hide a chuckle.

Tate shoots me a side glance, rolling his eyes at my morbid humor. "Why do you have to be so dark? That's just wrong." He shakes his head. "I'm young, hot, and so not ready to die. Just a few more years, please, Rae," he pleads dramatically, his black hair falling over his forehead before brushing it aside. "I have big plans for when I'm Bonded," he adds, waggling his eyebrows and eliciting more laughter from the team.

"Yeah, okay. I've got your back, Tate. Nobody's dying today." I focus on the potential collision course with a comet.

"I think Lover Prince would be quite sad about your death, Raea," Ciara hums through the headset. Trysten just chuckles beside me while heat rises on my cheeks. I ignore her.

When our transport arrives, Cresnigan's atmosphere is all white, covered entirely in a wicked-looking storm that swirls with intensity. Ciara is hovering over her screen, still trying to contact the tower, when another transport bursts through the storm system and out into space. If they can make it, so can we.

Trysten is busy instructing Tate to report the wind speed before the atmospheric temperature fluctuations, as I hear the all-clear through the headset, finally receiving clearance to make a landing. Ciara cackles when Tate mutters something about superiority. Quiet falls over us as I take a deep breath and lower us down, my hands steady on the controls.

"Just like before. Nice and slow. It's easy," I mutter to myself. "The transports are designed for extremes. The alloy protects us from the burn of reentry, and in case of extreme temperatures, we're fine. We will be alright." I trust the safety of this mission and of our transport, but deep within, there's an unsettling stirring, some instinctive warning telling me there's danger ahead.

"Quit muttering and focus, Raea," Trysten growls from his position beside me, his voice tense and clipped. His body becomes rigid as his hands hover over the secondary controls, ready to take over if needed.

"Not helping," I snap back. As soon as we break free of the atmosphere, violent gusts of wind hurl us off course. "Shit." My heart races as I engage the thrusters, correcting our trajectory with urgency. I squint through the blizzard outside, scanning for the launch pad, now a mere outline in the raging storm. Visibility is near non-existent; the conditions are so severe that it feels like the planet has been swallowed up. It should be midday here, but it feels like night outside.

The green landing box flickers on my display, bouncing erratically as I struggle to align it with the launch pad below. Every gust of wind throws our transport, making it a challenge to maintain stability. My heart pounds in my chest, thumping furiously and drowning out everything. It's fine, though; I focus solely on the steady rhythm of my breath. I focus on the black launch pad, praying to the gods that we land safely on it.

It'd be nice if they could at least turn on the lights for the pad. I remind myself to breathe, inhaling slowly through my nose and letting my lungs fully expand before releasing the tension, which eases the knot in my stomach. Each gust of wind feels like it's trying to force us further down the mountain. Thankfully, our transport thrusters are powerful.

I can do this. It's why I'm here, after all.

With another breath, I silence my mind, focusing solely on the black pad as I align our transport above it.

Relief washes over me as the transport touches down, and I become all too aware of my vice-like grip on the steering stick. With a loud thunk, the magnetic locks engage, latching us in place, and a collective sigh resounds through the cabin.

The howling wind outside pounds against the side of our transport, causing it to creak and lean.

"I think I just had ten years shaved off my life," Ciara whispers.

"I'm okay with never coming back here. Let's get our token and get the hell out of here," Tate says.

"We go together on this one," Trysten orders. "Walk as one unit."

We all slip on our winter coats and snow boots before opening the transport ramp. With the live feed running, we pull up our hoods, activate our energy shields, and brace against the wind. Trysten follows closely behind me.

Outside on the pad, the wind gusts make it almost impossible to stay upright. We huddle together, fighting against the wind as we make our way to the control room in a tight formation. It's so cold that I can feel my teeth chattering and my whole body shaking despite our flight uniforms.

Our steps are slow, and when one of us wobbles, we hold on to each other for support. When we reach the metal door, it swishes open, granting us access to the dark room.

"What the—" Tate mutters, his voice echoing off the cold walls as we survey our surroundings.

A suffocating sense of wrongness hangs in the air. The long, narrow hall is cloaked in an unyielding darkness, a chill rattling my bones that has nothing to do with the temperature here. I glance toward the adjoining rooms, finding them empty, their doors ominously ajar as if everyone had left in a hurry.

As we make our way to the control room, we find that it, too, is empty. The air inside the room is frigid, enough to have a bite even through our heavy winter gear. Outside the building, the wind continues to howl like a restless spirit, sending goosebumps racing across my skin.

"Well, this is new," Trysten states, pulling out his Hallo. I follow suit, gripping the familiar sleek frame. Behind us, Tate and Ciara press together, their backs flush and expressions full of anxiety.

Something about this feels wrong, making my stomach swirl with unease. I approach the control panel, my breath catching in my throat when I see everything shut down. A fresh wave of panic courses through me as I look out over the launch pad. There should always be at least two personnel stationed here for emergency landings. The stillness around us feels unnatural.

"Are we at the wrong one?" Ciara whispers, her voice trembling, teeth chattering, probably more from fear than the cold.

"No," Trysten and I reply in unison, our voices hushed. I can feel the weight of the darkness pressing in around us.

"Let's go," Trysten insists, an urgency creeping into his tone. "Something is off, and I'd rather not stick around to find out what. We'll call the school as soon as we're free."

We exchange nervous glances, each of us agreeing with a slight nod. Our footsteps become frantic as we retrace our steps back toward the exit.

Then, just as we approach the door, a whisper slices through the silence, sending chills crawling across my skin—"Soraea." My heart races, and fear grips me as I spin around, searching the eerie shadows for the source. But there's nothing there.

Trysten pushes me forward, urging me out the door. As we burst into the open, the merciless wind and cold are overshadowed by an overwhelming instinct to flee and get off this planet as quickly as possible. Without thought, we sprint across the blanket of snow, no longer huddling together.

Ciara stumbles, but Trysten is already there, reaching back to grasp her arm and pulling her along as we race toward the ramp already lowering at our approach. Once inside, I don't even bother to shed my coat or gear. All I want is to escape this nightmare of a planet.

"Get us out of here, Raea," Trysten commands.

I nod and hurriedly activate the emergency launch sequence. The ship hums to life around us as I brace for the violent jolt of the thrusters engaging. With a shuddering roar, we ascend, our backs pressed into our seats, the force holding our breaths captive until we break free from the grip of Cresnigan's gravity. In under two minutes, we're free.

Once clear, I stand and peel off my heavy coat and boots along with the others. Adrenaline courses through us all, leaving us all trembling.

"Ciara, you need to warn the other transports. We can't let anyone else risk landing. Send out a message as soon as possible. Trysten, can you contact the school and notify them of the situation? And Tate, find us a clear path to Cidal. We still have a few planets to go before we're in the clear," I instruct, my voice steady despite the unease running rampant within me.

As I take a moment to collect my thoughts, my mind races, replaying the events that just transpired. We had received clearance to land; I remember that clearly. There was a voice, authoritative and unmistakable, granting us permission. Then, there was that other transport—its insignia flashing on my screen, unmistakably linked to the academy.

"I've already sent the message to Professor Brendn and Chancellor Xara," Trysten replies, his ever-calm demeanor a welcome comfort. I nod, grateful he's here, and retake my seat, trying to focus.

"Can we look into getting clearance for the recording from the landing? I can't be the only one who heard the transmission," I suggest.

Trysten shakes his head slowly, his brows pinching together. "We don't have direct access to that data; the school does. And to answer your question more directly, I didn't catch it, but I wasn't exactly focused. I was trying to coach Tate on delivering the weather report," he admits, a hint of regret in his tone.

I turn to Ciara, hoping she heard it. She shrugs, admitting she was focused on their conversation, too. Frustration bubbles beneath the surface, but I remind myself to breathe. There's no point in worrying about permissions or recordings—not right now.

Cidal is a planet I'm intimately familiar with, and perhaps the familiarity will ease this gnawing anxiety inside of me. I scan the navigation system for a clear path before engaging our reactor, initiating the hyperjump sequence. The distance from Ateria to Treon is quick but not without its challenges. We will need to thread our way around Mori and Thirik, skirting the edges of the Storm Nebula before entering Treon's airspace. With hyperjump, we have a little more than an hour. I plan to use every minute to reorient myself.

As the transport begins to decelerate, the vibrant hues of Cidal emerge from the darkness of space. From this vantage point, the planet appears as a translucent, mint green hue, brushed with wispy white clouds that dance across its surface, interspersed with wide bodies of glittering blue water. Instantly, my nerves start to settle.

"Ciara, please clear us for landing," I instruct, my eyes fixed on the planet's surface. As we approach, Cidal's diminutive moon, Zaria, comes into view, peeking out from behind the planet.

Its small size is overshadowed by its stunning features—swirls of vibrant pinks and purples intertwined with cobalt rings. Though Zaria is beautiful, its waters are toxic, and gas emissions from vents prevent habitation. Instead, the moon serves as a storage site, repurposed for our waste materials before they are recycled.

"Cidal, pad twelve, this is Academy Transport Five. We are requesting access to land for a brief period of five minutes," Ciara communicates through the console, her tone professional yet smooth. I hear the all-clear echo in my headset, confirming that the others also received the message.

As the green light flashes, I prepare for atmospheric entry. Pad twelve is situated in the heart of the city, the location chosen for this exact exercise.

I notice Trysten holding back his instinct to take over the controls, his fingers twitching above the flight console. I glance at the ink swirling on his hands, wondering if it's just for art or if it has meaning. Shaking off the distraction, I redirect my focus to the landing pad. The stakes are significantly higher here, and it would be deadly if I made a mistake. Even with computers managing most of the landing procedure, I need to be ready for any shift that could pull us off course.

I steadily reduce our speed, expertly guiding the transport until we touch down seamlessly on the designated pad. The sense of relief that washes over me is palpable.

"Nice job," Trysten sighs, and I see his body visibly relax. "Gods, why is this so much harder on this side?" He chuckles as he brushes his hair back.

"I don't envy you right now, but you can trust me a little, can't you? I mean, we only have three planets to go. We'll be back at school just in time for breakfast." I smile at him, unbuckling my harness.

The air outside smells like fresh rain and damp forest, despite it being the largest city and colony on the planet. Tate and I make our way to the tower.

"Let's hope someone is here and there's not an imp waiting inside," Tate whispers. When I shoot him a glare, he chuckles. "Too soon?"

"First off, imps don't exist. Second, the lights are actually on this time," I note.

As the sun gracefully descends behind the colony's skyline, the city comes to life, sparkling with a kaleidoscope of lights that dance across the towering structures. Each time I visit Elran Asari, I am struck by the sheer height of the shimmering glass towers that seem to stretch endlessly into the sky. Personal pods zip through the air, adding to the chaos of the already crowded streets.

In Elran Asari, rain is as common as the sight of the never-ending crowd. Residents here have adopted a rather—unique style. Their daily attire consists of vibrant neon trenches, and they wear their hair in a variety of bright colors—electric blues, fiery pinks, and vivid greens—as if to compensate for the continuous lack of sunlight. Their choice of makeup here is equally extravagant; both men and women adorn their faces with dramatic hues, painting on thick layers of blush and lipstick.

Their fashion choices are a stark contrast to those on my home planet of Kyrr, where our lifestyles revolve around the lushness of the rainforest and the cascading waterfalls that define our landscape. In Kyrr, the colors we wear are influenced by nature, with palettes consisting of forest tones—muted greens, warm browns, light blues, and soft beiges that blend into our surroundings. Clothing is typically functional and straightforward, featuring cotton and linen tunics and skirts, as well as thick sweaters when needed. Leather belts and brooches are also included, allowing for easy movement through the dense foliage and rugged terrain.

"Princess Raea," Private Johanson greets us with genuine surprise. I wince when I realize I didn't put my hood up. At least my hair doesn't stand out here.

The man before me is one I've known for many years. His father once served as one of our trusted guards, and it's hard to forget the fond memories we share of teasing his father and giving him a hard time. Johanson is a bit taller than I, his golden locks shining beneath the bright lights of the control tower, but the scar down his left cheek is new.

He's wearing the typical uniform of our Terra quadrant, the camouflage fabric making him appear larger than I remember. The insignia of his rank is proudly displayed on his sleeve.

With a deep, respectful bow, he steps forward and extends his hand, presenting a green token. One side is adorned with a tree signet that symbolizes Treon's landscapes, while the reverse side bears the Kingdom crest.

"Thank you, Johanson," I reply, keeping my voice warm and filled with gratitude. "Are you well? I didn't know you had graduated already."

He beams back at me. "Yes, thank you. I graduated last year and was posted here about four months ago."

After a few minutes of letting him speak about his new position, I ask him to kindly forget I was here and not tell anyone, logging my name as Cadet Elara Maddix. He nods eagerly, assuring me of his silence, and with another grateful smile, I wave goodbye.

"Here," Trysten says, handing me a tray of food.

The aroma wafts up, mixing with the faint scent of metal. We are nearly to Ista, and the reminder of Anders and me discovering the older temple and the books on magic brings a fond memory to mind.

Sitting on the launch pad for hours with him had done wonders for our friendship. Not that I'd admit it, but I do miss him. I feel silly since it's only been a day, but I wish he were beside me. At least his best friend is here. According to the displays tracking our hyperjump progress, we should only have a few more minutes before we drop in.

"Thanks," I reply, taking the tray.

My stomach grumbles at the sight of food: a melted sandwich oozing with cheese and roasted vegetables. We were supposed to eat after Cresnigan, but food had been the last thing on our minds in the aftermath of events. I sink my teeth into the sandwich and can't help but groan appreciatively, earning an amused smirk from Trysten.

"So tell me," I say after I swallow down my bite. "How did you and Anders become best friends?" I take another bite. It's so satisfying, and I feel like my whole body reacts to the food despite my exhaustion. The energy shot I took earlier has helped, but I know nothing will satisfy my exhaustion like a good rest in my bed.

"Our fathers were close friends. We were raised like brothers in a way. I don't know, not much to tell," he says, his words trailing off. The way he avoids my gaze suggests there may be more to that story.

I swallow the last satisfying bite, sad that it's all gone, and take a long sip of the hot, rich coffee. "Mmm…so good," I hum. "Were you close with his father?" I'm curious about his relationship with King Aki.

Trysten only nods, something unreadable flickering across his features.

"Fine, no talking," I tease, sensing his reluctance to dive deeper. I take the last bite of cinnamon cake and return my tray to the cabinet. Clearly, he doesn't want to talk. Which is fine—it's not like anything is going on between Anders and me anyway.

The transport rattles violently, each jolt sending me sprawling across the metal walkway. I curse under my breath and catch myself against the hard surface of the cabinets before I risk turning my gaze to the displays. The screen flickers erratically, the marker dancing chaotically within the system's grid.

"What's going on?" Tate shouts, his voice barely rising above the cacophony of alarms blaring around us. I struggle to regain my balance as the entire transport feels like it's being hurled through space.

"We're still jumping," I call out, urgency fueling my movements as I race back to the console.

Red lights flash above it, accompanied by a deafening blur of alarms. Trysten is already at the controls, furiously tapping on the glass interface, his eyes scanning the rapidly scrolling code and alerts.

"We're off course," Tate yells. The gravity of his words sinks into my stomach.

This isn't possible. Transports can't alter their course mid-jump. I glance at the countdown timer—ten seconds left in this jump. Fear knots in my stomach.

"Tate, find out where we are now! Raea, sit down," Trysten barks, his usual calm cracking under the pressure as he goes through the alarms with a panic-stricken face. Another violent shake rattles the transport, sending me stumbling once more.

"Where are we, Tate?" I shriek, watching the screen with dread as it continues to glitch and sputter, unsure of where to place our location. Meanwhile, every sensor is going crazy, lighting up and blaring at us like I don't already know something is really, really wrong.

"The computers are going haywire. It's throwing our location all over the place. I don't know," he responds, the anxious tremor in his voice echoing my own fear.

When the jump ends, the sky shifts from black to a vivid blue, and I can hardly believe my eyes. The sky transforms again, morphing into an expansive body of water charging toward us with terrifying speed.

"Brace for impact, now!"

twenty-six

. . .

THE SOUND of the transport hitting the water is like a bomb; the impact is so loud that I feel it reverberate through every part of me, silencing everything for a moment, aside from a high-pitched ringing in my ears. I'm still recovering from the blow, too stunned to care that my ears are ringing or that I seriously hurt myself by not being strapped into the harness. Honestly, I'm lucky to be alive. I should have crashed into the glass.

Instead, my body is thrown up against the console despite my holding onto the harness I grabbed at the last minute. Thankfully, my corset took the brunt of it. I've never been more thankful for the ridiculous contraption I've been required to wear for the past eleven years. The Nakata plates potentially saved my life. I'll probably have a bruise, which is nothing compared to what it could have been.

When I glance beside me, I find Trysten unconscious, his face bleeding where he hit the panel, rivulets of crimson blood draining down the side of his face and covering the cracked glass where his head lies. In front of me, I notice the water level rising over the glass window, alerting me to the fact that our transport is sinking quickly. The water rises every second, revealing clear blue water and glowing white moon jellies swimming toward us. In moments, they've surrounded the glass, their bodies brushing up against it and molding to it, interested in who and what we are.

With another breath, I calm myself, realizing I need to take control. We'll die in here if I don't. The ringing in my ears subsides enough for me to gain clarity. "We need to get out now," I yell over the sound of rushing water that begins seeping through the cabin's cracks.

Anxiety and fear push in around me, threatening to drown me, but I can't let it win. *I will not be weak.* I take a moment to look around, take everything in, and then begin giving orders. We have minutes at best before this transport is sucked down to the bottom of whatever body of water we landed in. I only hope that someone will notice and send emergency vehicles to find us.

"Ciara, grab the bags," I keep my voice calm and clear. "Tate, I need your help with Trysten. He's stuck." I yank on his harness, but it doesn't budge. On the other side of Trysten, Tate pulls a blade from his waist and begins cutting through the thick fabric. On the edge of my control, panic threatens to take hold again, but I fight against it. Panic will not help us get out of this situation.

I gasp when chilly water fills the space around my thighs, my flight uniform doing little to ward off the cold. Finally, the harness snaps free, and Trysten sags out of his seat. His head wound does nothing to ease the grip on my chest.

"Can you lift him?" I ask. Tate just nods, lifting Trysten with incredible strength over his shoulders like a sack of grain. I glance back at the ramp and nearly groan. The angle at which we are sinking means we will have to climb.

"C'mon," Ciara cries. "Let's go."

Using the cabinetry, I pull myself up the steep path, reaching into one of them for the med pack, and reach with my free hand to grab Ciara's outstretched hand. Once I'm pulled to the edge and suspended above the water, we both turn, lying flat to reach for Tate, where he's propped himself and Trysten against the third row of seats.

Both of us cry out, using what strength we have to pull both men up. It should be impossible, but I know that the adrenaline coursing through me has made it possible. When Tate gets to the ledge, we help him stand as the three of us look out over the back of the transport.

"We have to jump," I say with a shaky voice.

Out the back ramp, there's about a twelve-foot drop, the ship almost vertical in the water now, and my breath catches. We'll need to clear the transport before we get sucked under. I don't hesitate, knowing that I'll get trapped in all the what-ifs if I think too long. "On three." Both of them nod just as I begin to count. On three, we all jump, Tate still holding Trysten around his shoulders.

I hold my breath just as my feet hit the surface, and a moment later, I plunge into the icy water. The water is so cold it steals my breath instantly and sends searing pain through my body. I break the surface and inhale, my body already numb in places. My limbs can barely function, but I know I need to get everyone to shore as quickly as possible. Staying out here is deadly. As I glance around, I don't spot Tate or Trysten.

Shit. Shit. Shit.

With another deep inhale, I dive back down, searching the clear water, thankful I can see, and find Tate struggling to reach the surface. It takes two strokes to reach them before I pull on Trysten as Tate pushes. Once we surface, I flip Trysten on his back and wait, praying he's still alive. Another heartbeat passes before he inhales, thank gods, but he's still unconscious. I turn in a panic and see Ciara swimming toward me with all the bags dragging behind her, their weight slowing her down.

Glancing around, I notice a shoreline not too far from our current position. "C'mon, it's like a two-minute swim," I sputter, fighting back against the cold. "Tate, switch with Ciara and get a break. Ciara, come help me pull Trysten." I inhale sharply. "We have to swim, don't stop."

Ciara nods, her teeth chattering and her lips already blue as she switches places with Tate.

My vision starts to fade at the edges, darkness threatening to pull me under. I fight against the encroaching weight of sleep with every ounce of willpower I can muster. "Kee-eep go-ing," I whisper, my voice barely audible over the rhythmic lapping of the water.

I'm completely numb, the cold water no longer biting into me. In some ways, it's a blessing, offering me a reprieve, but in other ways, I know it's hazardous. I need to get out of this water before my body shuts down.

As our feet finally make contact with the soft sand of the shore, a whimper of relief escapes my lips. Ciara and I cling to the last remnants of our dwindling energy, working together to drag Trysten's limp form from the water. Behind us, Tate struggles, his muscles straining as he hauls all four bags to the beach. The air wraps around us like a comforting blanket, surprisingly warm against our frozen skin.

"Ci-ar-a," I chatter, "Geeet h-hi-m un-d-resss-d."

Tate stumbles over, leaving the bags to help her, both of them fighting against shock and hypothermia.

It's midday, wherever we are, and it seems we are on a tropical island. Noting the humid air and knowing we need to dry off and warm up, I pull off my flight suit and corset as quickly as I can, fighting against that lull of darkness. As the soaked suit hits the sand, I slap my hands to my face, waking me up for just a moment.

We need a fire.

Dropping to my knees, I yank open the med bag and find the emergency blankets—they'll have to do. We didn't grab the survival bag, which has all the necessities for surviving in the wild. I toss the six blankets on the sand, moving to care for Trysten while the two of them can strip. Yanking the last part of his suit off, I take note of his blue lips and shallow breathing.

"We neeeed–tooo–gett himm warm," I say to nobody in particular.

Already pulling off the last of her suit, Ciara drops down beside him in the sand, wrapping her arms around his pale body. Her eyes flutter closed, and it takes me a moment to pull the blankets around them, tucking them in, before turning to find Tate kneeling beside me.

"Heeerrre," I chatter, my voice barely above a whisper as I pass him a crinkled, reflective blanket, its metallic coating gleaming in the sunlight.

I slowly unwrap my own, the weight of exhaustion pressing down on me like a weight. I have never felt this drained, a deep fatigue settling in my bones. Sleep beckons to me, but there's one more thing I need to do. Trysten's head is still bleeding, but at least the flow has slowed thanks to the ice water.

Stumbling, I reach for the emergency kit and nearly collapse on top of Trysten as I wrap the blanket around myself, trying to cover my body in warmth. With trembling hands, I pull out the glue patch and cleanser, my mind racing despite the fog of fatigue. I'm teetering on the edge of unconsciousness, but there's no time to rest. I squirt the cleanser onto a gauzy pad and, with a sense of urgency, slap the glue patch onto his injury, hoping it will seal the cut before any more blood can escape.

Lying down beside Trysten and Ciara, I can feel the chill radiating from his body. Just then, I hear Tate collapsing beside me and then feel the weight of his body pressing against me from behind.

At last, I give in to the pull of the darkness just as I reach out, finding Ciara's hand over Trysten's chest. I clasp it gently, drawing strength from this small connection.

This isn't how we die.

There's only eternal darkness, a never-ending void that sucks every bit of light out of everything around me. As I strain to see, an endless expanse of black swirls eddy like a living, breathing thing, resembling an onyx-colored mist that consumes the very essence of life.

Even though my eyes are blind to my surroundings, my other senses are heightened. I can feel *his* presence behind me, an undeniable warmth radiating from his solid form, a reassuring wall of muscle, offering me strength when I feel as if I have none. The fragrant scent of fresh citrus mingling with warm sandalwood envelops me, embracing me, filling my lungs, and easing my frayed nerves.

"Wake up, Soraea," he whispers tenderly, his voice soothing, like honey dripping over warm tea, right into my ear.

His large hands find their way around my waist, tugging me closer and holding me against his protective body. Another wave of calm washes over me, loosening the tension as I instinctively lean into him, a soft hum of contentment escaping my lips.

But underneath this strange, fuzzy warmth, panic lurks as I attempt to wade through my foggy thoughts. I need to save them—I can't let this horrible destruction continue. Only then do I hear the distant screams and desperate cries piercing the strange darkness.

Like a jolt to the system, I tense up and twist in his arms, grasping tightly onto the lapels of his jacket. "We have to help them," I plead, my voice trembling. "Help me."

I struggle to regain my bearings, but that never-ending darkness solidifies, becoming an impenetrable wall of obsidian. All I can feel beneath my feet is the solid, warmed stone—a reminder that I'm on the palace terrace in Mori, here for a party for the Queen.

Memories ebb and flow, becoming more clouded by the second, but the weight of his presence against mine shifts my anxiety into something bearable. I place my hand over the steady rhythm of his heartbeat, allowing it to ground me.

"Please, help me," I beg, my voice cracking.

"I am," he responds, his tone gentle and unwavering, as he brushes a few errant strands of my white hair away from my face, the only thing I can see in the dark. His fingers linger momentarily before his hands slide to the nape of my neck, sending a searing heat down my spine. I feel the soft press of his lips on my forehead. "Now wake up, beautiful."

With a gentle shake, he nudges me from the dark abyss. My eyes fly open with a startling gasp.

As I glance around, I note that the sky is cloaked in shades of deep blues and pale pinks as the sun sinks below the horizon, its shimmering water glistening like scattered diamonds. Reality slams into me, crushing me. Our crash landing here was not just a nightmare, but reality. I shift slightly, catching a glimpse of Tate, his arms wrapped securely around my waist. Then I glance to my right, where relief washes over me when I feel the rise and fall of Trysten's chest, assuring me he's still alive. My hand is still linked with Ciara's, and she, too, is steadily breathing beneath the blanket.

My body aches everywhere as I struggle to sit up. A painful headache jabs at my temples, making it feel like my head is splitting in two. The air around me is thick but warm, and there's a strange, persistent sound like a bug buzzing in my ears. I begin to absorb the little details of my surroundings; earlier, I had been too overwhelmed.

To our rear, a dense forest of tangled trees with pulsing bands of light and vines stretches up to the sky. To my left, a jagged rocky outcrop juts toward the glowing cerulean water. My mind races, desperately trying to map it all and piece together the hazy memories clouding my mind. I can still feel the lingering touch of Anders' lips on my forehead, but I know for a fact I haven't been to Mori in the past year, and definitely not with him.

I shake loose the confusing memories and instead focus on the environment. I have no idea where we've ended up. Fragments of images flash back to me—screens flickering with alarms, the sky going from black to blue in an instant, then...I push at my temples, trying to recall the flash of land I saw just beyond the water.

Where are we?

I see the displays of our position—first, we were in Treon, then Ateria, a moment later in Thirik, and then we crossed into Kadora. The jolting of the transport definitely fits with what the displays showed.

I carefully move out of Tate's arms, leaning over Trysten, and, with a trembling hand, peel back the bandage. Relief surges through me when I find that his wound is nearly closed up and the bleeding has halted. Sinking back onto my ankles, I exhale deeply. My survival instincts from Recon rush to the front of my mind, and for once, I'm grateful we were forced to learn them.

"Fire. Food. Water," I remind myself.

I'm not sure if we can start a fire with damp wood. I really wish we had the survival bag. I scowl out at the frozen water where our transport has found a watery grave. *Well, no use dwelling on it.* Instead, I focus on what we do have, unzipping each of our sodden bags and dumping their dry contents onto the sand.

I count five bottles of water, a change of cold-weather clothing, a second headset of mine, a pack of dried fruit, and a notebook, which might come in handy. I also gather six weapons: two Hallo guns, mine and Trysten's, and four daggers. It's not much, but we'll have to make do. I'm sure our trackers will bring help soon, especially when we don't check in on the next three planets.

"Raea?" Ciara groans, her voice low and raspy. I race over to her, dropping to my knees, and help her off Trysten.

"Thank you," I whisper, my voice barely above a breath as I hug her tightly.

Trysten is alive because of her and Tate. Though she's taller than I, she leans against me, her body still unsteady as she attempts to regain her balance. Once she steadies herself, she stands tall, her dark hair a wild mess around her shoulders and her rich, caramel skin flecked with grains of sand from the beach.

"Where are we?" she mumbles, her voice thick with confusion and exhaustion.

It must be the shock of everything finally breaking through, but I can't help it; I burst into laughter. The sound spills out of me uncontrollably until my stomach cramps. Her lips curl into a smile, and gradually, she joins in my laughter, her eyes sparkling with relief. In this moment, despite the chaos surrounding us, we find a reason to laugh.

Maybe it's because we're both stripped of our clothes, standing in our lacy underthings, lost somewhere in space with two passed-out men behind us, or maybe it's because we're trying to hold the hysteria and panic at bay. Either way, I let the light moment flood my system like a balm over my wrecked nerves. I'm sure if anyone saw us right now, they would laugh, too.

I take in her wild hair, the strands are as dark as night around us, each splattered with grains of sand like those clinging stubbornly to our skin in various places. The dark bruises beginning to form on her arms and legs make me wince, but I continue laughing as we scan each other, looking for more injuries. It's then that I finally notice the nasty purple and black splotch taking up my left side and part of my abdomen.

Pain courses through me, awakening at the sight of where I hit the console. I lay my palm flat over it, laughing through it because if I don't, I'm not sure I'll regain the control I currently have over the lingering horror of what happened.

"Gods," Tate groans, "what are you guys laughing about?" I glance over, only to realize that he, too, looks to be covered in various bruises. "Dammit," he hisses, finally sitting up and gripping his throbbing head with both hands.

The sight of him, disheveled and struggling, only makes us laugh harder, even as I feel the edge of panic tightening in my chest. The line between laughing and crying is beginning to thin.

Ciara must sense it because she says, "It'll be alright," as she dusts me off.

I nod, taking a much-needed deep breath, and shove everything back into a box, only feeling a slight burn behind my eyes.

Tate manages to prop himself up further, his fingers still clutching at his face as if that could somehow stave off the headache. When we drop down in front of him, he lifts his gaze to meet ours, his eyes widening in shock and mock horror. "Put some clothes on," he hisses, turning his head away in a mixture of embarrassment and disbelief at our state of undress.

"We literally have nothing," I say, letting a chuckle bubble up. "All we had were our suits, and they're still soaked. It'll be a while before they dry out fully." I let my mind wander momentarily, my lessons returning to me, and I can't remember the last time a transport crashed. It's literally been centuries. "Just pretend it's just our swimsuits." I shrug, offering him an amused smile. Beside me, Ciara tucks her lips in, attempting to hide her laughter, but it comes out anyway.

Tate turns to face us. "Fine, but don't blame me for how my body responds. Besides, swimsuits cover a lot more than—" he gestures toward our lace-clad bodies, "that. Gods, does anyone know where we are?"

"No. Are your trackers still working?" I look down at my hand where the gold band sits.

I'm not sure whether it's functioning or not. Ciara holds up her necklace shaped like a crescent moon, but there's still no way to tell. Tate displays the gold band wrapped around his wrist. "So, we don't know. Okay, what do we know?" I pull out the notebook from the pile of things I've gathered.

"We were jumping, and our transport apparently got lost. Was it the nav system?" Ciara asks Tate more than me.

"It was fine. I was watching us slow down when it started to shake. When I looked back, we were all over the system."

I nod in confirmation. "Okay, let's try this: planet trivia." There's a bit of excitement in my voice as I plop down beside Tate. "Maybe we can figure it out this way. We know the atmosphere is breathable, and we aren't in a desert. That rules out all planets in Mori and most of Kadora. This doesn't look like a volcanic planet, and I think all the beaches are cold with black sand, so I'm ruling out Kadora. Ateria's planets all have huge mountains and are in perpetual winter. I didn't see mountains or snow, and it's way too warm." I glance around in the dark; all I can see is the horizon of water in front of me and trees at my back.

"You know more about planets than anyone," Tate says as he digs his hands into the moist sand, watching as he lifts them, letting the sand fall in clumps back to the beach. "Which planets have humid air?"

I inhale, using my sense of smell to help narrow down the options. "Okay, so we aren't anywhere in Thirik. All of their planets smell like Hawkthorne weed. Oris is a possibility, but all of their planets are in perpetual fall, and the winds never stop. That leaves us with Treon and the Okenen Kingdom." I turn to a blank page in my notebook and start writing down every planet in both kingdoms.

When I'm done, I have forty planets to narrow down.

I look up at the night sky, and when I spot three moons, I start crossing off half of Treon's planets and a third of Okenen's. My mind feels tired, but I flip through the pages of my planet tome at home. I envision the wooden table in my study, where the light dances around the room throughout the day, and the scent of old pages from the ancient books on the high shelves before me. My tutors claim real books are better than digital, even though it's slower; I have to agree.

I recount what I know. Humidity fills the air, and three moons hang overhead. It's warm, but there's ice-cold water nearby. Glowing moon jellies thrive here, surviving only in freshwater. I cross out another six planets from my list that I know lack such large bodies of water with moon jellies.

"Okay, so here's the good news." I look at them. "We are on one of the nineteen planets I've narrowed it down to."

twenty-seven

. . .

ryker

I'M COMPLETELY EXHAUSTED, and my body is aching from sitting so long. We arrived home sometime in the early morning hours, and I took a long, hot shower to wash off the long day of travel before I collapsed into bed. With a rare day off to recuperate, I planned to spend the first half under the blankets, avoiding the rest of the world —and my responsibilities.

It's around midday when I finally groan awake, reluctantly peeling my eyelids apart. As I adjust to the light, another loud bang reverberates against my door. Maybe if I ignore it, whoever it is will just give up and go away. I shove my head deeper into the pillow, but another forceful knock echoes even louder this time.

Dammit.

"Open up!" a voice barks from the other side. My stomach twists at the sound of Kellan's voice.

With a heavy sigh, I push myself out of bed, grabbing the first pair of pants I can find, jumping into them and completely disregarding whether I look presentable.

"Yes?" I shove every bit of annoyance into the single word as I swing the door open to reveal Kellan standing there, looking far from his usual self. He appears almost sickly, his face pale and drawn. I might be the dorm leader, but I'm not a damn nurse.

"Where is she?" Kellan demands, his eyes narrowing as he looks past me into my room as if expecting to find Raea hiding in the corner. The idea strikes me as almost absurd—there's no way she would ever be in here. But then my mind comes to a sudden halt.

Why is he so desperate to find her here?

"What do you mean? Why would she be here? Have you checked her room?" I keep my tone calm, even as dread washes over me like a cold wave. Of course, he's already checked her room; the frantic look he gives me says enough.

"She's not there. Nobody has seen her. Is it possible she's still flying?" The edge of panic in his voice makes my blood run cold. They should have been back by now. I leave the door open, my mind racing with hundreds of possibilities, as I fumble through my clothes to grab a shirt, pulling it on in a hurry and searching for my boots. Once I'm dressed enough to face the world, I strap on my weapon belt and shut the door behind me with a loud clack.

"Let's go," I bark, anxiety already swirling inside me, as I take off at a brisk pace toward the launch pad.

If her transport has arrived, it means they're back. If it hasn't, well... Why the hell are there so many people in my way? Nobody else seems to share my rising panic as I weave through the throng of bodies filling the corridor. I ignore the surprised gasps and protests from other students as I shove them out of the way. I hear Kellan behind me muttering apologies as we go.

Always the simpering fool.

I reach out for the Bond between us—both of them—and can't get a reading on either. I calm the storm already brewing within me; no need to tear the school apart if she's here. She could be in the healers' center again.

My pace quickens as we leave Taeolyn, heading straight for the launch pad. The transport bay comes into view, and one by one, I count the ships docked and ready for cleaning. I know Raea has been assigned to transport five, which is located at the end of the long pad.

My heart races as I sprint down the hallway, urgency fueling my every step.

There is an oppressive silence that blankets the launch area. The Sky Division's launch pad remains unlit, everything shut down for the day as we all recover. As I approach Launchpad Five, dread uncoils in my chest—it's completely empty.

My instinct drives me toward the control tower, where they'll hopefully have answers. My heart pounds in my chest as I storm up the six levels, Kellan trailing anxiously behind me.

"You can't come up here," the guard stationed at the entrance warns me. I know I could easily shove him aside without a second thought.

"Call Chancellor Xara," I demand, brushing past him without waiting for a response.

His sigh of resignation accompanies my ascension as he reluctantly pages the Chancellor. I don't bother knocking when I reach the control room, finding only one tower controller, sitting casually, halfway through a sandwich on the opposite side of the room. He doesn't see me, and I don't bother wasting my time striking up a conversation. I head straight for the console and pull up the transport log, scanning the data relayed from her ship. There's no current flight signal, and their last known location was Cidal.

The knot in my chest tightens as images of what could have gone wrong flash through my mind. Perhaps they faced mechanical failure, though surely they would have called for help if that had been the case.

"Prince Anders," a voice interrupts my spiraling thoughts. It's Paulson, the tower control operator, his brow furrowed as he approaches me, still wiping his mouth. For some damn reason, the sight irritates me. We have a missing transport, and he's just in here enjoying his damn lunch.

"It's an emergency," I reply, not caring much about my flippant tone. Much to my surprise, instead of taking the controls, he pulls up a seat next to me. I can sense his gaze studying me, weighing his options.

"Alright, what are you looking for?" he finally asks.

"Princess Raea Tierson's transport never landed," I explain, my words tumbling out in a rush. "There's no signal." Paulson inhales sharply, a flicker of concern crossing his face as he turns in his seat to page Professor Brendn. I quickly find the tower number for Cidal and initiate a satellite communication.

After a few agonizing minutes, the response crackles over the intercom. "This is Tower Twelve, Cidal," the voice on the other end states, echoing through the room.

"This is Drithm Academy Control." I force myself into that steady calm required of a prince, of a king. "We are looking for an academy transport—number five."

Silence descends upon the room, every ear tuned to the transmission as we await news.

"Copy that. Transport five was here last night," the tower operator continues, each word feeling like a blow. "They launched after Private Johanson gave them their token."

A chill runs down my spine. The transports are equipped with a fail-safe beacon; we should be able to locate them anywhere in the system, and yet...

"Thank you, Tower Twelve," I respond, the words feeling hollow. Just then, the doors to the control room swing open, and Chancellor Xara strides in, flanked by Professor Brendn.

"What the hell is going on?" Chancellor Xara demands.

I stand quickly, noticing the pale, strained expressions on everyone's faces. Beside me, Kellan's composure is slipping.

My hands curl into fists as I say, "Chancellor, Transport Five, Princess Raea's transport, went missing sometime last night. Her last known location was Cidal. We spoke with the control tower, and they confirmed that the launch went smoothly. But now, *we*," I shoot Paulson a cold look, letting my barely-checked anger at him show just a bit, "can't track them." The gravity of the situation sinks in, and everyone's faces morph with horror.

I grind my molars as thoughts race through my mind. The first thought is that their transport could have exploded mid-air, or they could have been sucked into the Drennik Straights, an expanse infamous for lethal radiation levels.

Chancellor Xara's eyes widen momentarily in shock, but she swiftly masks it, pivoting her attention to Paulson as if searching for someone to blame. If I weren't so tired and sick with worry, I might have let a smug smile pull at my lips, but right now, I just don't care. "Why didn't you report a missing transport immediately?" she demands urgently, using her authoritative voice. Paulson blanches and cowers.

"Step aside," Professor Brendn interjects, addressing Paulson with a commanding tone. He strides forward, fingers moving over the control screen as he inputs a password.

Instantly, the room dims, cloaking us in shadows and casting a projection of the entire system around us. Raea's image flickers to life at the bottom of the display, accompanied by Trysten, Tate, and Ciara's faces. To my relief, their heartbeats pulse steadily beside their photos. *They're alive.* A wave of emotion washes over me as I gaze at her photo and Trysten's.

Thank fuck.

"Interesting," Professor Brendn murmurs, making his way through the holographic projection, manipulating the displayed planets with practiced ease to examine various sectors more closely. "I can't seem to locate them. They all had their trackers on, yes?" He throws me a questioning glance.

I nod in affirmation, recalling how Raea had played with the ring on her finger, stealing little glances as I pretended not to notice each of her moves.

Raea has so thoroughly gotten under my skin that I swear, my eyes find her before I even have a chance to consciously catch up. I notice everywhere she is, and everywhere she isn't. It's not just the Lumos Bond and the wave of translucent colors that seem to wrap around us —it's something else. Something deeper. I find that the only time I feel like myself lately is in her presence. I love teasing her, getting under her skin. She makes it so damn easy. But the way she looks at me, her glittering green eyes heat with a fire that only urges me on.

Chancellor Xara gasps. "Explain yourself, Professor," she commands.

It's rare to witness the Chancellor lose control. As long as I've known her, she's built a hard wall of adamant between her emotions and who she presents herself as. I can see her jaw tightening, her eyes narrowing as she fixes an intense glare on Professor Brendn.

"Well, it appears we have four missing students," he responds, his voice steady, almost amused by the predicament. "You mentioned Raea was last seen on Cidal?" He looks at me for confirmation.

I nod again. Every minute we sit here wasting time, the growing headache presses in.

"Ryker, please pull up her flight test schedule. I need to confirm her intended destination," he says, a hand stroking his chin.

I drop into a chair, fingers moving swiftly over the controls, pulling up the list of planets and projecting it onto the glass panel before us. The glass darkens to onyx, the projection lights becoming a bright teal.

"She was supposed to head to Ista, and she would have been hyperjumping to reach it," he mutters under his breath.

As I look at the flight path, my mind races, unable to keep pace with the unfolding realization. The jump from Cidal to Ista crosses Sgya airspace—a forbidden region. Everyone in the system is strictly prohibited from venturing into Sgya or any of its three moons. They all should have known this. Did they, though? Tate is the one navigating, and Raea would have had to approve the change in course. She's one of the most intelligent people I know, so I have to believe she would have avoided that area at all costs.

There's a reason nobody has been granted permission to fly there —not even our most experienced pilots or astrophysicists. Surely, they wouldn't attempt it just to save time. Trysten would never allow it, especially when they would have had to override the alarms and commands. Not with the history of missing fleets, transports found years later discarded like trash—with the crews long since perished.

An inexplicable feeling tugs at my insides, and a strange sense of knowing fills my chest. I shut my eyes for a moment, seeking out that unsettling pull, and though I can't articulate it, a profound certainty begins to crystallize within me. I know, somehow I just know, that she is on Sgya. My stomach plummets at the thought.

"I know where she is!" I blurt out, instinctively rising to my feet as if that unseen force is urging me toward her. I barely make it halfway to the door when Chancellor Xara's grip tightens around my arm, a fierce determination set in her expression. As Chancellor, she's obligated to keep me safe as one of her students. But I'm not just a student; I'm the future king of Okenen, and I could easily pull rank.

I watch the war of emotions flicker in her eyes. If she doesn't let me leave, the alternative is to inform King Bastian. The academy could close if news like this were to leak. Before she can determine which route she's willing to risk, I interrupt. "I'm going. I can reach her. I at least have to try."

Her amber gaze searches my face, and I can see the moment her resolve loosens.

"You have five hours to make contact and bring her back, or—" She pauses, her expression shifting to one of sheer dread. "Take two of the guards with you."

"I'll reach her." My voice is unwavering as determination settles over me. How I plan on making it happen, I have no godsdamn clue, but I'm just going to assume that little tug means I will. Hell, I've been listening to the subtle tugs and changes in the air, and they've always led me straight to her, like a personalized beacon.

For the past few years, I've built walls of arrogance to hide the truth: from the moment I saw her, she became the only war that mattered, and I'm not going to lose her now that I've finally let those walls fall. "The guards will only slow me down. We don't have time, Chancellor."

Without waiting for her response, I push through the door and sprint toward the school's transport bay. If I truly only have five hours, I know I'll need a much larger vessel to cover the distance. Time is already slipping away, and with every second that passes, she's at further risk.

"I'm coming with you," Kellan declares as he steps out from behind me just as I approach the ramp.

I turn to face him, a sense of purpose fueling my strides. "You have little to no flight experience," I remind him, letting my frustration creep into my voice.

I don't have time to debate with him. If she's on Sgya, if they're on Sgya, the very thought brings another wave of anxiety. Call it intuition, or something even deeper binding us together, but I won't leave her there, no matter the cost.

"I can handle it," Kellan says. "I flew enough in Specialists. Plus, you'll need help. You can't go in there alone."

With his mind made up, he pushes past me, reaching the ramp before I do. Unfortunately, he's right. There are four of them, and if even one is hurt, it could take too long.

I inhale sharply, checking my anger before gritting out, "Fine. You're in charge of comms. I'll handle navigation and take the controls. Once we're airborne, get the med packs ready. We need to be prepared for anything." I run through preflight procedures in my head, systematically ticking off tasks as I flip switches. The transport hums to life beneath me. "How many weapons are you assigned to carry?"

"A single short sword," he replies, taking a seat next to me and slipping on a headset.

I mutter a curse under my breath at today's turn of events. I'm not even in a proper flight suit, just barely dressed, and the exhaustion from lack of sleep hangs heavy on me, while this godsforsaken headache just keeps growing.

"Tower, we are ready for launch," Kellan announces as I snap together the last part of my harness.

"Drithm Transport, you are cleared for—" I cut Paulson off, slapping the emergency launch button without waiting to hear the rest of the clearance.

Every second matters, and I can't afford to delay. It might be reckless not to alert their parents, but my priority is getting Raea and Trysten, as well as the others, home. I know only one person who has managed to survive Sgya, and that's my father. According to the vague notes he left on his desk, he's been there before. How he managed to get in and out undetected is beyond me.

Once we clear the atmosphere and are free from Baedyn's gravity, I initiate a hyperjump toward Sgya. I override the error messages that attempts to stall us from plotting a course there. The ship's console throws a barrage of error codes at me, but thankfully, I know how to break through them, charting us a path. Sgya lies at the center of our solar system, surrounded by our seven suns and kingdoms that encircle it like spokes on a wheel.

As we jump, I move to the back of the transport. I draw my Hallo, checking the battery levels, and holster it on my thigh before going through the cabinets and taking stock of our supplies. The academy transport is significantly larger than the student models, featuring an impressive layout that can rival smaller planet transports.

On one side, seven bunks are neatly arranged along the wall with an office just beyond. Behind me, a glass-partitioned medical bay is fully stocked, with a larger medical bed at its center. Upstairs, I know there's plenty of seating, allowing this particular transport to haul up to fifty students.

"Do you know how to use one of these?" I hold up an additional Hallo, scrutinizing him for competence.

He shakes his head, and frustration grips me.

Breathing heavily, I swallow the tide of my anger. "How the hell are you supposed to protect Raea?" My voice comes out like ice, and I watch as Kellan subtly takes on a defensive stance. "Fine," I grunt, shoving the extra Hallo into a holster at my hip. "You take the sword." I secure daggers around a tactical vest for additional weapons.

"Where are we going?" Kellan asks, his eyes widening as they take in my weapons.

"Don't ask questions I can't answer right now." I clip on the last dagger. "Just know that for every minute she's there, she's in danger." I head back to the console, focusing on the tasks at hand. "Fill canisters with water for them. They'll likely be dehydrated when we arrive."

What little we know of Sgya is that the planet was not designed for human life to exist. The gods created the planet for themselves and kept Einvald, one of their moons, nearby.

The sheer size of the planet is intimidating. I don't even know where to begin looking for them. Hopefully, their trackers will pick up on the ping and alert me once we draw near—that is, unless some unseen force blocks them. I watch our location near Sgya airspace when the transport icon on the display glitches and flickers.

We know very little about Sgya's other moons, Evello and Pripeon, as both are off-limits—even to the imperial and royal families. What we do know is that both moons have breathable atmospheres, but as far as we know, nobody has ever returned—except for my father. That is not public knowledge, though. All three moons and Sgya, even the entire airspace between the seven suns, are restricted.

According to the notes I found on my father's desk, Pripeon has a dense atmosphere and isn't suitable for long-term habitation. His notes claimed he was on the moon for a total of five minutes before he was so exhausted he could barely move. His other notes, however, showed that he was studying Sgya and Evello, flying and testing the limits—until he didn't return. I know it's a risk, but I must try. I know she's alive, and that's the only thing propelling me at this point.

My head is pounding, and nausea slams into me. I've been awake too long and haven't slept enough—that's all this is. We flew for sixteen hours yesterday, and after we landed, we heard about Cresnigan. It didn't make sense. Someone was there when we landed. Sure, the guy was acting weird, muttering to himself, and his eyes looked completely black and glazed over, but he handed over the token just fine. Raea's transport called it in.

Dammit. Nothing makes sense.

I swipe a hand down my face and run it back through my hair.

I stand up, grab a coffee, and down it in two gulps. *I need to focus.*

Kellan is silently filling bags with water and food behind me. As the thrusters slow, the identifying white planet with five golden equidistant rings of Einvald—which wrap around like protective bands—come into view, and beside it, Pripeon's surface of swirling clouds in shades of slate, with a thick band of teal wrapping around the center and deep red at the poles. Finally, Evello's orange surface comes into view. They would be beautiful if they weren't deadly.

"Where the hell are we?" Kellan asks, sitting beside me. He knows; he just hasn't come to terms with it yet.

A minute later, the strange planet fills our view. Despite its beauty, there's something otherworldly about it, like there's an invisible warning telling us to stay away. From space, Sgya's atmosphere appears almost translucent, revealing two distinct spheres, the outer layer thinner than the inner, and, at the center, a thick ring of land encircling an expansive, turquoise ocean. Smaller islands are scattered throughout the water, and what appears to be a mountain range nearly bisects the sea.

Kellan and I are both silent as we come face-to-face with Sgya. There's no tower to alert, so I descend into the thin atmosphere. It's so clear that the single landmass looks like it's floating in space. The transport shakes, rattling everything within as I grip the controls tightly. I flick on the homing beacon for the tracking devices, hoping we catch a signal.

"Kellan, keep an eye out for any heat signals or transport beacons. We need to locate them quickly," I instruct as I scan the terrain below.

The planet looks unlike anything I have ever encountered before. The surface seems bright, suggesting it's mid-morning down there. The landmass is strange, resembling a gigantic, elongated ring of land intertwined with lush forests and sparkling lakes, surrounded by the various blues of the ocean on either side. The ground is blanketed with towering, bioluminescent trees, their trunks pulsing with veins of light. The valleys, however, are terrifyingly deep, with nothing but darkness, and according to our scanner, they plunge thousands of feet deep.

Our search for Raea's team will be nearly impossible unless we can pick up a signal guiding us closer. As I lower us above the thick canopy, I engage the transport's mapping system to help with topo-graphical mapping functions.

"Anything yet?" I glance at Kellan.

He shakes his head, allowing his stress to crease his brows and pull at his mouth. I grind my molars and face back to front as we continue our search. I can see Kellan's screen displayed on the console, and the creatures we pass are not normal forest creatures. The beasts below are the size of the trees, some with wingspans over twenty feet across. I also notice that the trees pulse with a rhythmic glow synchronizing with my heartbeat.

If I focus hard enough, I can feel the planet's pulse coursing through me, just like I feel on all of our planets—but here, it's stronger, wilder. We glide past another deep valley, its walls so steep that nothing grows on them, and then over a lake that catches the sunlight like a mirror. The water glitters like a pool of quicksilver.

"There!" Kellan exclaims, pointing at the screen.

My heart races as I see two small heat signals shaped like humans flickering near the ocean's edge below us. I lower the transport further, scanning the environment for a viable place to land. Unfortunately, the trees are too dense and too tall, their trunks intertwined, making it challenging to find a spot to set down. The desperation in my chest mounts as we navigate further from them.

I locate a small field not far from their heat signatures, just barely big enough for the transport. I grab the medkit as I exit and make my way toward the shore.

"Do you think we need to be careful of the creatures here?" Kellan whispers.

"I think we need to be wary of everything here," I reply. "What do you know about Sgya?"

I feel the pulse in the ground beneath my boots. It's a thousand times stronger than anything I've experienced on other planets. Usually, it feels like a slight tremor, but this is different. I can feel the hum and vibration in my bones as though I'm somehow connected to it.

"Sgya is the home of the gods. We aren't supposed to be here—that sums up my knowledge," he answers with a shrug.

My feet move quickly over the thick moss-covered ground, my eyes scanning the horizon for the quickest path and for any lurking dangers.

I keep my free hand near my holster as I scan the forest ahead. "The gods created Sgya, taking on mortal form, but their energy is too much for humans; that's why Einvald was the seat of power, not here. Be wary of every step, every sound," I say. We find a path along a rock formation leading us to a beach.

Moments later, the thick moss gives way to fine, grainy sand that shifts under the weight of our steps. A few yards away, two figures emerge from the chaos of the beach, sprinting towards us with desperation.

"Thank the gods," Ciara gasps, reaching us first.

Her appearance is jarring. Scrapes and bruises cover her skin, and her clothing consists of nothing more than a tattered oversized shirt, revealing her undergarments below. The sight of her makes my gut clench. She looks like she has been dragged through the mud and has been here much longer than a day or two. It makes me wonder how long a day on Sgya is, especially if all seven suns are rotating around it.

Tate approaches as well, his expression mirroring my own dread. My heart almost stalls when I realize that Raea and Trysten are nowhere to be seen. Panic threads through my thoughts like a fraying rope.

"What happened?" I demand, clenching my fists. "Where are they?"

Ciara's face crumples. "They went in search of water yesterday morning, or I think yesterday morning. The hours are different here. I–I don't know what happened to them. We tried to find them but couldn't. Something happened to our transport. We lost control, and then we crashed..."

Before she can finish, a chilling, blood-curdling scream pierces the air, coming from the dark, tangled forest beside us. The sound reverberates through the trees as the four of us instinctively turn toward the gnarled branches and begin to run.

For a moment, I allow my eyes to close. Maybe if I concentrate hard enough, I can sense her through our Bond and somehow follow those iridescent waves right to her. Just then, another haunting scream echoes. Without another thought, I launch into the dark forest. Kellan is a few steps behind me, and Tate and Ciara are drifting further and further behind. I don't have time to ask why they've stopped when another shrill scream pierces the air.

"Raea," I call out above the cacophony of snapping twigs and gasps of air.

I force myself to focus on our Bond, wrestling down the overwhelming fear that I won't reach her in time. As I navigate the tangled roots and slippery moss beneath my feet, I slow just a bit, knowing that if we aren't careful, we'll easily get lost in the labyrinth of twists and turns. Branches reach out for us like skeletal hands, pulses of light flickering with each thrum of the planet.

twenty-eight

. . .

raea - the day before

As I LIE next to Trysten, the hours stretch on, and sleep continues to evade me. My mind races with a whirlwind of thoughts, particularly on the texts I have mentally scattered across my study.

Trysten remains unconscious—his face pale, yet peaceful—but I'm grateful to see that his blood pressure and temperature are holding steady. Earlier, I used a cautery tool to close the wound on his head, sealing the edges into a neat, clean line. He'll most likely have a scar, but at least it will be a small one now.

I had to carefully clean the area and ensure no trace of sand lingered. It was slow work, all the while suppressing memories of the crash and his limp body bleeding on the glass console. Now, all that's left to do is wait, praying that he will awaken and that I can figure out where the heck we are.

I can see the pages clearly, each vibrant with photos of the planet and facts surrounding it. I know Oxorion has five moons, all of which can be seen from the planet's surface. Clearly, that's not where we are, as I've only seen three. Kliax has three moons, but the planet consists of islands peppering the unending sea. I saw an island in the distance just before the sun set, but Kliax doesn't have any freshwater lakes this large.

As my thoughts continue down this path, I am startled awake by an overwhelming rush of sunlight, warm and more vivid than any I have ever encountered. It dawns on me that I must have finally fallen asleep. Unfortunately, I feel as if I haven't had enough, like it should be the middle of the night, yet I have no way of tracking time. I wish I had memorized Professor Mathison's instructions for building the solar clock.

Beside me, Trysten gasps sharply as he draws in a sudden breath, his eyes flying wide and bewildered, taking in the surroundings. He sits up slowly, confusion etched across his features, his hair matted and covered in sand; the piercing on his left brow is red and angry, but otherwise, he looks fine.

"Hey, hey, you're okay," I say, keeping my voice low. "We crashed, we're okay. You hit your head." I wince when his hand flies to the bandage, and I swat it away.

"Where are we?" he rasps, still looking around like we must have those first few hours.

There isn't much to look at from this little beach. Today needs to be the day we scout the surrounding forest for food and water. Without a fire, this water is unusable.

"We don't know...yet," I clarify. "As soon as they wake up, we are going to have a look around."

Trysten's eyes go wide, and his face flushes as he gazes down at my body, and I remember I am still in my underwear. At least this set covers more than usual. The white undergarments are made of silk and lace, hiding the most intimate parts.

I wrap my arms around my chest and stomach in an attempt to cover myself. "Our suits were soaked, and we only have winter clothes in the bags," I chuckle nervously. "I guess next time we should pack for multiple seasons." Trysten nods, refusing to look at me now.

"Here, let me get you some water." I stand, taking the blanket with me and covering my bare backside.

At our bags, I see a trail of glowworms crawling around our bags. When I pick one up, little tentacles reach for me. "No, no, little guy," I sigh, setting him back down with a huff of frustration. I didn't know they were on beaches, too. Last I read, glowworms were only found in caves in Treon and Kadora.

I return with water and take a moment to check on our suits. They're damp, and getting into them will be a hassle. Then I have a laughable idea. I walk back to our bags, pull out my long-sleeve shirt, and use the blade in my bag to remove the sleeves. There we have it— a summer shirt. I try the same with my pants, grateful they aren't my Xori ones, but the blade can't cut through the thick, strong material. At least the shirt is long enough to cover most of my bottom. It'll have to do.

When I return, Trysten looks much better. His once-pallid complexion returns to a warm, golden tan. Even the intricate lines of ink that snake across both arms and extend onto his chest seem darker. "Thank you."

I nod in acknowledgment and settle beside him, relieved he's awake.

Tate jolts awake a few feet away, his eyes frantic, before the reality of our surroundings snaps back into focus. "You good?" I ask softly.

"Shit, I thought this was all just a bad dream," he breathes out as his shoulders fall.

"Unfortunately not," I sympathize.

Tate rises to his feet, his movements a bit unsteady, and heads off to the forest, clearly needing a moment to himself.

I take a deep breath, gathering my thoughts as I prepare to address the next pressing matter. "So, I plan on taking someone with me into the forest. We need to gather food and water. Do you want to come, or would you rather stay here?" I'm already searching for my boots.

Normally, I'd insist he remain to recover, but as the senior here, it feels right to respect his choice.

"I'm coming. There's no way I'm letting you out of my sight. Ryker would kill me," he sighs, running a hand through his hair, wincing a bit where I'm sure he still has a bump. "Hell, he still might kill me. I was supposed to protect you."

I chuckle at the thought, though he doesn't share my amusement.

The notion of Anders getting pissed over something out of Trysten's control is ridiculous.

It would be easy to tell myself that Anders being concerned about my safety strikes me as absurd, but I'd be lying to myself. Our connection isn't going away, it's getting stronger. He might have a grumpy demeanor and often act like a complete ass, but underneath that tough exterior, I see him—the real him, the vulnerable side. I see the prince who loves his family and his people. The man who's willing to go above and beyond. He let me in, first on Kliax, then the night he took care of me and carried me across campus. Deep down, I know Anders does care. Or maybe I'm just deluding myself into thinking I'm special.

"Yeah, well, Ryker can get in line," I reply, trying to sound light-hearted. "I'm pretty sure our parents have the quadrants out looking for us already."

I spot my boots tossed haphazardly near the line of moss and sand. "I'll talk to Tate while you get dressed. Just so you know, the suits are still wet, so take your pick." I pat his shoulder and turn, leaving him on the beach where Ciara lies sprawled in the sun, blissfully unaware. I glance back at Trysten, finding him staring out at the horizon, deep in thought. I wonder what he's thinking. Is he searching for the quadrants like I have been?

The quadrants, the kingdoms' military, are organized into four distinct branches. Protos are our space force, monitoring the kingdoms from above. Terra oversees our ground forces, extending their watch to the skies. The Regils serve as the royal guards, loyal yet terrifyingly deadly, while the Fari keep watch over our seas. I know our parents won't leave even a single area unchecked in their hunt for us. Honestly, I don't know how we haven't been discovered already.

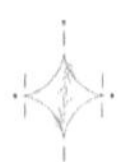

The forest is like nothing I've ever encountered. As we venture deeper, it becomes clear that we are far from any planet I recognize. My books and ancient scrolls don't mention trees with spiraling branches resembling thick cords and glowing vein-like strands that pulse gently, synchronized to the soft humming of the planet beneath us. Branches adorned with luminous green leaves feel alive in the canopy above, attracting both bugs and animals.

With each step, I feel the moss squelching under my soggy boots, but it's the strange energy that gives me pause. It's a sensation that mirrors a slow heartbeat reverberating through the ground. It pricks at the edges of my awareness, sending shivers up my spine and leaving my hair standing on end. Here, there's a wild energy that flows freely. It's a little unnerving. It's so similar to the lines of energy I saw on Ista.

Every twist and turn of the winding path reveals more unfamiliar trees, vibrant plants, and a spectrum of wildlife and insects. Creatures that remind me of butterflies flit gracefully through the air, their indigo wings trailing shimmering dust with each flap. They dance and swirl around us before landing on the gnarled roots of ancient trees. I wish I had my Prism to capture a photo of them. Above us, I can hear the rustling of animals hidden among the leaves.

"Where are we going, Raea?" Trysten rasps from behind me.

I glance down at the forest floor, where the branches twist and intertwine in the velvety green moss. We need to find a source of water, and we need to do it soon. We're down to the last of the water. I crouch down, letting my fingers sink into the cool, damp moss, feeling the moisture beneath. It's wet, but not nearly enough to hint at a nearby stream or pond.

"Just keep your eyes peeled for moss growing on tree trunks or maybe the sound of trickling water," I reply, ducking under a knotted branch that stretches like a gnarled hand from an ancient tree. "We really need fresh water. The survival bag is still in the transport," I add, pressing forward into the underbrush.

He mutters behind me, reminding me that he's the expert in Recon.

"So," I say a little too brightly, "what's your favorite food?"

If I'm going to be stuck with Trysten on this planet, we might as well use it as an opportunity to get to know each other better. Besides, he's been training me for weeks, and we've barely scratched the surface. Trysten is quiet, but observant, and I know there's a lot more to him than he lets on. I guess that's what makes him the perfect friend for Anders.

Trysten curses under his breath when he nearly trips over a hidden root. I can tell his head is still hurting by the way he keeps wincing, but if he needs a break, he'll let me know. "In the whole system or just Okenen?" he asks.

"Both."

He's quiet for a few seconds before he pauses, breathing a little harder than I'd expect him to. He drops the bag we brought and pulls out the bottle of water, taking a long gulp before offering it to me. I take it as he says, "Out of all of our planets, I love the food on Mystel in Kadora, but in Okenen," he swipes his longer hair out of his eyes. "I'm going with the palace cook, Mari. Besides, no place like home, right?"

I hand the water bottle back to him, swiping at my wet lips as I watch him screw on the lid. "Mystel? You need a Mesh to even get around. I've never been."

He nods and begins walking again, this time falling into step beside me. "Mystel has some of the prettiest landscapes. Black sand with lush green plants, massive waterfalls that are the clearest blue you'll find in the whole system, and the volcanoes. I guess I'm a sucker for them. They have the most active volcanoes of all of Kadora's planets. And their food, well, it's just hearty. Spiced lamb dishes with potatoes and cooked vegetables."

I look up into the canopy just in time to see a winged creature larger than the tree line flying overhead. I suck in a sharp breath and continue walking, hoping we're not prey.

"What about you?" I offer him a small smile, thankful that his mood seems to be improving.

"I—"

Suddenly, a loud, thunderous drumbeat echoes from deep within the forest, sending vibrations pulsing through the ground and through me. My heart quickens, thumping in sync with the drumming that seems to beckon me forward. There's a tension in the air, like an invisible string tugging at me.

"What are you doing?" Trysten's voice shifts to a frantic whisper as he takes on a fighting stance and reaches for a Hallo that isn't there. His eyes widen with my first step.

"I just need to—" My words falter as I take another step forward, my feet moving almost of their own accord. "Umm, Trysten." My voice trembles slightly as an unseen force pulls me closer. In an instant, Trysten's arms wrap around my waist as he attempts to anchor me.

"Fight back!" he growls.

The scrape of his combat pants against my bare legs sends goosebumps rising along my legs. I should be terrified right now, should be struggling against this strange pull, but instead, a sense of wonder envelops me. I feel as if I'm watching myself from the outside, mesmerized by this strange tug.

"Trysten, let go. It's okay…I think—" I try to mask the uncertainty that gnaws at my insides, but gasp as I feel a powerful wave surging up my spine, emitting warmth and energy that trickles through every nerve ending. It creates a tingling sensation that races from my fingertips to the tips of my toes. It's similar to the energy that sparks between me and Anders when we touch. Except this time I'm completely consumed, overwhelmed by a power I've never known before. It's hot and uncomfortable, but only for a second.

As I move forward, Trysten keeping a step behind, a dark clearing comes into view, almost as if we've found a cave, but it's the thick canopy high above that has somehow blocked out all the daylight. The trees surrounding us hum with life, their roots intertwined with those strange pulsing veins of light that weave through the underbrush in vibrant shades of indigo and azure, leading us to the heart of the clearing.

At the center stands a majestic, ancient tree, its trunk hollowed out and glowing with hues of indigo and azure from the veins, and adorned with thick, radiant tendrils of shimmering starlight.

"What the hell?" Trysten murmurs.

My breath catches in my throat as tears begin to well in my eyes; not from fear, but from sheer beauty. Something deep within me whispers that I have a connection to this place, even though I know logically that this is my first time setting foot here.

My feet carry me further into the clearing with Trysten trailing closely behind. It is then that I notice it. A swirling mist, dark as exquisite onyx, floating languidly around the base of the tree. It moves almost as if it possesses a consciousness of its own, curling and stretching with a sense of curiosity. A thrill of fear dances within me as I study it; it's not human or animal, but rather something *other*. A prickle of unease crawls along my neck as I realize this mist seems to regard me as much as I regard it.

Trysten collapses at my side, his body suddenly going limp as his eyes roll back into his head, his body curled up on the moss-covered ground. Panic washes over me, and for the first time, a chilling thought crosses my mind. Maybe we aren't meant to be here. Perhaps I should have run. My heart races as I struggle to comprehend exactly what I'm seeing. I glance first at Trysten, his chest rises and falls, steady yet distant, and then to the onyx mist that seems to move excitedly as I continue forward despite my unwillingness.

I try to fight against the pull, but with each step I take, it feels laborious, like wading through thick, clinging tar. "No," I plead, my voice echoing in the stillness. "No!" The pull lessens, but my feet remain rooted to the ground, immobile.

The clearing is dark, with barely any light to be found aside from the glowing light; still, I search, taking in my surroundings. Tears well up in my eyes at the sudden helplessness I feel; my eyes catch a shadow creeping from behind the tree before it coils around me. A shrill scream escapes my lips, piercing the oppressive stillness of the air. The scream feels distant, almost as if it's not my own.

In an instant, the world around me dissolves into consuming, endless darkness, a velvet void that swallows everything, including every bit of light.

twenty-nine

. . .

raea

THE GRIP on my body feels inhuman, an unyielding force that seizes me with sharp, piercing pain as though claws have sunk deep into my sides. I can sense something tugging at my legs, pulling me deeper toward an abyss. At the same time, a weight crushes my chest, like a heavy band constricting my breath and pinning me in place as I attempt to fight back.

Power surges through me again, a chaotic energy burning like a wildfire, consuming everything in its path. I can't be certain, but I think I'm screaming, though the sound is lost in a cacophony of whispers. It's as if there's an iron dome encasing my mind, but the whispers grow louder, hammering against the walls of my mind, demanding entrance. The whispers grow louder, the indistinct voices fill my ears, pulling me further into this nightmarish struggle for control as I battle the darkness threatening to keep me.

"Soraea."

"Light-bringer."

"The new dawn."

"Give it to us."

"I'll destroy them all."

Over and over, the voices repeat, overlapping and driving me madder than I already feel with the hammering in my head, the loud buzz of the planet, and well…everything else. I'm tapped out on sensations, overwhelmed, while my heart continues to pound violently against my ribcage.

Darkness continues to envelop my vision like an endless void. I'm haunted by vivid flashes of war, scenes of death and destruction unfolding before me as I watch helplessly. I see homes and villages engulfed in flames while horrific creatures born of nightmares gnash their teeth in a frenzied display of hunger. A strangled sob escapes my lips as I lie here, powerless and lost in images I can't comprehend.

"Give it to us," the voices echo around me, some demanding furiously, others with a voice laced with deceit and false sweetness. Their incessant demands twist my insides, fueling my fear.

Desperation wells up as I cry out, "I don't know what you want!"

In my search for something to hold onto, my hands grasp at what feels like a root, its rough bark biting into my palm. I can feel the damp ground beneath my fingers, the solidness grounding me even as my body writhes in agony as I teeter on the edge of unconsciousness. My fingers intertwine in an attempt to anchor myself.

"Give us the light!"

The command reverberates through my mind like a thunderclap, leaving me gasping. A chill settles into me, bone-deep and unending, as the darkness around me deepens, consuming me whole.

"Have strength, Soraea, daughter of the forest," a sweet, calm voice murmurs softly from somewhere nearby. It brings a sense of quiet comfort despite the unending pain and terror.

"Who are you?" I manage to bite out, the grip on my chest escalating to unbearable levels. "Please, make it stop," I plead, desperation clawing at me.

Suddenly, a gentle hand rests on my head. The soothing touch momentarily eases my torment. The relentless pounding in my skull subsides, and the disorienting buzz of distant planets fades into silence.

"We cannot," she replies softly, her voice soothing like a lullaby. "This is your path. Have strength. He'll be here soon."

"Who?" I sob.

My voice trembles as I feel jagged claws dragging down my legs. The presence of whoever is hovering over me begins to pull away, leaving me as the whispers surrounding me turn taunting and vicious. They chant their malevolent refrain, repeating words about light and a new dawn, twisting them into a cruel promise that *she'll* make me suffer if I don't comply.

The band around my chest feels like it's constricting further, the pressure building as the tugging on my legs pulls me deeper into despair. I scream, the sound leaving my throat raw as it echoes through the void. I grip the root beneath my fingers with all my strength. I can't let go—not now. I just have to hold on, that's what she said. Then, without warning, the darkness envelops me once more. Utter and complete nothingness.

I wake to more haunting visions of wastelands stretching endlessly through my mind, but these desolate landscapes belong to no planet I've ever known. The people who inhabit this miserable realm are different—taller, faster, and more beautiful. I feel like I'm glimpsing at a photo of a long-lost family. There's something familiar about them, but I know my parents were both the only children born to my grandparents, just like me.

A profound sadness settles against my heart as I silently plead for this torment to cease. This is just another ploy to get me to break. I can't discern how long I've been unconscious, or even how long I've been trapped in this hellscape. I can feel my strength dwindling, and the reserve of energy I felt earlier seems to drain faster than the well can replenish. A soul-rendering sob escapes my lips, my vision still shrouded in darkness, and all I can feel are the deep, sharp talons raking mercilessly into my skin, leaving behind a burning trail of agony.

Poison.

It has to be some kind of poison that makes those claw marks burn with indescribable heat.

Maybe this is death. Or perhaps I'm merely caught in a dream. I don't know, but I cling desperately to that root, a fragment of something real and tangible in this sea of cold darkness.

Seconds stretch into minutes, minutes spiral into hours, and hours blur into a formless expanse that renders time meaningless. Those eerie whispers penetrate my thoughts like an insistent wind. My mental shield holds strong, muffling their cries of outrage.

My vision flickers back to life for a moment, but the only thing illuminated is the glowing tree at my side, casting an ethereal light in an otherwise suffocating darkness. Just when I try to focus on it, a fresh wave of pain surges through me, and once again, I'm cast into the void.

My thoughts drift to my parents and friends—will they be okay when I am no longer here? Will Trysten, with his unwavering loyalty, and Ciara, with her fierce compassion, find a way to escape the hellish nightmare we've crashed into? And what of Tate? Will he remember to laugh when I'm gone?

Will my parents survive my death, or will they die with me? My safety has been my mother's sole focus, and my happiness my father's. Every moment, I have felt their undeniable love for me as if I were their sole reason for continuing on. They have to live.

A deeper ache settles in my heart when I think of Anders. Will he understand that in the end, it was his presence, his quiet strength, his comforting hold that I yearned for the most? That in my last minutes, it was he that I craved more than anything—his warmth, our Bond, our relentless teasing. Will Kellan forgive me? Does Kellan know how deep my love for him is and that even in death, he will always hold a piece of my heart? The weight of so many unanswered questions presses down on me as I feel my fingers begin to slip.

"Oh, how she'll enjoy torturing you, devouring you, Little Light," a sinister voice whispers, dripping with malicious glee. "It won't be long now."

The words coil around me like chains, tightening their grip. Before I can fully comprehend their implications, I'm pulled into unconsciousness once more.

I awaken to the distant echoes of voices calling my name, pulling me from the depths of nothingness. I can only focus on the overwhelming shouts and mocking sneers that claw at my mind. The sharp pain of talons digs into my sides with a frantic desperation, as if trying to keep me in this nightmare.

"Raea!" I hear Kellan's voice pierce through the chaos.

But can it truly be him?

It feels like I'm hallucinating, trapped in a twisted reality. That surge of power I felt before pulses within me, the fire building with each passing second, hotter and hotter, igniting a nuclear heat deep within my core. I gasp just before a roar escapes my lips as the waves of agony mount.

My back arches involuntarily away from the damp, soft ground, and I feel my fingers slip from the ancient root that has been my lifeline. Panic floods my thoughts, but that unyielding heat seems to burn away those poisonous talons, incinerating each deep gouge. I claw at the ground, desperate to hold onto something, anything.

"Soraea." Anders' voice echoes in my mind, penetrating the iron dome that has shielded my mind like it's nothing more than a sheer veil. I feel him kneel beside me, his presence unmistakable even in this endless expanse of hell. Almost as if I summoned him.

Cool, soothing hands embrace me like ice has wrapped around my burnt flesh. I can feel the sharp claws lodged in my sides withdrawing, allowing the jumbled chorus of voices in my head to retreat, their terrifying screeches fading into the distance. The raging fire, that insatiable flame consuming me from within, flickers and then extinguishes, as if a splash of water is all it took, as if *he* were all it took.

A sensation similar to cool water floods through me like a stream, healing me with every heartbeat as it surrounds my nerve endings, my muscles, and even my soul. Slowly, so slowly, I peel my eyes open, and all I see is him.

Anders.

My breath hitches as my gaze catches on him. He's devastatingly handsome, his presence consuming. His dark hair is windswept, and purple bruises underscore striking sapphire eyes, but he's nothing short of perfection.

His gaze roams anxiously over mine, searching, probing. For a fleeting moment, I wonder if I am merely hallucinating his presence or if he has truly come for me.

"You're here," I rasp, tears welling in my eyes. It's not a question. My words seem to wreck him, his features falling as he nods.

After an agonizing pause, he releases me, but echoes of pain surge back through my body, and a desperation wells up inside me. "Don't leave me," I plead, my voice raw and raspy. "Don't let go. Please, stay. Just stay."

He runs a soothing hand down my cheek. "I'm not leaving. Never," he replies shakily. "I'm here. I've got you. I'll always come for you."

A flash of pure white catches my eye, and I turn to see that the world around us has transformed into a mesmerizing cocoon of pure starlight, swirling and twisting on an ethereal breeze.

With a tenderness that steals my breath, he lowers his head to mine, inhaling deeply as if drawing strength from my very essence. He pulls me into his lap as though I am the most fragile thing in the universe, something precious and irreplaceable that he cannot bear to relinquish.

Moments later, the starlight begins to fade, leaving me to wonder if it was all a beautiful illusion conjured to shield me from the agonizing reality. My entire body aches, and a heavy weight of exhaustion settles in, mingling with the numbing aftermath of pain. Have I died? The thought flits across my mind, unsettling yet oddly calming.

He reclines back, cradling me against him, holding me close as if the simple act of touching me will ward off all the lingering darkness. "Not dead," he coos softly, his voice a gentle balm as he brushes a tender hand down my arm, anchoring me in the here and now. "I'm here."

I hadn't realized I had spoken my fears aloud.

My body trembles against him at the mere thought of experiencing that pain, that suffocating darkness, that evil again. As if sensing my unease, he shifts onto his side, pulling me close so our bodies align perfectly. In this moment, I am blissfully detached from everything—my fears, my memories—like the gods themselves conspired to send him to me just when I needed him most.

In the recess of my mind, I know we should run, but before the thought can materialize, I feel Anders pull me impossibly closer.

My thoughts blur and dissolve, leaving only the warmth of his embrace as my anchor. I rest my head against his heart, feeling the erratic thump lulling me into a deep sleep and into a realm bathed in warmth and starlight, far removed from the gaping pit of emptiness that filled me before. Exhaustion settles over me like a heavy blanket, and I willingly surrender to it, letting my consciousness slip away.

I find myself floating on an undulating sea, the sky above a breathtaking tapestry of muted colors as trillions of stars twinkle like diamonds, casting soft glimmers upon the water's surface. So many worlds beckon to be explored out there, yet I remain cradled by the gentle waves, feeling an overwhelming sense of safety that envelops me. I surrender to the much-needed rest my body demands. But like whispers carried across the water, I hear the voices of Trysten and Kellan, cutting through the peaceful silence.

"RaeRae," Kellan whispers, and the concern lacing his voice has me turning my head toward that voice.

"Are they alive?" Trysten rasps.

I can hear the fear in his voice, but I keep drifting. My heart aches for a moment at the thought of them worrying, but the comforting weight of exhaustion pulls me further into this dreamlike sea. I want to reassure them that we're fine, but the tide of sleep keeps rolling in, lulling me deeper into forgetfulness, where the demands of reality cannot reach me.

"Raea," Ciara's voice echoes faintly from far away.

"We need to leave now," Kellan warns. "I'll carry Ryker. You carry Raea." His choice to lift Anders instead of me surprises me momentarily, but then again, I don't care. Not when I feel so warm, so safe, like I can just forget.

My quiet vision of warm waters lapping gently at a starlit shore is violently shattered when unfamiliar hands seize me, yanking me away from Anders'. Something inside me snaps, a fraying thread of composure giving way to raw desperation.

A primal instinct surges within me, compelling me to claw and scream, to fight back. *Not helpless.* I must get back. Back to Anders, back to that feeling of safety I so desperately need.

Panic grips me like a vice as the arms around me tighten. Trysten's voice cuts through the confusion, barking insistently for me to calm down, but I fight with every ounce of strength I have, recalling that time I was cornered and how that felt. I refuse to be taken against my will again.

I will not be weak.

My sole focus narrows to getting back to Anders.

"Raea," Kellan admonishes, his voice strained with exasperation.

My vision blurs, the harsh light around me colliding with the throbbing headache that pounds in my temples. In a desperate attempt to escape the brightness, I slam my eyes shut.

My screams pierce the air as I throw my elbow backward wildly, feeling more hands restraining me. "Let me go!" I shriek, kicking and clawing, desperate to escape.

Phantom claws pierce me as chains wrap around me, restraining me in the depths of hell. A sob breaks free from my lips, a plea escaping as I thrash beneath the weight of outstretched arms.

Distantly, logically, I know it's not the shadows, but my body and mind have been so thoroughly wrecked that I can't make it all make sense. Suddenly, the grip holding me falters, and before I fully comprehend, a pair of strong, comforting arms envelop me.

The familiar scent of warm ocean water and a hint of citrus envelope me like a tether in the frenzy. I stop fighting, surrendering to the warmth radiating from him as he lifts me effortlessly, cradling me against him. Sobs wrack my body as he whispers over and over that I'm safe, calming the fire of panic. I breathe in Anders' scent, relaxing into him.

Safe.

Safe.

Safe.

"I've got you," he whispers softly.

As the last bit of my energy slips away like sand through fingers, I surrender once more, drifting back into a peaceful sleep among the midnight waves and the glow of the endless stars above.

thirty

. . .

ryker

"WHAT THE HELL IS GOING ON?" Kellan barks, stepping closer as if he might leap forward to snatch Raea from my arms.

I dare him to try.

Whatever he sees on my face has him reconsidering as he takes a half-step back, palms raised despite his accusatory glare. I woke only moments ago to find Raea thrashing, as if some part of me knew she needed me. Whatever this strange magic is, I feel it's pull on us dissolving.

Trysten, Tate, and Ciara stand a few feet away, their eyes wide with confusion, searching my face for answers I don't have. I feel the weight of their stares, the burden of their expectation pressing down on me. Exhaustion clings to my bones, yet the adrenaline coursing through my veins drives me to move as quickly as possible. I have to get us all off this gods-forsaken planet.

I glance down, my heart rate gradually stabilizing as I absorb the sight of Raea nestled against me, peacefully asleep despite the shit-storm around us. Her pale skin is mottled with cuts and bruises, and her shirt is ragged, too short, torn in several spots, and revealing enough that I can't keep my eyes from drifting to the black ink-like

claw marks that trail down her thighs. Fury at whoever—or whatever
—hurt her has me working my jaw.

A vicious protectiveness wells up within me. One hand is clenched
in my shirt, her nails bloodied and caked in mud. Despite being
trapped on this planet and the torment she has just endured, her delicate scent wafts on an invisible breeze, settling something deep within
me. A dewy forest mixed with fresh blooms—her.

I tighten my hold on her gently, mindful of her injuries, and shift
my gaze back to Kellan. "I can explain everything once we're away
from here." My voice is steady despite my uneasiness. "But we need to
move now. If we don't, we could be trapped here for good." The
shadows and the mist are already here, and based on her injuries, it's
come prepared to attack.

I feel the shadows creeping around us, dark tendrils slithering
through the underbrush, watching and waiting, eager to snatch her.
Why they want her, I have no godsdamn clue. Witnessing her entan-
gled in those shadows and shrouded in that mist, her eyes glowing
with an otherworldly golden hue, nearly shattered me. I've never seen
anything like it.

Her magic was trying to protect her. But mine...it responded to
her. It's the only explanation for why I could draw the raw energy
coursing through her and channel it back into Sgya. She had been
pulling it from the veil. The intensity of the energy was almost
unbearable. How she managed to contain it is beyond me. But when I
wrapped my hands around her, it was as if a hole opened up—the
energy surged through one arm, a deluge of raw power that flowed
from her and through me, finding its way back to where it belonged.

As I glance around, anxiety claws at my chest. We've been here
much longer than I intended. "Run, now!" I command. "Get back to
the transport!"

Kellan grits his teeth, a flicker of hesitation crossing his face before
he sprints ahead. He knows the way, having helped me locate our
clearing in the first place.

Navigating the gnarled branches with Raea cradled against me is a
nightmare. Trysten and Tate flank us, working in tandem to push aside

as many branches as they can to clear a path, their muscles straining as we move as quickly as possible. One nearly scrapes Raea, but I dodge it just in time, letting it snag on my stomach.

We rush past a towering tree swarmed with coral butterflies, all making a home in the bark. Something deep inside me stirs, a memory of my mother whispering from the shadows of my mind. I yell over my shoulder to Ciara, urging her to grab a branch as we rush by. Thankfully, one of the smaller branches snaps under her weight, leaving us with a decent-sized twig.

"We were in hyperjump," Trysten gasps, struggling to catch his breath as he bends over, his hands on his knees. He's more hurt than he lets on. "Something pulled us here mid-jump."

"We crashed in the lake," Tate cuts in, gesturing to the sea. They must not have seen it from above. "The transport is at the bottom, but the water is so cold it nearly killed us."

My thoughts are a whirlwind as I take in all this information, not that I plan on ever returning again. The dense trees finally give way to the beach, and relief washes over me momentarily when I spot Kellan leading the way around a rock formation.

Ciara barrels past me, grabbing four flight suits drying on a rock ledge. My gaze sweeps the beach around us. Clothes and blankets are strewn across the sand, and a med pack lies abandoned, half-buried. Trysten darts after it, snagging the med pack I had dropped alongside the other before rushing after Kellan.

We have only a few minutes of light left at best. Shadows swirl at my ankles, taunting me with their insidious whispers. Over my fucking dead body will I hand her over.

"Leave her. Let us have her," the alluring voices say into my mind. I can feel a slimy temptation attempt to wrap around my resolve. Icy dread slides down my spine as I tighten my grip on Raea.

"We can keep them both," another voice snickers.

As I stagger forward, the sand makes each step harder, and fatigue weighs me down. Tate gives me a gentle but firm shove, pushing me onward.

"It's only a matter of time," the sinister voice warns, and I know in my gut that every second we waste brings us closer to the darkness waiting.

When I finally emerge into the clearing, the ramp to the transport is wide open, but it begins to close with a low hiss as we hurry up the incline. Kellan and Trysten are already seated at the console, fingers flying over the controls.

"Hold on!" Trysten shouts back to me, his voice cutting through the din.

I barely manage to collapse into a bunk, cradling Raea in my arms. She's still sound asleep, her petite form a comforting weight against my chest. I close my eyes tightly, focusing all my energy on hoping we break free of the planet's atmosphere.

"Let us go, please." I direct the prayer to the gods. It's the first time I've asked them for anything in over four years.

I stopped praying, stopped asking for anything after my father never returned, and my mother's depression took her from us. But right now, they have complete control over our fate. "Let us go." I don't know if they can hear me, but I'm willing to try.

The shake of the transport slows momentarily, as if sludging through mud, and then—without warning—it feels as if we're being catapulted into space. My stomach lurches violently with the sudden shift in momentum.

"Tate, set a course back to school. Ciara, inform them that we're on our way," Trysten commands.

He's not just great at being a friend, he's a remarkable pilot, and I trust him to get us back to school. As I close my eyes once more, some unknown weight pulling at my consciousness again. I let the steady rhythm of Raea's breathing draw me under, if only for a moment. I feel mentally drained, as though every thought has been siphoned away, leaving only a dull ache in my head. All I need is a moment to gather my scattered thoughts and breathe.

My mind drifts on a midnight sea, the sky shrouded in an endless blanket of stars, daring to show off their beauty. I feel a profound sense of peace wash over me, as if a deep, healing rest has descended upon my soul. I shift slightly on the warm, undulating surface of the water, and there, shimmering about thirty feet away, I see a brilliant orb of white light glowing softly, inviting me closer.

As I lazily stroke the water, the gentle waves caress my skin with a soothing warmth, drawing me nearer to the mesmerizing sphere of starlight. Just as I sense that I'm almost within reach, a loud voice shatters the silence, ripping the landscape apart. The world shifts abruptly, revealing an unnatural, brightly lit space with a metallic scent.

"Ryker," Trysten's voice calls, pulling me from sleep.

I blink my heavy eyelids open, struggling momentarily to clear my blurry eyes. The familiar sight of my best friend hovers above me, concern etched across his face. I blink again, and my gaze settles on both Kellan and Trysten standing by the bunk. While Trysten looks worried, Kellan seems torn between being pissed that Raea's wrapped up in my arms and being confused why she reached for me instead of him.

A soft, settled hum releases from Raea where she's still tucked into my side, her face mere inches from my neck. It feels so natural to have her next to me, as if this is where she's always belonged. Her snow-white hair is a disheveled cascade, strands escaping from her braided locks, yet she has never looked so beautiful. The soft warmth of her breath tickles my skin, and I instinctively squeeze her a little tighter, savoring the moment. I choose to ignore the fact that she's hardly dressed and practically lying on me under the shared blanket someone draped over us. It's then I realize my hand is gripping her bare thigh across my stomach, and damn if I don't go semi-hard.

I give myself two seconds to get my shit together, forcing myself to face everything I despise. My mother's tears, the relentless disappointment etched on Cole's face every time I fail him. An image of Clara, sitting alone in the quiet palace as she holds all her joy close, stubborn to fall into a depression of her own, while my mother deteriorates in her room, a ghost of herself. Then there's Kellan, his arms embracing Raea as she smiles up at him. I grind my teeth as the scene sends raging hot jealousy coursing through me.

That worked.

Taking a long, steadying breath, I reluctantly shift my gaze to the two men looming over us. Their expressions are a mix of curiosity and exasperation. Kellan is seething, his rage barely contained within him. Trysten appears almost amused, despite the dried blood caked into his hair and the large bandage wrapped around his head. He understands my feelings for Soraea—he has for years. He was the one who called me out on my bullshit three years ago when I made excuse after excuse to visit Cole in Betas.

Trysten has been persistent in his pursuit to get me to admit my feelings for her, urging me to stop being a little bitch and to face her. The weight of my family's issues coupled with the kingdom's demands—it's been too much. Plus, I can't afford for the media to catch wind of any romantic entanglements, specifically with another royal, especially not while my mother battles her depression. It would only bring more attention to Okenen.

Raea's fingers tighten around my shirt as if she senses my intentions, a gentle reminder of the connection between us I've been trying to navigate. I wrestle with the impulse to lean down and kiss her again, but Kellan's presence holds me back. Not that it stopped me earlier when I swept her into my arms without a second thought. With a reluctant sigh, I slip out from beneath her, carefully prying her fingers from the fabric of my ripped shirt.

As I stand, I catch sight of the angry red and purple scratch marring my stomach from where that branch caught me. I'm just glad it was me and not her. Ignoring their stares, I grab a medkit and attend to the wound.

"We'll be there in five. If you want to talk, now's your chance," Trysten remarks casually, as if our entire future hangs in the balance, and he couldn't be less invested in the outcome. He plops down onto the bunk opposite mine, while Kellan lingers, arms crossed in a protective stance, his gaze firmly fixed on Raea. At the front, Tate and Ciara remain seated, monitoring the consoles.

I run a hand through my hair, a habit that has become all too familiar when I'm backed into a corner. How the hell do I even begin this conversation?

"I'm still trying to make sense of it all," I admit. "After my father went missing, I spent countless hours poring over his notes and journals. They were filled with cryptic messages, maps marked with strange symbols, and supply lists that seemed to make no sense."

"What does any of that have to do with this?" Trysten interjects. Before I can respond, Kellan shoots him a sharp look that silences him instantly.

"Listen," Kellan snaps, his voice low but commanding.

Trysten's eyes widen, and he quickly averts his gaze back to me. I almost allow myself a chuckle at the sight. I feel a flicker of gratitude towards Kellan. Despite my reservations about him being Raea's so-called best friend, he's been unexpectedly helpful. "My father's transport didn't just vanish without a trace—he left of his own accord. The specifics aren't crucial right now," I continue, my voice steadying as I gather my thoughts. "What really matters is that Raea and I found something. And with that something—"

I glance back at Raea, and my heart squeezes. Despite the bruises that mar her creamy satin skin, she's perfection. Her time in the sun seems to have kissed her cheeks, giving her a warm glow. Has it really only been a day or two since she left?

"I think we both have magic," I finish, frustration tinging my voice as I shake my head. I broke my promise to her that we'd keep this between us, but they need some answers. "I don't know why or how since we're still unBonded, but there's something between us, like our magic seems to work only around each other."

Trysten whistles softly.

Kellan shifts uncomfortably.

Despite how much I hate the bastard, I can't help but feel a pang of sympathy for Kellan. She didn't tell him, and by the look of disbelief on his face, he's hurt over it.

"Anyway," I continue, "the books gave us more insight into the veil and the shadow forces. There's even information on the gods in them. There is something wrong that either the crowns aren't telling us, or they're oblivious to. The veil has been flickering in and out more frequently than we know. I can feel it. Raea does too. The shadows are just the beginning," I add, burying my face in my hands and releasing a groan of exasperation.

"How the hell did we end up on that planet?" Trysten mutters, his anger simmering just below the surface. I can sense his hurt that I didn't share this with him sooner, and honestly, I can't blame him.

"The gods brought you there—at least, I think so. That was Sgya," I explain, allowing the gravity of my words to settle in the air around us. "My father's notes speculated that access to Sgya was a privilege granted only by the gods, and it might be why we managed to escape it. According to his notes, he's been there before." Both Kellan's and Trysten's eyes go wide. "Bonding magic feeds the veil's power, but it's not enough. It was never meant to be permanent."

"Trysten," Ciara calls out. "Time to land. Unless you'd prefer I do it."

He stands with an air of reluctance, leaving Kellan and me behind.

"Tell me about your Bond?" Kellan's hands turn to fists at his side as he glances between Raea and me.

I shake my head slowly, feeling a weight in my chest. If she knew the truth, she wouldn't be avoiding me like this—wouldn't constantly evade the connection that seems to pull us together and push us apart simultaneously. At least, I don't think she would. I recall her frustrated rants about Bonding being forced upon us without our consent.

"I...it's complicated." My words barely pierce the silence. The truth has been gnawing at me for weeks. "We, uh..." I pause and draw in a steadying breath.

Gods, please don't let her hate me for this.

"The Bond between us is powerful, but it's more than that. When we were in the field, we were channeling energy back and forth; that's how she managed to break free from those mist and shadow things. I still can't fully grasp what it all means, but our Bond is intense—we've felt it since our first night at school. Well, technically, it was morning...when we touched..." My voice trails off, lost in the haze of memories of her running into me.

I had shown up at her door, flustered and annoyed at how I even ended up there, floundering like a teenager over what I wanted to say to her when she bounced off my chest. She was so pissy about the whole thing, I just kept my damn mouth shut and decided to let her hate me. It was better than her ignoring me. Being assigned as her escort was a complete surprise, and I knew that by accepting the role, it would only make the situation worse. But I did. I took on the role to make sure she was safe, but also so I could get to know her.

Kellan clears his throat, pulling me back to the present.

What does he want me to say?

Everything felt right in that moment—the energy, the safety, the inexplicable connection between us. But it's not only my story to share.

"Why didn't she tell me?" Kellan's eyes blaze with a mix of anger and heartbreak. He's breaking.

"She loves you." I hate that she does, but I know it's why she hasn't said anything. She's scared of hurting him and admitting her feelings for me, even though she's been so damn persistent in avoiding all of this. I take a few more steps toward the consoles and raise my voice above the hum. "Let's all agree on a story before we land, all right?"

Everyone around me nods.

I brace myself as the transport's landing gear touches the ground with a subtle shake. I open the doors to a chaotic crowd of anxious faces—some familiar, some not. Among them, I spot a furious Kuron, Raea's personal guard, and a visibly worried King Bastian and Queen Amaya.

We're walking straight into a shitstorm.

thirty-one

. . .

raea

I WAKE up with a pounding headache, disoriented, and instantly aware of the sharp needles protruding from my arms. There are also tight bandages wrapped around my hands, hips, and ankles. The rhythmic beeping from the heart monitor hovering above me has me pinching my brows together. I don't remember how I got here.

As I glance around the dimly lit room, I see my parents at the foot of my bed, their voices low but tense, and engaged in a heated discussion with Chancellor Xara. I catch fragments of their conversation floating through the air—words like "irresponsible" and "unacceptable" come to me, but as I strain to listen, I decide I don't actually want to know what they're arguing about. I have a good enough guess. "We should have this school shut down—"

Kuron is also here, hovering in the corner, keeping watch. His dark, rich brown skin glimmers beneath the light. His black beard is new, cropped close to his face, and his hair is pulled tight in seven braids. He's taller than everyone around him, and his presence only adds to the tension in the room.

And boy, does he look pissed.

My heart rate picks up as I sense something is off, but I just can't remember what. Suddenly, a warm hand envelops mine, grounding me. I turn to find Kellan seated beside me. He holds a finger to his lips, urging me to be quiet. I nod, squeezing his hand for reassurance. As I examine his features, I notice how fatigued he looks—his eyes carry dark circles, and his usually neat hair appears disheveled. Despite the confusion, his familiarity wraps around me like a comforting blanket. Rain or shine, my best friend is always here.

"You're awake," he whispers, his voice shaky with emotion, before he musters a smile. "You scared the hell out of us, RaeRae."

As I meet his gaze, a familiar ache settles in my chest, tightening my throat. How did I end up with this man as my best friend? The warmth of his hand gives me some solace, but I can't shake the nagging question—how long have I been here?

As I glance down at my body, currently covered in warm blankets, and take in the bloodied nails and scrapes on my arms, flashes come back to me, making my stomach churn. I squeeze my eyes shut, seeing Trysten's bleeding head on the console.

"We crashed," I croak, my voice raspy, as if that single admission can encapsulate the unexplainable days on that beach. I wonder how long it took for them to find us.

"You can't pull her out," Professor Brendn protests, his voice firm and steady. Kellan and I turn toward my parents and staff, their faces half shrouded in shadows, illuminated only on one side by a soft, golden glow from the flickering sconce. "She needs to finish the year. Wait until next year if you want to withdraw her. There are only a few months left." He crosses his arms defiantly, seemingly unfazed by the presence of the king and queen of the most powerful kingdom. I let out a weary sigh and glance back at Kellan.

His golden-brown hair is matted with mud in places, reminding me of our childhood days spent climbing trees and splashing in the streams that wound through the palace gardens until dusk, when we'd chase firebugs and laugh until our sides hurt.

"What are you doing here?" I ask, a realization dawning as though I'm beginning to piece together an unfinished puzzle.

"I was there, RaeRae. Care to explain?" Kellan's voice trembles slightly. "Anders—he didn't—"

A vivid and overwhelming rush of memories floods my mind, accompanied by a wave of nausea. The crash, the tangled trees of the glowing forest, shadows, and the mist, distorted voices echoing in my mind, flashes of chaos and war. It's all too much. I can barely keep my breath steady, feeling the walls close in around me.

"Anders…" I sit up abruptly, scanning the room, panic clawing at my chest.

The incessant beep of the heart monitor fills the silence as it moves out of the way, avoiding collision with my trembling body. He saved me. He pulled the burning power from me. Flashbacks attack my consciousness—the towering tree, the haunting whispers, the energy clash between light and dark, good and evil. The screams, the devastation that followed. Astor and Calia…and then there's Anders—*I need him*—the thought crystallizes in my mind.

"Where is he?" I demand, adrenaline coursing through me as I rip the needles from my arm, ignoring the shock on Kellan's face.

My mother gasps as she rushes to my side. "Raea!"

I glance to where Kellan now stands, his eyes churning with what looks like devastation.

My mother is dressed in a cornflower blue gown, its edges delicately embroidered with shimmering gold silk, reflecting the room's soft light. It's rare to see her hair loose and flowing, the dark waves reaching her mid-back and swaying gently as she leans over me, her fingers cupping my face with familiar tenderness. She's always been overly fussy.

"How are you feeling, dear?" my father asks. His large, familiar hand envelops mine, soothing some of my frayed nerves as he stands beside my mother. Their concerned expressions make it seem like I've been lost for a month, not a few days. A fog of confusion clouds my memory as I grasp for some sense of clarity.

"I'm fine, I promise! Please, let me stand," I insist, waving them off gently.

I love my parents, but their hovering can sometimes feel overwhelmingly suffocating. Habitually, I take Kellan's hand for support, but then I freeze instinctively like I do with Anders. I brace myself for the familiar jolt of energy, but nothing happens. I catch Kellan's gaze flit from our intertwined hands to my face. The way his expression falls tells me he knows more than I had hoped. My eyes plead with him to understand, but for the first time ever, Kellan drops my hand, stepping away from me like I've become a complete stranger. The weight of his gaze crushes me.

I'm about to plead for him to give me a chance to explain, but Chancellor Xara interrupts. "Princess Raea." She steps up to stand at the foot of my bed. "When you feel well enough, we want to discuss what occurred."

I nod in acknowledgment, but before I can speak, my mother interjects fiercely, "Absolutely not." At her side, my father lets out a long sigh and gives her hand a reassuring pat, as if trying to temper her.

"I'll do it," I declare, my voice stronger than I feel. Panic begins to seep back in as I realize I need to find Anders. "Where's Anders?" I repeat. "I need to talk to him."

The tightening sensation in my chest grows unbearable as more fragmented memories flash through my mind—the crash, Trysten and I searching for water, the drum beats, an image of the indigo and azure glowing tree encased in darkness emitting unrestrained power, followed shortly by a consuming mist, pain, so much pain, and Anders freeing me from the agony.

"He's outside in the waiting area. We've already taken his statement," Chancellor Xara explains.

I need to verify what everyone said when they provided their statements to ensure my account remains consistent. At least that's what I tell myself to excuse the almost demanding need to see him.

"Please, I just need five minutes with him," I plead, ignoring how desperate I sound. I don't dare look at Kellan. I'll have to find him later and explain everything, including my Bond with Anders.

"Let her go," my father says, surprising me. He grips his wrist with his opposite hand, assuming the kingly stance he uses to assert his authority in the room.

My bandaged feet meet cool stone as my long hair, now brushed and clear of debris, sways around my arm. The Bond flickers between

Kellan and me, a shimmering green light that pulses with potential. I exhale slowly, grateful it's still there, and allow my defenses to drop. I turn back toward Chancellor Xara and Kuron, picking up on the weariness etched into Kuron's features. I'll need to spend some time with my guard later and reassure him I'm okay and there's nothing he could have done to prevent it.

I feel everyone's gaze locked on me as I push open the door on wobbly legs and find Anders seated across the hall, shoulders hunched and head hanging loose between two clasped hands.

As if he can sense me, he looks up, and I see tired eyes staring back. He swallows thickly, standing and closing the gap in a single, purposeful stride before wrapping strong arms around me, embracing me like it's him who needs me and not the other way around.

For reasons I can't fully grasp, a rush of relief floods me. I can feel him relax as though my presence has calmed the storm within him. He leans back slightly, cradling my head in his hands, and presses a gentle kiss to my forehead.

"We need to talk," he whispers, his breath tickling my skin. I nod, unable to find my voice, and let him take my hand as he leads me down the dimly lit hall.

He opens a door, and we slip inside. My senses come alive as I step into the golden, filtered light, absorbing the scene around me: brick floors, shelves overflowing with potted plants, and greenery cascading from the glass dome ceiling. This is the medicinal greenhouse.

It feels as though Anders instinctively understood my need to be surrounded by nature. I exhale a long, shuddering sigh and turn back to find him leaning against a worn wooden work table, hands tucked into his pockets, and his dark gaze focused solely on me.

"Thank you," I whisper, my voice barely rising above a rasp, thick with so many emotions I can't even begin to convey.

I reach for my throat, my pulse quickening as memories wash over me—I had been screaming. Hot tears spill from my eyes, tracing warm trails down my cheeks as the reality of what I experienced, what I saw, what was demanded of me, crashes over me. I had come so close to losing everything, and it was Anders who had saved me.

It was Anders who reached into the dark, into that all-consuming fire, and rescued me. He reaches out, wrapping a hand around my waist, and gently tugs me between his outstretched legs.

Something has changed between us. This change in intimacy and friendship blurs the lines. My lips quiver as the hold I had on my emotions breaks. I crumble, burying my face in his chest, tears soaking into his shirt as he holds me tightly against him. I sob for everything I've endured, the horrors of the last few days, and the thought of never seeing any of these people I love again. Just when I think I've reached the end, fresh waves of grief and confusion sweep in. I had made myself a promise to never be weak, and I couldn't keep it when it mattered.

My body feels weak and cold, the kind that goes beyond logic, so cold that I feel as if I might never understand what being warm feels like. I know it's just the effect of trauma, but I tremble at the thought nonetheless. Anders remains silent, anchoring me as my knees give out beneath me. His arms are the only thing keeping me from collapsing entirely. Time stretches, and the minutes bleed together until I finally feel strong enough to stand on my own.

When I finally look up, I find nothing but understanding etched on Anders' features. He cups my face tenderly, brushing away the remnants of my tears with gentle fingers. As we stand there, it feels as if the world outside has faded away, leaving just the two of us wrapped in a cocoon of our Bond's iridescent light.

For the first time since noticing them, I smile softly at the beauty of all the colors. The muted purples and wispy greens intertwined with soft pinks and blues all faded beneath a shimmering white cloud. It's so unlike the dark shadows I almost died in.

My tears dry as his hands find their way back to my waist, settling there as if that's where they belong. "I'm grateful I found you," he confesses. I watch as he grapples with memories—assumingly those of finding me—his jaw flexes, and his grip tightens slightly. "I sensed that something was wrong. I heard you screaming—"

"Wait," I cut in with confusion. "What exactly happened? My memory feels like a hazy dream."

He runs a hand up my spine, causing goosebumps to break out over my skin, and I lean my head against his chest, allowing him to hold me against him. His warmth seeps into me, and to my utter surprise, it chases away the chill that feels bone-deep. I'm sure things will return to normal tomorrow. Right now, though, I plan to savor this moment of vulnerability and honesty between us.

His heartbeat is a steady thump beneath my ear as he begins to recount the events of the past few days. The timbre of his deep voice is soft and soothing, as he continues to gently run his fingers along my spine, touching me as if he is afraid to let go. He starts with the night his team received the notification about Cresnigan before heading to bed. He continues with waking up to a frantic Kellan.

I remain silent, my hand resting against his chest, listening as he opens up about his father. Shock and then empathy wash over me, and my heart breaks for him.

"I've known about my father, or at least had an idea about what happened, since he went missing. I couldn't be certain, but once I realized you were gone..." He exhales heavily, his hand moving up to cradle the nape of my neck. "It felt like instinct; I don't know how else to explain it. I realized I had to get to you. It was reckless and irrational, but I knew it had to be me."

His words swirl in my mind, and I sense that I know what he's talking about, that it had to be him. I don't think anyone else would have made it. Though the notion that anyone could survive Sgya seems almost unfathomable. I'm still struggling to believe it myself.

"Raea, I found something in the books," he murmurs. "I was going to tell you, but then you were dealing with your cycle, and then this." There's sorrow there, not because of his father, but over me. "I think..." he pauses. "I think that the prophecy we found is about us. Which means—"

My chest aches, but my heart flips excitedly that he's allowing me in. I reach for his hand, intertwining my fingers with his, not shying away from the energy this time. The familiar energy flows between us, but now I realize something I hadn't known before. The energy feels remarkably similar to the raw energy of Sgya, as if it's all part of the same network; yet this feels dull and manageable. It's another thing to add to the growing list of questions.

"That we're fated to Bond?" I ask with a little squeak.

I bravely glance up at him, craning my neck, and my heart nearly skips a beat at the look in his eyes. The guarded masks he wears like a second skin have vanished, leaving behind a raw and vulnerable Anders, his gaze silently pleading with me to stay, not to pull away.

For too long, I've dismissed the strength of our connection, yet hearing him articulate this pull ignites a warmth that flushes my cheeks. The brooding hot prince could become my husband? I almost giggle at the chance that Anders is the one I'd be destined to Bond with.

"We still have to go through The Ceremony. It might not even be us," he assures me, though I catch the hope in his tone.

I nod slowly, understanding that he's trying to soothe the tension between us; still, I can't help but feel the gravity of it. In all my studies and research, I have yet to find anything that captures the unusual intensity of what I share with him. I think I've known from the beginning, deep down, that it was more than just a regular Bond, even on the first day of school, though I've done a lousy job accepting it.

He finishes recounting the events that unfolded in the clearing, the impenetrable wall of shadows that kept my lower half shielded from sight, and the way the mist had completely enveloped me. He shares, with a bit of guilt, that Trysten had remained unconscious across the field, but he had chosen me.

Anders didn't hesitate to reach for me, feeling the power burning within me, and instinctively, like his body knew what to do, he began channeling it out. As he did, he watched as the shadows and mist retreated. He finishes off by retelling those short minutes before we had to get back to the transport.

I can't bear to meet his gaze, the weight of my actions crashing down on me. I not only struck Trysten for yanking me out of Anders' arms, but also allowed myself to curl up against him for comfort and sleep beside him on the bunk. Though I wonder if there's more to it as I watch some memory cross his eyes.

When he's finished, he gently brushes a strand of hair from my face, tucking it behind my ear in the same way he's done countless times before. "What did you tell them? They want to question me." I attempt to divert the conversation. Avoidance feels like the safest path for now, but I'm not ready to let go of him just yet.

Whatever he sees in my eyes has him leaning down, wrapping his palms around my thighs, lifting and spinning me to the table, and stepping between my thighs before pulling me firmly against his chest. My breath catches in my throat, and my toes curl at the heat I find in his gaze.

I lean back on my palms, attempting to put some distance between us despite my body coming alive. I'm still dressed in nothing but a modest nightgown. Still, it's just soft fabric with no underthings.

"We all agreed to keep it simple for now." His gaze drops to my mouth. "Your transport was in hyperjump when it got trapped by Sgya's gravitational pull, and you crashed. You saved Trysten. We only found you by sheer luck, picking up your heat signatures. We managed to escape before anyone realized we were ever there." He shrugs nonchalantly, as though what transpired was nothing more than a minor inconvenience. I have no doubt that every kingdom will know about this by tomorrow.

His hands wrap around me, lifting me back to him, my breasts nearly brushing him. I gulp down the simmering desire building in my core. "So, no mention of your father's notes? Or the nightmarish shadows that sought to pull me into that glowing tree?"

A disbelieving chuckle escapes my lips as I run a palm down his chest, feeling every toned muscle beneath. Our chests brush together as I lean in, looking up to fully face him, and I wish I could crawl back into bed with him at my side.

The desire to be near him is a consuming force of its own. It's unlike any emotion I've ever experienced. It almost feels like an essential urge woven into the very fabric of my being, as necessary as breath itself. He lets out a soft hum, his gaze shifting toward the door momentarily before returning to me, filled with a restlessness of unspoken thoughts.

I'm not sure if he's aware of his hands, but they move to my hips, his thumbs making idle circles on the lower section of my abdomen. "There's also notes about your magic, or at least I think it's your magic." A flicker of something unreadable crosses his face as I tug him closer, wrapping my legs around his. His eyes drift down to where our bodies are joined.

My palm brushes against the scratchy shadow of his beard. The sensation ignites an awareness within me. As I run my thumb along the pronounced contours of his high cheekbones, he leans into my touch, his sapphire eyes devouring me. They glimmer like deep pools, and I find myself lost in them, captivated by how they shimmer with unspoken want.

"It's real," I mutter, not as a question, but as an understanding, an acknowledgment.

This magnetic pull between us transcends the Lumos Bond. It's a fulfillment of an ancient prophecy ordained by the gods themselves. Usually, I would be terrified, instinctively wanting to run in the opposite direction, hating that once again my life is dictated by the gods' plans, but right now, I simply can't resist, and I don't want to. Acceptance floods my mind as an unexpected calm washes over me.

It's real.

I'm unsure who moves first—maybe it's me, perhaps him—but suddenly our noses are brushing, the whisper of shared breath hanging between us as if time has slowed. Our lips are so tantalizingly close that it would only take a minuscule shift to close this insufferable distance. His breath grazes my lips as he whispers my name.

"Soraea," the sound so much like a prayer or maybe a desperate plea, as his hand moves to cup my neck, his fingers weaving through my hair, as his thumb brushes over a very sensitive spot on my neck. The intimacy of his touch tugs at something deep within me.

In that same heartbeat, I lean forward, letting our lips graze like they did at the resort. I crave this connection, and as my eyes flutter closed, I feel a euphoric haze settle around me, my body coming alive with anticipation. His lips brush against mine again, soft yet fervent, and I am swept away by the sweetness of it.

But just as I feel ready to surrender, he pulls away, a pained expression crossing his features. "I really want to kiss you." He sighs, running a hand through his hair. "Gods, I want to kiss you..." I see the longing and truth of that statement in his eyes, but he continues, brushing a hand down my shoulder, "but not like this." The weight of his frustrating words hangs in the air. "I don't want our first real kiss to be tainted by this trauma."

The tension in his jaw reveals the restraint he's forcing upon himself, as if he can't believe his own words. I can't argue with him. I want to kiss him desperately, yet I understand.

"Don't look at me like that," he chuckles softly. His gaze is full of mischief and a searing heat as he leans in, his mouth brushing against my cheek. "I plan on kissing you the moment you're ready, but when I do," my whole body erupts in goosebumps as his breath and lips brush over my cheek, "it won't be soft or sweet, Princess."

A gasp, or maybe a moan, escapes my lips as he pulls away. A darker glimmer flickers in his gaze this time, and a seductive grin spreads across his lips.

"When I finally kiss you, Soraea, it will be a claiming. There won't even be a hint of doubt about my intentions or feelings." His promise sends a thrill coursing down my spine, setting my already heated core ablaze.

I shift slightly in his arms, my core brushing against his hips, and a knowing smirk curls at the corners of his mouth. Just as I'm about to demand that kiss, my body betrays me as a pain I hadn't noticed before, which feels like a stab wound at my hips, causing me to clutch his shirt in pain. He swears under his breath, drawing me against him as he runs a soothing hand down my spine. I can feel the unmistakable evidence of his desire pressing against my belly, but he's right, I'm not ready.

"Let's get you back to bed," Anders teases. "That's enough excitement for today."

I mock gasp, half-heartedly slapping his chest, the pure strength of him beneath my palm igniting a flurry of butterflies in my stomach. Just as I lean back on my hands again to catch my breath, the door swings open with a creak, and my father steps inside, his presence instantly commanding the room.

I immediately shoot up, sitting straight and attempting to wiggle free since Anders is still between my bare legs. His annoyingly sturdy, impressive body doesn't budge an inch. Something like amusement flickers in my father's gaze as I squirm, pushing at Anders; it almost makes me turn my stubborn glare on him.

He clears his throat, and Anders finally turns, keeping a possessive palm on my thigh as he stands beside where I'm still seated, shifting my thighs closed and crossing my ankles. Embarrassment floods my cheeks.

"Thank you, Prince Anders, for rescuing my daughter," my father says genuinely. "But if you wouldn't mind carrying her back to her bed, her mother would be extremely grateful for her return."

I can hardly believe my ears. Did my father just say that? The man who should be storming in, demanding that Anders release me, is instead suggesting he carry me? My jaw drops in disbelief.

"Yes, your majesty." Anders' grin widens as he bows before effortlessly scooping me into his arms in one fluid motion. His audacity renders me both impressed and flustered.

My father holds the door open, a small smile playing at the corners of his mouth, while I sit stiffly and awkwardly in Anders' arms.

"Relax," Anders whispers, his breath warm against my ear.

But I can't let go of my tension; instead, I press my lips into a tight line. If I had been caught in that position with anyone else, I'm not sure they would have survived my father's wrath.

Anders chuckles softly at my discomfort, and for a moment, the atmosphere softens with amusement. That moment dissipates faster than my next heartbeat when the door swings open. Kellan sits at my bedside, his face pale, his eyes wide, as his gaze shifts from Anders' arms around me to where my palm is flat on Anders' chest.

The silence that follows is far worse than any shout.

thirty-two

. . .

raea

IT HAS BEEN three days since we returned to school, and the bruises covering our bodies have turned dark shades of blue and purple. I didn't realize how much we had been hurt in the crash.

For the past two nights, my sleep has been plagued by nightmares that replay fragments of Sgya. My memories blend our time there into blurry bits. It's always flashes of glowing trees and the sound of the drums. Then, as if my mind can't fully grasp all the trauma, I only remember segments of that clearing.

I can hear that soft, feminine voice saying, "This is your path... he'll be here soon." Although I never saw her, I can't shake the feeling that it was Calia who touched me and alleviated some of my pain. I relive the power surging through me, burning me from the inside out all over again. In the depths of my nightmares, I hear those whispers weaving through the mist and the deep claws sinking into my flesh all over again.

It took an hour of negotiating, but my parents reluctantly agreed to let me remain in school, albeit with the stipulation that I would forgo any off-planet missions for the remainder of the year unless accompanied by Kuron. Speaking of Kuron, he had the hardest time leaving my side despite my dancing and spinning around the room to show off how alive I was.

That night, I returned to my room and discovered Kellan waiting for me in the living space. He told me his version of events, which lined up with Anders', though Kellan had a lot more to say about Anders and me. Then we talked about the Bond and our magic late into the night.

A sense of resignation settled over him when I mentioned the prophecy Anders and I found. I've never seen Kellan like that, but he held me and didn't let go, even when we had both fallen asleep on the sofa, until Aolyn woke us.

I haven't talked to Anders since the day in the greenhouse. At first, I wasn't sure if he was avoiding me or if it was something else. I found myself dwelling too much on whether I said or did something wrong until he messaged me that we would talk soon and that he's been pulled into palace meetings every morning—and that he misses me.

Every morning since, I have opened my door hoping to see my assigned escort, but it's been Trysten every time, with a tea in hand 'from Anders.' I've attempted not to dwell on why my heart aches, though it's impossible.

The bright side? It's allowed his best friend to become an unexpected anchor in my life, grounding me each morning and reassuring me I'll be okay.

He has insisted he's alright and begged me to let it go, yet this does little to quell my endless apologies. Each apology feels inadequate, so I keep saying it...every morning.

Trysten meets me at my door again, ready to lead me to the Executive Hall for Bonding class. I offer him a bright smile and follow him out.

"How's your day so far?"

"Fine."

"Hey Trysten," I halt, making him pause as we near the stairs. "I'm sor—"

He groans, rolling his eyes with a smile and keeps walking, making me giggle. I'd be lying if I said he hasn't become a good friend to me. It won't just be Anders I miss when the school year is over.

We meet Ciara and Tate by the door, interrupting their hushed conversation. As we step into the hall, a wave of gasps washes over the four of us. I cringe, suddenly remembering that the other dorms haven't seen us in a while, primarily because we've been dodging the dining hall in favor of someone's rooms to eat in. The last thing any of us has wanted is a room full of whispers and prying eyes.

"It's getting old," Ciara grumbles at my side as she finds an empty row near the top.

"Speak for yourself," Tate chimes in with a cheeky grin. "The ladies love it."

Ciara and I roll our eyes at him, but I can't help but smile at his unwavering optimism. We make our way up, sliding into empty seats and inching toward the center. My eyes lock with Anders at the end of the row, talking with Trysten.

To my surprise, they both decide to join us. Trysten takes a seat beside Ciara, while Anders settles in on my other side. Just my luck, Kellan chooses that moment to join us, filling in the only empty seat next to Tate.

I catch Ciara's eye, and she shoots me a sly smirk as she looks back and forth between Anders and me. I can feel the energy radiating from him, but it's our Bond that has me stifling a smile.

The wave of pastels surging around us goes wild, like our Bonds have missed each other. Our pinkies brush against each other, and I pull my lips in to stifle a gasp. It's strange how quickly it can feel familiar. Without a thought, our pinkies intertwine, reminding me of the Bubble Village, where we held hands openly without a care in the world.

"Where have you been?" I whisper, trying to keep my voice steady as I turn to face the dais.

"Researching," he replies softly, his gaze focused on something far beyond the classroom walls. "You needed time."

Something similar to disbelief and anger flooded my chest. "So you decided for me?"

His mouth twists up as his eyes meet mine. "Raea," he murmurs, the sound searing every nerve ending while soothing that ugly, hot anger. "I promise, it was for your own benefit, not mine. I—"

He's cut off, but my body relaxes into the seat now that I know things between us are exactly as they should be. He wasn't avoiding me. Or so he says. Either way, my whole body relaxes at his confession, settling a part of me that I don't fully understand.

"Settle down," Professor Becca instructs as she takes her position at the front of the room. She scans the three dorms gathered here, her eyes sympathetic and understanding when she reaches us. "I'm glad to see you all alive and well," she adds, addressing the six of us individually with a gentle smile that softens the tension in the air.

"Today, we're going to shake things up a bit with a fun exercise," she continues, her enthusiasm palpable. "In just a few minutes, we'll walk over to the Academy Hall, where tables have been set up for an interactive Bonding session." The crowd begins to share whispers, making our professor chuckle. "Not that kind of Bonding session. Ladies, you'll take a seat at one of the tables and stay put throughout the class. Gentlemen, you'll be moving around—find an open seat and sit across from one of the ladies. You'll have exactly two minutes at each table to learn more about the person in front of you."

My eyes drop to her Bonding mark that winds up her middle finger to the back of her hand. It's strange to see hers so dark. I'm used to my mother's and the other women in our court. Their Bond marks are lighter shades of silver and gray, blending in effortlessly. I've seen darker marks, so I know they aren't rare, but I wonder if the color carries any significance.

"You'll all be looking for the Bond—this can be something subtle, like a faint buzz in the air. If you feel it, make a note on your tablet. If you don't feel anything, move on to the next table. This exercise will help you narrow down the choices for your upcoming ceremonies. Now, juniors, don't worry if you don't feel much, or anything at all, at this stage—just jot down whatever you observe. Remember, depending on your birthday, you still have another year, or possibly two."

A hand shoots up from the corner of Taeolyn's section.

"Do seniors only match with seniors?" a woman asks, her tone dripping with impatience. "I mean, I don't want to waste my time with a junior."

I immediately recognize her; it's Sienna.

When I lean forward to see her, I note the bitchy smirk on her annoyingly beautiful face, and it takes everything in me not to roll my eyes. I sit back and face forward, biting down on the inside of my lip hard enough to draw blood. I don't know what it is about her that gets me riled up so easily.

"Don't let her get to you," Anders murmurs from beside me, leaning in close enough that I catch his masculine scent that I often dream of. My shoulders relax instinctively as warmth radiates from him, comforting me even on a soul-deep level. "There's no Bond between her and me." Our knees brush together, and the energy that pulses between us is both exhilarating and grounding. "I'm yours."

Anders interlaces his fingers with mine, wrapping my hand in his. A rush of emotions floods me. We've gone from merely acknowledging an attraction to an undeniable need for each other that feels overwhelming, yet exactly right at the same time. Those two words play over and over in my head.

Mine.

"Good point, Sienna," Professor Becca continues, her tone shifting to a more serious note. "Senior men will have the opportunity to visit tables for both juniors and seniors. Junior men, however, should stick to junior ladies."

Professor Becca answers a few more questions, and soon we move as a crowd toward the Academy Hall. Anders walks at my side, no longer holding my hand, but close enough that I can feel his heat radiating against me while Kellan trails closely behind us, silent but observant. I feel both of their Bonds reaching for me—the iridescent light from Anders envelops me in a protective cocoon, while Kellan's soft green Bond attempts to weave its way toward me. It's a peculiar mix of comfort and agony to have them both beside me. I'm not even sure if they're aware of it. I've never asked.

If someone had asked me a few weeks ago, I would have confidently declared Kellan my choice—if I had one. He's always been my best friend, and my heart feels safe with him. Yet, somewhere along the lines, the dynamics have shifted. Anders has somehow woven himself into the fabric of my life, becoming an all-consuming need that I can't seem to satiate.

The Academy Hall is lit brightly when we arrive. The roofline is sloped, resembling a gentle wave in the forest, with glittering walls of glass and windows. Inside, I can see soft lights illuminating the open space that awaits us.

As we enter the space designed to accommodate the nearly two thousand students and faculty on campus, I take in the hundred or so tables decorating the usually expansive floor and along the walkways, separated by lush planters that typically line the edges of the room. The balconies that rise above on the three sides are shadowed, and behind the dais, the wall of windows reveals the twin moons in a blanket of stars.

I find a seat in the corner near the dais, not nearly as excited as my classmates for this exercise, as Professor Becca uses her projection magic to display clocks above each desk.

Once all the women have settled into their seats, Professor Becca takes up a position behind me on the dais. "Gentlemen, you may now find a seat," she relays.

The men shift awkwardly, their shoes squeaking on the polished floor. Just as I catch a glimpse of Kellan and Anders making their way towards me, a man from Veker slides into the empty seat across from mine, blocking them from view. I suppress a sigh, forcing my lips into the best smile I can muster.

Despite the mess of all this bonding stuff, I remind myself that I am still a princess, and there's a chance that the prophecy may not even link to me. And, as Anders said, we still have to conduct The Ceremony, which means I will eventually have to narrow it down to a large group of men to undergo the testing with.

For the next couple of minutes, the man I've learned is named Arne launches into a series of clumsy flirtations, each one more uncomfortable than the last. I grimace inwardly as he chuckles over his attempts to impress me with the significance of my name and his.

"Raya," which isn't even my name, but not that I'll point that out. He claims it means queen, and his means eagle, and with the Treon family crest being an eagle, well…it's a stretch. Just when I think I can't endure anymore, I'm rescued when the timer signals the end of our interaction. Relief washes over me. I just hope that they get better from here on out.

As Arne shuffles away, another man takes his place. "Princess Raea," Lord Syzmon greets me with a deep bow. He's a senior from Ateria, and I immediately sense we have no Bond. I muster a patient smile while he stumbles through his own round of flirting. Meanwhile, I burn under the intense gaze of either Kellan or Anders, their eyes boring into me from across the room. I resist the urge to look.

When the two-minute timer is up, I relax and roll my shoulders.

I can do this.

The new kid, Gunnar, takes a seat next before a junior boy from my politics class can. Gunnar's blue eyes light with arrogance as he leans back, relaxing into the chair.

"We haven't had the pleasure yet, Princess Raea," he says flirtatiously. "I've heard nothing but intriguing tales about you." His tone drips with narcissism, and I can't help but wonder how Anders could be friends with someone like him. Then again, I feel the same way about Sienna, who's currently glaring at me like she's plotting my death.

"Gunnar," I reply, sliding on my facade as the poised princess. "Tell me more about yourself."

I straighten my posture and tilt my head, trying to maintain an air of indifference. He's cute in a way, with an air of don't-give-a–shit—a fact he's clearly aware of. He has ice-blue eyes, and his tousled auburn hair falls in loose waves around his face. A hint of scruff frames his jaw, and his fitted navy shirt reveals toned muscles beneath, contrasting with the paleness of his skin. I almost ask why he isn't tan like the other Okenen men in my life, but then I realize I'm just comparing him, and unfortunately for him, I find him lacking.

"I think I'd rather hear about you. What's your favorite color?" he asks, quirking an eyebrow with his teasing smirk.

Oh, he's definitely a flirt, but two can play the game. At least he's keeping things interesting.

"Green," I reply casually, "like the fever thistles that blanket Kyrr in the summer. Or the pale pink Azaleas in Okenen." I lean back in my chair, feigning boredom, but inwardly I can sense that he sees right through me and is ready for the challenge.

"Favorite book?" he fires back.

"The Tales of Emberlee Rose." I'm aware that it's not my definitive favorite, since my love for literature spans many genres, but it would be impossible to choose just one. Still, that novel has left me with a severe book hangover.

"Romance. Steamy. Okay," he says with a seductive pull of his lips, making me blush.

"Ten seconds," I tease, pointing to the timer above us.

"How would you feel about taking a walk after this so we can get to know each other better?"

I momentarily freeze. Did he just ask me on a date? Heat rises in my cheeks for the second time in under two minutes.

"Think about it." He winks, standing just as the timer sounds.

What. The. Hell.

The dumb ripples of light hit me like a shockwave, sending waves of yellow crashing over me.

Damn it.

Reluctantly, I mark him down on the app open on my tablet. If I don't, I won't get credit.

Six more men sit in front of me. They're all kind but more interested in touting their accomplishments and accolades. Only one of them do I sense even the slightest flicker of light. Or maybe it's fatigue. I mark him down anyway and look up, knowing we have time for about four more.

"Princess," he purrs, the word rolling off his tongue with a velvety smoothness that sends a jolt of energy through me.

My heart races as our eyes lock, his stormy blue depths captivating me completely. I can't help the smile that spreads across my face. He looks devilishly handsome, especially in the warm, golden light that accentuates every angle of his chiseled features. The formal black attire clings to his tan, inked skin in a way that stirs something deep within me, igniting a flame low in my belly as I think of the strength of his arms around me. There's a rush of pure happiness in seeing him, my friend, my…maybe something more.

He returns my smile, a look of wonder playing across his face, his gaze unwavering. I notice his breath hitch, and he nearly stumbles as he takes a seat across from me, making the air feel thick with tension.

"What?"

"You've never smiled like that at me. Everyone else. Never me," he admits, his voice carrying a blend of surprise and admiration. "It's beautiful."

The weight of his words sinks in, and suddenly my smile falters. A heavy stone lodges in my throat at his admission.

Have I truly never offered him my full, unguarded smile before?

It's one I typically reserve for those closest to me. Realization washes over me, and I can't shake the feeling that I've been such a bitch and a terrible friend. I set my pen down, flipping the tablet over to hide the list of names I've been scribbling—names that now feel trivial compared to the feelings flooding my chest. We're fated to Bond, and all I've done is push him away.

His hand covers mine, and it's a cataclysmic event. Longing. Fear. Hope. Comfort. Heat. Desire.

Forever.

It's as if each nerve ending in my body awakens, sending a delightful shiver racing through me. I try to convince myself that I'm overreacting, but every second he holds my hand reminds me that this connection is far more intense than I've ever allowed it to be.

A sharp gasp escapes my lips, and warmth floods my cheeks, the kind of heat only he seems to elicit. His fingers interlace with mine, flipping the tablet over. The movement is slow, almost sensual. When I dare to look at his mouth, my curiosity piques—I wonder what he might taste like. Does he have that lingering minty freshness from earlier? The thought makes my pulse race. I want to know. Hell, I want to feel his mouth all over me.

"Interesting," he remarks, breaking my reverie.

I snap my gaze to his eyes, confusion swirling within me. His grin surfaces, and that irritatingly charming dimple makes an appearance. If I weren't already seated, I might just float away from the sheer effect he has on me.

"What?" I manage to ask, my voice unintentionally breathy, betraying the whirlwind of erotic thoughts playing out in my mind.

"Your list," he says with a playful lilt. "What else would I be talking about?"

As if he can sense my thoughts, his eyes darken. My stomach twists at the mere mention of it, but not in a bad way. My body seems to have a mind of its own, finding new ways to self-destruct, reacting to his words with reckless abandon. I press my thighs together, desperate to regain some semblance of composure.

"Seems I have a few options," I respond with a touch of sass, but inside, I cringe at my choice of words.

Options? Gods, open the ground and swallow me whole. When did I lose my ability to talk to him?

"Princess, we both know that's not true," he counters, his tone carrying an undeniable certainty that feels a lot like a promise.

My heart does a little flip as butterflies take flight. I clear my throat. Pulling my hand away from his feels like a frigid gust of air cutting through the warmth, leaving me immediately clearer-headed but unbalanced.

"I have some questions for you," I say, aware that time is running out: twenty-two seconds left. "Tonight. After dinner. Can we meet down by the river at our spot?" The words tumble out, and I almost blush at the idea that we would have a *spot*.

"See you there." He stands while taking my hand. The air fills with iridescent waves, buzzing with unspoken words and possibilities. Every cell of my being hums with anticipation.

Then, as if the world around us slows, he leans down, turning my hand over, and presses a soft kiss onto my palm. The touch reverberates through me, all the way to my soul. My jaw drops to the desk, and I can't help but notice the hushed gasps from those around us. When the shock fades, laughter bubbles up inside of me—nervous, giddy, and undeniably excited.

Is this how it feels to have someone pining for you?

I feel multiple pairs of eyes on us as he turns, casually sliding his hands into his pockets while that infuriating yet enchanting air of confidence surrounds him as he saunters away, leaving me breathless and filled with a longing to chase after him and finally discover what it would feel like to have him claim me like promised.

Later.

Later, I will find out.

Three additional men sit across from me, their presence hardly worth noting, but they're all sweet nonetheless. They're all from my kingdom, so I thank them for their time, knowing that I'll be their queen one day. By the time I reach the final spot on my list, I've gathered a respectable number of candidates. Kellan claims the last seat, and a contented sigh escapes me as I sense our Bond coalesce in the air. He greets me with that same warm smile he's worn every day for the past fifteen years, a smile that instantly soothes me.

I know it's selfish, this desire to keep him close while still knowing it's Anders I'll be Bonding with, if the prophecy is true. But I'm not ready to let Kellan go. Not yet. The idea of him Bonding with anyone else makes my stomach turn.

"Saving the best for last?" I let a teasing smile dance on my lips, both a challenge and an invitation.

"Raea, you don't have to choose Ryker just because of some prophecy." Okay, I guess that's how we're doing this. It's the same conversation we had the other night in my room. My brow furrows at his bluntness, irritation bubbling beneath the surface.

"Kellan, you know it's not up to me. When the time comes, I don't actually get to pick, do I?" I lean back and cross my arms over my chest defensively, annoyed by this conversation and the whole scenario. I hate feeling like I'm toying with his emotions, but he has to understand there was always a possibility we wouldn't Bond even without the prophecy.

Kellan looks exhausted, like he, too, has felt the invisible weight of the Bond this year. His freckled face looks a little flushed, and the longer strands of brown hair seems as though he's been tugging at them repeatedly. His hazel eyes, usually bright, look dimmer today, but there's a desperate plea written across his features.

"RaeRae." He leans closer. "You know how I feel about you. I don't want to Bond with anyone else. You're my best friend. Screw the prophecy. Just tell me I can make you happy." His words wrap around me, squeezing my heart, and I reach across the table, taking his hand in mine.

With Kellan, everything feels softer and warmer, like a cozy blanket on a chilly evening or a gentle hug when the world feels overwhelming. Things feel so right with him, I don't know how I can feel so strongly for two different men. Lifting my gaze to meet his, I see a world of unguarded emotions reflected back at me—hope, love, and a hint of despair.

"Kellan, I love you. You have to know that," I confess, my words spilling out in a rush. "We still have a year left. Things can change. I'm not making any decisions, okay? Not until The Ceremony."

He nods, but it's clear it's only to pacify me. The weight of this brokenness between us weighs on my chest, crushing me. In a simpler life, one where Kellan and I weren't tied to a crown, I would be perfectly content to settle down with him in a little cabin on the edge of the woods and raise a few children as we grew old together.

A sob almost escapes me at the thought. The idea of Kellan not being in my life just doesn't make sense, but if Anders and I Bond, where does that leave him?

"I love you too, RaeRae," he whispers, his voice deep with emotion. A heavy sigh escapes his lips as resolve washes over his face.

"And that's time. Please hit submit on your lists before heading out. Class is dismissed," Professor Becca announces.

As the crowd disperses out of the hall, filtering back into the dorms and dining hall, Kellan keeps hold of my hand, ignoring the glances from those who notice.

Before we step through the door, I pause and bury my face into his chest. I'm not sure what to say, but in a way, I know I'm letting go of years' worth of hopes and dreams that he'd be mine.

"No matter what happens, you'll always be my best friend," I whisper, my voice barely above a murmur, before pulling away to wipe away an unexpected tear.

Nothing has changed, but I can feel it coming. There might be burning heat and ice between Anders and me that are undeniable, exhilarating even, but Kellan holds my heart in a way that Anders never could. Kellan leans down, pressing a tender kiss on my forehead before leaving me alone to gather my emotions.

I can't be sure, but it feels like its own kind of promise. He won't let me go without a fight.

Kellan and I walk in silence, the heavy doors of the Academy Hall echoing shut behind us. My footsteps fall softly against the marble, but I can feel the weight in every step—not from exhaustion, but from the way he looked at me. The way I looked back.

Kellan walks just behind, close enough that I can hear the controlled rhythm of his breath, but not close enough to touch. He hasn't said a word since, and he doesn't need to. We reach the archway leading out into the moonlit path when I finally speak. "You didn't have to say what you did…in there."

He doesn't answer immediately. Instead, he stops walking. I turn, and he's standing in the silvery light, jaw tight, eyes shadowed and unreadable.

"I didn't say everything," he mutters, voice barely above a whisper.

My breath catches. "What does that mean?"

He takes a step closer, not enough to close the distance, but enough that I feel the pull of it. His gaze finds mine, and it's raw—vulnerable in a way I've never seen from him.

"It means I can feel you slipping through my fingers, Raea, and I don't know how to stop it. It means I've been watching you fall for someone else, and it's killing me." His voice breaks slightly, but he doesn't look away. "It means I don't want to be just your best friend anymore. You think I don't care, but gods, Raea...I've cared every moment you looked past me. I just didn't know how to say it...until now."

Silence falls between us like a blade.

He doesn't wait for my answer. He gives a small, pained shake of his head and walks past me into the night.

thirty-three

. . .

raea

I SNEAK out of the dorms when the moons are high enough to light the way. I hadn't seen Anders leave the dining hall, but when I checked, he was already gone. Clad in the same delicate gown I wore to dinner earlier—a soft, flowing white fabric adorned with intricate, leafy green embroidery that highlights the green of my eyes. Thankfully, the night air remains warm since I didn't think to grab a cloak.

Navigating the well-worn trail that leads down to the water, I gingerly slip off my shoes, conscious of the uneven stones beneath my feet. My mind is so focused on the damp embankment ahead that I nearly miss the energy in the air around me. It's a subtle, yet tingling sensation against my skin, alerting me that I'm not alone. When I finally look up, there he is, leaning casually against a tree trunk and draped in shadows. One forearm is pressed into the bark, while his other hand rests nonchalantly in his pants pocket. The picture of confidence. He looks absolutely divine, and deep within me, an almost primal instinct screams, *mine*. My tongue flicks out instinctively, wetting my lips as I feel his smoldering gaze intensify.

"You wanted to talk?" he purrs, stepping out of the shadows with a seductive grace that makes my heart race.

Each purposeful stride toward me ignites a fire within me, coating my body with a warmth that spreads from my core. I clear my throat, desperate to summon my thoughts that seem to have fled altogether.

With a mind gloriously distracted, I cast my gaze toward the shimmering water. Perhaps the cool water will help clear my head. I tread carefully down the embankment, the fabric of my gown trailing behind me.

"You look beautiful," he murmurs, moving to stand beside me, his voice low and velvety. I smile softly.

As I settle onto the rocky shore, I gather the flowing material around me before dipping my toes into the chilly water. He shifts closer, his nearness only intensifying the charged atmosphere between us.

"I don't really have a question as much as—" I pause, searching for the right words. "Well, I don't know. I want to explore...this." I gesture between us, trying to articulate the pull between us, perhaps to convey that I want that kiss now.

His head tilts slightly as if weighing the sincerity of my words. Then, with deliberate slowness, his hand rises toward me, fingers gently tugging at the ribbon that binds my hair in a braid. It untangles with ease, allowing the strands to cascade down my back, making me shiver.

"Whatever you're comfortable with," he says, his voice deep and resonant. "I won't Bond with you, at least not right now, so don't worry about that."

I believe him, but a strange tightness grips my chest, making it hard to breathe. What is it I truly want from him? I cast my gaze back towards the water, taking a few calming breaths to steady the molten core of my anxiety.

"Soraea," he whispers, his breath warm against my ear, causing a delightful heat to trace along my neck as he gently brushes my loose hair aside.

Panic seizes me as I pull back. "What's your favorite color?" I blurt out, desperate for a delay to gather my courage. He pulls back slightly, a smile playing on his lips as he considers my question before responding.

"Green," he replies, his eyes lighting up. "Or maybe white."

I purse my lips, scrutinizing him closely, only making him chuckle.

"What do you like to do for fun?" My nerves soften as he leans back on his elbow with an effortless grace. It's the air and attitude of the dark prince, cocky and assured.

He exudes total confidence, the kind of princely charm that captivates everyone around him. Instead of feeling annoyed, I am surprised at how endearing I find it. Anders carries himself with a barrier between him and everyone else—except Trysten and me, allowing us glimpses of the authentic man beneath the title.

He reclines on the boulder, one leg bent and looking comfortable, while I remain seated, the rough texture pressing into my palms as I steady myself. His button-down shirt, a soft charcoal, clings to his broad shoulders and chest and is unbuttoned just enough to reveal a small patch of skin. If the gods had crafted a man specifically for me, I'm sure he would be the embodiment of that ideal. A lock of dark hair falls across his forehead, and without thinking, I sweep it aside.

He sighs at my touch, but his reaction quickly shifts to one of pure awe, as if my simple gesture struck a chord within him. He swallows thickly, and I sense that the distance between us is beginning to dissolve.

"FinSurfing, reading, flying, and playing with my sister," he replies.

The last one surprises me. Princess Clara can't be more than nine years old. The thought of him spending time with her fills my chest with a strange warmth I didn't expect. He had taken her to Kliax, and I wish I could have met her, but my temper always seems to get in the way.

"What's FinSurfing? You've mentioned it before."

He looks at me in disbelief for a moment before sitting up straighter, bringing our eyes to the same level. "You've never—" he hesitates. I see excitement cross his features, as if he can't wait to teach me. "You're coming with me over break. Most of our planets have regular whales, the kind we all hear about, but on Kolari, Aquarion, and Malaya, we have Tesinik Whales. They're smaller than the whales you might think of, but they're incredibly fast. If you time it just right, you can ride on their fins. They seem to enjoy it just as much as we do, but it takes skill to balance without slipping off."

As he speaks, his eyes light up at the memories of FinSurfing alongside Trysten and Cole during their childhood. I watch him, excited to see the real him, the man who isn't burdened by a crown. I find myself completely captivated. The prospect of watching him in action excites me. Maybe I'd even let him teach me.

"Why do you prefer 'Ryker'?" I let the question fall out of me. I've been so torn since the start of school.

Everyone calls him Ryker, yet I can't seem to figure out if he actually likes it or not. I stopped using Soraea because it was a mouthful, but I still use it...sometimes. I remember the day I told my parents I wanted to be called Raea. They seemed so sad, but they respected my wishes, introducing me as Raea from then on. At home, though, occasionally, they'll slip and call me by my full name. I wonder if it's similar for him. When I glance back at him, his expression shifts, becoming distant for a moment as he contemplates the question.

"Prince Anders is my official title, the name I present to the entire system. But for my friends, and those closest to me, 'Ryker' just stuck. It was the first time I could feel like someone without the weight of my crown." My heart sinks a little as I absorb his words.

"I'm sorry." An unexpected guilt creeps in. I've demanded to be called Raea, yet I haven't offered him the same respect. It never occurred to me that he might actually prefer Ryker over Anders. "What do you want me to call you?"

His gaze meets mine again, and he offers a small, gentle smile. "Whatever you want." He means it, and I can sense the sincerity behind it. I know that feeling—the longing to be a person instead of a title. Deciding to give it a try, I turn and face him.

"Ryker," I say, feeling slightly self-conscious. The name feels weird on my tongue. He laughs softly and pulls me closer, wrapping his arm around me as I settle snugly into his side.

Ryker.

Ryker.

The more I say his name, the more it settles over me.

"Ryker."

I continue the questioning until a chill in the air has me rubbing my arms to keep warm. Without a word, he brings our bodies together. The cool air is no longer an issue when I settle into his heat, all the while continuing to talk as if he didn't just shift the whole atmosphere around me.

I remain quiet, savoring the warmth radiating from him—it's more than just physical. I love hearing his voice and the stories he shares. Thoughts of Professor Becca's advice replay in my mind. If we are indeed fated to Bond, then I want whoever I give my heart to be a choice, not a consequence. I want to be sure that, should I give it to him, it's done with full intent and understanding. I want control.

It's late when my resolve steals my spine. With the twin moons casting long shadows, I twist up to my knees. He promised me no Bonding, and…well…it's time for that kiss that keeps me daydreaming. There's only a heartbeat's hesitation before my mouth slams into his. For a second, he doesn't move, probably from the shock of it, and then he cups his hand under my hair, tugging me closer, demanding total control.

For him, for this kiss, I relent.

A burst of energy shakes the trees around us, its power exploding outward like a wave. His fingers tug at the strands of hair at my nape, tilting my head back so he can deepen the kiss. His lips are soft and gentle for only a moment before a sort of desperation takes over, and that claiming kiss he promised…he delivers tenfold.

I never knew a kiss could be like this, but I surrender as a raw hunger overtakes him. Our mouths meld in a deliberate slide and press as a need and want so powerful reverberate through me. I can feel him. Not just the heat of his skin, or the rough rasp of his stubbled jaw, but his emotions. I realize the potent blend of desire and fierce protectiveness isn't mine, but his. I only hesitate for a moment before he's pulling me back so that my body is flush with his.

The revelation is startling, but when I go to pull away again to tell him, his grip tightens. His want for me is a tangible thing, primal and deep, an almost desperate need to brand me as his. My lips part willingly, an invitation on my part, and the first velvety slide of his tongue sends a deluge of heat through my core, radiating outward. He tastes of mint and something inherently male, a wild, coastal scent that pools low in my belly. We're a whirlwind of seeking lips, a clash of teeth, and soft moans as he devours me, a delicious oblivion that scatters every thought. He moves with expert precision, exploring every inch of my mouth.

I can feel the tug on my Bond, but every emotion is so heightened and overwhelming that I can't pick out which one it is and tell it to calm down.

"Raea." His voice is a ragged whisper against my lips as he breaks our kiss, and we share the air between us. "Your Bond. You're losing control."

"Okay," I gasp, my breaths coming in shallow, uneven bursts. "Thanks."

The words are barely out before I tug him back, my focus shifting, however hazy, to the Bond in my mind. An array of light and colors ripples in the air around us so beautifully, so peacefully, as if it's dancing to the sound of us. Meanwhile, the strange well of power deep within me, one I'm still exploring, begins to replenish itself, flooding my body with a warm, intoxicating sensation.

A gasp escapes my lips, maybe it's a moan, as something in my core pulls taut, like a silken thread of life attaching itself to his very soul, binding us in a way that I know, deep down I know, is irreversible. The shift within me feels like something ancient, yawning awake, as a deep-seated ache settles in my bones that only he can fulfill. The forest, the moons, the weight of all my responsibilities—everything fades, leaving only the two of us beneath the blanket of stars, the twin moons as our silent chaperones.

With a need to get closer, I straddle him. I tell myself it's because of the uneven rock and the awkwardness of kneeling while he's seated, but my lie is pretty flimsy, even to me. That fierce, almost unbearable urge to be closer, to meld our bodies, our souls, has taken root. The silky skirts of my gown bunch around my thighs, though Ryker doesn't seem to mind, his movements betraying a practiced ease as he thoroughly tastes and claims me. His hands slide up my bare thighs, finally settling on the curve of my ass, his fingers digging into the lace with a guttural groan that vibrates through my core.

I shudder, and my hips slide forward along the hard length beneath me. Another warm surge of energy runs up my spine, this time from the delight that I can make him feel like this. His grip on my ass tightens as he begins to rock my hips back and forth, his kiss moving in rhythm with my hips. I can feel how wet I am, and much to my embarrassment, I know it's soaking the front of his pants. I shift, finding a hard edge, and grind myself on it.

"Damn it, Raea," he groans, his voice thick with strained restraint. "Don't move."

He leans back slightly as I go still, my body humming with unsatisfied desire. Gods, I can't think when he touches me like this. I only feel.

It's a heady and dangerous combination. After a few ragged breaths, his mouth is back on me, skating to the sensitive area on my neck while I tangle my fingers back through the short, silky strands of his hair, pulling him impossibly closer.

My skin erupts with goosebumps as his hands move out from under my gown, his grip tightening over my waist. I can feel his hands as if there were no delicate layers between us, as if his very skin is pressed against mine. His mouth returns to mine and my thoughts dissolve, lost in a heady mix of lust and a growing sense of power. His tongue withdraws from my mouth, leaving a slick trail as his lips move to my jawline before dipping into the spot just below my ear, into that overly sensitive curve, and using a mixture of hot breaths and sucking to send sparks dancing beneath my skin.

I've never begged for anything in my life like I'm about to beg him to release me from this all-consuming burn. Unlike the power I felt on Sgya, this feels delicious, like sitting too close to the hearth on a cold winter night. My body moves of its own accord, rocking, begging, pleading, and gods, every inch of it feels dangerously alive. It's a current of pure energy, and every time we touch, the universe threatens to come undone.

His hands keep me pinned against the glorious, hard length of him as I rock, chasing a release I so desperately need. Ryker's bite on my neck drives me into a frenzy.

"I need—" I nearly sob.

He leans back just enough that our gazes meet, and it's not shame that I feel, but power. I don't care, not at this moment, what I look like or what I'm doing. I have just let go of all my self-imposed expectations and surrendered to the moment. And the way he's looking at me, he loves this; however, I can't be sure, since his lust is as deep as mine.

"Your Bond," he responds, his voice thick, "It's not worth the risk." When my face falls, he adds, "We'll practice your shield." His hands move, wrapping around my back and holding me close. "I want every part of you." He kisses me tenderly. "Your heart." Another soft kiss. "Your soul." Another kiss. "Your pleasure." He grins against my lips. "Everything." His words summon a flood of emotions that has a tear falling down my cheek, getting caught between us. "I want you forever."

Another tear falls, and all I can do is bury my face in his neck and let him hold me.

We stay that way for long minutes, neither of us moving, allowing our breaths to sync, our bodies to adjust to this newness between us. I may not be ready to express my feelings in words, but I can show him. So I squeeze him tighter, putting my feelings on display. When he does pull back, his sapphire eyes seem to almost glow in the moonlight.

"Be mine, Raea. Let me in. Let me take you on dates. Let me show you why we're perfect together." His voice is barely a whisper, laced with desperate vulnerability. "This, us, I want to drown in you and never come up for air again."

His hands, still stroking my spine, tremble slightly. My heart leaps, and fresh tears leak from my eyes, but when I look into the swirling silver of his blue gaze, that invisible tether between us tightens. Something like a silent language passes between our two souls. It's an understanding and a profound sense of belonging, as if we are two halves finally reunited.

It isn't the obligation of the Bond that stirs within me, but a more profound yearning, a fierce desire to be his, wholly and completely his. It scares me. This depth of my feelings. How did we get here so quickly? Without a word, I lean forward, offering him another slow, deliberate kiss.

Our mouths mold together once more, a soft sigh escaping my lips as he seems to memorize every curve and contour of mine, a promise for the future. An embarrassing whimper escapes my throat at the thought, and a ghost of a smile touches his lips against mine.

The kiss deepens into a slow, languid exploration that leaves me breathless in a completely different way and strangely content.

Finally, with a bit of reluctance, I pull back, resting my head against the solid warmth of his shoulder, my hands draped behind him, content to remain in his lap.

"I'm scared," I admit softly, my fingers idly toying with strands of his hair. I feel a sense of vulnerability—mine, not his—wash over me. I've never done anything like this before, never allowed myself to feel, and yet it feels so intoxicating and addictive.

His.

Can I be his?

His hand glides over mine, a gentle but purposeful movement, drawing it down between us.

"I know," he finally responds. "You don't have to answer tonight. But you wanted honesty—there it is." His body is so relaxed despite the confession. "You're so beautiful," he whispers, tucking a loose strand of hair behind my ear, his touch so tender. "I love your hair. You hardly wear it down."

"It gets in the way," I reply with a chuckle.

My fingers wander up his arm and into the crook of his neck, seeking the warmth of his skin. I watch as his eyes flutter closed, his breath hitching slightly as I trace his jawline with a delicate touch.

In a voice that's low and breathy, he asks, "Can you feel that?"

"The energy or your emotions?"

"The energy. It's amazing." His grin broadens, and for the first time, I notice how his eyes crinkle at the corners, an adorable detail I've overlooked in my previous obsessions. How have I never noticed it before? Perhaps it's because he rarely smiles, or maybe it's that I'm perpetually distracted by that infuriating, addictive dimple on his right cheek. "What do you mean, your emotions?"

I brush my fingers lightly over his lips, recalling the sensation of their warmth against my own. Leaning in again, I let our lips collide gently, and suddenly, his emotions are laid bare before me. The depth of his feelings for me scares me, but it's the need that gives me pause, as if he requires me to breathe.

"When we kiss, I think I can sense your emotions. I don't know how or why, but I just can." His gaze locks onto mine, filled with an intensity that makes my heart race. It's not fear or even confusion, but admiration. Those blue swirls pull me in, dragging me down into a depth I know I won't ever escape. I will never tire of looking at them. I want to study them in every light. I watch as the dark blue swirls with the white and silver mini storms. "Your eyes look like a storm over the ocean," I whisper.

"That's what my mom used to say." For a fleeting instant, I see a flicker of pain darken his expression before he masks it. "Yours reminds me of the forest. The way the green swells with light and illuminates flecks of gold looks like shimmering sunlight filtering through the canopy."

The compliment catches me off guard, and I suddenly find myself staring at his fitted shirt, overwhelmed by a rush of emotions I don't know how to articulate. I push them aside, choosing to focus on this moment instead.

"Thank you," I murmur around a lump in my throat.

"For what?" He brushes his fingers through my hair, and the sensation sends waves of delight coursing through me. No matter where or how he touches me, I feel that energy, but right now, it feels subtle, as if all the pent-up energy has finally been released.

"Everything. For Sgya. And after. For—" I chuckle softly, a warmth creeping up my cheeks. "Tonight."

"Anytime, Princess." A smirk dances across his lips.

Lying my head on his arm, I bury my face in his chest, breathing him in. I close my eyes, feeling his arm wrap around me, pulling me closer as if shielding me from the outside world, while a strange, warm breeze surrounds us.

I know we should head back to the dorms, but I'm not ready to let reality intrude just yet. Here, in this fleeting moment, I can pretend to be a normal girl. No prince and princess roles, no prophecy looming over us, no weighty expectations concerning whom I should Bond with or how I should carry the fate of the system. I can forget it all in this peaceful cocoon—at least for a while.

thirty-four

raea

I WAKE UP, stretching and sinking further into the silk sheets at my back with a sort of contentment I haven't felt before, definitely not since school started. My mind drifts back to last night, with Ryker's mouth exploring mine, down my neck, settling over my heart. And his confession...gods, it was so unexpected and tender, and I think it made me fall harder. It's exactly what I needed from him.

Because that's what's happening, I'm falling for him. I feel giddy as I get ready for the day, slowly showering, washing my hair twice, and then spending extra time braiding it and letting my natural waves hang loose from the ponytail. Aolyn hums with a knowing smirk when I brush on my blush and swipe my lips with a bit of lip stain.

My bruises have mostly faded from my face, and the cuts on my hands have closed up. Now, if my torso and arms could get the memo. I look like I was beaten up from the bruises peppering my chest from where I hit the console, and the bruises on my arms—well, who knows?

"You seem chipper," Aolyn teases as I grab my bag from my desk. I roll my eyes and give her an amused smile.

"Have a good day," I sing back to her as I close the door behind me.

Ryker is across from me, holding out a tea, looking devilishly handsome in his athletic shorts and a backward hat I've never seen him in, his chest gloriously bare. Gods, why is it so attractive? His muscled legs and arms are on full display, and the deep contours of his chest and abs are still glistening from whatever workout he just finished. His heated gaze tracks down my body, taking in the skirt and top I chose today.

"Morning, Princess." His voice is deep and husky, a sound that melts my insides.

I try not to look at his lips, remembering how they molded against mine, how thoroughly he claimed me last night under the moon and stars, but I fail. I can't help it. His mouth is perfect, and for a first real kiss, well, it was out of this world. I can't imagine it gets any better than that.

"Morning." I flush from head to toe when I realize I've been staring at his mouth this whole time.

He chuckles, his mouth tilting up at the edge as he turns. Instead of leading me downstairs, I find myself at his door. With a backward glance, there's nobody around. He opens the door and tugs me inside.

I don't even have time to look around before I'm pinned against the door, the hard lines of his body pressed into me as his mouth moves to mine. I hold out my tea, careful not to spill it, but apparently, I'm too distracted—I hiss when a scalding splash hits my hand.

Ande—Ryker...gods, I've gotta get used to that—pulls away briefly, taking my tea and setting it on an end table near the door before returning to me. With both hands free, I let my bag drop and slide my palms up the warm contours of his chest, wrapping them around his neck. Gods, I love the feel of his heated skin on me. My thoughts drift to what it would be like to feel his entire body pressed into me sans all clothing.

I'm knee-deep in highly inappropriate thoughts when he tilts my chin up so that I can look into his eyes. "Will you come to my game today?" he asks. He sounds confident and sure of himself, but I can see his underlying vulnerability. There's something so sweet about Ryker being nervous.

I slide my fingers into his hair, lifting onto my toes and placing a soft kiss on his cheek. "I'd love to."

His hands tug on my hair, tilting my head back further, fusing our mouths back together, and deepening the kiss. Gratitude and excitement are pouring off of him in waves. I'm already on my toes, so he's setting the pace. Once again, we become a frantic mess of tongues and teeth, his emotions mixing with mine, and the heat within me ignites like it's just been lying in wait.

As if sensing where my thoughts have gone, his hands drift down to my ass again, tugging me impossibly closer until I feel how hard he is against my stomach.

A gaspy moan escapes my lips as he pulls back, his whole body taut and restrained.

"That fucking sound," he growls.

I chuckle lightly, falling against the door for support while I breathe through the energy build-up. "Can I ask you something?" My cheeks heat, but it's been nagging at me all night. He nods, and I continue, "Will we have sex before our Ceremony?"

I swear I watch his eyes darken exponentially as his nostrils flare, his palms coming up and planting on either side of my head.

"Do you want to have sex before *our* Ceremony?" he asks, his voice low, almost a whisper. My chest heaves with the air I'm attempting to inhale, but failing to do so.

"I don't—I haven't—" I take a deep breath, finding my courage. I'm a princess, and he's my fated future, so I'd better learn how to talk to him. "I've never even kissed anyone until you," I admit. "But this fire between us—I want you like I've never wanted anyone."

His features lift with a small smirk. "Good." He shifts, pressing his body into me again, the proof of his desire, pinning me in place against the door. "I want all of you to myself. Every kiss, every touch, every heated moment, every gasping moan—I want them all to belong to me." My cheeks flush as I attempt to breathe, his face so close I can feel his hot breath tickling my cheek. "And if you ever learn to control that Bond of yours, then we can talk. I won't push you farther than you're ready to go."

"And if I want to?"

He chuckles, the sound wrapping around me. "Then who am I to deny you? Trust me, Soraea, I cannot wait to sink myself so deep in you that you forget the rest of the galaxy exists. I want to hear you screaming my name as I make you come on my cock, giving all of you over to me."

I'm pretty sure I stop breathing as my toes curl. I've never heard such filthy words and been so turned on at the same time.

Ryker leans in further until his mouth brushes the shell of my ear. "When you finally give yourself to me, whether it's before or after, I'm going to roar so loud, and mark you so thoroughly, that everyone in every corner of this system will know you belong to me."

My head turns so that our mouths are so close, sharing the same air. "And do I?" I ask breathlessly. "Belong to you?" I swallow thickly, running my fingertips along the grooves of the door at my back. I've never allowed myself to be this vulnerable with anyone.

Ryker stands to his full height, making me crane my neck. "I've belonged to you far longer than you know, Princess." He reaches out, brushing his thumb along my jaw. "The question only you can answer is if you're ready to belong to me."

"I—" His finger presses down on my lips, silencing me.

"I told you to think about it. Because when you say yes, there's no going back, there's no changing your mind. I do not share, and I will not stand back silently watching as other men try to flirt with you. You will be mine and only mine. So think about it." He removes his finger from my mouth as I draw in a shallow breath.

What is it that I want? If I have over a year left, am I ready to commit to Ryker? Should I be using this time to flirt and enjoy being single? Dread sinks in my stomach. I don't know what I want. I don't know what I'm ready for.

I do know that the idea of him taking those same luxuries has me wanting to vomit, but it would be wrong of me to ask that of him if I am not ready for that level of commitment. It's not that I have this sudden urge to flirt with society, but belonging to a man before The

Ceremony has just never been a possibility, and right now, it's scary as hell.

As if sensing where my mind has gone, he leans down, placing a quick but tender kiss on the tip of my nose and offering me a smile. "There's no rush, beautiful," he mutters. "C'mon, let's get you some food." He takes a step back, effectively releasing me, and hands me my tea. I'm too stunned to do anything more than accept with a small smile as I follow him out, my mind still reeling.

So fast. Everything that has happened between us has been so fast. Even if we've known each other since we were in diapers. Even if I know the truth of my fate. He's right. I need to take some time to think about it. In the meantime, I need to take things slow with him. I want to be sure about taking that step.

He walks at my side, slowing his steps to match mine as we make our way down the hall toward the dining hall. He remains quiet, watching me from the corner of his eye, but I hate this awkward tension between us.

"I'll think about it." My slippers tap on the stone floor. "You're right. It's a big decision, and I don't…I mean, I haven't even considered the possibility of being serious with someone before The Ceremony. I've always expected to wait for any sort of relationship until The Ceremony was complete."

His hand brushes mine, our fingers briefly tangling, careful of watchful eyes. "Take as much time as you need. There's no rush. Like I said," he pauses, his voice turning to a whisper. "I've belonged to you far longer than you know."

Before I can ask what he means, Ciara bounces up to my side, taking my hand and squealing about something. Ryker's lip tilts up slightly as he winks, then saunters away. Ciara's still babbling about something I'm not hearing as I watch him fill a plate of meat and eggs, his team gathering around him while most women's eyes drift in his direction. I can't blame them; a shirtless Ryker with a backward hat is the best kind of innocent fantasy, but it doesn't stop me from seeing red. This is going to be a lot harder than I thought.

"Hey, RaeRae," Kellan says, coming to my side as I take in the dining options. I don't know why I bother looking. I know it will end the same as it does most mornings. A bagel, some fruit, and possibly some yogurt.

"Hey, Kel." I shoot him a quick smile before grabbing a plate.

I ignore the red, blaring alarm going off in my head. If I say yes to Ryker, what does that mean for Kellan and me? Wasn't it only last night that I promised not to make any decisions? I shove aside the guilt, finding a nice little box to lock into and focus on the present.

Kellan grabs a plate, following me to the self-service spread. I grab a bagel and a spoonful of fruit. "What are you doing today?" I ask.

He mutters something about needing meat before responding that he's studying today and wants to head into town to get out for a bit. I follow him to the window, serving a sort of meat and potato hash.

Ryker walks by subtly, brushing a hand across my lower back as he reaches for a pre-filled plate as if possessively already laying claim, and then disappears, leaving my whole body alight with energy and heat. A thrill courses through me at the thought of a possessive Ryker. Kellan doesn't miss the contact, his face becoming a mottled shade of red as he grinds his molars.

"Come with me?" he asks as we take slow steps back to our tables.

I wish we could sit wherever we wanted on weekends. Ryker's little rule is absurd. Perhaps I could convince him to lay off, at least for one day of the week.

"I can't," I sigh. "I'm headed to the game this afternoon." I don't bother explaining why. I probably would have gone with Kellan if Ryker hadn't asked me already.

"You don't even like AerBall," he snaps, making me flinch. "What now, because you find out you're possibly fated to Bond with him, you're an AerBall fan now?"

His words sting like a physical blow. Kellan and I never fight, and he's never talked to me like this. I told him about the last game I attended and how much fun I had. The fact that he's questioning me now just hurts.

"You can be a real jerk sometimes," I whisper, holding back tears. "He's not the only reason."

"Just the main one," Kellan turns and finds a seat at the Intel table.

I fight the urge to rub the spot where it feels like my heart hurts. I hate all of this; I hate how much it's hurting my best friend. I just don't know what to do about it. I can't deny what's happening between Ryker and me, but that doesn't make my feelings for Kellan disappear, either. I plop down into a seat beside Ciara, the giddiness from the morning already gone.

She bumps my shoulder with hers, offering me a piece of sausage. I accept it, biting into it, ignoring the burning in my throat. "He'll be okay."

"You heard?"

She nods her head, offering me a small, gentle smile. "Not all of it, but it was pretty obvious. Ryker isn't as subtle as he thinks he is. I'm sure half the room saw him touch you. I only happened to hear the part about the game."

I sigh, falling onto my folded arms. I'll need to make it up to Kellan, but also, why should I? He's the one hurting me. I could have been doing anything today. Just because I didn't drop everything to go with him. "I'm going to the game because I want to." I sit up, forcefully unraveling my linen napkin. "And because Ryker asked. I don't want to go to the village."

"Then we go to the game," Ciara says, shrugging and tossing some potatoes into her mouth. The rest of breakfast I spend trying to recover my mood, but if I'm honest, I'm still upset over the whole interaction.

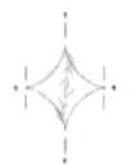

There's a storm coming in this afternoon, so I slip into my Xori pants and wear a long-sleeve shirt under the Drithm Academy jersey I ordered. Aolyn has a matching one, with the Drithm crest covering our chests.

"Sit," she orders.

I take a seat on the tall stool in front of my vanity as she paints my face with blue and gold stars and the number seven on my cheek.

"You can't!" I gasp. "No. Aolyn, what if I'm pictured or something? I can't wear his number."

She ignores me, humming as she paints the other cheek with a stencil, painting the Drithm crest. "You'll be fine," she responds. "Besides, who cares?"

I groan and look in the mirror. "I can't, I'm sorry, but it's just going to start rumors, and none of us need that, especially with what just happened."

She rolls her eyes and sighs, relenting, and wipes my cheek, painting another star in its place.

I steal the paint from her and trade places, painting her face in a similar fashion. As I do, we talk about Ryker showing up earlier and letting us know he reserved a row of seats for us directly behind the pit. It's some of the best seats in the arena.

Kamden, Tate, and Ciara are meeting us there. I messaged Kellan to see if he wanted to come, but I haven't heard back. I'm going to assume it's a no.

When we're both done fixing our hair and makeup, I brush my teeth once more just because. Not that I plan on kissing him again, but just in case.

We make it out to the arena and find our friends among the crowd at the front of the gates. All of us are dressed in academy colors. Today, we're playing against Coriat, one of the academies in the Okenen kingdom. Their fans are among us, dressed in light blue and white. I groan when we make our way to our seats and find Ryker's dumb cheer team only three rows behind us.

thirty-five

. . .

ryker

"LET'S DO THIS," I roar across the arena to my teammates.

We're up thirteen points in the last period. The crowd goes wild, and my personal cheer team starts chanting something about me being the best. I glance up to the stands, my eyes immediately finding Raea there with her usual group of friends, her white hair like a beacon.

She's changed out of that cute skirt I wanted to strip her out of and is now wearing her Xori pants with a Drithm AerBall jersey. Her hair is pulled up, and she has a sparkling tattoo on her cheek with the school insignia. She looks like a damn fantasy. The only thing that would make it better would be if my name and number were printed across her back.

I'll have to beg, probably, but it's something I need to see. Hell, maybe it'll be a birthday present for me. Just her in the jersey, some pretty white lacy panties beneath, and sprawled out in my dark sheets. The image has me growing hard again, but I'm learning to live with it. It seems that's a new constant state for me.

Her asking me earlier if we would have sex before The Ceremony almost made me drop to my knees before her and beg her to let me take her right then and there, but that would have made me an asshole. Not for her first time. I knew she was a virgin, but never kissed anyone else either—hell. I've never been so godsdamn possessive in my life, but when she told me that, I almost demanded she not even look at another guy. It took every bit of restraint to hold that weird possessive shit back.

It doesn't help that I can't stop thinking about the way she was grinding herself on me last night. The filthy thoughts filtering through me ever since have kept me in a constant semi-hard state.

Raea's gaze meets mine, and I watch as her creamy skin floods with pink as she smiles shyly at me. If it wasn't against regulations for royals to be dating, hell, for us to even be friends, I'd run over there so fast and kiss that shy smile right off her face in front of everyone, making sure they all knew who she belongs to.

She might not be ready to admit she's mine, but it's just a matter of time. I'm going to do everything I can to prove to her she can make the jump, and I'll be there waiting, ready to catch her.

"You ready?" Savenne asks, breaking me from my thoughts.

I nod and focus back on the bunker just before the bell sounds. Just having Raea here watching and cheering me on has kept my energy levels up the entire game. I beat their guardian to the balls and scoop them up, heading back to the water.

I don't feel the burn of the ice-cold water when I jump in, moving quickly toward my teammates. I make it back to Orion and Breckn, the junior who replaced Cole. They grab the ball and dive over me into the water, swimming around the island to the far side where the obstacle ring is located.

I swim after them, keeping the AerBall tucked away in the net on my stick. I catch up to my team and spot Savenne already climbing a tree, but one of the asshole defenders pulls her down, slamming her onto her back. The crowd gasps, and my anger simmers. She groans as she rolls to her side. She throws out a hand to signal she's okay and doesn't need the healer.

I hoist myself up out of the water, nodding for the groundball attackers to move on. The defender comes straight for me, and I can't dodge him. My only chance to reach Savenne is to knock this guy down a notch. I toss my stick and drop my shoulder, throwing my weight into the defender.

He goes down like a felled tree, hitting the dirt hard. Savenne pulls herself up to relax against the tree out of the corner of my eye. The defender beneath me throws a punch to my kidney, and I wince but knee him in his gut until he groans. I stand and grab my stick, making sure the defender stays down before checking on her. Her right pupil is dilated, and when I hold her head, she brushes me off and starts vomiting. She is most likely concussed.

I signal for a healer, and for Kalli, one of the senior girls, to come take her place. Savenne whines, but I tell her to knock it off and get help. She nods and groans again. The defender hovers near us, no longer allowed to attack during the pause in the game. Once the bell sounds for us to resume, he's going to be the next to be hauled off on a stretcher. I play by the rules only as long as the others do. Hurting one of my ladies is completely unacceptable, and he's about to learn that. I can't afford to be thrown out of the game, so I make a quick plan to keep it all legal.

I position myself in front of him as the switch happens and jerk my head to the right, telling Kalli to go that way. When the bell sounds, she sprints right and disappears into the forest of obstacles while I use my stick to shove the defender. I'm bigger and stronger, and his feet slide against the hard path. He throws a punch that I dodge, throwing my elbow right into his face, making his nose bleed. Once the trail is clear, I shove hard and then take off running for one of the traps. It's my nemesis, but if I time it right, I can get clear just in time for the restraints to wrap around him instead of me.

I suck in a sharp breath just before I step into the trap zone and launch myself across just before the restraints fly out from the ground. The defender did precisely as I hoped and followed, not paying attention. He screams when the restraints wrap around his arms and legs, sending him face-first into the ground. The more he fights them, the tighter they get. The trick with the restraints is to relax long enough for them to loosen. One by one, you can slide your limbs free slowly.

Once he's down, I kick dirt in his face as retribution, holding my anger back from kicking his head in, and instead take off before I do something that will end with my name in the media. I'm sure my publicist would love that. I have seven minutes left to get past the bladefish and get the AerBall into the net.

The opposing team cheers, and I look up to see they've scored a groundball. One point isn't going to get them close enough. A collective groan comes from the crowd, and I smirk, guessing they just missed the AerBall.

I dive headfirst into the bladefish, ignoring the burn of micro-cuts against my skin that won't be healed until after the game is over. Orion and Breckn are fighting off the second defender, keeping him busy.

The goalie sees me, and his face pales. He has twenty seconds at best to decide if he's going to leave his goal unattended and come after me or just attempt to block. I run close and release the AerBall. His stick flies up but misses, and I whoop once the AerBall hits the back of the small net. Orion and Breckn cheer, running after me, clearly giving up on the groundball. The buzzer sounds, and we dive back into the water, ignoring the bypass, and head for the island where the rest of our team meets us.

We've only lost one game this season and are well on our way to winning the championships if we keep this up. After the formalities are done, the rest of the team heads back to the locker rooms, our high from the win still pumping through our bodies, but I pause at the steps just as Raea comes down with a flirty smile on her face. Gods, I wish I could just hug her right here in front of everyone, but she'd probably kick my ass. It'd still be worth it.

When she reaches the last step, I keep eye contact with her, grab her hand, and tug her down the last step. Her breath hitches as her chest brushes against me, and she's forced to look up at me. Neither of us says anything despite knowing we're drawing the attention of the crowd around us.

I lean down, brush her cheek, and whisper, "Meet me at the gates in twenty."

She nods and blushes when I let my lips softly graze her ear, careful that nobody else sees it. She smells so good. I wish I could just bottle the scent.

"Good win," she says breathlessly.

I don't care that I'm wet and dirty and probably stink. I pull her in for a hug, tucking her into me and allowing myself three seconds to soak it in, soak her in, then I leave, glancing back and watching her cheeks flush, both of us ignoring the questioning looks on everyone's faces.

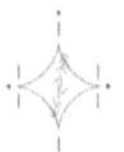

Thirty minutes later, we're sprawled out in the living space of my room, the books and scrolls spread out before us. Even the Book of Beginnings is humming with its mysterious power.

"Here," I say, handing it over with the prophecy page open.

She rereads it, chewing on her lip. I've studied it so many times that I've memorized it. "What do you think it means?"

I shake my head. I don't have a single clue other than knowing deep down it's us.

"I think I found the answer to your magic." I grab a hefty tome that looks seconds away from falling apart. "It mentions the gods mentioning a gift of starlight heat. You said the shadows kept repeating Light-bringer. And you've been called the harbinger of light." Her eyes widen, grabbing the book from my hands, making me chuckle.

She reads through the page I marked quietly, nodding. "Okay, but I don't have light."

"Yet," I say. "You don't have light yet. Raea, we shouldn't even have these powers yet, and here we are. What if we need to complete the Bond to gain access?"

I've been practicing my own powers in secret, eager to finally show them to her. With her face buried in the text, I open my palm and send a chilly blast of air her way. The pages ruffle, and she drops the book, looking at me questioningly.

"You—" she squeals, bouncing on her knees. "You figured it out. Do it again," she breathes out.

Her excitement brings a smile to my lips. I love her like this. Hell. I think I love her. I shake the thought away, adding it to the growing pile of things I feel for the woman in front of me. She's not ready for that.

With another wave of my hand, a cool blast of air *whooshes* her way. "I can't figure out how to get warm air," I admit, the chill lingering on my fingertips. "But I'm close."

Her face scrunches adorably, a thoughtful frown creasing her brow. "When we were on Sgya," she begins slowly, her gaze distant, as if reliving the moment. "Did you heal me?"

"No?" I shake my head, the memory hazy. "I don't think so."

"But when you touched me," she insists, her curious eyes meet mine. "I felt a cool wave flow through me, like a soothing balm, and it healed the pain, that burning sensation." She pauses, a new idea sparking. "Can you summon water?"

My focus immediately shifts inward, to the well of magic within me. I try to think of water, envisioning a clear stream, but nothing happens. I groan, frustrated when I can't figure it out. She picks up the ancient book, biting down on her lip as she reads.

"Can I try summoning it with you?" The words tumble out as a hopeful question.

Without a response, the book falls to the floor with a soft *thud*, already forgotten. Her eyes heat in a way I've never seen and there's something seductive about the way she crawls to me, feigning innocence, but I see the smile she's attempting to conceal. She knows exactly what she's doing. The air between us crackles as she slips into my lap, her legs bracing my hips.

Fuck me.

"What do you need?" she asks breathlessly.

I growl, tugging her body flush with mine, my mouth immediately claiming hers. Her lips part, a soft sigh escaping as I bury my tongue in her mouth, *tasting* her. She gasps, her body melting against mine in an instant.

As our kiss deepens, I reach for that well of magic within me. Beside the strand I instinctively tug for air, a new one shimmers—a vibrant blue. I pull on it, willing warm water to my palm. Nothing. No sensation of power, no shift in the air. Yet, she smiles against my lips.

"Do you know how good that feels?" she murmurs, her voice thick with pleasure as I draw back just enough to see her face. "It's like a warm shower, soothing over my nerves."

I had no idea anything was even happening. "I don't have control over it," I confess.

"Yet," she responds, her eyes sparkling with challenge. She kisses me once more, a soft, deliberate press, then climbs out of my lap, reclaiming her space.

"Now," she declares, turning her back to me, "I need to read without distractions." The lingering heat in my lap and the imprint of her body keeps me distracted, though.

thirty-six

. . .

raea

HAVE I spent the rest of my evening thinking about Ryker's magic? Yes. Yes, I have. Out of every book we went through, the only things that stood out were the prophecy and the paragraph about the balance of starlight being a gift to the second daughter.

Cryptic, as always.

I can't help but wonder if Professor Becca was right. Spending time with Ryker is proving to be an awakening. Beneath the dark, asshole exterior, he's full of life and emotions, and he's everything I could want in a partner. I could spend hours with him and never tire of talking to him.

Trysten drops padded gloves at my feet as he stalks into the gym. "Today, you'll be learning how to use your fists." He straps the gloves to my hands before positioning me in front of a punching bag hanging from the ceiling.

With his guidance, I learn how to strike and recover, shielding my face and body properly. Once he thinks I have the basics down, he leads me to the center of one of the training mats.

He goes slow at first, his strikes coming at me in almost slow motion as he teaches me how to dodge and when to strike. I can't help but appreciate all the time he's spending with me and training me. I can feel my body moving in muscle memory. I don't tremble when he throws a real punch at me, either.

I can see why he's Ryker's best friend. He's quickly becoming a great friend to me as well—not that I have admitted that. I should probably tell him, but I don't want things to get weird. Plus, what happens on the off chance that Ryker and I don't Bond? Would Trysten still want to be friends?

When he claims I'm stepping before throwing my punch, he moves me back to the bag, asking for permission before gripping my hips and kicking out my legs. After several rounds of adjusting to the correct position, we return to the center mat. I can feel the difference with each punch to the pads on Trysten's hands as he swats me away.

"You're doing great," Trysten praises. "And getting stronger, too." I smile at the praise before asking to go again.

By the time we call it quits, I'm exhausted, but I feel strong, I feel alive. Trysten and I are stretching when Ryker enters the gym, looking like he's been napping. Trysten teases him about it.

Before I leave with Ryker, Trysten says again, "Great job. We'll keep working on different attacks and how to get out of holds, but I think soon, you'll even be able to fight Ryker off." The beaming smile I give Trysten makes Ryker scoff.

"We'll see about that," Ryker teases. "C'mon, little warrior, let's get you to bed."

"Can I tell you something?" Aolyn asks as she sits down on her bed, brushing out her long, dark hair. She looks nervous as she glances at the door once.

"Yeah, what's up?" I slip into a black nightgown to dress for bed. She grabs our tablets and Prisms, shoves them into the bathroom, turns on the water, and then closes the door. My full attention falls on her.

"Raea, I think…" She shakes her head. "I think something bad is happening with my father. I was talking to him about your Sgya inci-dent, and he mentioned that she wasn't happy about it. When I asked him who, he said," she gulps, "the dark one." Goosebumps erupt over my arms, and the hum of my power rushes to the surface.

"The dark one?"

She nods. "Over break, there was a lady in the palace. I never saw her face; she was always cloaked in dark robes, but something was off with her. And her powers—" She shudders. "I think she controls the shadows."

Bile rushes up my throat at the same time I hear the voices in my head. I focus on Aolyn. "Why are you telling me this?"

"Because," she moves to my bed, sitting beside me. "I think," she swipes at a tear. I've never seen Aolyn cry. "I think they're planning an attack or something big. I overheard her speaking with my father about the veil being close, and then he said something to her about you." She looks up at me, those icy-blue eyes shrouded in tears. "I'm sorry I didn't say something sooner, but I don't think it's safe for you to stay at school."

"A," I whisper, "I need to tell you something too."

So I do. I tell her everything that happened to us on Sgya—the real story—and then about the magic and prophecy. I don't know why I tell her, but she's my friend, and she betrayed her father's trust by telling me.

"I think it's time to go home, Raea," she sighs. "I don't want you to get hurt."

That night, I go to bed thinking of a girl shrouded in shadows, whispering to them like they're her pets, ready to do her evil bidding.

"Please, help!" I scream.

"Stop fighting us," the eerie voice snarls, wrapping around my mind.

I grab my throbbing head and bend over, willing the voices to stay out. Around me, the colonies are arguing with each other. Some have been consumed with anger, tearing into the next person they see. Some are filled with lust so intense they seem almost inhuman, animalistic in the way they move, like nothing else matters but fulfilling their deep-seated desires.

The one thing they all have in common is that they aren't themselves. Onyx mist fills the air with its nefarious voice and tangy taste, and there's nothing I can do but watch the colony destroy itself. Swirling onyx mist sits like a blanket between the shops and homes, forcing people to walk through it.

Whispers and voices chanting *Kill...Take...It's all yours,* filling the space between the shouting and chaos.

"Give it to me, and this will all stop," the voice chants.

I feel like I'm going to be sick. I scream, squeezing my head because it feels like I'm being ripped in half, and my body feels like it's burning from the inside out.

"Give it to me," it demands.

"No!" I shout. "No!" Hands wrap around me, gripping me tighter. "No!" I shout again, thrashing to get free.

My people need me. My whole body shakes, the grip growing tighter. I summon my heat, ready to burn, when I feel a cooling calm wash over me.

"Hey, hey."

I snap my eyes open to see Aolyn and Ryker standing over me. Ryker has his hands on me, pinning me to the bed. Aolyn looks terrified, her fists clenched at her chest, a look of pure terror in her eyes.

"I'm sorry you wouldn't wake up," she whispers, terror lacing her voice. My chest heaves as I gasp for air. It was just a dream, *right*? I look around in the dark and realize I'm still in my room. It was just a dream. I swear it felt so real.

"Raea," Ryker says softly, releasing me.

I take another cleansing breath and close my eyes, willing my trembling body to calm the hell down. It was just a dream. Maybe if I say it enough, I'll believe it.

Gods, it felt so real. I swear I can still taste the tangy air and feel the unsettling chill in my bones. I breathe in for three, holding it before blowing it out for three, willing the adrenaline to leave my body. I groan, dropping my face into my palms. Ryker pulls back the covers and sits beside me, tugging my trembling body into his. I don't fight it, and I don't stop to question why Aolyn went to Ryker. She goes back to her bed, leaving him and me alone.

"I've got you," he whispers against my temple.

He doesn't say anything else. He's just there, and I let his scent wash over me, and the charge of energy in the air warms me like a soothing blanket. I close my eyes and feel my body relax more with every breath.

It was just a dream.

I sink into the warmth of his body, letting his steady heartbeat lull me back to sleep.

I wake up to an empty room, the sun already high enough for me to realize I slept in. I shower quickly, washing off last night's sweat, and dress in a simple navy shift dress that brushes my mid-thigh. A simple gold necklace and a waterfall braid finish my look. If I hurry, I can make it to the tail end of breakfast. But after last night, there's something I need to do. Every secret, every impossible truth, now demands to be shared.

I'm calling a meeting.

thirty-seven

. . .

ryker

GODS, it took everything in me to pull myself out of Raea's grasp this morning. I had fallen asleep beside her and woke before Aolyn or Raea and snuck out. Last night, she scared the shit out of me. Aolyn showed up at my door, looking terrified and begging me to help. I found Raea thrashing in her bed, but I couldn't get her to wake up. She was screaming, crying, and fighting. The energy surrounding her body had burned hot like the day she was on Sgya.

It took several minutes before I was able to wake her, and then, just like before, she crashed into my arms. I don't know what to do about it, but we need to get her powers under control before she hurts someone or damages something. Hell, it's time we all talk. She'd been thrashing, screaming words I couldn't decipher, but the air around her room had thrummed, the crystals in the sconces vibrating with latent power. It wasn't just a nightmare—it was a manifestation.

I sit down beside Trysten in the dining hall at breakfast. He's tearing pieces of his honey roll off and tossing them into his mouth while he concentrates on something in the distance.

"Trysten." He doesn't look at me. He just continues the same mindless routine. "Trysten." I shake him this time, and he snaps out of it. His eyes move to mine.

"What?" he answers.

"What's up with you? Wanna talk about it?" I stab a piece of meat and toss it in my mouth.

"What's up with you two?" he asks, taking a long pull of his coffee. "You're not being careful." He looks around the table at the other leaders, all of whom are chatting.

I take a sip of coffee before saying, "Not here. But," I pause and look around, "after Sgya, everything's different."

He nods, then his face falls. "I'm sorry I couldn't protect her." He sighs. "I keep hearing her screaming, and each night, I can't get to her."

His hand unconsciously rubs where the bandage was on his head, his eyes distant as if reliving the memory. "The voices were telling her that she would watch her kingdom burn, and then every other kingdom after it. Then there were other voices." He looks around. "Ryker, I have a bad feeling something big is coming."

I take another sip of my coffee despite the urgency I feel thrumming through me. He's right. I can feel the shift in the air. I just don't understand why every daily report about the veil shows no change. Nothing makes sense.

"C'mon, we have to get to the briefing." I nod and take a few more bites of food before discarding the tray with the rest of the crowd.

Before lunch, Raea messages a group of us, asking us to meet her in the first-floor study room. Trysten and I get there last, finding the room full. Kellan sits near her, Tate and Ciara arguing about something, and Aolyn and Kamden are even here.

"Hi," she says with a blush, though a faint shadow still lingers beneath her eyes. Her shoulders are squared, but I feel the subtle tremble as I hug her. "I think it's time we all talk."

"Thank the gods," Trysten says, dragging a seat back before dropping into it. I pull her to the front, keeping an arm around her because I can't not touch her.

"You okay?" I ask quietly.

She nods, stepping back out of my arms.

"Okay, well, I called all of you here because you're my closest friends, and well, a lot has happened, and I don't think I can do this alone anymore," she says.

Raea looks up at me, a silent apology written on her features. My hand slips to her lower back unconsciously, but she doesn't pull away. I don't miss the look of death on Kellan's features or the questioning gazes of her friends.

"Mind if I start?" I ask. She shakes her head. "There's a lot that has happened, but the main point is the veil is going to fall. It's not a matter of how or why, but when. Second, Raea and I have…abilities," I pause, glancing at her. She's chewing the hell out of her bottom lip. "And I think it's because there's a prophecy about us being fated to Bond that has a lot to do with the veil. It's the only thing that makes sense, as we haven't Bonded yet."

Kellan mutters something unintelligible, his brows knitted in confusion that mirrors his rage. He knows of the Bond, and us being fated, but this is clearly something else.

"Ryker and I went to Ista," Raea cuts in. She tells them about the books, her starlight heat sans the light, and the voices on Sgya, but when she mentions Aolyn claiming her life might be in danger, I nearly come undone.

"I spoke with my father," Aolyn says, looking ashamed, like she's torn between her father and Raea. "I told him I had a bad feeling about the veil, just trying to gauge his response." She shakes her head. "His response was that I was safe for now, but not to worry. All would make sense soon." She looks at Raea. "Please, go home or call Kuron." Tears fill Aolyn's eyes.

Ciara sits up. "Rae, you have to tell your parents."

Raea looks up at me, questioning what I think. Pleading for help.

"We call our guards, keep them stationed in the halls and the yard. You don't go anywhere unaccompanied by anyone not in this room. In the meantime, we need to up your training. Trysten, what's your assessment of her progress?" I look to my best friend, who looks more lost than I've ever seen, but something settles over him.

"She's doing great. I'd like to test her skills, though. Maybe you and I can tag team a surprise attack?"

"Absolutely not," Kellan barks. "Are you out of your damn minds? She's not doing that."

I chuckle, feeling the urge to put Kellan in his place. Raea isn't his, and as far as I'm concerned, she makes her own damn decisions.

Kamden surprises the hell out of me, though, when he speaks up. Honestly, I don't even know why he's here. "You'd rather she get attacked again by strangers?" I watch the blood drain from Raea's face, and memories of seeing their bloodied bodies still aren't enough to quell the rage inside.

"What?" Everyone seems to glance at her as she whispers, "How did you find out?"

Kamden admits he was on the roof that day and only reached her when Cole arrived. He thought it was best to stay out of it. Raea shudders. I wrap my arm around her, tucking her into my side.

"Since we're on the topic of secrets," I say, "My father is alive, I think, and living on Evello. Why? Not a clue, but he's not missing." Raea wraps her arms around my waist, resting her head on my chest.

"So where do we go from here?" she asks softly, her heart rate slowing to match mine. I don't even know if she knows it.

"Let's start at the beginning," Tate says, letting the front feet of his chair drop back to the floor.

thirty-eight

. . .

raea

AN HOUR LATER, we've recounted almost everything since the start of school. It feels good to get it all out, even if the looks Kellan keeps shooting my way are filled with betrayal. I need to talk to Kellan *again*. I hate this valley between us. He needs to hear from me about my heart and what I've decided. But if I've learned anything this past hour, it's that I need my friends in this with me, him included. We can't keep doing this alone. I think Ryker agrees—if the looks of approval and pride he keeps casting my way are any indication.

"I keep having visions," I start. "You were there in one of them." I glance up at Ryker, who's still hovering at my side. "I mean, we both were. In Mori, at the palace. There was a party or something, but you and I were out on the veranda, and everything was cloaked in shadows. There was screaming, but you said something."

I close my eyes, allowing the vision to replay in my head as tears well up in my eyes. My heart sings, not in fear, but with an overwhelming sense of safety. Ryker has been with me every step of the way, even if unknowingly.

I glance at Ryker, letting a tear splash down on my cheek with a smile. His brows furrow in confusion. "You told me to wake up, and I did. I don't think my mind just conjured it," I continue. He's studying me when Kellan clears his throat.

"What other visions are you having?" Ciara asks.

I tell them about all the strange dreams and visions of another girl —the one who I think is the same one Aolyn keeps talking about.

"The voices, though," I finish. "That's the mist. On Sgya, they were trying to penetrate my mind, but it was like an iron dome around my thoughts. They kept claiming things like 'Light-Bringer' and 'The New Dawn.' I keep hearing them."

"The prophecy," Kellan says, looking at Ryker. "What does it say?"

Ryker moves to the other side of me, leaning down on the console and typing it out. His hand brushes over mine as he does. Instantly, all my frayed nerves calm. As if he feels the same, I watch his body relax.

Ryker spends the next minute typing it all up before projecting it on the board behind us.

The days are numbered before the skies fall to night when Myrkr rises.

When the souls collide and the land trembles, will the new dawn begin.

The crowns of the seven will turn to ash. The empire reborn after the life gift restored.

The fate of the two crowns will destiny unite.

Long-forgotten answers will be revealed, an awakening bestowed.

The birth of the firstborn will the veil be complete.

Light and dark was balance made, but one will fall, one remain.

We all sit in silence for a long minute, reading through it. The entire time, Ryker stays at my side, his fingers toying with mine below the console, as if he needs my touch as much as I need his.

"I'm going out on a limb here to say that skies falling to night has something to do with the shadows," Tate muses, breaking the silence.

"Wow, great observation," Ciara teases, pulling her braids over her shoulder. "Souls colliding, maybe your Bond?"

I look up at Ryker, but he's shaking his head.

"I don't know. Everything I know about the Lumos Bond has more to do with the gods pre-ordaining specific Bonds between people; that's why there's The Ceremony. You have to find the strongest one. The Bond has nothing to do with souls, but it could just be wording." He shrugs, dropping a hip to lean against the console.

I nearly stumble as I'm tugged along until I'm standing so close my arm brushes his stomach with every breath.

"Well, it mentions the new dawn, and if the mist was calling you that," Kellan says, "I'm going to assume that line has to do with you. If you're the new dawn, maybe you'll complete a mission or something?"

Shrugging, I look to Ryker. "The next line is pretty obvious. The kingdoms won't exist if an empire is restored," he says. My mind tries to make sense of all of it, but it feels like a dream I can't quite grasp, like looking at a broken image in a shattered mirror, all jagged and wrong.

"Einvald," I mutter to myself. If the empire is restored, Einvald would be opened again. There would be ancient texts there that could help.

"Two crowns," Tate exclaims, gesturing to the two of us. "So obvious. Destiny has united you both." He grins, and it's almost enough to make me chuckle. I love his enthusiasm. I know I'll need to tell them soon that Ryker and I might be a thing. But that's a conversation that needs to happen with the man whose arm is wrapped around my waist.

"The rest of it is still cryptic," Ciara sighs with a frown.

"Back to the mist," Ryker says, looking at me. "The old man in Seamark Shallows." A full grin spreads across my face, making him chuckle. "What? I do know the actual name," he teases.

I roll my eyes and look at our friends. Ciara is grinning, Tate looks amused, Trysten looks relieved, Aolyn has seen it all, Kamden doesn't seem to notice, but Kellan—Kellan is furious. Honestly, he's going to have to accept this sooner or later. I'm not ruling out the off-chance that Ryker and I aren't destined, but I'm not going to pretend to hate Ryker either.

Ignoring Kellan's glare, I say, "An old man approached me in the village on Kliax. He said, 'The *birth of the new dawn is coming, Light-bringer.'*"

"So many titles," Ryker teases, poking my side. "So special."

The second poke sends me into a fit of giggles as he continues poking my sides below the corset.

"Anyway," Kellan states sternly, sucking all the joy out of the room. "Great, you have all the titles about being the light or whatever. Will that be your Bonding magic?"

I stop laughing, feeling a little lightheaded as I try to compose myself. "I mean, maybe," I respond a little breathlessly. "The mist said it wanted me to give it to them. If I don't have my magic yet, then why would they say that? Maybe it's something else?"

"It might not even be light," Trysten says. "Light can be a whole lot of things."

"Great, so we're back to nothing," Ciara says dramatically.

The room has a weird tension again as Ryker glances at me and then at the projection. "Raea, did you feel the energy on the planet before you went into the clearing?"

I nod, tilting my head. "It was stronger than here." My memories of that pulsing power surface. "On Sgya, I felt like it consumed everything."

Ryker's gaze goes distant as if he's thinking.

Kamden puts his Prism down. "Wait, hold up. What energy?" he asks.

"It's like a heartbeat," I say, studying Ryker. "The air, the ground, everything—there's so much energy there." Something passes over Ryker's features as if another piece of the puzzle has slipped into place.

There's a memory that is on the edge of my mind, just out of reach, but the emotions surrounding it are there. A fondness and friendship with Ryker as kids. The image is surrounded by a haze I can't penetrate. Ryker tilts his head as if he too can see it. "Did you—"

"Yes," I say, feeling perplexed. "I can't remember or access them, but I feel them sometimes."

"You two are super weird," Ciara mutters, earning a "You have no idea," from Trysten that's seconded by Aolyn.

"She's right. It's like a heartbeat," Ryker says, finally breaking our gaze and looking at our friends gathered around the table. "It's a distinct pulse, and it's in the plants, the ground, everywhere. It's here too, but Sgya was the strongest I've ever felt."

"Well, okay then. The two freakshows over here can feel the planet's heartbeat," Tate mutters.

"You guys do realize that you both feel the energy or whatever, and you're able to channel that energy from the planet and back into it?" Ciara looks between us. "Or were you stealing energy from those shadow things?"

"I think it was from the planet. I think—" I pause and turn away from them. My mind is reeling from all of the possibilities. The thing is, I already *know* the answer. "It's the same energy that powers the veil." I release my hands, noticing that I have been clenching them too tightly. "I think Sgya is the energy source or stores it." It's insane, but the moment I say it, I know it's true. "That's why the mist and shadows were there." I'm talking more out loud than to them as I think through everything. "They can't access the energy. They knew I could, which is why they were trying to take me. I can unlock the power of the veil."

I turn around, and everyone is lost in their own thoughts. This sounds crazy, but it's starting to make sense.

"If," I look at Ryker, conveying my apology, "the prophecy is about Ryker and me, we would need to have access to that power source. That's why he was able to touch me, and Kellan wasn't. If the mist is alive—" I gulp back down the bile in my throat. "It wants to consume the energy. Which means, technically, we are all in danger. Not just Ryker and me. All of the Bonds are energy sources." My hands find their way to my hair, where I fidget with the tied ribbon.

Oh, gods.

"The strongest ones are said to burst out and can sometimes be felt for miles. I don't know if they'll wait for the Bonding Ceremonies, but anyone who has a Bond is tapped into Sgya, just in smaller amounts. That's why the gods required it of royalty. We have blood-lines to uphold, to keep pure, and a duty to our kingdoms. If they knew the empire would eventually fall, they created a failsafe—us," Ryker finishes for me, putting it together.

I sit down in the chair and pull back Sgya's size so that I can see the whole thing. "Bloodlines..." I mutter as my mind spins.

"Every time we Bond, we give energy to the veil. The energy is at its highest on the woman's twenty-third birthday. It's why we have to wait," Aolyn says, but her voice is distant as I'm gripped with another image, this time recalling the same strange people I saw on Sgya.

Immortals.

"So if the Bonds are a failsafe, why is the veil losing energy?" Tate asks.

I suck in a sharp breath, gaining Ryker's attention. "We need to go to the Isles and use that pass. The bloodlines and immortals," my head spins. "What if...what if they never surrendered to the veil?"

thirty-nine

. . .

raea

KELLAN STANDS, gripping the back of his chair as if it's the only thing keeping him grounded. "The reality is, there are fewer and fewer Bonds every year," he begins. "Kingdoms are no longer producing bloodlines with the same frequency as they once did. It's been six decades since the last royal family had more than five kids and a decade since one had three. Plus, the last time a royal Bonding occurred was over a century ago."

As he speaks, Kellan's jaw tightens, a sign that he's just putting it all together and attempting to keep his calm. It's clear he now understands the implications of this revelation just as much as we do. "Royal bloodlines," he continues, a sigh escaping his lips, "are renowned for producing stronger and more enduring Bonds." His grip becomes white-knuckled.

Ryker exchanges a knowing glance with me, our silent communication growing increasingly easier with each passing day. Royal babies are becoming rarer with each generation. My parents said they struggled to conceive me for years. Queen Meganna still hasn't been able to conceive.

"And with everyone willing to lose their Bond early," Trysten supplies, leaning back in his chair until the front two legs are lifted from the floor.

"So what? Ryker and Raea Bond, they restore the veil, and everything goes back to normal?" Tate asks.

As if it were that simple. I feel like the answer is right in front of me, but I'm just not seeing it.

"No," Ryker chimes in, coming to sit in front of me, his knees trapping mine in place. The heat from his body makes the fine hair on my arms stand on end. It would be entirely inappropriate to lean in right now and steal some of that warmth. "The prophecy says the days are numbered. The veil was never meant to last. It bought us time." He looks at me, keeping his gaze locked on mine. "The birth of the firstborn will the veil be complete." His eyes swirl, taking on an otherworldly look. "A baby."

My heart stutters to a complete stop. *A baby?* Oh, my gods. They want me to have a baby...with Ryker? I mean, obviously, if we were Bonded, but—suddenly, the air in the room is not enough. I want to have sex with the man—who wouldn't—but a baby? I haven't gotten that far yet.

"It doesn't say it will be fixed." Ciara tilts her head like she does when she's thinking.

Ryker stands in front of me, his eyes relaying an apology. He moves so slowly, pulling me from my chair and blocking the others from view. I don't have time to respond, but the second his palm is on my waist, I collapse into his chest. It's completely illogical, but it's exactly what I need.

His hand strokes up and down my spine with understanding as my mind swirls, drowning out the discussion happening behind him. It's not hard to guess this is affecting him too. I inhale a lungful of sandalwood and citrus notes with a hint of fresh ocean air, and my whole mind goes silent. As if the scent alone somehow grounds me.

"I'm sorry," he whispers into my hair.

I don't reply, but I don't move either. I just hold onto his shirt that's fisted in my hands and continue breathing until the prophecy and all that it entails falls away. I don't have to worry about this. Not right now. First things first.

"Schedule our trip to the Isles," I say to Ryker before pulling out of his arms. "We're going to call our guards. In the meantime, Aolyn, try to figure out what your father is planning, or who that woman is. Can you go home without telling them?"

She nods.

"We all need to stay vigilant. Trysten, plan the attack with Kamden. I will feel Ryker's presence if it's him," I look up at Ryker, "And in the meantime, we all pretend. Tate, Kellan, I could use another set of eyes on the books that are in the common language. Ciara, any chance you can search The Link for anything strange going on in Ateria?"

She nods, gleaming. With something for all of us to do, everyone files out of the room, heading off for lunch.

"Raea," Ryker says.

I wait until we are alone and then walk back over to him. I sit on the console beside him, my gaze tracking the movement of my swinging feet. Why does this all feel so heavy?

"I'm sorry about all of this," he sighs. He's looking at the console, not me.

"Together." If I've learned anything, it's that fate has brought us together for a reason, and I don't plan on testing it now. The prophecy doesn't need to tell me what I already know, what I feel. Ryker will be with me every step of the way, and I won't even have to ask.

I can't not touch him. I slide my hand across his back and shift over so that I can rest my face on his shoulder. He sighs and turns to come and stand in front of me so that we're facing each other. His hand slowly slides behind my neck, bringing me closer to his lips as he leans over me, our foreheads pressed together.

"Are you okay? I need to know you're okay," he whispers. His voice sounds so desperate, like it pains him to think I might not be.

"I will be." It's the best I can give him right now.

I close that final gap and melt into him, letting our lips brush once, then twice. His grip behind my neck tightens as his mouth slants over mine, his other hand tilting my chin up to deepen the angle.

Our mouths meet again and again, heat and raw need filling every nerve ending, building to a crescendo. My lips part, and instantly, his tongue brushes mine. Claiming my mouth, his kiss promises me he is falling just as hard.

Sgya's power radiates through us, a seamless conduit flowing between our merged forms. A flood of feelings crashes through my senses: longing, hope, desire, desperation. The same as mine, yet distinctly his.

Unlike the other night, his emotions, now a shimmering blue in my mind, are sharply defined. He wants me to love him. Tugging him closer, his palms catch on the console as our lower halves meet. He groans, wrapping his arms around me, pulling me tighter as if it still isn't enough. It never is.

Still holding me, he shifts, settling into a chair, pulling me onto his lap, my knees bracketing him. He holds me as if I might float away. My hands slide up his chest, tangling behind his neck, thumbs cupping his jaw. *More.* The word consumes me, echoing from both of us, crowding my mind. He groans when I lift, readjusting, seeking to deepen the impossible closeness. Our bodies are as flush as they can be, yet it isn't enough.

Strong arms squeeze me tighter in response, his hands splayed wide. The neckline of my dress dips barely an inch, but his mouth moves to my chest, and almost all thoughts fade except one.

"Wait," I gasp.

Ryker pulls away quickly, holding me still pinned to his chest.

"Yes," I breathe, my stomach fluttering. "Yes, to us."

My smile breaks free, radiant and raw. "I don't have sweet words or grand declarations. But I am willing to surrender to this destiny, utterly and completely. I want to be yours, Ry. Only yours." Tears gather, blurring the world. I can't ignore my feelings anymore, and with the memories of our childhood flickering in and out like they have, I know he is who I'm meant to be with. Sure, it's fast. It's terrifying how fast, but the gods chose him for me.

I'm done denying fate.

The love in his gaze is my undoing, a culmination of every desperate hope, every unspoken dream. A gasp tears from my throat as profound heat blazes along my spine, and the tether between us surges, solidifying into an immutable stone bridge.

"Are you sure?" he asks, stumbling to find the words.

Tears fall when I nod.

"Yours," I mutter, and then the world around us disappears, and I'm only here, in this moment, with him.

Nothing else matters. I feel the walls of my Bond rippling. I mentally stack more bricks in front of my iron gate for good measure. My hands find his hair, and the loose strands flow between my fingers before I grip down. My back arches into him, and he doesn't hesitate to slide his hands down my ass, gripping me tighter, bringing me toward him.

I lean over him, deepening our kiss again. He tastes like mint and something masculine, filling my body with a need so intense that there's nothing beyond it. A primal knowing settles deep in my bones: he is my other half, the one meant to claim every want, every need. I will never desire another. I tug on his lip, my teeth dragging along the edge, eliciting a groan from him, making me smile.

"Gods," he pulls back just enough to bury his face in my neck and inhales. "I don't know how to wait a whole year for you."

Something ancient, a forgotten chord, vibrates deep within my chest. When he says things like that, I know he's slowly taking pieces of my heart for himself, claiming them like they belong to him, and maybe they should, maybe they already do. A clarity settles over me as he holds me, breathing me in like I'm his very breath.

We're both breathing heavily, unwilling to separate our bodies, and we stay like that for minutes, who knows, maybe more. My stomach growls, making him chuckle, and it's my turn to bury my face in his neck out of embarrassment. His soft, inked skin smells of sandalwood soap and that distinctly Ryker scent. I inhale deeply, settling further into the comfort of his embrace, feeling a sense of belonging fill a part of me deep within. His steady breathing calms my own, and I feel the rhythm of his heart against my chest, slowing mine to match. I untangle my fingers from his hair and reluctantly pull away, leaning back until our faces are close enough that I can run my nose along his, making him grin.

"I messed up your hair," I giggle softly as I try to flatten it back down, but I don't know how he does it.

A small smile tugs at his lips. "It's fine." This time, he kisses me slowly. "I want you to know I won't let anything happen to you. You aren't alone in this." He goes back to the crook of my neck, breathing me in.

"Together," he repeats what I said earlier.

A profound rightness settles within me, everything falling into place with astonishing speed. It's terrifying, yet I feel ready. The moment those three words find a voice, I know he will be there, and then, forever—a promise that wraps around my heart.

I'm still straddling him in his lap, pressed into his chest in a tender embrace, his mouth to my neck, his teeth grazing a very sensitive spot, eliciting a gaspy moan when the door opens.

"There you are."

forty

. . .

ryker

"THERE YOU ARE," Gunnar says. His eyes go wide as he takes in Raea and me in this intimate position.

Shit.

I've been meaning to catch up with him, and it slipped my mind that I agreed to meet before lunch to go over his training on how to carry a Hallo.

Raea's cheeks flush as she climbs off my lap, adjusting her dress and clearing her throat. Her lips are swollen from our kiss, and her hair is a little wild from my hands. There's something about the soft, white strands that drives me absolutely crazy.

"I think I should go," Raea whispers.

She glances over at Gunnar, but I know she's talking to me. I stand and pull her back in for another hug, placing a quick kiss on her hair. I don't care if he sees. Besides, he and I have a lot to talk about.

"I'll see you in a few minutes," I promise, releasing her.

Even as she leaves, the raw essence of her lingers, every curve of her body etched into my vision, intensifying the relentless ache that has become my constant companion since she agreed to be mine. Gods, the need to claim her fully, to complete this Bond, is a torment.

Gunnar clears his throat in amusement. "So, Princess Raea, huh?"

He leans against the glass with his thumbs tucked into his pockets. He grins and wags his brows like he's just walked in on something more than a heated kiss. "She's a catch. I'm assuming you're the reason she turned me down the other night?"

My eyes narrow at him as my jaw ticks. Is it acceptable to knock out a friend over your fated future wife? That weird possessive side of me hovers like a beast waiting to pounce. I inhale deeply, calming myself, and respond, "It's a story I don't have the time, nor energy, to hash out right now." I grab my bag and head over toward him. "We need to reschedule."

"That's actually what I was coming to talk to you about." He stands, opening the door for us. "That guy…starts with a T… always with Raea." He snaps his fingers as his eyes close.

"Tate?" I offer.

"That's the one." His eyes open as we turn to head for the dining hall. "Anyway, he said you might still be here. Off-topic, though, I actually need to head home for the week and check on my father. He got hurt after he hit his head on the boat. I guess he's been having severe headaches."

We both turn left, following the steps up to the bridge that takes us to the dining hall.

"Okay. I can speak with Chancellor Xara and inform her that you need a pass, and I'll arrange for the transport. This works out perfectly," I reply, the truth of Raea's confession still humming in my veins. "I need to go home. There's an urgency that demands I be there now."

I need to speak with my mother about the veil reports, and I should probably tell her about Raea. It has to come from me. I just hate leaving her so soon.

Gunnar nods. He leaves my side and finds a seat with some of his friends as we enter the loud hall. I find my seat with Trysten as he slides a tray in front of me with a plate of meat and vegetables.

I down a glass of water before asking, "What's with the smirk?"

"Nothing. Just happy for you. Not only do you know who you're going to Bond with…" his voice drops as he leans closer, "you also get some action beforehand. Don't think I didn't notice her walking in, all flushed several minutes ago."

"I'm not sleeping with Raea."

He chuckles as if I'm being ridiculous. "Nobody said you were."

The Royal Palace of Malaya, a breathtaking vision of white and gold stone, shimmers into view as our transport descends. Its crystalline spires seem to pierce the pale blue sky, crowning a forested peninsula that is surrounded by a cerulean sea. Nestled into the cliffside, the palace feels as if it has risen from the very waters it commands.

Below, the fading sunlight shimmers across the pearlescent glass domes of the lower palace. Soaring white stone pillars rise from interconnected seawater pools that feed waterfalls, cascading endlessly into the ocean. From the white sand beaches of the north to the sun-drenched southern lagoon, the entire structure is a breathtaking extension of the natural landscape, defined by its flowing waterways and endless ocean views.

When the transport lands, and the doors open, filling the transport with the scent of home: salt, brine, citrus, and sandalwood trees, with a hint of an afternoon storm in the air.

My footmen, Leif and Bo, and personal guard, Rune, meet me at the base of the ramp and bow before the former head into the transport to grab my bags, leaving Rune at my side. It's always a shock coming home and resuming the formalities after being on my own for several months.

I'm happy to be home, even if just for the night, but how can I even begin to tell her? Not just that the prophecy has claimed me, but that my fated partner is the princess of Treon, a revelation that will shatter every carefully laid plan she's made for my reign.

"Anders," Clara squeals as she comes running into my arms.

I swing her around before bringing her to my chest, the scent of sugar and strawberries enveloping me. I set her down so she can run around while I hug my mother. She's looking better than she did when I last saw her.

Her blonde hair is pulled up and braided into an elaborate style, and she's dressed in a deep blue gown with the family crest displayed on a necklace. A spark of recognition jolts me.

The Sgya branch. The Butterfly Bindwood.

I'd researched alternative healing ideas for depression, finding an old text that mentioned Butterfly Bindwood as a cure for ailments of the heart and soul. While on Sgya, I had seen those weird branches and their vibrant butterflies, wondering if that was it. No amount of archive research had yielded definitive answers, yet seeing my mother now, a desperate hope ignites within me. That is the missing piece. I need to bring it to her.

"Son." She wraps me in an embrace, her coconut and jasmine scent wrapping around my senses. "I'm so glad you could come. What has brought you all the way home?"

"I think we should all go inside." I turn her and walk toward the stone palace ahead. The salty ocean air calms all my senses, and the quiet rush of the waves acts like a balm for my worries. The only thing that could be better is having Raea here with me.

She acted like it wasn't a big deal that I was leaving, except that I know her. I could feel her worry before she sealed it up with a practiced smile and quick dismissal. Though she tried to hide it, her breathing became shallower, her shoulders slumped for half a second, and her microexpressions weren't as easily concealed.

The white stone walls tower over us as we walk toward the private entrance. The guards pull open the ornate glass doors, and the aqua arches inside come into view. The white columns, the turquoise arches with domes filling the room, and the murals of our kingdom's past are painted on the walls. White marble floors fill the space with soft light, the walls illuminated by a gentle glow. Each dome is filled with murals and stars. The columns are adorned with sea creatures that wrap around them. All of it is grand and tastefully lavish, but to me, it just feels like home.

The sound of my mother's heels clicks against the tile as we navigate toward the private living space at the back of the palace. Clara runs ahead of me and giggles as she twirls. Her honey-blonde locks fly out around her.

"Clara, dear, don't make yourself dizzy," my mother calls out. "She's delighted you're both home. It's so quiet around here when you're gone. Cole and Linnea stick to their wing. You hardly notice they're around."

My jaw ticks at the reminder of Cole and Linnea. Cole claims a Bond forged between them during an intimate night when the intensity of their connection proved too much for her mental shield. An unforeseen consequence, but a Bond nonetheless. This is exactly the reason I won't risk taking Raea to bed. Very few women have the ability to keep their Bond behind their mental shield when in a fit of passion.

I spent hours in the gym that night with Trysten, taking out my anger and worry on him, all while feeling as if I had failed Cole. He was so reckless and irresponsible. The weight of my failure felt suffocating.

And it was all because my father had left, abandoning his responsibilities, and forcing me into this role. Then those thoughts turned dark and ugly when I remembered that it was *his* responsibility, not mine, to care for us. I never asked to be a parent to my siblings, yet I've been forced into it for five years. I've been angry with my father for years, but now, if he ever returns, my forgiveness won't be easily earned.

He failed us.

I don't know much about Linnea aside from what I learned from Rune and at school. She's from Thirik and has dark hair, dark-tanned skin, piercings on her nose and brow, and a few tattoos. Her fierce, independent aura seems so opposite of who I'd think he'd go for, but who am I to judge?

The doors ahead open, and the glass wall that overlooks the ocean is open, allowing a fresh breeze to flow through the room. My parents had made this room a place for the family to come together at the end of the day and read and talk.

As we enter, the doors close behind us, and I know we're finally alone. My mother takes a seat on the white chair across the room. It's where she always sits. Clara sits on the floor with her dolls, and Cole and Linnea take the oversized sofa across the room from my mother.

"So, ready to explain?" my mother asks as I drop into another stuffed chair.

When it's long past the time when everyone has gone to bed, I shower and crawl into the dark sheets, feeling the breeze pass through the open doors on my terrace. Waves roll in slowly outside, sending a fresh breeze and the sound of a deep, bassy rumble through my chamber.

I pull up The Link for a distraction, needing something to put me in a different mental state. I decide to add Raea as a friend, figuring I'd better just own it, and she accepts my friend request immediately, which makes me chuckle. Looks like she's up, too.

Ciara tagged her in a post from break. It's a photo of her and Raea with Tate and Kellan behind them, hugging them both. They're all laughing and smiling on the transport with the caption saying: EXCITED FOR THE BREAK! #FountainIsles #holydaysfordays

The soft blue gown she's wearing brings out the hint of blue in her hair. It's not always easy to see, but in certain situations, such as with her gown, her hair appears more blue than white. My once-simple attraction has grown into an uncontrollable need for her.

Mine.

It's like some beast inside of me keeps chanting that ever since she agreed to be mine earlier.

I keep scrolling through Raea's feed. She shares numerous book recommendations and photos of plants and tea. She hardly shares pictures of herself unless she's with someone else. There are a lot of her and Kellan, which doesn't sit well in my gut. I find a few of her that she was tagged in from the media at balls and different events.

Gods, she's gorgeous.

When she's dressed in a royal gown with her crown, she looks like the most beautiful princess. There's something ethereal about her and the way she smiles and holds herself. It's so different from how she is at school.

I get a notification about her liking a photo of me. I click on the notification, and it's a photo of me from an AerBall game last year. I'm celebrating with my team, and they have me on their shoulders.

I chuckle and shoot her a message:

Anders Rykerson: Stalking me, are you?

Raea Tierson: You wish. It popped up on my feed now that we're acquaintances.

Anders Rykerson: Acquaintances? It's a friend request, not an acquaintance request. You accepted to be my friend. In fact, I distinctly remember you agreeing to be more.

Raea Tierson: Whatever makes you sleep better, Prince. Why are you awake anyway?

Dammit, I love her sass.

Anders Rykerson: I could ask you the same thing.

Raea Tierson: Why do you answer my questions with questions?

I laugh out loud, filling the large room.

Anders Rykerson: Did you just respond with another question?

Raea Tierson: So did you. Gods, you're annoying. I'm going to bed. Bye, not-just-my-friend.

Anders Rykerson: Friend? You're right. That title doesn't fit. But one title does…

Raea Tierson: Oh? And what title is that? Boyfriend?

Anders Rykerson: I'm not a boy.

Raea Tierson: You're right. Let's see… handsome Prince? No. Cocky, beautiful, annoyingly distracting man who consumes my thoughts?

I can't help but smile.

Anders Rykerson: While I appreciate the honesty, how about an easier title: Yours.

It shows she read my message and started to respond, but then it disappears. I groan and roll over, dropping my Prism onto the bedside table. I wave a hand over the light panel just as my Prism dings with an alert.

Raea Tierson: Mine.

Raea Tierson: And I'm yours.

It takes me over an hour, but finally, I drift off.

forty-one

• • •

raea

ZAYLA LOOKS SO beautiful from the sandstone castle. The desert here is home to wild animals grazing on the sparse plant life, visible from the terrace as far as the eye can see. Overhead, there are four moons varying in size. The sun is setting, and it's that beautiful time of day when the skies are pink and the moons are out.

Baedyn doesn't have this.

Behind me, the party is still going on. It's Queen Meganna's thirty-fifth birthday, and her husband, King Osiris, is dancing with her. They are so at ease in front of their guests. I guess having a kingdom of only eight planets helps with that.

The heat from the day is still radiating off the stone, and sweat trickles down my spine beneath my corset. I'm wearing a blue and cream gown in the loose style of the kingdom that lifts and flows with my movements. It feels magical. I only wish Ryker were here to see. He'd appreciate it. The blue of my gown reminds me of his eyes.

I close my eyes and try to picture where he is. I can't remember Malaya, even though Father has said I've been there several times. I was just too young. I wish I could access the memories. I sway with the music even though I'm alone.

A chill races down my spine, and fear seeps into my bones. I turn just as the music halts, and screams fill the dance hall. Darkness swirls, and one by one, royal members fall to their knees, begging for life. A scream ripples through the darkness before it's silenced.

I feel the power radiating up my arms. It's not enough. I slam my back against the wall, hiding myself. I need to calm myself down. Breathe in for three. Out for three. My fingers tingle, the power waiting to be released.

"There you are," it hisses.

The eerie voice is neither male nor female—just something ancient and evil. A dark, hooded face appears from the mist. It's as if life and color have been drained from it. Its hand wraps around my throat, the grip unrelenting, and my vision starts to go black on the edges.

I release my power and throw my palms to its chest. It screams, but its grip only tightens. It's a war to see who will give out first. I reach for Ryker. I need his help. My skin burns from the release of energy, and my vision goes dark. I can still feel, but everything else is gone. There's only that endless void of noth-ingness.

"You have to fight!" I hear Ryker's voice in my head. "Fight, Raea."

I inhale sharply as I am jolted awake by Aolyn. She's standing over me with worry in her eyes. Dammit, not again.

"Are you okay?" she asks.

Her eyes skate around my face. It's barely first light, and the room is still cast in shadows. She's dressed in her white nightgown, her slender arms hugging her center as she looks upon me with frightened eyes. I scrunch my face, trying to recall my dream.

"I'm fine. I don't remember it," I lie.

"You were screaming for Ryker." She sits beside me on the bed. I bury my face in my hands and sit up. "Are you going to tell me what's been going on with you two? I know it's more."

"It's a long story, but the short version is that I agreed to be his… girlfriend? I don't know. We haven't said anything about titles."

She doesn't say anything as she looks me over and then smirks. "Is that all? I've seen the way you two look at each other. Everyone can see it. Why do you think I went to him instead of Kellan? I think that ship sailed long before you agreed to it."

"It's the Bond. That's all. He makes me crazy." I slap my hands down on the sheets and groan. "I don't know how else to explain it." I throw the covers off myself, feeling too hot all of a sudden.

"Some days I can't stay away from him, an invisible string pulling us together. Other days, I just want to slap his beautiful face." I pace the room. "At first, I thought he was cocky, but he isn't. After he saved me, my thoughts became a tangled mess. Now, I can't breathe without him, and I can barely breathe when he's near. I'm losing my damn mind, and I just...I just *need* him. It's so intense. I want to be his, because the idea of being with anyone else makes me sick."

Aolyn just laughs, bringing her knees to her chest. "Oh my gods, you're in love with him."

I roll my eyes and crawl back into bed. "I'm not. I'm going back to sleep." I throw myself against the pillow and roll over so my back is toward her. She giggles and curls up behind me, wrapping her arms around me.

"You know, for someone so intelligent," she whispers, "you are pretty clueless. Don't worry, I won't say anything." She makes a delighted hum as she pulls the blankets over herself.

"I don't love Ryker. It's too soon."

"You know it's okay to love Kellan; he's your best friend, but you're *in* love with Ryker. Sleep now, my young Princess," she trills.

I chuckle and close my eyes.

I'm not in love with him, right?

It's still early when I wake up; Aolyn is still asleep beside me. I have to get ready because today I'm headed to Onyxera to visit the village in the lava tubes with Paxton, Korē, Thriven, and Aurora for our assignment for Ethnography.

I slip into a maxi dress made of thick, all-black material. The material stops at the top of my breasts, where the corset lifts them, and from there, a series of ropes drape over my shoulders and chest, creating a cage appearance. Apparently, this is typical fashion for the

Kadorian nobility. I twist sections of my hair and braid others, bringing them together in a coronet at the back of my head.

I paint my lips a soft pink and brush on blush before lining my eyes with coal. I slip my diadem over my head, letting the jewel fall over my forehead, and slip on a few bangles and a necklace. I'll be representing my kingdom today. I grab my cloak and Prism, along with my bag, on my way out.

Ryker is there waiting for me. I didn't expect him back yet, so I can't help the giddy smile that spreads across my face as I launch myself at him, wrapping my arms around his neck with a giddy squeal. "You're here!"

He chuckles, wrapping his hands around me. "Just came to see you off, but I need to head back to Malaya." He squeezes me as my heart does a little dance. He came all the way back just to see me.

"Gods, you're breathtaking," he groans, leaning down, wrapping warm hands around my waist. "Have fun today, and be careful."

I inhale a lungful of him before pulling out of his arms. One heated look from him steals the breath from my lungs. I could just stay right here, and I'd be perfectly happy, and, well, that scares the hell out of me.

He grins, tugging me down the hall toward his room before I can say anything. His door opens as he places a gentle hand on my lower back, escorting me in. Once the door is closed, gone is the facade of calm and collected, and in its place is something carnal.

The back of my thighs hit the edge of his desk, and my freaking core ignites. There's something predatory about the way Ryker leans over me, leaving no space between us for the way my chest is heaving. His eyes drop to my mouth in question.

"Tell me to kiss you," he pleads.

I'm not sure if it's a question or a demand, but the choice is mine. In response, I lean up on my toes, giving him what he wants. I still have a few minutes before I need to be downstairs.

He doesn't hesitate to claim my mouth. My lips part, and his tongue sinks in, stroking and claiming me with the taste of fresh mint still lingering in his mouth. *Yes.* This is what I need more of. It's a dangerous game we're playing, but I don't care right now. I just want to burn.

Warm hands find the backs of my thighs as he lifts me to the desk, spreading my legs so he can step between them. My dress rides up to my thighs as I wrap my legs around his waist, locking my ankles at his back, my slippers falling to the floor with a thud.

Nothing exists beyond us, beyond this door. The veil could fall, the planets burn to the ground, and I wouldn't have it in me to stop. Not with the way he's holding me and kissing me like I'm the very air he needs. His breath mingles with mine as his tongue strokes mine, making my body putty in his arms.

"Your Bond, Raea," Anders mutters, pulling away just enough to brush his mouth over my lips.

I nod and then lean back in for more, sliding my fingers into his hair and tugging on the silky strands.

He tastes so damn good, I could live with my mouth attached to his. There's so much energy flowing between us that we could sustain life itself. His mouth leaves mine, skating across my jaw, peppering kisses tenderly and so at odds with how I feel. His hands flex on my thighs as I rock forward, my core finding friction along his waistband. My power surges through me.

I'm.

On.

Fire.

"Raea," he growls.

Right, my Bond.

I stack more bricks, noticing the wall has been blown apart. Gods, if he wasn't paying attention, I'd have given my Bond to him. For some reason, I can't find it within myself to care, not right now, not when I know this can very well be my future. Driven by the escalating friction, my hips move forward. I feel the soft graze of his teeth along my neck, sending a delicious spark of heat dancing along my spine.

"Ryker," I breathe.

In one swift motion, he's carrying me across the room.

He sits on his bed, keeping me in his lap, pinning me in place with his hands firmly on my waist. I shift, rocking my hips, uncaring when a breathy moan escapes me. He lifts his hips into my core, and I feel the hard length of him beneath the combat pants.

"Watch your Bond," he rasps, grinding against my sensitized core.

I gasp, gripping his arms while focusing on the not-so-stable brick wall in my mind. I lean forward, bringing our bodies flush; his solid length rubs against me as he holds me in place and presses all-too-gentle kisses along my neck. Once he reaches my shoulder, he holds his mouth there, breathing, his whole body still.

"I can't," he says raggedly. "The first time I get my hands on you, it will not be like this."

He pulls away, those deep sapphire eyes studying me as he cups my cheek. Emotions I'm not ready to name threaten to break loose. "Our first time will not be rushed. When I finally take you to bed, Soraea, I'm going to need hours, if not days, to worship every part of you before starting over again."

He kisses me again, all too gently, and the fire within me dulls to a simmer. My breath slows to match his while he holds me in place, gently cradling my face as he studies me.

"I am trying to do the honorable thing," he explains. "But make no mistake, Princess, I've been worshipping you in my dreams for far too long."

A warmth blossoms along my spine. I don't know what to say, so I cup his cheek, brushing my hand along the stubble, before bringing our mouths together one last time in a sweet and tender kiss.

"Mine," I whisper.

"Yours," he promises as I sit up. Amusement dances across his face as we openly gaze into each other's eyes.

"So," he starts, sitting up so he's leaning back against his hands. "What do I have to do to be your friend?"

I don't know why, but I find myself laughing. A huge smile spreads across my face as I look down on him.

I slide my palms up his stomach, over his chest, settling them on his shoulders. "Why would you want to be my friend when you're more than that?"

His lips quirk up. "Questions answered with questions. Hmm..." He brushes my hair back. "What if I want to be more *and* your friend? Can't I be both?"

I drop my lips to his, smiling against them. "Okay, Prince," I say, kissing him softly and sweetly before crawling off his lap and heading for the door, leaving him rumpled and utterly gorgeous on the bed with a smile.

When I open the door, a guard, whom I assume belongs to Ryker, gives me a questioning look but doesn't say anything. I find Kuron, my guard, lingering at my door, doing a once-over before following me to the dining hall.

forty-two

. . .

raea

THREE HOURS LATER, Paxton, Aurora, Korē, Thriven, and I sit in the library that's built into the cliff face over a glacial lake. Apparently, this is the safest place for the books to be. We spent the first hour touring the lava tubes and meeting with their officials and professors.

They all seemed extremely welcoming to me, but then again, I do represent the entire Treon kingdom. Seeing their homes carved out like little caves with fire and sconces placed everywhere to illuminate the space felt oddly inviting. They haven't been able to implement modern touches like electricity or heat, but I kind of liked it.

The people who live here in the tubes wear thick linens and tunics made from animal skins to keep them warm. Both men and women wear their hair long hair in various war braids or shaved short with tattoos covering their skin. They all have glacier-blue eyes and shades of blonde or light brown hair. Genetics is an amazing thing I'd love to study.

Their language is breathy and full and so beautiful. There's something so familiar about it. I wonder if I've heard it spoken at the summit balls before? Or maybe at an event with my parents? Either way, the words settled over me and within me as if they were speaking to a deeper part of me.

"So what are we looking for?" Aurora asks as we take over the larger wooden table at the center of the room. She's a rail-thin blonde in Intel Division. She's really lovely.

"Well, I think we need to focus on their way of life. Their government and traditions are amazing, but it would just be too much for the time slot we've been given." Not only is a report due, but we have to present it in front of the class.

The five of us break apart, each going in different directions to cover the shelves of books that line the walls of this massive space. I find a section on the furthest wall, reading the spines. I've never seen so many ancient texts before.

My fingers brush against the spines, amazed at their collection. I stop on a large book, the text worn on the spine, and pull it off the shelf. I blow off the dust before carefully opening the book. It's written in Elvisiah. Strokes of ink in various patterns and lines fill the pages. It's so pretty. Something whispers in me as I scan the page; the words fill my mind. It's a children's story.

The librarian passes by, halting to look at the text in my hands. Her peppered hair is braided into one long piece. Her clothes are held together with leather straps matching her boots, which are covered in what I think is rabbit fur and lashed with leather ties.

"Interesting," she muses, coming to stand at my side. Her eyes search my face before looking back at the open book. "The Fable of the Primordial Orum," she says with reverence in her voice. "An ancient fate of two harbingers of light and dark. One day, the two shall engage in a war so bloody, only one will remain." Her intense blue eyes meet mine. And something twists in my stomach. I mask my face in naïve interest.

"Why would the gods let that happen?" Fear settles in my bones.

If the gods were truly good, why would they create something so inherently dark?

The librarian tilts her head as if thinking whether or not she plans on answering. "The Primordials are all about balance, my young Princess."

I nod.

Balance.
I understand.
She is my balance.
Light and shadows.

"On your feet, Raea," Trysten says as he circles me later that night in the gym.

I roll to my stomach and push off, landing on my feet. A frustrated groan leaves my throat. "Why can't I stay on my feet? What am I doing wrong?"

Trysten laughs. "You're small. I've told you, use that to your advantage." He stops moving and crosses his arms, daring me to argue with him.

"I'm not small, just vertically challenged," I retort.

He laughs at me as he swings forward, knocking the air out of me with a punch to my ribs, hitting the Nakata corset that I'm training in tonight. I'll give him this: he doesn't hold back, and he hasn't turned on my energy shield. Sparring with him has become more than routine. I actually enjoy it—I enjoy him.

"I've told you," he starts. "Strike first, strike fast, and get away."

I nod and take him by surprise when I slip past him and elbow him in the kidneys before kicking at the back of his knee. He manages to stumble instead of fall as he swings around, his fist coming fast at my face, but I launch out of the way just in time.

"Watch it," I snap.

"Ooh, the feisty princess has come to play. I like it. You should get angry more often, Raea," he taunts.

I step with my left and spin toward him, and my fist connects with his jaw. He just chuckles as his hand rubs the spot.

"You fight better when you're angry. So get angry." He punches for my ribs, but I sidestep him.

I groan. "But I'm not angry," I say bitterly.

His responding smile is laced with knowing mischief. "Did you know that Sienna is only here to try and get closer to Ryker?"

He is taunting me. How he knows I despise her, I can't fathom.

My sharp inhale gives me away. "Yes," I bite out. "Pretty sure she's made everyone aware of that fact."

He's circling me like prey. "Did Ry tell you that he's the reason she's in Taeolyn and not Veker with Cole?" Something ugly twists in my stomach. Jealousy. Always jealousy when it comes to her.

"He doesn't even like her," I snap. "Stop it!"

He shrugs as if this is amusing to him. "Maybe," he says, but I attack, fed up with the taunting.

If he was trying to get me worked up, he succeeded. I can't stand her. For the next few minutes, I allow my anger to build, fueling it with images of her hugging him and making her flirty comments; all of it makes the rage burn hotter.

Finally, I catch Trysten by surprise and knock his feet out from under him. He lands with a loud thud on the mat, and he groans. I drop my knee into his chest and give him a saccharine smile. I know that I'm boiling hot when a drop of his sweat hits my hand outstretched on the mat near his head.

"Anger is good," Trysten grunts. "But that magic of yours, not so good." He stands when I lift off of him. "You and Ry need to get that under control before you explode."

I nod, chewing on my lip. I look down at my hands, shaking my head. This heat, I have no control. I know I don't, but I can't exactly ask for help. "I don't know how." I feel more on edge than I should. "I need to go. I need to cool off."

"Good idea." When I turn away, he stops me. "And Raea, Ry only put Sienna in Taeolyn so he could keep an eye on her. He doesn't have feelings for her, never has."

I don't respond and just keep walking. I need to get to the river as quickly as possible.

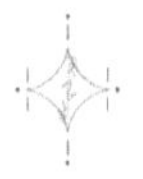

"Who can tell me what the Treaty of Kenaf is?" Professor Isik asks.

The room is quiet. He looks around the room of juniors, and nobody raises a hand. I roll my eyes and lift mine. Tate chuckles beside me as I shoot him a playful glare.

"Princess Raea?" he asks as I send an elbow into Tate. It only makes him chuckle again.

"The Treaty of Kenaf is an agreement between all seven kingdoms to use the same calendar system. Isn't that right, Tate?" I turn my head and smile. His chuckle ends, and his face falls.

"And why is that important?" Professor Isik prompts.

"Without the treaty, the kingdoms could use their own time and calendar system. In the first fifty years after the empire's fall, the kingdoms operated independently. Once trade agreements were in place, shipments were lagging, and there was no way to correctly track shipments between kingdoms. The Treaty of Kenaf allowed the kingdoms to use a universal system so that shipments were on time and, therefore, there were no breaches of contracts on trade agreements."

"Showoff," Tate mutters.

"Very good," Professor Isik says.

I sigh and sit back in my seat. Treon Kingdom was the one to initially draft the treaty. Had we not, there's no telling how trade agreements could have succeeded.

All seventy-two planets must have been designed or subjected to magic because, since the veil went up, all the planets have the same length of days and weeks. We know that planets used to have different lengths of days and years, but now, it's just all the same, as if we're all rotating on some invisible spoke. For the rest of politics class, we learn about drafting our own trade agreements and how to give and take to get what we want. Our assignment is to draft an agreement for something we want with another student.

Intel remains as boring as always, and we continue to learn about how to handle classified information and what to do if it's ever leaked. How Kellan does this as his Division is beyond me.

As the day passes, I find myself constantly glancing outside the glass walls of the classroom, looking for Ryker. I hate that he isn't at school. Instead of torturing myself, I pull out my Prism, hiding it behind my tablet, and message him when I drop into my seat.

> Raea Tierson: Hey, I just wanted to check in and make sure everything was okay with you.

> Anders Rykerson: All is well, Princess. Miss me?

I roll my eyes and scoff quietly, but I grin. I love teasing him. It's become one of my favorite activities.

> Raea Tierson: I'd have to actually like you to miss you.

> Anders Rykerson: So you're finally admitting you like me, then? Finally!! Princess Raea finally admits her feelings for me. I never thought I'd see the day.

> Raea Tierson: How in the gods' names did you come to that conclusion? I was merely checking in on you since I currently don't have an escort. Nothing more. Kuron and Ezra are boring me.

> Anders Rykerson: Well, your escort is fine. I needed to be here for something. I'll tell you when I'm back. And in case you don't know this... I do, in fact, miss you.

My cheeks heat, but I can't fight off the grin that takes over my face. Gods, I have some big feelings for him.

> Raea Tierson: ...

> Anders Rykerson: Don't overthink it. You know how I feel.

> Raea Tierson: Fine…I might miss you, but don't let it go to your head. And how do you feel, Prince?

> Anders Rykerson: I suppose I'll have to remind you when I get back. ;)

Professor Trygg, my Aeronautics professor, clears his throat from the front of the class, crossing his arms over his chest. "Raea." He tilts his lips like he's caught me finally. "Care to elaborate on the design dynamics of the transport pods?"

I clear my throat and put my Prism down quietly. For once, Tate is the one to save me by whispering where we are.

"Yes, the transport pods use a combination of older technology and newer anti-gravity technology. The transport pods have two fans located at the back, which are used for steering, while the anti-gravity system keeps them hovering, allowing the pods to travel anywhere on the planet. The glass dome allows for the air to glide right over it, with the aerodynamics keeping it low-energy."

Professor Trygg hums like he's upset he didn't catch me off-guard, and I whisper my thanks to Tate as he goes back to explaining why we no longer use aircraft with blades.

"Listen up, class. Today we will be learning about the eight different types of transports," Professor Brendn says a few days later in Sky Division.

The fine hair on my neck and arms stands, and the air buzzes to life around me. My scalp prickles as I turn and find blue and silver eyes looking back at me. My heart leaps involuntarily.

I am not in love with him, I just like him…a lot. But, gods, those blue eyes and those lips. He smirks as if reading my thoughts and makes his way over to us.

My body should not be responding this way, but then again, the last time I saw him, I was literally rubbing myself all over him. Then he confessed he'd been dreaming about *us*. I clear my throat, rubbing my palms over my pants. It's so damn hot in here.

"The school transports are the smallest of the fleet—" Professor Brendn's voice fades as the ripples of electricity drown him out. Colors flood the edges of my vision, and I have to roll out my shoulders.

"Princess," I feel his breath on my ear like a full-body caress. I keep my face forward while my lips curl into a full grin.

"I thought you weren't going to be back until tonight?" I ask.

He sits beside me, and the heat from his body surrounds me.

"Also, aren't you supposed to be in Aeronautics right now?"

"I didn't see the point in staying. Plus," he leans closer. His lips barely brush the shell of my ear, and my body goes crazy. "I missed you. And I'm ditching Aeronautics."

I close my eyes and press my lips closed, sealing in the gasp that threatens to escape. He should not be doing this during class. I reach my right hand over to him, linking it with his under the desk.

Energy surges between us, and I'm drowning in him. I don't let go, though. Neither does he. We both breathe erratically, consumed by the spiraling energy and vibrant colors of our Bond.

Okay…fine, I more than just 'like' him.

The power subsides, becoming more manageable after a minute or so, and I can open my eyes. Ryker chuckles low so only I can hear. I smile again. He missed me. Ciara and Tate are hiding their own chuckles at my side. I want to glare at them, but that would attract more attention.

My grip tightens, my arm protesting the lingering connection. When I let go, I take a deep breath, willing my emotions to subside. After class, he tells me to clear my schedule for the night because he's taking me on a date.

forty-three

. . .

ryker

I AM TRYING to focus on reading these new reports about the veil instead of the smile on Trysten's face. I didn't plan on returning early, but for some damn reason, I missed her and couldn't wait. Do I care one bit? No. I'm man enough to own how thoroughly she owns me. Bond or no Bond. Prophecy or no prophecy. I've been falling for this girl for years. And then last night, gods, I couldn't keep my hands off her.

Last night, we wandered into shops looking at trinkets and books. I told her about the tree on Sgya, the one I had been searching for, and explained my mother's depression to her. Thankfully, the bark from the Butterfly Woodbine was exactly what my mother needed. By the time I had left Malaya, my mother was already feeling much better.

The rest of the evening, we sat at a bar and ate pub food that was a little too greasy, and she may have gotten a little tipsy from the dryerstead. She made me dance with her, and she had rested her head on my chest.

Visions of our future and what it could be assaulted me. By the time we returned to the pod, she was exhausted and fell asleep with her head in my lap. This time, I did carry her straight to bed, and Aolyn just cooed like she'd been witnessing a fairytale.

"This doesn't make sense," I say, slamming my Prism onto the desk. The reports show no new activity, but I can feel it. It's as strong as before. An icy rage trickles through me.

Trysten leans against the wall, crossing his ankles. "Ry, we need to talk about Raea's powers. She almost lost control." That gets my attention as I look up. I'm about to respond when there's a knock at the door. "I'll be on the terrace and give you two some privacy." He slaps my shoulder, disappearing as I reach the door and swing it open.

It isn't Raea standing there, but Sienna. "Hey." I lean against the door, blocking her way in.

"Aren't you going to invite me in?" she asks. I shake my head, shoving my hands into my pockets. "I just need to tell you something personal. Please."

I stare at her for a moment, grinding my molars. Then I step back —not to welcome her in, but to make it clear there's no invitation in my silence. I put as much space between us as I can without making it obvious just how badly I want her gone.

"Talk, Sienna. I have things to do."

She pouts. "Why are you being like this?" she says, voice all hurt and soft. "I thought we were friends."

Godsdamn.

"We are. And I said I'm busy."

She grins and pulls open her cloak, revealing her naked body. Her robes slip from her shoulders in one fluid, practiced motion, pooling around her bare feet.

"Sienna." I hiss, turning away, my body going taut. Not from desire —never from that—but from the effort it takes not to throw her out myself. "Get dressed and get out, now."

Fingertips glide up my back. My skin crawls. "I want you," she breathes. "Let me make you feel good. You've been so tense lately."

Trysten makes an appearance then. His eyes widen for a heartbeat before narrowing into something sharper with understanding.

I shake my head, and his gaze falls on her. "Sienna," he says coolly.

There's a false smile on his face that doesn't reach his eyes. He hates Sienna more than I do, which is a recent development for me.

I've always pitied her. He, however, hasn't ever given her the time of day.

"Trysten," she responds coyly. "Wanna play with us?"

A low growl works its way up my throat.

"I'm not really into forcing myself upon people who don't want me," he says flatly.

I take another step, boxed in between my bed and the disaster she's making of my night. "Leave, Sienna. I don't want you. This is the last time I'll say it. I won't offer you this kindness again. Now get out."

She scoffs. "How would you know? I'd be the best lay you've ever had. Is it because of that pathetic princess who keeps following you around?"

That does it. That cold, quiet part of me rises—the part that doesn't yell. Doesn't plead. Only ends things. Too many times has she shown up at my door wearing thin clothing that leaves absolutely nothing to the imagination, and too many times she has attempted to seduce me. But now she's going to bring Raea into this? I rake my hands through my hair, already regretting not calling Rune minutes ago.

"I'm done asking." My voice is deadly calm. "Get out. Now. Or I'll call Rune and let him drag you out by the hair." My hands curl into fists. There's no way I can remove her myself without giving her the satisfaction of looking at her. "I'm serious," I growl. "Get. Out."

Trysten snorts, crossing his arms. "Bye," he says, waving his fingers.

Melodically, she replies, "You're not a good liar, Ryker." She drags a nail down my back. "That haughty bitch doesn't even know you."

Another long drag of her nails. Her touch makes me want to vomit. Anger floods in—cold, sharp, and final. Like steel drawn under moonlight. If she ever comes close to touching me again, she's done.

She steps back—maybe sensing it, maybe just out of smug satisfaction—but as luck would have it, the door clicks open. I turn at the same time everyone looks to see Raea entering my room. I added her fingerprint to the lock and told her to use my room whenever she needed to be alone. Never pictured this being a scenario she walked in on.

"I—" Raea starts, eyes flicking between the three of us.

Sienna's cloak is draped over her arm, and what she *is* wearing barely qualifies as clothing. The whisper-thin silk robe hangs open, revealing everything.

"It's not what it looks like." I stride across the room, my steps eating up the distance quickly.

Raea looks to Trysten, who immediately nods. "It's not," he says firmly.

Sienna's voice slices through the air. "Why does *she* have access to your room, Ryker? Are you bedding her now?"

Trysten moves first. "He told you to leave. You're humiliating yourself."

I wrap my arms around Raea, feeling her tremble. "I swear, she just showed up. Nothing happened."

She barely nods before turning to Sienna. "Guess you won't be bagging yourself a king." She's trying to hide the tremble in her voice, but I hear it.

Trysten coughs, hiding a chuckle.

"And since Cole isn't here to fall for your act, maybe you'll have to settle for a Lord. I could help you find someone...if you're that desperate."

I bite the inside of my cheek. Gods, *who is this girl?* Raea is usually poised and reserved except when it comes to me.

And I love this side of her.

I curl a hand around her waist, pulling her back against me. If we didn't have an audience, I'd consider throwing her on my bed and worshipping her, mental shield in place or not. It shouldn't turn me on as much as it does, but then again, everything Raea does turns me on.

Sienna scoffs. "Desperate? If I was desperate, I'd be on my knees again, sucking him until he was growling my name. He liked it well enough last time."

Raea flinches while I sigh.

"That was six years ago. I was drunk. It meant nothing." I turn to face Sienna fully now, my voice like ice. "I don't even remember it. But clearly, you do. If that's what you're clinging to, that one mistake, then that says everything."

Sienna's cheeks flush with color. She yanks her cloak around her. "Enjoy the bore," she snaps. "You'll grow tired of her soon enough."

She throws the door open—only to find Kuron and Rune outside, trying their best to look serious. I know Rune well enough to catch the amusement he's failing to hide. The door slams closed a moment later.

"I swear—" I start, but Raea's already pulling away. Hurt. Confusion. Fury. It's all written across her face, cycling too fast to pin down. "Please," I say, reaching for her wrist. "Let me explain." She turns, tears already streaking down her cheeks. "It's not what it looked like," I whisper, hating how raw I sound. How vulnerable.

"Why? Why was she here?" she asks, her voice breaking as she pulls her arm away before shoving me.

I step back, more from fear that I've lost her. Betrayal settles on her face as she pushes me again. Her palms are hot against my chest. More tears fill her eyes, but the hurt on her face wraps around my heart like a vice.

"All year, I've had to watch her flirt with you, and you just let her, and now…" Her chest heaves. "What do you want from me? I can't be that." She gestures for the door.

"Everything!" I snap. "I want your pain, Raea, the darkest parts of you, even your tears as long as I'm not the one putting them in your eyes. I want everything. And I want you to believe me that nothing happened just now. I want you, not her. It's always been you, Raea. Always."

She shakes her head. "Are you sure?" she cries. "I trust that nothing happened, but she was naked in your room, and I can't compete with her." She swipes angrily at the tears streaming down her flushed cheeks. This all happened so damn fast.

I reach for her again, slowly, waiting to see if she'll pull away. When she doesn't, I take her hand, guiding it to my heart, sending a wave of cool through her. She whimpers, attempting to swallow her tears. When she refuses to look at me, I tilt her chin up. "There's no competition, there never has been, and if you believe anything I say, believe that." I grind my molars, hating all of this. How can she not understand that she's perfect for me? She's everything I've ever wanted.

Everyone might see a crown on my head, but she is the only kingdom I would burn the world to protect. I'd risk it all—for her. My duty, my honor, all that I am. "You, Raea—you're it. The only thing I want. I can't undo what I've done. I'd rip time apart if it meant erasing that look on your face, but I can't. I've got nothing to give you but what's left of me. And every damn bit of my future is yours if you want it."

I watch the fight drain from her, see her face crumble just before she buries it in my chest. I wrap my arms around her as she starts to cry, holding her like I can somehow fix this. Gods, she doesn't deserve to be tethered to someone like me—but I'm going to hold on to her anyway.

Her body shakes against mine, and every second of it guts me. I did this. I broke her. And yet, the way she clings to me—it's the only thing keeping me from unraveling completely. Maybe I haven't ruined everything. Not yet.

I never thought Sienna would become this much of a problem. For years, she's thrown herself at me—always circling, always waiting for a yes that never came. I kept the line clear. Except for that one godscursed night when I was drunk and she was willing. The worst mistake I've ever made.

I've been with women before—ones who understood what it was: one night, nothing more. They moved on. She didn't. I don't know what's twisted in her head, but if I don't put a stop to this, it's going to get worse.

And I won't be the reason Raea cries. Not again.

After long minutes, Raea's sobs turn to sniffling, but she remains in my arms, her breaths shuddering as she tries to regain her composure. "I hate her," she hiccups. "I really hate her, and I don't hate anyone."

"I know," I soothe, running a hand down her hair. "I'm sorry. I'm so sorry."

She remains pressed into my chest as I continue to run a soothing hand up and down her spine. Over and over again until I feel her body relax and the last of her hiccups dry. I bring my hand to her nape, running my thumb along her neck, causing her to shiver.

"I was just coming to tell you that I think we should talk to Professor Ainslyn," she whispers.

Trysten moves closer, stopping before us. I had forgotten he was here, and based on the shock on her face, I'm assuming she did, too. "I was here the whole time," he reassures her. "Ry refused to even look at her until you came in." She gulps and offers him a wobbly smile as she steps out of my arms. "I'll see you both later."

When he's gone, I pull her back to my chest. "I'm so sorry," I repeat, rocking her back and forth.

She sniffles but nods before pulling out a scroll from her bag.

Three days later, we're escorted to the Isles with Professor Ainslyn at our sides. Raea said she wanted someone seasoned to work with us because she believes we'll find an immortal species here. The scroll mentioned some of the lesser fae still being scattered around the system. We didn't learn details about what lesser fae are, but I guess we'll find out.

Not knowing what we're up against, we agreed we needed more than just our friends. Professor Ainslyn has always been on our side, and when we told him all that had transpired, he just shook his head and asked what we needed. I swear, nothing surprises him.

The beach comes into view from where we're seated atop what appears to be some sort of ray. It glides just beneath the water, but the harness strapped to it has a platform with two benches.

"What if this was all for nothing?" Raea asks.

"It's not. We'll either find answers or we won't. Either way, we'll know for sure, and then we can move on." We both fall quiet as the ray slows, gliding onto the beach where it comes to a stop. Six men and women greet us in a language I don't understand. We both bow, offering them thanks for allowing us to visit.

Raea and I are allowed two guards to escort us to the elder's hut, which is nothing more than a stick room built over the water with a fire in the center. The roof is made of large leaves from local trees, and the floor features a few worn rugs that serve as a barrier from the hard floor.

Kuron and Rune stay with us as the ray disappears back into the water after the harness is removed. The four men and two women appear to have spent their whole lives in the sun, with dark, wrinkled, and weathered skin, and wearing animal skins to cover themselves. They look human, yet a closer glance reveals something 'other' I can't quite place.

The two women have tusks through their noses, their long, dark hair now mostly grayed, and red paint under their wild eyes. The men's bodies are covered in the same red paint, portraying symbols and pictures I recognize as a language, but it's incomplete, and I can't read it. The tallest of the four is their leader, as indicated by the symbol on his collarbone and something that tugs at my awareness.

When they speak, they start in their native tongue. It's some sort of prayer to the gods, offering their knowledge freely to save their people.

"Prince Anders, we welcome you. Princess Raea, we welcome you," one of the women says in the common language. "We have waited generations for the ones foretold. Your Bond was felt here, and we knew you would come." Raea shifts anxiously beside me.

"Our Bond? How did you know we would come?" Raea asks.

The woman smiles. "Your Bond has been awakened. You feel it. That bridge between your souls. The first elder saw you two in a dream many millennia ago and was told that when the war came, and all peace was lost, you two would be mated and restore what should be."

...Mated?

Raea's face scrunches in confusion while Professor Ainslyn shifts to her other side.

"Tell us, why have you come?" one of the men asks, sticking with the common language. I relay our findings of the books and our magic, but it's Raea who asks if they are human.

The six look around, silently communicating with each other somehow. "We serve the second council and the true heir," one of the women says.

The second council. We read about them. There were three. "And what is the second council?" Professor Ainslyn asks.

Instead of answering, the first woman moves to the fire, stroking it. "What are your powers, Prince?" the woman asks, studying me.

Good question. What are my powers? I know I can sense the veil and magic, Raea's aura, apparently wind and water, but only with her. I've been trying to figure it all out myself for so long that I'm not really sure what's real and what isn't. It all kind of blends into something that doesn't make sense.

Even as a boy, I can remember being faster and stronger, but is that part of this, too? Are Raea and I even human? Our parents are human —I think. Raea was right to come here.

"I think," I pause, looking at Raea. "I think I can manipulate air."

The elder hums as if this doesn't bother her one bit.

One of the men steps forward; he's the youngest-looking of all of them. He also looks the most human. It's only then that I realize that the woman at the fire shimmers beneath her dark skin, like pearlescent scales. I must be hallucinating, right? She looks at me then and nods as the man says, "Your lifeforce must be restored. The ancient blood calls to you, even without it, and with the gifts bestowed upon you by Astor and Calia, you have magic, even without your ancestral birthright."

"Is that why I can sense the veil? I feel its power waning, and sometimes, I think I can hear it." I shake my head. I sound insane.

One of the men responds from the other side of the room, "It is your job to protect her until she is ready." He points to Raea.

The woman shifts her gaze to Raea, who is nibbling on her lip nervously. "And your light, why do you fear it?"

Soraea winces like she's been slapped. "I don't," she whispers.

It's the man who answers, "You're scared of your powers, Princess. Magic is not something that has been given to you. It flows through you, just as your blood does. It is you. You must embrace who you are."

Raea falls quiet for a minute, still nibbling on her bottom lip. I grip her hand tighter, running a thumb over her hand. "And who is that?" she finally asks quietly.

It's the other female who answers, "Our savior and mate to the young Prince." Her head swivels back to me.

"What's a mate?" Professor Ainslyn asks on our behalf. Raea's gaze remains fixed on me, but something washes over her. An understanding, maybe. It explains the otherness we feel that isn't a regular Lumos Bond. "They aren't Lumos Bonded?"

Their leader, the eldest male, then speaks, crossing his arms as something akin to anger fills his features. "The Lumos Bond is a pathetic excuse for a mating Bond. It's blasphemy. Mating Bonds are rare. Two souls united as one. Powerful. You do not have a Lumos Bond."

My attention moves back to the elders. "So what do we do now?"

The second woman kneels beside the fire, and the other woman follows. "Our own powers have never been fully revealed outside of our people for a millennium, but we will now unveil their secret to you." They gather around the fire, holding hands, including us in their circle.

The fire at the center of the room flashes, rising to the ceiling before slowly shifting to a picture of the first elder's dream of Raea and me. The image changes to Raea radiating her starlight and projecting it from her body while I stand at her side, a tornado sweeping past us. The third image shows us with a little baby in Raea's arms as the three of us stand before a crowd of people.

More images—past, present, and future—of Raea and me, weaving our lives together. Us as kids, wrapped in that cocoon of starlight. Another of us at school, down at the river, sharing our first real kiss. The next is another image of us fighting back to back as shadows swarm us and creatures crawl from it, with her starlight glowing to keep them away.

"You have been given great gifts with great responsibility. We share our knowledge with you now," the second man says. "You must restore what is yours. Dangerous days lie ahead."

Their skin changes before us, almost dissolving, becoming scales. Only their faces remain "human," but large gills cover their necks, and their hands and feet become webbed. Along the women's backs, a spine of sharp fins pokes out. The men have hardened cone-like spikes protruding.

Professor Ainslyn gasps alongside Raea; behind us, Rune and Kuron shuffle uneasily, but I just sit, watching, studying. My people. These are my people. Not just because they live in the Okenen Kingdom, but because of the second council. My blood sings at their reveal.

The first woman studies me, tilting her head. "You're not afraid," she says. "We serve until our last breath."

Their leader says, "You must train if you are to win."

"But our powers—" I feel more confused than when we first arrived. "Do we need to do something about the…*mating* Bond?"

He shifts his gaze between the two of us. "The trial of the Bond will be completed in due time. For now, to harness your powers, you must ground yourself in all the elements. Feel them around you, as a part of you."

They wait expectantly, so I close my eyes and envision burying my feet in the sands of Malaya and then feeling the wind, the power of the oceans, and every living animal. I feel the heartbeat of the planet. It comes so naturally, as if their powers are guiding me, heightening what I see.

"Separate them," one of the women says. "Envision each of the elements in color. Blue for the water. Red for fire. Gold for energy."

"White for air, green for the planet, silver for lightning," the other woman coaches. I keep my eyes closed and, in my mind, give color to all I see and feel. Raea's excitement radiates through me as I share with her what I'm seeing.

I open my eyes and turn toward the water. I reach for the blue, twisting my hand and raising my palm, and the water rises in a small column. As I move my hand, the water follows, obeying my command. The connection feels like communication. The elements want to obey me. I twirl my hand, and Raea giggles beside me as the water column becomes a small spout.

"Very good," the leader says. "Remember, the greatest strength of your power will come when you remain calm and one with the planet. Trust in the gift the gods have given you."

For the next hour, they share their knowledge of the veil, explaining the two races, fae—which I guess is my ancestral line—and Elven—Raea's line. Both races gave their immortality, or their impossibly long lifespans, to power the veil. We are then given a map, and told not to show it to anyone. After staying for a luncheon of fresh fish and wild berries, we are given a tour of their island and their people, who all know who we are.

Raea was right. They aren't human. They are fae, *my* people, and knowing the truth, I feel a sudden, fierce need to restore them to their true heritage. Every single one, even the babies, pulses with inherent magic.

Humans, the third council, possess no inherent magic. Yet, despite this, the three races have always lived in harmony, with the Fae and Elven promising protection and sharing their knowledge. In return, humans have agreed to serve and fight alongside us.

As we navigate through the village, the women offer us food they've prepared in baskets along with chains of flowers, and the men offer gifts of spears and fishing tools. They're all in their human form, but I see the pearlescent scales hidden beneath their dark skin. Raea plays with the children and braids a few girls' hair before we thank them for their hospitality and promise to try our best to keep them safe.

Before we board the ray to take us back to the mainland, where our transport waits, one of the elders stops us. "Soraea, Light-bringer, do not fear your gift, or what is to come. You were chosen for this long before your birth. And he—" she looks to me, "is your mate. Your true match in every way. Take this and find your light, Soraea, or we're all dead without it."

Raea opens her palm to see an orb, milky white with streaks of gold, but it moves like a mini weather system inside. Without a second glance, the woman leaves us.

forty-four

. . .

raea

As soon as we're launched, Ryker and I find a quiet room upstairs. He looks exhausted, yet there's a light in his eyes that I haven't seen before. "So that was a lot." I look up at him. "I don't even know where to start. But your powers," I shake my head and grin at him. "You were amazing." Seeing him manipulate the water was so mesmerizing.

He chuckles and slides down the wall, propping his knees up in front of him. "I think they helped me somehow. I've tried seeing the strand for water before, and all it did was run through you."

"We'll keep practicing."

He nods and pulls me down into his lap, burying his face in my hair. Something settles in me. *Mating Bond.* As if reading my thoughts, he says, "So, our new titles," he teases, his fingers dancing along my ribs, tickling me until a smile blooms across my face, and I beg him to stop. "Mate. Should I start calling you my mate?"

Something funny happens to my insides, and now that stone bridge between us makes so much sense. Not a Lumos Bond, but a mating Bond. Stronger. "Not yet. We have to do The Ceremony, or ritual, or whatever he called it. Then you may use whatever title you wish."

His grin becomes lethal, stealing my breath.

A moment later, his lips settle over my cheek as he whispers, "Mate. Wife. Princess. Queen. Mine," punctuating each one with a kiss somewhere on my face.

My body erupts in goosebumps. "Who knew you were so romantic?" I tease. My pocket makes a crumpling sound. "The map," I gasp, pulling out the detailed map they gifted us.

It's not just our system, but the entire galaxy. The closest system to us is named Auralan. It appears there are only seven planets there. In fact, out of the four different systems, ours is the largest by far. Helix and Sotas have thirteen between them. They're close together, but sit at the opposite end of the galaxy.

Despite our advancements in hyperjumping, I'm not sure any of the transports could make it there. I don't even know if they could make it into Auralan. "We have to go to Auralan. That's where the councils are," I whisper. "Maybe we'll find more answers."

He nods and pulls me closer until my head is resting against his shoulder.

"We'll figure it out. We have time."

We've been back at school for two weeks now, and we haven't learned anything more about the mating Bond or the lifeforce. Even Professor Ainslyn has been assisting us. I wave goodbye to my running team as I head back to Taeolyn.

The evening breeze cools my heated skin. We've been practicing my gifts, and no matter how hard I try, I can't control when I get hot, and I still can't summon the light. Every failure feels like I'm letting the entire system down. I can't figure out what's holding me back; I feel fine. I've accepted that I have some strange bloodline that makes me Elven, or whatever, and I've accepted that my unnaturally long life is gone. But I can't find a light within me to summon.

The wards cling to my skin the moment I step into the Executive Yard

—cool, invisible threads weaving over my arms, curling around my throat, brushing across my spine like a spiderweb laced with static. A whisper of ancient magic pulses against my senses, alive and alert. I doubt I'll ever stop feeling them—like they're watching, weighing, waiting.

After opening up to our friends, I learned no one else feels them. No one...except Ryker.

My mate.

I still don't know what that means.

But I like saying it. *My mate.*

I reach the steps of Taeolyn and freeze when a sudden, icy shock drenches me from head to toe. The gasp sticks in my throat as something thick and wet coats my skin. I blink through the blur, vision swimming in crimson. My power stirs, drawn from its well like a blade unsheathed—primed to defend. I swipe at my eyes, but my hands come away slick, glistening red.

The crowd around me erupts in laughter and whispers. Students press in, delighted, horrified, their Prisms already recording. At the center of it all stands Sienna. Her smile is all teeth and malice, her icy blue eyes locked on me. She hoists an empty paint bucket like a trophy.

She lifts a brow before saying in a melodic, cruel voice, "Did you know that when you have sex for the first time, you bleed?" Her head cocks to the side. "Oh, but you wouldn't know that. Don't worry, it's not a lot." She steps toward me, her boots making the paint squelch on the stone steps. "A little birdie told me you're still untouched. Still intact."

The laughter grows around me as Sienna takes another step. "Shame. I really thought he was into you. Guess not."

I steady my breathing and look around. My voice is razor-thin and shaking. "Why—Why are you even here?"

My fists curl so tightly at my sides, my nails bite into my palms. Heat surges through me, a wildfire under my skin.

Hold it together, I scream inwardly. *Not here. Not now.*

The paint slides down my body in thick, mocking streaks—hot, nearly scalding. My pink running top and shorts are destroyed. My hair drips red like blood.

And still, I stand there. Burning.

Sienna laughs—low and sharp. "You know why." She takes the final step, her smile turning into a cruel, vicious thing. "And I'm not giving up. It's only a matter of time before he tosses you aside. You don't know him like I do."

I swallow down my insecurities. *Mate.* He's my mate. We're fated to Bond. "I know him better than you think." I take a shuddering breath. "All of this over something you have no control over? Like I said, desperate."

The words come out smooth despite the shakiness I feel. My anger flares the longer I stand here, the longer everyone stands here recording my humiliation.

"I'd call you a whore," she sneers, "but I guess you can't be if you're a frigid little prude."

More laughter bursts from the sidelines.

I smile, slow and sharp. "No. That title already belongs to you." Her face contorts. She shrieks and lunges, fist swinging. It never connects. Trysten's training takes over. She swings again, and I twist, sweeping her leg and stepping back, laughing. This time, the crowd laughs with me; something in my veins sings.

Sienna launches herself at me, knocking us both into the dirt. I hit the ground hard but roll, flipping us so I'm on top, pinning her down. "Stop embarrassing yourself!" I yell. Her wrists are trapped above her head, and she's thrashing, screaming. Trysten shouts behind me, but he's distant, muted. All I hear is the power rising—slamming into me like a wave breaking on stone. "He doesn't want you," I seethe.

Sienna's screams turn feral as she writhes beneath me, but it's not until I glance down that I understand why. Blisters bloom where my hands are pinning her wrists—angry, red, bubbling beneath my touch.

A jolt of panic snaps through me. I try to let go, but my body doesn't respond. My limbs are locked, frozen in place by something far greater than will.

Move. Move.

My chest heaves in shallow gasps. There's no air—only fire. The same searing flood that overtook me in Sgya rushes through my veins now, scorching, unrelenting. The crowd behind me vanishes into silence.

And then, I feel it—an instant shift in the air. A heartbeat later, Ryker is there. He drops to his knees and wraps himself around me, shielding my body with his own. He hisses at the contact, but he doesn't let go. Instead, his power meets mine—cool, steady, and sure. It flows into me like water over a flame, dousing the inferno inside.

I gasp as my muscles finally release, and Sienna slips from my grip, rolling over, attempting to push off the ground but collapsing into the dirt, half-conscious and gasping for breath. Ryker stands, lifting me into his arms like I weigh nothing. I can't stop staring at her. At what I did.

"I almost killed her," I whisper.

"She's alive." He cups my face tenderly despite the sternness of his voice. "That's more than she deserves after what she pulled."

Trysten approaches, expression unreadable. "I'll get her to the healers." He glances between Sienna and Ryker. "And I'll call Rhoan."

Ryker nods, already turning with me in his arms. We pass Kuron and Rune on the steps. Kuron's eyes are wide, his jaw clenched. Ryker speaks calmly, "She's okay. I've got her."

Neither of them responds.

No one says a word. No one meets our eyes. As we pass, they vanish into the stone and shadows like they were never there at all.

Inside his room, Ryker carries me to the bathroom and turns on the shower. Steam curls up, fogging the mirror. I stand motionless. Numb. Somewhere deep inside, I know I'm shaking, but I can't tell if it's from cold, shock, or horror. All I see is Sienna's face, twisted in agony. Blisters. My hands. My power.

Ryker's hands, cool and firm, lift my paint-soaked shirt. I feel the slow drag of fabric against my skin, a stark contrast to the burning shame that still prickles inside. "I almost killed her." I murmur again, the words tasting like ash. "And it's recorded."

His gaze, unwavering, follows the path as he lifts my sports bra.

"They'll know," I whisper, a single hot tear tracing a path down my cheek. "Everyone will know."

My sports bra lands with a splatter sound on the tile just before his warm hands cup my cheeks. "What will they know?" he asks, his voice so soft and sweet.

"That I'm a monster." The words tear from me, trembling and broken. "They recorded it."

Ryker's expression doesn't flinch. "No," he says, voice low and firm. "The recordings were shut down a minute in, right after she swung at you. I made sure of it. And my people are already on the rest. Nothing's getting out." He says it like a promise. Like an order already fulfilled. But it doesn't quiet the voice in my head.

Monster. Monster. Monster.

I look away. "Maybe the elder was right. Maybe I do fear my power. Because I could've—" My voice cracks. Ryker steps closer. His thumb brushing away a tear. But there's no fear in his eyes.

"You think you're a monster," he murmurs. "But all I saw was strength." His voice lowers, reverent. "Don't be afraid of what's yours."

When I turn my face, unable to look at him any longer, he says, "Soraea." His voice is low and commanding, yet not unkind. Ryker cups my cheek, turning my face back to his. "We'll handle it. But right now, get in the shower." He starts to move away, but I lunge forward, clutching his shirt.

"No," I whisper, breath catching. "Please...don't leave me." I'm standing before him in nothing but my soaked shorts. Paint-streaked. Broken. Vulnerable. Yet his gaze doesn't waver—not once. There's no shame in his eyes. Only heat. And something raw.

Pride.

"I'm not going anywhere."

He walks me to the shower and checks the temperature before guiding me under the spray. The water hits me, and my shoulders tremble. I reach for the waistband of my shorts, peeling them down slowly. I stay in my underwear. I don't even care anymore. Ryker steps in still fully clothed. The water soaks him instantly, but he doesn't flinch. He pulls me against him, his hand firm on my back.

"I see you, Soraea," he murmurs, voice thick with something reverent. "I *know* you. You're not a monster." My resolve finally breaks. The tears I held back crash into him like a flood. He just holds me tighter.

He stays like that—anchored to me—as the water runs hot over both of us. For what feels like an hour, he doesn't move. He doesn't speak. He just holds me as I shatter. And when my sobs begin to slow, he presses a kiss to the top of my head. Then, gently, he reaches for the shampoo.

He washes my hair. Once. Twice. A third time—each time softer than the last, until the red paint is gone. Then my back, slow and methodical.

When his hand hovers at my front, he doesn't touch me. He offers the sponge, silent, eyes locked on mine. The intimacy of it all kills me. Not because it's too much. But because part of me wants it. Wants *him*. Even after everything.

My hands tremble as I clean myself. I keep seeing it—Sienna's face twisted in pain, the blistering heat under my hands. All of this— over *him*.

When I'm rinsed, he shuts off the water. Before I can even think, he's wrapping a towel around my body. Then, without hesitation, he strips, discarding his soaked clothes in a pile at his feet. His body is powerful, and he looks...dangerous. My eyes drop, involuntarily taking all of him in—and when they rise to meet his again, he's watching me with something unreadable.

Not shame.

Not restraint.

Almost...regret. But also desire. And something more dangerous— *certainty*. He gives me a sad smile. "C'mon. Let's get you dressed."

A few minutes later, I'm curled up in his bed, swallowed in one of his shirts. I'm waiting for clean clothes from Aolyn, but I can barely keep my eyes open. Ryker pulls the blankets over me and slides in behind me, wrapping an arm around my waist. He's warm. Solid. Unmoving.

But I can still feel the echo of fire in my veins. The look in Sienna's eyes. My own hands. Her screams. "Sleep, Raea," he says softly, his lips against my ear. "I'll still be here when you wake up." His grip tightens ever so slightly. "*Always.*" And I do. Eventually, the pull of sleep drags me under.

But my dreams are anything but peaceful.

A battlefield stretches before me—charred hills and rivers of blood. At its center, a girl stands draped in black. Shadow curls around her like smoke. When it parts, I see her face.

Mine.

Hair dulled to silver ash. Black war paint slashed across my eyes. And a smirk. Not kind. Not soft. Predatory. Certain. Powerful.

I *am* the monster.

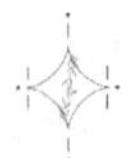

I wake up feeling warm and safe. When I clear my eyes, I find Ryker asleep beside me on his stomach, an arm draped over my waist. Yesterday, I was too wound up to speak, but he took care of me. Without needing to be told, he just knew what I needed. It has to be the Bond between us. It's the only explanation.

He sighs, his eyes flickering open before settling on me. "Hi," he rasps. He pushes up, revealing his bare chest. "How are you feeling?"

Nervous butterflies take flight inside of me. "Okay," I respond, a little breathless. He nods, turning on his side and pulling me closer until our bodies are flush.

"Are you hungry?" He brushes my hair from my face. "You missed dinner."

I shake my head, suddenly aware that I'm in nothing but his shirt, and morning Ryker might just be my favorite sight.

I gulp. "Is she okay?"

"She's fine. Just a little burn. Trysten told the healers you had your Prism in your hand, and it was overheating."

I nod and close my eyes, taking a steadying breath before opening them again. "And the recordings?"

"Rhoan took care of them. Cassia messaged you and wants to talk. Kuron called your parents and relayed that you were attacked, but it was handled quickly. Everyone's okay. You're okay."

I shake my head. "I lost control."

He tips my chin up until our eyes meet again. "Then we find control."

I roll out of his arms and sit up, brushing back my hair, feeling scared and lost and so damn confused. My chest squeezes. "We've been trying," I say, defeated. "The only reason I lost control yesterday is because she embarrassed the hell out of me, telling everyone that I'm still a virgin because you don't want me." I groan, burying my face in my hands. "I know it's not true—"

"It's not."

"But it still got to me." I turn to look at him, pulling my knees to my chest. "I let her get to me. I felt it, and I couldn't do a damn thing about it."

He sits up, the blanket falling away as he scoots closer. "There's something we're missing. We'll figure it out. Until then..." He swipes a hand through his hair.

"Until then, what? You can't protect me or, I guess, protect everyone else from me."

"Don't," he says sternly. "Don't go down that path."

My body hums with energy as if the magic is summoned again with my emotions. I gasp, feeling my panic consume me as I jump from the bed, shaking my arms out and blowing out a breath. *Calm. Stay calm.* I inhale and exhale, counting to three. I hear Ryker come to me, but I keep my focus inward, searching.

I search for that well of power, and when I find it, I nearly sob. It's full, overflowing, in fact. Pure white heat pours from it, flooding my system. "Get control," he commands.

"I can't," I sob, watching the molten heat pour into me. His hands grip me, shaking me. Instead of the cooling sensation, he just grunts.

My eyes spring open. He's not using his power to counteract mine. "Stop!" I shriek.

He just holds on, grunting through the pain. "Get control of it." Panic becomes a tangible thing. Internally, I beg myself to stop. "Raea," he pants, "this hurts. Please."

I gulp and breathe through my nose. *Get control.*

Just like on Sgya, I clear my mind, settling myself. I hear the elder's words in my head. It's *a part of me, not gifted to me.* It's a part of me, which means I can decide. Sweat is beading on his face.

"Please," I plead, "Let go."

He shakes his head, groaning again. I find that well of power and look around. I don't know what to do, but maybe it's like my mental shield. I blink, and an iron lid appears. I slam it closed, feeling my body cool instantly. When I'm pulled back to Ryker, I blink at what I'm seeing. His hands...

I run to the bathroom, vomiting into the toilet. He steps up to my side, pulling my hair from my face. "You did it," I swear there's pride in his voice. He drops to his knees beside me. "I'm okay." My mouth waters as I turn to face him. He's holding his hands up in front of me, the skin perfectly healed.

"Don't do that again." I rest my head on my arms. He shrugs and mutters something about it working before pulling me to my feet. I slam my palms into his chest before flushing and walking away.

"So violent," he chuckles.

The burning memory of his hands, blistered then instantly whole, lingers in my mind. How can I possibly face everyone now, knowing what kind of power truly flows through me?

forty-five

. . .

raea

A FEW DAYS LATER, I settle into my chair, Ryker at my side, Kellan at my other, as Professor Becca discusses the Bonding serum. Its classified ingredients prevent us from completing a Bond until the seers finish their measurements. Once recorded, the individual with the highest reading receives a counter-serum, and the Bond is completed. My body physically recoils.

It feels so…systematic.

I wonder if we can avoid The Ceremony altogether. If Ryker and I are mates, it's all for nothing anyway. He's my future. I accept that, even if a pang of loss hits when I glance at Kellan. He knows, yet he clings to hope. He doesn't know about the mating Bond, just the prophecy. Where the once green light was so easy to detect, it's now vacant. I should have known it was coming, but it's still a shock nonetheless.

"You'll be required to kiss each of the potential Bonds, linking your hands together…" Professor Becca says as I gasp, too audibly.

Everyone around me turns, glaring. It's been a rough few days, and I'm pretty sure everyone hates me. If I thought everyone whispered about me before, now it's tenfold. My cheeks flush as I sink further into the seat. Kellan wraps an arm around me, rubbing my arm as he mutters that it will all work out.

I swear I hear Ryker growl. The thought has me tucking my lips to hide a smile when I look at him. He only lifts a questioning brow. I shrug but offer him my hand. He rolls his eyes but takes it, resting our interlaced fingers on his thigh.

"So what happens if your Bond is so strong that none of the other men even come close?" Ryker asks, interrupting the professor. Everyone shifts their focus to him. "I mean, do they stop The Ceremony right then and there? No need to waste time." He grins knowingly as a flush fills my cheeks and my gaze bores into him. If looks could kill…

"Well, since that's never been the case, I wouldn't know," Professor Becca responds. "There are always two or three who are close runners-up."

Kellan makes some indistinguishable noise beside me.

Ryker winks at me before responding, "Is there a way to test ahead of time?" He leans back as if comfortable. "I mean, I don't like sharing."

This earns a few giggles and whoops around the room.

"Unfortunately, Prince Anders," Professor Becca argues, clearly annoyed with the display. *Join the club.* "A Ceremony is required of all royalty."

She's about to change the topic when he cuts her off. "But rules can be changed for specific circumstances."

She sighs, pinching the bridge of her nose. "Prince Anders, if you'd like to discuss this further, my door is always open." He sits back with a smirk.

"See you on Veilan," he replies. Professor Becca groans, then continues as if he never interrupted.

Veilan. The second day of the week. He's always in meetings on Tempas, the first day of the school week.

"What are you doing?" I snap. "Don't be an ass."

His mouth comes intimately close to mine. "But you love it when I am." He offers me that classic smirk before pulling away. "Mine," he mouths silently.

I roll my eyes, focusing on the dais.

"For today's exercise, you'll be paired off with someone you reported feeling a Bond with during the last exercise." She looks at Ryker and narrows her eyes. "And no, you don't get to pick."

I almost chuckle.

"You'll find a spot somewhere in the room or out in the halls, and all I want you to do is focus on your Bond. Feel your mental shield fall into place, and then lift it and watch how your Bond responds." She pauses in the middle of the dais. "We are not Bonding today, people." This gets a good chuckle from the crowd. She grabs her tablet and tells us our partner has been sent to our devices.

When I open mine up, it's blank. So is Ryker's. When we look down on Professor Becca, she's watching us, her hand on her hip. She purses her lips and then taps a button. Both of our devices populate with each other's names, but below it is a message for us to see her immediately after class.

"You got us in trouble," I whisper-shout at him.

"I'm not practicing Bonding with anyone other than my mate." This side of him makes my heart do some weird routine because, if I'm being honest, I love it. There's something about his possessiveness that makes my toes curl.

The professor dismisses us to connect with our partners. Ryker finds a private nook in the entry, pulling me into his lap before I can protest. "Possessive flirt," I tease, shifting off his lap so that we're sitting knee to knee.

I link our hands, amazed at how he still manages to leave me breathless at a single touch. At least I can now handle the surge in power. Ryker lowers his forehead to mine as my eyes fall close.

"I'll find a way out of this," he promises.

I nod, tilting my head until his mouth meets mine. His tongue brushes along the seam of my lips and I open for him. He sweeps in, stroking and tasting with a low groan that makes me smile. At the sound of footsteps, we pull apart.

"Focus," I command, "you're distracting me." I close my eyes again, focusing on the iridescent colors that wrap around us and flow on an invisible wave. "I love it."

"I felt it that first day," he admits. "When Cole had to open his damn mouth. The moment you looked at me, I saw it."

I inhale deeply, letting my forehead rest against his. I then search for that stone bridge between us, and for the first time, I step onto it. I test my weight, then take another step and begin walking. It feels weird to be standing on a bridge within myself—especially knowing it somehow connects my soul to Ryker's.

Around me, there's an endless void, but the bridge is illuminated with a soft, warm light. I reach the halfway point only to be met with a wall, extending into the void and impenetrable. It rises around us, not just a blanket of fog, but a living, breathing entity. It swirls and shifts, tendrils curling, imbued with a shimmering, iridescent dust that catches the ambient light. It tastes of ancient earth and raw magic, cool against my skin. It pulls an invisible tether, drawing me forward, and I take a physical step, then another, walking toward the unseen. I reach out, hoping to get through it, only for my hand to bounce back. Maybe if Ryker meets me in it?

"Go down the bridge," I whisper. One second. Two. When nothing happens, I open my eyes. "Did you go?"

"It's blocked." He sighs. "The mating Bond?"

Immediately, the world around us shifts. My head swims with the sudden change. I tighten my grip on Ryker, only to realize that he's in it with me.

We are standing on a mountain peak, the air thin and crisp. Below us is a thick, ancient forest that stretches to the horizon. A strange circle of glowing markings surrounds our feet, pulsating with a soft, rhythmic light. My spine tingles like an itch I can't scratch, but it also burns—a painful, searing heat radiates from my skin.

"My back." I hiss, reaching for it.

Ryker spins me around, his hand tracing the line of my spine. "Raea." I hear the confusion in his voice. "Your spine is marked with glowing tattoos."

"What?" I attempt to look over my shoulder, but the vision holds me captive. Some ancient knowledge whispers, *Complete.* This is the final piece of the mating ritual.

The mountain peak dissolves, throwing us into a whirlwind as the sky turns a bruised, angry gray. I stumble into Ryker as he steadies me. When I look around this time, we're on a battlefield. Scorched grass stretches in every direction cloaked in a sickly, green mist. Across the clearing, a girl stands. *Me.* But different. Her hair is dulled to silver ash. Black war paint slashes across her eyes. And a smirk. Not kind. Not soft. Predatory. Certain. Powerful. It's the same woman I've been seeing this whole time.

Ryker looks down at his hand, his right arm is now inked from his wrist and into his sleeve, the tattoo swirling like it's alive. He now has sleeves up both arms, but the tattoos on his right look like runes. He lifts his palm, and the air itself obeys, spinning as the skies darken, rain pelting us from above. He releases it, and I feel a burst of power, raw and untamed. The air around us charges as starlight swirls in the wind, meeting his gale, devouring enemy forces like a life of its own and out to do his bidding.

"What the hell is going on?" Ryker asks, his voice thick with awe and confusion, his eyes completely white and silver, like the flecks have taken over.

My gaze falls on the woman across the clearing. The shadows curl around her, a living extension of her will. Before I can say anything, or learn anything, my head spins again as we're thrown back into our bodies, both holding each other and gasping for air.

Still breathless and a little dizzy, I look over my shoulder, hoping to catch a glimpse of my spine. I don't know why my response is disappointment when I realize it's completely normal, no markings in sight. Ryker leans over my shoulder, noting the same thing. He must sense my disappointment because I'm yanked into him, my face buried in his chest while he strokes a soothing hand down my back.

After a few quiet minutes, he asks, "Does that happen often?"

When I shake my head, I tell him about the woman and the shadows. He claims he didn't see her. But how could he not? The images

stay with me long after, my thoughts spinning in search of answers I
know won't come.

forty-six

. . .

raea

I'M SWEATY AND TIRED, and my whole body hurts. I know why we're out here with Recon, but still. The afternoon sun beats down on us relentlessly, the black material of my uniform making me wish I'd gone with the standard-issue dress. At least then I'd get some air flow.

Our dorm has been divided into groups of six, comprising a mix of juniors and seniors, as well as a blend of all three divisions. Leading my group are Trysten, Cas, another senior in Intel, and Knox, the senior Recon representative. Ciara and Tate are also in my group since they're part of my flight team. Ashton, a senior girl who is part of Ryker's flight team, is also here. We were pulled from bed for an early training exercise—a surprise to all of us. Well, not Ryker. No, he was fully aware and decided to hide this little exercise from me. Last I saw, he was with the other two dorm leaders talking with Professors Ainslyn and Brendn this morning.

Once we find our flag, our flight team, including Trysten, along with Freya, a girl from Intel, is supposed to rush back to the launch pad to start searching for the other flags, while our Intel counterpart decodes the coordinates. It's a game of capture the flag and a race against the other teams and dorms. Since Ezra needs a seat in my transport, we don't have the extra space for Recon, so Trysten will double as our Recon expert. The ground crunches under my boots as Trysten and Knox discuss the route on the map we've been given.

"It's hotter than Mori's asshole out here," Tate groans. "When is our little march through this forest over?"

I snicker when Knox shoots a glare over his shoulder.

"You okay?" Ciara asks quietly, slowing her steps to walk beside me.

I offer a small smile to my best friend and bump her shoulder.

"I'm okay. Just thinking." We both fall into silence for a moment.

With a grin, she asks, "About a certain prince?"

I can't hide my own as it spreads across my face. Last night I had been practicing with my magic in his room, and when I could barely keep my eyes open, he asked me to stay. He gave me another one of his shirts to sleep in. I woke this morning, tangled in his arms, mortified by our compromising position. Yet, all I could think about was spending every morning like that.

We stayed like that for another hour, reluctantly rising, knowing I'd have to sneak back to my own room. Blessedly, Ezra said nothing when I slipped into my clothes and showered. I spent the morning berating myself for putting us back in the "not-so-safe zone."

By the time I dressed in clean clothes, Ry knocked on my door with a smirk, announcing a surprise training session. If Professor Brendn wasn't part of the entourage, I'd have given Ryker a piece of my mind for not warning me.

"Things are...complicated." I hike my backpack higher. It holds pre-packed meals, water, a notebook, and a pen (our tablets were temporarily confiscated so nobody cheats), and our tracker jewelry.

"When have they not been?" she asks, wiping sweat from her bubble-braid crown. "You two are the epitome of complicated."

She's right, and I hate it. I wish this were easier. I still need to talk with him about Sienna. She's gone. Not just skipping classes—*gone*. Her room's been emptied out, and no one knows exactly why. The rumors claim she was expelled, suspended, or exiled to one of the outer moons. No one says it outright, but it's because of what she did to me. Apparently, she moved out the same night as the paint incident.

My guess—it was Ryker. Or Kuron.

Ciara pauses, halting me as well. "Look, Rae, I know you love Kellan, but you have to let him go. He's really hurting right now and you owe it to him. And with Ryker, there's literally a prophecy about you two. We only have a few months left of school, so just enjoy it. Besides," she grins, "I know where you've been sleeping. Came to check on you after Sienna's paint show and Aolyn said you were in Ryker's room and he had just left after grabbing your clothes."

I roll my eyes. "It was two times." She squeals and heads turn.

"Shh..." I warn, slamming my palm over her mouth. I feel her smile and lower my hand. "And you're right. I need to let Kellan go, but I don't know how to. I don't love him like he loves me, but he's my best friend, and I'm scared this will ruin us."

Ciara offers me a sad, knowing smile.

Ahead, Trysten turns to tell us we're almost there, so the sixteen of us in this group fall silent, knowing that any of the other dorm teams could be around.

Baedyn's energy pulses softly around me and beneath me, grounding me in a way that I don't understand. Ever since I got back from Sgya, it's like the further from Sgya, the weaker the energy. Maybe that's why the veil is so weak? The further out, the less power? I know I need to go back to Sgya for answers, but every time I think about it, my pulse races, and I feel like I can't breathe. I can swallow down gulps of air, and still, I find myself gripping my center, waiting for the panic to pass.

Trysten holds up a hand, halting all of us as we come around a turn in the path. Ahead, there are two flags. One for Taeolyn, one for Veker. I thought they would all be spread out. I wonder what happened to Bragr. Did they already come and claim theirs? And if so, why did they leave ours?

"It might be a trap," one of the men from Intel whispers to Knox.

Trysten and Knox nod to each other, spreading out on either side, looking up and down for any traps that might be set. Trysten crouches low and makes a bird call, which gets Knox's attention.

Together, they clear the pile of leaves to find a cord that is attached to an animal trap. Gods. I haven't seen one in person before, but it's barbaric. The two metal rings are lined with large iron spikes waiting to be spring so they can close over someone's leg.

"Is that even allowed?" Freya gasps, covering her mouth a little late. All eyes shoot to her, and she winces.

It takes us a few more minutes that we don't have to spring the trap and check for more, finding none, before we tuck both flags into Ashton's bag. She'll be taking them back to our meeting spot located in the AerBall arena. Some of the Intel seniors claimed it as our home base since setting foot back in the Executive dorm yard is forbidden until the games are over.

Our Intel team makes quick work of decoding the complicated message, which has been scrambled up and uses code words in place of names and locations. While they finish decoding the last of the locations for us to go find, Ciara, Tate, and I eat a quick lunch, knowing there may not be time once we reach space for part two of our little exercise.

"Got it," Trysten says, heading to us. "Let's go."

He takes one step, and the scream that pierces the air steals the breath from my lungs. Trysten falls to his knee, gripping the sides of the trap as rivulets of crimson trickle down his leg, pooling in his boot and staining the ground around him. It takes two heartbeats before I'm in front of him, my fingers interlacing with the spikes as I assist, trying to pull it back. Others surround us, gasping and calling for help.

Annika, one of the girls from Recon division who's on my running team, stabs a branch between one of the spikes, using it as leverage. Knox is next to Trysten, pulling as the three of us work to free Trysten's leg. Trysten screams again, the sound piercing my chest.

There's no way this is part of the games, *right?* I don't think our parents would approve of this, but then again, they did say it was supposed to be a real-world experience. We get the trap open enough so that he can escape, while Tate and one of the other men assist him.

"On three," Knox says, looking at me.

I nod as he counts, both of us letting go at the same time, and the branch that Annika was holding smashes into the trap. That could have been any of us. Why is there a trap like this hidden for a bunch of students?

"Don't move," I shout, looking around at the sixteen of us who are scattered about. "There could be more."

Carefully, I stand, wiping my hands on my pants and ignoring the blood staining them and now the tips of my hair where it sopped it up from the ground. First red paint, now blood. Maybe I should just dye my hair.

Trysten groans as he bites down on a strip of leather given to him by Knox. We all have medical training, but not enough to handle this. My thoughts spin quickly, but I inhale, finding my center, reminding myself not to let my emotions and thoughts control me. "Okay, I'm going to run back to command. Knox, Tate, you both start carrying him in that direction. Annika, you're with me." I look around, finding pale faces, and one girl is puking in the bushes. "Ciara, you got her?" My other best friend nods. "The rest of you, get back on the trail we got here on and tread carefully, but hurry."

I drop my pack, grabbing my water from it. Annika does the same as we both turn, sprinting for control, Ezra staying silent behind us. He's not allowed to intervene unless it's me in danger. We run, knowing the healers won't find them unless we bring them back. I set an urgent pace but keep my reserves, knowing it's a long run. We've been hiking for two hours or so, and we are definitely off campus.

Annika stays two steps behind me, both of us pausing once to breathe and take a sip of water before we run again. My lungs burn, and my legs protest, but when the academy comes into view, I sigh in relief. We both find the energy to sprint the rest of the way to the academy grounds, the wards making my skin tingle as we cross them. She falls behind, but I don't slow. Once on campus, we sprint past three other dorms and arrive at the Center. Once the control tower is in view, I push myself, throwing open the doors and praying to Astor that I make it up the stairs without puking.

I make it to the last landing when I hear Chancellor Xara talking. I push open the doors and fall to my hands and knees, gasping for air. Ezra steps in behind me.

"Raea," Ryker is at my side first, the Chancellor gasping somewhere above me. Every breath burns, and my throat is raw, but Trysten needs help—immediately.

"Trysten," I rasp. "He's hurt." Ryker helps me stand, keeping an arm wrapped around my waist, the only thing keeping me up. "Traps." My vision blurs, and I bend over, finding a waste bucket.

"Traps?" Chancellor Xara gasps.

Professor Ainslyn speaks next, or at least I think it's him explaining that it could be traps from the village. It's all I hear before Ryker is rubbing my back and instructing me to slow my breathing.

Annika finally makes it to the room and drops into a chair. "Sorry," she wheezes. "I couldn't keep up."

I shake my head, allowing Ryker to help me stand. He helps me to a chair, turning a fan on me. "Did you just run the whole way?" he asks. I nod, and then he tells me our flag was dropped five miles off campus. That makes sense since we started the hike from the stadium.

"Healers. He needs healers now, Ry. His leg." My vision swims again. It's so damn hot. Ryker nods but keeps his gaze on me before pulling me from my chair and into the bathroom, closing the door behind us.

"What are you—" My shirt is ripped off, so I'm only standing in my corset, but he makes quick work of the laces, loosening it until we can pull it free. I instantly cool ten degrees, and I can breathe again.

"You just ran five miles in a corset," he growls.

He flips on the water, running it cold while I rest against the cool tiled wall. I can't find it in me to care that I'm standing here in my bra or that my professors are on the other side of the door while Ryker is in here with me. Cold towels are draped around my shoulders, the water soaking my bra, but it's enough to bring my temperature down and my heart rate back to normal. He's gentle when he cleans off the blood from my hands. "Let's get your hair clean."

I lean over the sink, dipping my hair into the basin and watching the red float on streams that disappear down the drain.

I sigh as my adrenaline fades. "I have to go with the healers."

"I'll come with you, and we can take the pod."

An hour later, Ryker sits beside me in Trysten's spot. Trysten is sedated after the healers cleaned his wounds and stitched him up. Thankfully, the spikes missed his artery and didn't fracture any bones.

"I don't freaking get this. These coordinates lead to nowhere," Tate growls in frustration. We're all holed up in the transport, while our team tries to decode the coordinates they received from Cas and the other Intel team.

I keep banging my head on the console in frustration while Ryker tries to hide his amusement.

"Ashton, call Intel back and ask them if this is right. Tate's right, there is nothing here," Freya says. Ashton and Ciara exchange a quick glance and then call Cas, who reads off the same exact coordinates as last time.

"Ryker, seriously?" Tate huffs. "What is this shit?"

When I look over at him, he shrugs and ignores Tate, kicking his feet up on the console. I can't help but raise a brow in question. He only shakes his head, crossing his arms over his chest. My gaze falls to his right arm, thinking about the tattoo that was inked there in the vision. Was it a mating mark? The thought makes me blush. The idea that his will be visible for all to see makes me feel possessive. Typically, with the Lumos Bond, only the women's marks are visible. His hand interlaces with mine a moment later.

"Damn, this is annoying," Ciara groans.

"Guys, why don't we just fly there, and we can look around," I finally suggest. It won't hurt to just look. The information is either incorrect, or the computer is malfunctioning. Most likely the first, but it's better than sitting here.

"Fine, but I'm telling you. There's nothing," Tate sighs.

"Ryker, get off my transport," I tease with a grin. "Ciara, clear us for takeoff. Ashton, we'll see you when we get back." When I look back at Ryker, he's already buckling his harness and slipping on a headset.

"I'm actually staying." He clips in as he says, "I can't help, but I'm here just in case." I scowl at him. I already have one guard. "I won't say a thing," he promises with a chuckle. I roll my eyes and go back to the console, sliding the switch for launch.

"All clear, transport five," the tower says.

The console illuminates with a soft hum as it angles us.

"Take us up, Raea," Ryker orders.

I lift my brow again. "You aren't here, remember. My transport, now shush." Ciara chuckles behind me.

"You two done flirting up there?" Tate asks. I roll my eyes and hit the launch button a second later.

When we reach space, our team works seamlessly, navigating around the Westsea Cloud and the Lynx Asteroid field. We reach the destination forty minutes later, and all I can do is chuckle.

"Hey, hey, guess what's here," I tease Tate. "Feel free to say I was right and you were wrong."

Both Tate and Freya groan, and Tate mutters what sounds like, 'You were right,' back to me, much to my surprise. Everyone gathers around the front window to see the buoy that's been dropped here with a box we have to retrieve.

I line up the transport and let Ciara use the claw to reach out and grab hold of it, storing it in the compartment below.

"Hell yes," Tate whoops.

"For Trysten," Ciara claims. I turn to Ryker and wink before bursting into giggles. I think I love flirting with him.

"You're amazing." He reaches for me. Everyone is still talking behind us, but I unbuckle and step closer. I lean over him, kissing him, and when I feel the delicious slide of his tongue against mine, a warmth blossoms in my stomach.

Ciara whoops the loudest while Tate yells, "Finally."

I smile against his lips, kissing him again before whispering, "I really, really like you." He echoes the sentiment. "Okay, settle down," I laugh, getting back in my chair. "Tate, route us home. I'd like to be back before dinner."

That night, Ry delivers the news that our team won not only against the other dorms, but against the other Taeolyn teams. As a reward, our team was awarded a free day pass to leave campus.

forty-seven

. . .

raea

I'M CALLED home over the weekend when an article leaks about Ryker and me. The photo is of us on campus, and I have to admit, we do look a little…cozy. It was taken while on a run, and naturally, we're clad in very little material. He must have said something funny because we're both laughing, but it's the way I'm clinging to him that has the gossip already flowing around the system.

"Raea," my father sighs, knocking his knuckles on the armchair. It's his nervous tell. "What is really going on with you two? And don't say nothing because I saw the way you two were looking at each other in the Center." He means when he walked in on Ryker and me after Sgya. "You two have been friends since you were babies, and we've always hoped you'd Bond, but your actions—" He just shakes his head, and I can see the hint of disappointment, or maybe confusion.

I run a hand over my gown, my gaze settling over the waterfall near the window in my father's study. "We found some books," I start. "And well, one thing led to another, and we went to the Ancestor Isles."

"That's why Kuron reported you went to Demeter." I nod.

"The elders believe Ry-Prince Anders and I are fated to Bond, or mates, or something." I shake my head. "Our Bond isn't normal." I

450

look at my father, whose features soften. "I really, really like him. Maybe even more."

My father hums, settling back in his chair as he taps his finger once, twice, three times. "You need to be careful. Both of you. Your Bond is still intact?" I nod but feel a blush creep over my cheeks. "The crowns won't accept this. They'll still demand a Ceremony."

"Is there no way out of it?"

He stands, gathering his tablet. "I'll need to speak with my advisors and our media team. We need to get ahead of this. In the meantime," he pauses, "there's a historian, Elison Kolbek. Last I heard, he was living in Mori. He's loyal to our family. Let's see if we can find him and see what he knows."

Two hours later, I'm sitting in a meeting with Cassia, the palace media team, and some of my parents' advisors. I feel like I'm in trouble, yet my father keeps assuring me I'm not. I never thought I would end up in this position. Never thought I'd be falling for someone other than Kellan. Definitely not the one man who's entirely off limits. *Gods*. The worst part is that a meeting has been called between the two kingdoms, and as we speak, Ryker is on his way here with his mother.

I can't help but feel a rush of anxiety every time I think about seeing him. How am I supposed to act? Can I hug him? Definitely not kiss him. Do I pretend we're just acquaintances?

"Raea?" Cassia asks from my side.

I've zoned out again. I'm supposed to be searching for an assistant to take over my social media and ensure I'm posting and sharing more, so that I appear active and focused.

I let my gaze fall to the three photos and bios projected above the table. This is who the team has narrowed it down to. Someone trustworthy and able to create an image for me. This is what I wanted, though. I've been asking for months to have someone take over, except now it feels wrong.

"Anneli." I gesture toward the lady at the center. She has kind eyes, is a little older than I, and looks like someone I could be friends with. After all, she'll become part of my ladies. My handmaid, Mera, and my chamber ladies, Zhel and Aza, are the closest things I have to sisters. So, yes, Anneli will fit in with them—I think. I hope.

One of our guards opens the door and bows, welcoming Queen Priana and Prince Anders of Okenen and his staff. Queen Priana enters first, her navy gown clinking on the tiled floor as the gemstones sewn into her train drag behind her. My father welcomes her with a familiar embrace.

Ryker enters beside her a moment later, dressed in a black cashmere sweater with the sleeves pushed up to his forearms and navy pants, looking like my wildest dream. He looks the part of the prince about to take over the kingdom.

The second our eyes lock, a blush spreads across my cheeks, and I'm on my feet, giving a polite curtsy, which only makes his lips tilt up. He isn't looking at anyone else in the room, only me, and it doesn't go unnoticed. My father steps between us, breaking my line of sight as he pulls Ryker into a hug. They pat each other's backs like old friends.

My father gestures for me to come forward, and when I meet my father's gaze, he nods subtly. Ryker's hands twitch at his sides as if he's fighting the urge to pull me into his arms. I can't say I'm not feeling the same way, but he doesn't need to touch me to leave a mark. His presence alone is a brand on my soul.

"Hi, Princess." He bows deeply with a wink that flushes my whole body.

"Hi," I whisper back, wishing we were alone.

With all eyes on us, and the room unnaturally silent, I step to the side, bowing my head to the Queen. That familiar sensation that I've met her before strikes me as odd, but I still can't pull those memories forward. At least I can explain it away.

"Such a beauty you've become, dear," Queen Priana says, taking my hand in hers. Our party turns for the room and I find my seat again.

A chair is pulled out across the table from me, but my father insists that Ryker take the open one to my right. His team finds open seats around the large table, with the Queen at the opposite end of the table from my father. Introductions are made. His publicist, Kaes, already knows Cassia. She's about the same age, in her late twenties, with long black hair and big, wide eyes that tilt up. She's beautiful. Maya, his social manager, appears to be in her late thirties, with deep bronze skin and short black hair that brushes her shoulders.

"Well, let's not waste time," Hanson, the palace's lead publicist, starts. I'm pretty sure he hates me right now. "We have a problem on our hands, and one that doesn't look good. How do we spin this?" He somehow looks down at me from across the table, his overgrown silver brows pinching as his pointed chin lifts.

My fingers tangle nervously under the table. Ryker takes my hand in his, that little current not overwhelming me, but soothing me in an instant.

"Well, I've been thinking about the optics," Maya replies. "What if we turn them into the darling couple that everyone wants to see end up together?"

Hanson snorts, but my father responds, "How?"

It's Cassia who responds, saying, "We narrate their story. A real one. They're in love, but they know they have a duty and responsibility and won't risk their Bonds." She looks at Ryker and me. "You two make more appearances together. We want to show them you have a united front for ensuring the future of both kingdoms."

"And we do a live Q&A. Let the kingdoms ask their questions. Obviously, we choose which ones to answer, but we want everyone to fall in love with them and focus on being young and in love."

Hanson looks about two seconds away from bursting a blood vessel. "Her duty is to Treon and her Bond." He stands. "Excuse me, but if I may be blunt." He looks at my father, who nods. "These two are putting both kingdoms at risk. What does a future look like if the king and queen of two kingdoms become one?"

"A powerful one," Ryker responds. "I won't deny my feelings for Raea, and I won't risk her Bond. I've made that clear from the beginning."

"But you're setting a new precedent. Our nobility falls in line because we stick to the rules," Hanson replies coolly.

"And what of the other matches over the last nine hundred years where royals Bonded?" my mother asks as she gracefully strides into the room. The entire atmosphere changes with her presence. She holds herself tall as she moves not to my father's side, but behind Ryker and me, settling her hands on our shoulders. "There is precedence for royals marrying and Bonding."

Hanson looks like he's sweating now as his features soften. "But my Queen," he gulps, "those royals were not the heirs. They were second in line."

It's my father who responds, "So a new one will be set. That's how it goes. If these two Bond, then who are we to argue? Raea and Anders' Bond will be studied by our lead scientists. In the meantime, we will push this story." He looks at Ryker and me. "Do either of you object? To push your love story, that is?" His lips twitch as if he's fighting a smile.

Ryker squeezes my hand in question as he looks at me. "Any objections, Princess?"

I roll my eyes and then face the room. "I won't lie, but I don't object to the story either. Prince Anders and I are friends who share a strong Bond *and* are still loyal to our individual kingdoms. For now, we are getting to know each other, and when my ceremony happens—if it happens—then we will go from there."

My mother squeezes my shoulder before moving to my father's side.

Hanson pats his forehead with a handkerchief. "Well, I guess we need to come up with a response to the allegations then." He pulls open the article in question, causing me to cringe. It's the same leaked photo, but the headline claims Ryker and I are sleeping together, citing a source from Taeolyn who has seen us entering and exiting our dorms together at all hours of the night. *Not untrue.* But we aren't sleeping together, sexually speaking.

Ryker clears his throat. "This is nothing more than gossip. Okenen will not respond to the gossip blogs." He looks to his mother, who nods in approval. "We will run with the story and nothing more. If interviews are needed, fine. We will address specific questions, but I will not engage in this, nor drag Raea through it. As she said, we are friends with a powerful Bond. That's all anyone needs to know."

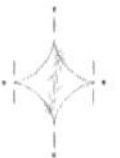

With Ryker staying on Kyrr with me, after dinner, I decide to take him to one of my favorite spots when I need to think and be alone. Today was a lot. And the word love was tossed around quite a bit. Ryker and I haven't even said those words to each other, and now we're supposed to share them with the whole system?

I'm wrapped in my cloak when Kuron leads me to the smaller pod. My usual pilot, Sam, is waiting with a genuine smile. I haven't seen him since I left for school.

"Princess Raea," he bows.

I smile back and accept his hand as he opens the door to the pod. The floors light up green as I walk to the front, where it opens into seats beneath a glass shell. These pods are used mostly for touring and therefore have the most visibility of them all. They can't leave the planet, so the glass body is perfect for on-planet transportation.

"Sam, please take us to the Drift." I throw my hood back. I settle into the seat and buckle. The hair on my arms and neck stands on end as ripples of light hit me.

"Princess," Rune says, taking the seat ahead of me.

Ryker sits behind him and beside me. Close enough that our knees brush. As soon as the pod dims, Ryker pulls me into his side, wrapping an arm around me. At this moment, words aren't needed, and he knows that.

We fly over the edge of the palace island before we begin our descent to the forest floor. The Drift comes into view once we break free of the cloud bank. The huge rip in the ground is such a mystery. Nobody has ever been to the bottom, or ever returned. I don't know why I like coming here, but I've always felt drawn to it.

People around the system refer to it as the heart of the system. I've always chuckled at the idea. Now, I hate it. After being on Sgya, my once safe world feels exposed and upended. I draw patterns on Ryker's thigh. The same ones I saw stamped on my spine in that vision. I've been thinking about it a lot today. That vision, our future, the prophecy. He was the arrogant prince assigned to guard my future. I never expected him to become it. And now, I don't know what I'm feeling other than being stuck, like sitting in a waiting room, waiting for my life to start. I may not be ready, but I'm willing to face what the stars have decided.

Before dinner, my father, my mother, Queen Priana, Ryker, and I met with our guards to plan a two-day trip to Mori to search for Elison. We sent word to King Osiris and Queen Meganna, requesting permission to visit and stay at the palace. We'll start our search in the capital. We haven't heard back yet.

Sam lands just outside the treeline, and before the transport is off, I grab Ryker's hand and lead him to the familiar trail that leads straight to the edge. Kuron keeps his distance as we navigate the moonlit path. Around us, the trees sway in a light breeze, filling the air with the scent of fresh rain and damp soil.

"It's up here." His grip on me tightens.

When the gaping hole in the ground comes into view, I lead him right to the edge, plopping down and letting my feet dangle into the cloud bank that stretches across the Drift. It's so thick, it's almost as if you could just walk across. No matter the time of day, no matter the weather, this cloud bank is here, so solid, blocking any view of what's beneath. No amount of technology can penetrate either. Ryker does the same, sitting close enough that our thighs brush against each other.

The sky is bright from the light of our single, large moon that takes up a quarter of the sky and makes the clouds in the Drift reflect the moonlight. Toward the center, you can make out the outline of a tree. We don't know if there are more. If they're really tall or if there's a ledge or a floating island. We don't know anything.

I've been here enough times to know pretty much everything there is to know. When it rains, the raindrops seem to disappear. When it's storming at night, there are flashes of light in the clouds. It looks like there might be some sort of electrical creature flying around. Nobody has ever seen them, though. In the early mornings, before the sun rises, there's a loud cry of something from the bottom. It doesn't happen every day, making it hard to learn anything.

"This is a mess," I sigh.

"Raea, look at me."

I look up into his sapphire eyes, and what I see nearly breaks me.

"Together. We do this together," he whispers, cupping my cheek. "So what. Let them find out. Let them see how madly in love with you I am. Because I am, Soraea." He turns to face me directly, taking my hands in his as I criss-cross my legs. He runs his thumbs over my hands, soothing my racing pulse.

"I'm in love with you," he says again, softly. "I have been, I think, for my whole life, and I'm done hiding it. You aren't some dirty secret or some scandal. You aren't a piece of gossip or whatever else they want to call you. What you are is mine. My friend, my future, my fate. You're my heart and soul, and I can't thank the gods enough that they chose me to be your mate. What a privilege that is. Even if I have to wait another year, and wait for some ridiculous ceremony to tell me what I already know, I will thank the gods for every second, because in the end, I'll have you. And if our lifeforce or magical bloodline is restored, or if it's not, I won't waste a single second. A human lifespan, or an immortal one, I will always love you. The stars may have already chosen me, but I chose you long before."

Tears track down my face, puddling in his hands where he's tenderly holding me. Something in me calms like never before. It's as if those were the words I've been waiting for my whole life.

"You love me?" I ask, my voice breaking despite the feeling of my heart taking flight.

"I do. To the very end, I will love you."

A whimpering cry escapes me as I lean forward and crawl into his lap—my safe spot. I hold tight, my voice no louder than a whisper. "And if the prophecy is wrong?" I don't think it is, but my heart and soul feel as if they already belong to him, and if we don't Bond, I think I might shatter.

"Then my devotion will be enough." Something ancient tingles at my spine, like the words have branded themselves on me.

"I—" I start, but his finger crushes my lips, pausing me as he leans back.

"No, not tonight. I don't need you to say it because I did. Not until you're ready to give your whole heart to me. I know your heart and soul, and that's enough for now. When you say those words, I want you to know without a doubt that you love me."

He holds me as both of us settle as the night stretches on in silence. Tears flow every now and then, and he silently brushes them away, but we stay here on the edge, at the heart of the system, where he gave me his heart. The night stretches on, silent save for the hum of the Drift and the beating of our hearts, finally, truly, in sync.

This is everything. This is forever.

But even as his words brand my soul, the weight of tomorrow presses in. Mori. Elison Kolbek. The desperate search for answers that might define our future, or end it.

forty-eight

. . .

raea

WE'VE BEEN GIVEN a pass from school for the week to visit Mori. The crown's response came the next day, and we boarded the Treon transport two hours later. I'll be honest. After all the dreams and visions of Mori, I'm a little on edge, but Ry has promised he'll keep me safe. And I'm not the same person I was when I started school. I might be forced to my knees, but I'll never yield.

The palace here is unique, situated right in the middle of their capital city, with towering sandstone walls erected in the shape of a large rectangle. The high afternoon sun's golden light streams through intricately carved archways and trellises, illuminating the calm waters of the numerous pools that dot the interior. Lush green vines cascade from high ceilings, wrapping around ornate columns—a stark contrast to the arid landscape outside. The air is thin and dry with the scent of dust and exotic blossoms growing in pots. Low seating that's piled high with plush cushions in rich, jewel tones fills the halls and rooms.

My chambers are equally impressive, offering two distinct perspectives of this city. From one terrace, the view stretches across a sea of ochre clay homes, their flat roofs creating a patchwork mosaic. In the distance, the vibrant green of the central oasis shimmers. It's the vital artery that feeds life into the sprawling city.

The other terrace offers a private view of the interior palace. It overlooks a lush courtyard, where the gentle trickle of water from a grand fountain at the center of a long pool can be heard. Here, mature trees provide generous shade, complemented by comfortable seating arrangements.

Mera gets to work instructing Aza and Zhel on where to unpack my belongings. Both Kuron and Ezra traveled with me. So did Cassia, Anneli, Kaes, and Maya, who will spend the week capturing Ryker and me together with the King and Queen and visiting the colonies.

Queen Meganna has already put out a memo searching for Elison. We have two hours before we'll be introduced at a feast they have planned for us, to celebrate our Bond, of course, and encourage the system to follow suit. Queen Meganna and I aren't close, but I'm grateful for her support nonetheless, and I plan on remedying our friendship while I'm here. Having a friendship with another crown, especially a young one, could prove beneficial in the coming war.

I slip into a lightweight cotton dress that leaves my back bare before heading to Ryker's chambers down the hall and up a flight of steps. I only knock once before he opens it. My mouth waters at the sight of his bare chest, making him grin.

"I love when you look at me like that," he confesses, pulling me inside. He dismisses Bo and Leif, his footmen, before capturing my mouth with his.

I melt in his arms. His kiss is slow and reverent, his tongue gliding gently along mine. I've wanted to return those three words for days, but he's right; I need time. His hands tangle in my loose hair, tugging until my head tips up, deepening our kiss.

I'm breathless when I step back. "Anneli and Maya want to take a few photos of us on the terrace in my room. Do you feel up for that?"

He sighs, interlacing our hands before pressing a kiss to my hand. "Do I have to get dressed? It's so hot."

My eyes drop, then widen. His pants are unbuttoned, hanging loose on his hips. My body flushes. I look up, giving him my best flirtatious smile, running a single finger down his chest, over the ridges of his stomach, and further still, until I tug on his waistband. He steps closer, his gaze heating and nostrils flaring.

"Careful, Princess," he purrs. "I might be tempted to see how well your little flimsy shield holds up." His fingers trace down my spine, then his hand cups my ass, pulling me flush against his growing desire.

I hold in the moan that threatens to escape. Instead, I grin. "That feels painful," I tease, my voice a low hum. "Guess you should take care of that before you come to my room—dressed." I step out of his arms, but before I make it three steps, he scoops me up, throwing me over his shoulder. He smacks my ass—a sharp, playful sting that makes me laugh—before dropping me onto his bed.

He's on me in an instant, his whole body covering mine, his weight a delicious press. My legs fall open, and he settles between them, a heated energy zinging through me. His teeth graze along my neck, and his fingers interlace with mine on either side of my head. When his tongue licks a sensitive spot, I arch into him. There have been so many times I've wished for this, and now, there's no reason why we can't. We aren't at school, and the elders of the Isles confirmed we are mates, so...

"Don't torture me," I demand.

He nips, moving south to my shoulder, then to my chest, taking his time to kiss and suck, careful not to leave marks. We're alone, in a palace far from home, and right now, I want him.

"Don't stop," I say breathlessly. It may have been a plea though.

"Raea," he groans, pulling away, but I tug him back down, too consumed to think straight.

Bond.

My Bond.

"Are you sure?" he asks into the crevice of my neck. I nod frantically. I feel confident in my mental shield until his mouth moves over the material of my dress, sucking my nipple into his mouth. I moan again, and the wall I've built in front of my mental shield shatters.

He chuckles but moves to the other side, giving equal attention. My body writhes beneath him as I try to construct another wall, as if it will help. When it comes to him, I'm hopeless. Forming coherent thoughts is a chore, much less building a shield meant to last a world-ending kiss, and dare I say, more?

When his mouth returns to mine, he mutters, "Raea, please, let me touch you. I need to feel you," the words a low thrum against my lips. I meet his blue gaze and smile. "Focus on your Bond, love. Let me take care of the rest." I sink into the silky sheets, loving the delicious weight of him above me, as he kisses me, his hand trailing down my thigh, finding the edge of my dress, sliding it up until my soaked, throbbing core is exposed.

He doesn't stop kissing me as his hand cups my center. A guttural groan rumbles from him. "So wet for me, Princess." He kisses me again, his fingers toying with the lace. I arch, needing more, focusing on the Bond, yet unable to stack bricks fast enough. I don't want to. I just want to let go.

He slides the lace aside, his fingers brushing against my bare center. I've never experienced anything like this, and for once, I'm glad I waited. Every first belongs to him—my mate.

My mind goes blissfully blank as a finger slips inside. I gasp, locking my legs behind his, my body flushing with the heat of my power. *Shit.* He doesn't hesitate to cool me, flooding my system with soothing water.

"Your Bond, love," he says musically, kissing my jaw. I gasp when his finger hooks inside, sending a hot thrill of pleasure through me, all the way to my toes.

My Bond floods my mind, escaping every wall and gate I've tried to contain it in, and now, the only thing I can do is slam an iron wall down. The Bond crashes against it, but doesn't escape. Ryker praises me, "Good job," before picking up the pace. His finger teases and twists, his thumb presses over the bundle of nerves at my apex.

"Please, Ryker," I cry out. The intensity of sensation is almost too much to bear. He clucks his tongue, and the wolfish grin he's giving me makes this feel nearly impossible.

"You can take it."

My eyes water as I shake my head. I don't think I can actually, but I do. Gods, somehow I do. My legs begin to tremble.

His mouth meets mine again, his free hand groping my breast, the other blurring my consciousness with blissful heat. "Let go, Soraea. I've got you."

I surrender. I give in to the building energy, and when that second finger pushes inside, I collapse.

My nails dig into his bare shoulders as he continues to stroke me over the edge. Colors and warmth flood my mind, body, and soul, and I find myself lost in it. Falling and falling. It's never-ending, but as I succumb to the blissful peace, he removes his fingers, and an emptiness replaces that fullness I felt.

"So beautiful," he murmurs, kissing me deeply, my satiated body and mind completely at peace.

I want to forgo all our plans and just stay in bed with him for the rest of the day. He chuckles, shifting off me as my eyes flutter closed, and I stretch out on the cool sheets. A cool breeze, too concentrated to be anything other than him, dries my sweat-slicked skin. The bed shifts, and I hear a faucet turn on from another room. I roll over, resting on a pillow, when the bed dips again, this time behind me, and he pulls me to his chest.

Remembering his own need, I reach behind, letting my palm slide over his pants. He groans, deep and guttural, but pulls my hand away, interlacing our fingers as he tucks our hands to my chest.

"Not right now." He pulls me tighter against him. "Later. For now, I just want to stay like this. I'll make sure we're ready in time."

"So, how is Professor Ainslyn doing?" King Osiris asks from Ryker's other side.

We're seated at a formal table set at the head of the room while their court is at tables stretched out before us. The tables are laden with platters of cooked meats, hummus, figs, and dates coated in sugar, vegetables of bright colors, and flatbreads…so much flatbread. The air is much cooler now that the sun has set.

"Well," Ryker responds. "He's our favorite professor."

I nod in agreement.

Queen Meganna leans forward, her heavy gold earrings swaying beneath her long, dark hair. "What is your Bond like? You say it's strong. How do you know?" Her accent is thick as she says, "I'd like to understand why you would risk it so close to The Ceremony." She looks at both of us expectantly.

I answer, "The Lumos Bond—we noticed it on the first day of school. It's bright iridescent white and soft pastels, but it's the energy that is exchanged each time we touch that alerted us at first."

"There's something deeper as well." Ryker takes my hand in his and kisses my knuckles. The public display has my cheeks heating. His words play in my mind. *I love you. A human lifespan, or an immortal one, I will always love you.* "I've been drawn to her for years, but this year, I can't not be around her. It's like a magnet."

I smile softly at him. "No matter how hard I fought it," I'm speaking to her, but keep my attention on him, "I couldn't stay away. I knew early on he was it for me. He would be my husband."

I don't say Bonded because I don't think the Lumos Bond holds any real power, not anymore. *Mate.* He was chosen for me long before the Lumos Bond was even created. It's not a flimsy Bond to power the veil, that's for sure.

"Wow," Queen Meganna says. I look her way to find her beaming. "How godsblessed you both are. I look forward to witnessing your story unfold. You two will be powerful leaders."

We eat and exchange stories for the rest of the evening, the air thick with the scent of Mori spices and quiet conversations. When the tables are cleared, Queen Meganna pulls Ryker and me onto the dance floor, and the music swells around us. She guides my movements with a warm smile, her own gold bangles chiming softly with each graceful twist. King Osiris, meanwhile, laughs as he demonstrates steps to Ryker, their shared amusement echoing across the hall.

It's a performance for the court, a public affirmation of our burgeoning 'love story,' yet beneath the watchful eyes of their kingdom, something genuine blooms—a friendship. Ryker and I move together, our steps improvised, our laughter blending with the traditional music, earning warm smiles from the King and Queen. Seeing their own deep, enduring love, so evident in their intertwined steps and tender glances, fills me with a quiet hope for our own future. That night, as I drift to sleep, I thank Astor and Calia, and the Primordials, for choosing Ry to be mine.

We're exploring Hiekka Torg, one of the underground colonies on Soren. The entire colony is an intricate network of tunnels and caverns, housing four distinct bustling cities. Vibrant markets draw in visitors yearly with goods that can't be found anywhere else in the system.

The colony houses hundreds of thousands of residents and just as many visitors, hidden beneath a vast and deadly landscape. On the surface, there's nothing for hundreds of miles except for sand dunes, deadly snakes and creatures, and the occasional shifting sand trap. If you didn't know where to look, you'd never realize it was there.

The King and Queen stayed on Zayla, as they needed to attend meetings, but sent a royal caravan with us. They've been instructed to remain out of sight so we can go about our business. Ryker and I are both dressed in traditional Mori garb, and I've included a headpiece that covers both my hair and face, leaving only an opening for my eyes. He has a cloth covering his mouth and nose. Hopefully, we can find some information on Elison's whereabouts. We've narrowed it down to Soren, but we haven't heard anything more yet. He's sure making it difficult to locate him.

A small transport carries us, along with Rune and Ezra, into a crevice in the landscape that conceals the entire cavern system below. It docks, allowing us to blend with the crowded market. Kuron is already here, somewhere, along with a few members of the Regils who are undercover.

Pathways, some cobbled and others smoothed by countless footsteps, wind through an intricate labyrinth of stalls and shops. The air hums with the lively chatter of merchants bartering their wares, the enticing aromas of exotic spices mingling with the damp scent of the cavern.

Overhead, dramatic stalactites hang like sentinels, while cleverly strung lights, reminiscent of festive lanterns, cast a soft glow upon the diverse goods laid out below. From rich textiles and gleaming metalwork to fresh produce and ancient artifacts, the market offers a treasure trove for every taste.

Ryker holds me close as he leads me through the crowded space toward a vendor that claims to sell ancient artifacts. Whether they're real or not, I have no idea. Despite being underground, the space feels open, with lighting that mimics sunlight, casting pools of warm light every now and then.

The market is loud and filled with the scent of spiced meats, garlic, and roasted vegetables. Nobody notices our small party as we move through the halls of shops and tents.

"This is insane," I say with a bit of awe. "I've always wanted to come here."

Ryker squeezes my hand in response. Finally, we come upon a shop carved out of the cavern and reinforced with steel. Above the door is a sign that reads "Artifacts and Books".

A bell dings as we enter the shop, and when the door closes behind the three of us—Ezra choosing to remain outside—the chatter of the room disappears with it. An older man behind the wooden desk at the back welcomes us without looking up.

Around the room, there are shelves and shelves of old books, jewelry, and artifacts made from wood, stone, and various metals. Some are large, while others are no bigger than my palm, but all appear extremely old. My gaze snags on a glass orb seated on the end of a bronze staff. The artifact is nestled on a bed of midnight blue silk. It reminds me of the one gifted to me by the Ancestor Isles elder, though I still haven't been able to figure out what its purpose is. It sits there day and night, swirling softly with white.

I reach for it just as the man appears beside me. "Ah," he says, startling me. "The orb of Elder Elric. The third member elected to the second council." The hairs on my arms stand up as my gaze swings to him.

"The second council," I repeat. "As in—"

"The fae one, Princess. He channeled his magic through the orb."

So that's its purpose?

Ryker appears at my side, wrapping a protective hand around my waist that does not go unnoticed by the man. "And what magic was that?"

The older man appraises Ryker with keen eyes. His monocle is pinched between unblemished, youthful-looking, pale skin, despite his age. "He could borrow other people's magic, but he had no way of controlling it without the orb. It was gifted to him by the Elven counsel, in fact." His gaze swings to me before going back to Ryker. "Tell me, to what do I owe the visit of both royal households today?"

"We're looking for Elison Kolbek."

The old man grins at me. "You've found him."

forty-nine

. . .

ryker

THE SUNSETS on Zayla are beautiful. Raea and I have to head back to school tomorrow, but our week here has been effective. I don't even know what to do with all the knowledge Elison shared with us. Artifacts and books were only the beginning; then he spent hours retelling us stories that had been passed down through his family, generation after generation.

His ancestors had given their lifeforce, but not without preserving the knowledge first. They were once tasked with ensuring that histories were recorded under the Fae king in Auralan, and now they pass it on verbally, sometimes in writing, to their sons. Over and over for almost a thousand years.

His suggestion to us was to find a way out of our system—Caelestis, he called it. He wants us to make our way to Auralan when the veil falls. He said it was essential we train our gifts. He's agreed to gather his things and is moving to Kyrr to live at the palace with his family, which we learned is relatively large. Raea's excited to have access to all the books. I'm interested in the artifacts that we learned are not for sale, at least not the real ones.

I stop along a section of the palace grounds dedicated to training. There's a cache of weapons at the far end, along with various rings dedicated to different types of weapons. Even in this heat, their Regils are out here weight training. I had asked King Osiris if he had a gym, and he sent me here. Kuron asked if he could accompany me, claiming he needed to move his body.

After a grueling workout, Kuron and I call it quits. I need to bathe before dinner. Before we can leave the training pit, one of the guards approaches, his uniform white like a typical Regil, but the style matches that of the kingdom. He bows deeply before handing me a written message.

"When we return to school," Kuron says, "will Raea be attacked by your friend again?"

The question catches me off guard as I scan the letter. I look up at him, and something like disappointment flashes across his features. Not at me, I realize, but himself for not being able to stop the attack.

If only he knew about the first one.

"Sienna no longer attends Drithm. I pulled a few strings." I pause our walk. "She matters to me—deeply. Not just her physical well-being, but also her mental well-being. I should have had Sienna moved much earlier. I take full responsibility for that incident."

Kuron nods, and we keep walking. I hand the letter to him. "What do you make of this?"

He reads it once, twice, flipping it over to see if there's more. There isn't. "I think it's time to head home tonight." I agree as our pace quickens back to the palace, and back to Raea.

I knock once before letting myself into her chambers. Her chamber ladies gasp when I enter. I offer a quick apology before finding Raea seated at a vanity, her hair being pinned by her handmaid. She smiles when she sees me in the mirror.

"Hi." My heart nearly beats out of my chest when she smiles at me like this.

I kneel beside her, asking Mera to give us a minute. "Time to leave. Kuron is giving the orders to everyone now." She frowns. "It's not safe for us here." I look around the room before dropping my mouth to her ear and whispering, "I'll tell you on the transport, but we need to say we were called back for an emergency. Don't hesitate, act calm. You're going to come with me to my rooms so I can get a shirt, and Ezra and Rune will escort us to the transport."

Her breath hitches, but she nods, taking my hand and plastering on a flirty smile, though I can feel the slight tremble. We find Mera and the two ladies loading Raea's bags haphazardly. Kuron nods to me as he watches over them. Ezra escorts us to my rooms, where Rune enters with us. My footmen have already packed my bags and are working on their own. Aksel, my butler, tosses a shirt at me, nodding to Rune. Aksel is an undercover Regil and a skilled warrior.

Rune follows us out, Aksel close behind with the others. Ezra leads the way, meeting up with Kuron and the rest of our party, including the media team. It takes five minutes before we exit the palace grounds, and it's three minutes until we reach the transport. The media team and Raea's ladies go ahead to ensure all the bags are secured, leaving us with only our guards and my footmen.

Once the transport is in sight, our path is blocked when three men, clad in all-black attire and their faces covered, emerge from the shadow of the transport. They stand before our party, swords and blades holstered at their sides. I put Raea behind me, and thankfully, she doesn't protest. She stays close, her breath becoming more rapid by the second.

"Move," Kuron says. "We won't ask twice." Their leader steps forward, breaking away from the other two.

"We have orders to bring her to the King." An inhuman smile crosses his face. "I don't fail." What little magic I have flares to life. Over my fucking dead body are they taking her.

Kuron steps forward again. "And which king is going to kidnap a royal?" he asks.

It's a distraction. Ezra unholsters his Hallo, passing one to me, keeping one for himself. I see Rune slipping his free as well. I don't have to look at Aksel to know he drew his the moment we stepped out of the palace. Raea touches my arm, and it nearly burns me. Thank the gods her magic decided to work here.

"Enough games," the leader mutters, and in a single blink, a blade comes flying through the air, straight for Kuron.

Call it instinct, but in an instant, I grip that strand of white, and my wind wraps around us like a protective shield. The men growl before running for us. I don't have to look to know Raea's energy shield is activated. I can feel the distinct hum vibrating through the air. I tap mine on just before my wind shield crumbles. I'll need to work on holding it in place.

Ezra fires first, the plasma bouncing off their own energy shields. Kuron wastes no time wrapping his hands around the first man, cutting off his air. "With me," I bark at Raea, turning to her and gripping her face. "Stay with me." She nods, her eyes going wide as I lead us away from the chaos, Aksel sticking to our side, Rune engaging with the third man.

Ezra manages to slip a blade past the man's energy shield, and a moment later, the hilt is the only thing sticking out of the side of the man's head. His eyes drain of life as he sinks to the ground. Raea screams.

I step into her field of vision. "Time to run, love. Don't look, okay?" She's gasping, her face pale, her body instinctively heating, becoming hotter and hotter by the second.

"Where the hell are the Regils?" Aksel mutters.

"They aren't coming." I tuck Raea under my arm, cooling my own skin, leaving her power to manifest. We run, it's thirty yards to the ramp. Fifteen, five. One of the women screams, halting Raea. I nearly take her out, pulling her with me. "Don't look," I command.

"Stop, Stop!" she cries. "We have to go back." She's pushing against me as I attempt to drag her up the ramp. "Please," she sobs. When another scream pierces the air, I turn to see Kuron with a sword hanging out of his stomach. "Please," she cries.

I hesitate for one second, and that's all it takes for her to break loose. She runs straight back into the chaos, so fast I can't catch her. "Raea," I yell, taking off after her.

The last of the king's men turns and raises a gun. I swear time slows. It's Kuron's Hallo. I keep running—toward her, toward that gun —but before the trigger is pulled, my beautiful, unstoppable mate erupts.

The air itself shatters. Light—pure, blinding, impossible—explodes from her, ripping through the twilight with a resounding whoosh as the air is displaced. It's not just light; it's the very essence of starlight, ancient and raw, tearing through the atmosphere with a heat so searing, I feel the bronze button on my pants melt. The sky above us *shifts*, purples and deep blues swirling, as if the heavens themselves have come to watch. There's a noise—similar to a gasp—and it's as if it comes from the universe itself, drawing in a deep breath. As if it's been waiting for this moment.

My eyelids slam shut against the searing light, but I keep moving, propelled only by instinct, pushing past the unimaginable heat. My vision returns, blurry, but I see her. My girl. She burns so brightly that everyone's clothes melt right off, smoking and dissolving into ash. The guns and weapons become molten liquid pools at our feet. But her focus is on the ground in front of her, on the man with the gun. Now he's nothing but ash and smoke taking flight on the breeze.

I reach her, wrapping my hand in hers, letting her know I'm here. I wait, watching her. I'm frozen in place with awe. Her eyes are pools of molten gold, swirling with power, her bright white hair glowing like the stars themselves, unbound and wild around her. That protective starlight cocoon of hers rises on a gentle wind around us, shimmering and ethereal, as she finally turns her attention to me.

Slowly, so slowly, she pulls in the beautiful light. It starts gathering back into her, a breathtaking reverse of creation, before I watch with amazement as the light drains from her fingertips, then her arms, revealing her perfectly creamy skin, completely unmarred. Like a wave being pulled back in, it drains all back to that place in her chest, right above her heart, right where her magic originates. When it's all gone, I take her in. My gaze falls frantically down her body, noticing she's fully clothed and unharmed. However, when I glance back up into those swirling golden eyes, I swear her hair lingers like strands of starlight.

She does the same. Her eyes roam over my clothes that are tattered and shredded, and barely hanging on. I have no idea how mine remained, but I'm grateful.

A small price to pay for such power.

In a blink, her eyes return to green, and it's as if reality crashes into her. The starlight cocoon fades as she screams into the night, bending over as she clutches at her chest, and then she moves for Kuron, finding him kneeling on the ground in a puddle of his own blood. My heart clenches. Even with all that power, all that raw, terrifying beauty, her worry for him overshadows everything. I kneel next to her, holding her as her body trembles with sobs.

"No, no," she cries. "Please, no."

Kuron's usually dark features and dark skin are soft and pale. Ezra and Rune stand, their bodies bare, but unscathed somehow. In fact, as I look around, everyone in our party is unscathed, not even a single blister to be found.

Ezra grabs Kuron, and Rune takes his other side as they lift him up, holding the sword in place. Pulling it from him would be lethal. "Princess, get on the transport, now," Ezra barks. He looks at me in silent communication, relaying that we go now, no more delays. I run, hauling her into my arms, and pull her into the transport. The rest of our party runs up the ramp just behind, Leif and Bo bringing up the rear.

"Hang in there," Ezra grunts under the weight of Kuron.

The ramp closes with a loud hiss, and we collapse to the floor as the emergency launch sends us into space a second later. Raea trembles in my arms, her body still wracked with sobs. The air tastes of metal and blood.

We are safe.

We are *out*.

But as the transport lurches, pushing us back into our seats, a new sound fills the cabin. Not the hum of engines. Not the rush of air. It's a low, guttural growl, echoing from the cargo hold below.

My eyes snap to the floor. The metal groans. Dark, viscous shadows begin to seep from the seams of the compartment door, spreading across the floor like spilled ink. They writhe, alive, their tendrils reaching outward. A faint chorus of whispers, bone-chilling and ancient, drifts from the darkness, weaving around a low, predatory snarl that raises the hair on my neck. It smells of rot and something old, something *wrong*.

Raea's head snaps up, her golden eyes—now returned and still swirling with residual power—lock onto the seeping darkness. Her sobs cease. Her breath hitches.

And then, from the depths of the hold, a voice. Low. Cold. And utterly foreign.

"You cannot escape what is already here."

The shadows pulse, coalescing into a formless mass. A single, monstrous shriek tears through the cabin. The transport shudders, not from the launch, but from something *else* waking up.

Something that shouldn't be here.

Something that has followed us.

Glossary

The Veil: A magical barrier protecting the system, now weakening. Loss of the veil means shadow forces may invade.

Lumos Bond: A faint connection between two people. Once the Bond is complete, magic is gifted to the two that will then power the veil.

Mating (Aethermark) Bond: A rare, soul-deep mating bond allowing partners to share power, emotions, and thoughts. Permanent and unbreakable for eternity. Completed after the trial period.

Bonding Ceremony: A formal event where Bonds are tested and recognized. Premature or forced Bonds can strip a person of their true match and magic.

Mental Shields: Protective barriers trained into the mind to prevent accidental or forced Bonding.

Transports: Disc-shaped space ships. There are eight different designs. The academy ones being the smallest with six seats, the largest being the royal transports. Can use a technology called Hyperjump to fly around the system in hours vs it taking lightyears.

Transport Pods: Egg-shaped, glass transports that seat up to ten people, used for planetary travel. They combine older and anti-gravity technology for movement and steering.

Energy Shield: Personal energy shields, often worn as a bracelet, that protects the individual from high-speed attacks and blasts. Can be penetrated if moving slower, like reaching through water vs bouncing off the surface.

Shadow Forces: Unknown enemy. The shadows can coalesce into eerie death-incarnate, has the ability to grab ahold and capture. The mist holds voices that have the ability to penetrate minds and drive someone to madness.

Glossary

Mesh Units: Created by the Kadora Kingdom, these units allow individuals to breathe in toxic atmospheres or surround colonies for free movement. They are made of plasma shingles that shield from radiation and recycle oxygen.

Simulator Room: A facility for combat training against holographic attackers and for flight practice in various weather scenarios.

AerBall: A high-intensity, fast-paced, brutal game played over one hour and divided into three twenty-minute periods, by two teams of eight players. The game involves two types of balls: the small AerBall, which is propelled into nets using a stick for five points, and the larger groundball which players shove into the ground goals for one point. The sport is played in an arena consisting of five rings. The island at the center which is surrounded by an ice-cold water ring, then an obstacle ring, another water ring of bladefish, and the outermost ring is the goal ring.

Prism: A personal communication and data device (similar to a phone/tablet) used for messages, photos, and uploading to The Link.

The Link: A popular social/photo-sharing network used by students and nobility across the system.

Trackers: Small nanotech devices placed on the body for identification and location tracking within the academy.

Hallo Gun: A rare and advanced weapon, difficult to master; passing the Hallo test is considered a great achievement.

Hyperjump: A rapid interstellar travel method that allows ships to "jump" between distant points in space in a matter of minutes/hours. It utilizes quantum folding bypassing traditional propulsion limits. May not work for traveling to different systems in the galaxy (untested).

Glossary

Divisions (Executive Level)

Sky Division: Focused on aeronautics and transport piloting. Students learn navigation, weather adaptation, and flight combat.

Intel Division: Dedicated to intelligence, politics, cultural anthropology, and strategy. Future advisors, spymasters, and leaders train here.

Recon Division: Specializes in security, combat missions, and physical operations. Often produces Regils (royal guards).

Quadrants (Military Forces)

Terra Quadrant: The primary on-planet military branch. Terra handles both land and atmospheric defense, including ground campaigns, siege warfare, border patrols, and sky-based protection. They form the backbone of every kingdom's defense, maintaining order on the home front.

Fari Quadrant: The naval branch, responsible for seas, rivers, and coastal defenses. Fari fleets secure trade routes, engage in ship-to-ship combat, and safeguard ports and coastal cities. Known for endurance, navigation skill, and mastery of maritime warfare.

Protos Quadrant: The space force, extending protection beyond the skies into the void between planets, moons, and suns. Protos patrol interplanetary routes, defend against external threats, and lead exploration beyond the veil. Highly technical, daring, and future-focused.

Regils Quadrant: The elite guard force. Regils are handpicked protectors of royals and high-ranking nobility, sworn to loyalty above all else. They specialize in precision combat, defense strategy, and personal protection, serving as both symbol and shield of the crown.

Pronunciation

Character Names

Raea Tierson: RAY-uh TIER-son
Soraea: SOAR-ay-uh
Kellan Hyston: KELL-un HIS-ton
Xara: ZAR-uh
Aolyn Seltn: Ay-OH-lin SEL-ton
Trysten Asgir: Az-gur
Tate Kinnunen: KEN-oo-nen
Ciara: See-AR-uh
Ainslyn: AINS-lyn
Jensn: JEN-son
Sienna: SEE-en-uh
Priana: PREE-ah-nuh
Kore: KOR-ee
Thriven: THRI-ven
Britta: BRIT-uh
Kristien: KRISS-tee-en
Aada: A-duh
Vori: VOHR-ee
Polk: POL-k
Dexen: DEK-sen
Kastiel: KAS-teel
Kuron: KUR-on
Linnea: LIN-nay-uh
Bastian: BAS-chen
Alexi: UH-lex-ee
Sava: SAW-vuh
Cassia: KAW-see-uh
Kaes: KAY-s
Maya: MY-uh

Aki: AH-key
Mera: M-air-uh
Aza: A-zuh
Zhel: Z-elle
Aksel: AX-el
Anneli: AH-na-lee
Izak: EYE-zach
Annika: AH-nik-uh
Arne: ARN
Elex: EL-ex
Corine Cazl: KOR-in KA-zeel
Anele: AN-ell
Urik: OO-rik
Mara: MAR-uh
Garrek: GAR-rek
Nalana: NAY-lawn-uh
Meganna: MAY-gon-uh
Leif: LAYF
Rune: ROO-n
Paxton: PAX-ton
Elison: EL-i-son

God Names

Calia: Kal-ee-uh
Ravana: Rah-VAH-nuh
Caelus: KAY-lus

Pronunciation

Place Names

Treon: TREE-on
Taeolyn: TAY-oh-lin
Veker: VEK-er
Drithm: DRITH-um
Bragr: BRAH-grr
Kliax: KLEE-aks
Kyrr: KEER
Malaya: MUH-lay-uh
Sagchyl: SAG-chil
Ateria: Ah-TEER-ee-uh
Thirik: THER-ik
Kadora: KAH-dohr-uh
Einvald: EYN-vald
Ista: EES-tuh
Auralan: OR-ah-lan
Sgya: S-guy-uh
Ael'drien: AYL-dree-en
Dionek: DI-O-nek
Cryos: CRI-ohs
Gowden: GOW-den
Mystel: MIS-tel
Elran Asari: EL-ran AH-sar-ee
Onyxera: ONYX-air-uh
Demeter: DEM-e-ter
Soren: SOR-en
Hiekka Torg: HI-ek-uh TOR-g
Ia: EE-uh
Ulen: YOU-len
Feandra: FEE-ann-druh
Chyr: KAI-r
Rayek: RAY-ek
Halgan Peaks: HAL-gon

Cultural and Lore Terms

Primordials: Pry-MOR-dee-als
Orum: ORE-um
Regils: REE-jils
Lumos: LOO-mose
Nakata corset: NAH-kah-tah
Elvisiah: El-VI-sigh-uh
(breathy, melodic)
Kaelish: KAY-lish
Aether: EE-thur
Veil: VAYL
Enotia: EN-oh-sha
Valoria: VUH-lor-ee-uh
Solara: SO-lar-uh
Asteria: AST-eh-ria

acknowledgments

Wow, this book is a dream come true.
Really.

As many of you know, I write books based on dreams. This story was nothing more than a glimpse of planets and magic and bonds. It has been so fun to bring this dream to life.

I first want to thank my family—without you, I wouldn't be able to live my dream. To my boys, who have filled my days with laughter, chaos, and love—you are my greatest adventure. This book was written between homeschool, sports practices, and snuggles, and I wouldn't have it any other way. You remind me daily of the magic worth fighting for.

To my husband, thank you for always encouraging me to pursue my dreams and cheering me on along the way. There were several nights where you delivered dinner to my desk or afternoon tea to keep me from bonking. There were days I was pushed out of the house so I could have some quiet time to write and think.

To my family and friends who never stopped cheering me on—even when I doubted myself—thank you for believing in the story before I dared to. To my sister, you've always been one of my biggest cheerleaders.

To my beta readers and critique partners: Maeghan, Christina, Jasmine, Niina, Haleigh, Bethany, Marilyn, Chelsea—you caught the cracks in the crown, you gasped in the right places, you made me giggle at your comments and laugh at your responses to Kellan. You encouraged and pushed me to try and try again, to grow and to write mystical lore that felt all too scary and beyond my capabilities. Your love of this story made me fall in love alongside you and you reminded me why I was telling this story in the first place. You made these characters sharper, stronger, and more alive. I am endlessly grateful for your time, your honesty, and your hearts.

To my editors, cover designer, and every creative hand that helped shape this book into what you now hold in yours—thank you for your vision and your brilliance.

To the writing and reading community, both near and far: your encouragement, advice, and camaraderie made this lonely process feel less like walking through shadows and more like stepping into light. LJ Claren and Penn Cole: your advice, your words, your shared experiences were gold for me during this process.

To Stephanie Meyer and Rebecca Yarros: you taught me to dream and fall in love with fictional men. First as a new college student finding my own way in the world, and then again as a healing mom who was just learning about the depths of my invisible illnesses. I'm an irrevocable Twihard and RY-hard...lol.

And to you, reader. Whether you stumbled into this story by fate or by chance, thank you for choosing to step into this world with me. You are the reason these characters breathe beyond my imagination. I hope that in these pages, you find something worth holding onto—courage, hope, love, the strength to rise again, or maybe just the reminder that even in the darkest night, there are always stars.

about the author

Eleni James is the author of both contemporary and fantasy romance. Her debut, The Sound of His Whisper (2024), introduced readers to her emotionally rich storytelling in a tale of love, loss, and resilience. She now expands into romantasy with her Of Light and Shadows series, beginning with A Fate of Two Crowns (2025), the first of a sweeping five-book saga filled with ancient prophecies, morally gray princes, and heroines who must choose between duty, destiny, and forbidden love.

Eleni became an author after years of dream journaling, where her imagined worlds and characters refused to stay silent. Whether in contemporary settings or star-studded kingdoms, her stories are bound by the belief that love—tested, challenged, and fought for—is always worth the risk.

When she isn't writing, she homeschools her three boys, curates music playlists that shape her books, and is rarely far from a pot of tea.

Trigger Warnings:

Explicit Language
Violence
Kidnapping Attempt
Assault
Anxiety, Fear, Panic, Dread
Bullying
Blood and Gore
Fantasy Violence and Combat